"A MIGHTY NARRATING EYE FOR HOT-BUTTON ISSUES . . . in this new novel Grisham also reveals for the first time a surprising knack for comedy."

—*Chicago Sun-Times*

"Passages in *The Rainmaker* are reminiscent of Pat Conroy. . . . This is Grisham's most barbed book since *The Firm*, and it is by far his most entertaining."

—*People*

HIGH PRAISE FOR
JOHN GRISHAM'S
#1 *NEW YORK TIMES* BESTSELLER
THE RAINMAKER

"Grisham's vivid minor characters and near-Dickensian zeal for mocking pomposity and privilege are apt to endear him to his many readers all over again."

—*Entertainment Weekly*

"MR. GRISHAM'S MOST SYMPATHETIC HERO AND MOST ENGROSSING PREMISE SINCE HIS FIRST RUNAWAY SUCCESS, *THE FIRM* . . . An event-filled tale that works hard to please and largely succeeds."

—*The Wall Street Journal*

"Melding the courtroom savvy of *A Time to Kill* with the psychological nuance of *The Chamber*, imbued with wry humor and rich characters, this bittersweet tale, the author's quietest and most thoughtful, shows that Grisham's imagination can hold its own in a courtroom as well as on the violent streets outside."

—*Publishers Weekly*

Please turn the page for more extraordinary acclaim. . . .

"John Grisham has combined many of the best qualities of his previous novels to write an entertaining and credible courtroom thriller."

—*Chicago Tribune*

"NEVER BEFORE HAS GRISHAM USED THE DAVID-GOLIATH ELEMENT SO CLEVERLY AND POWERFULLY AS IN *THE RAINMAKER*. And by combining it with nail-biting tension, wrenching suspense and unadulterated excitement, and by adding plenty of humor and a smidgen of romance, he has made this new novel his most sheerly entertaining and enjoyable to date."

—*Buffalo News* (N.Y.)

"Grisham creates courtroom scenes of high humor and intense drama. . . . A good time will be had by all."

—*Daily News* (N.Y.)

"ENTERTAINING AND WELL-WRITTEN . . . *The Rainmaker* marks a return to Grisham's snappy pacing and devilish sense of fun."

—*Memphis Flyer* (Tenn.)

"Grisham has constructed a case and a courtroom drama strong enough to grab our attention."

—*The New York Law Journal*

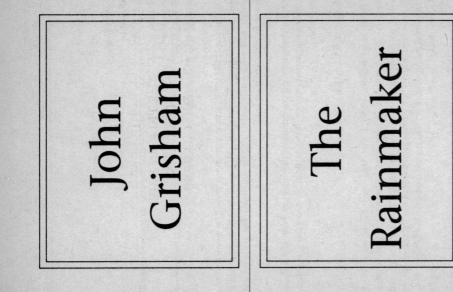

John Grisham

The Rainmaker

Island BOOKS

ISLAND BOOKS
Published by
Dell Publishing
a division of
Bantam Doubleday Dell Publishing Group, Inc.
1540 Broadway
New York, New York 10036

Copyright © 1995 by John Grisham

ISBN 0-440-22165-X

Reprinted by arrangement with Doubleday

Printed in the United States of America

Published simultaneously in Canada

February 1996

10 9 8 7 6 5 4 3 2

OPM

To American trial lawyers

In writing this book, I was assisted at every turn by Will Denton, a prominent trial lawyer in Gulfport, Mississippi. For twenty-five years, Will has fought diligently for the rights of consumers and little people. His courtroom victories are legendary, and when I was a trial lawyer I wanted to be like Will Denton. He gave me his old files, answered my numerous questions, even proofread the manuscript.

Jimmie Harvey is a friend and a fine physician in Birmingham, Alabama. He carefully steered me through the impenetrable maze of medical procedures. Certain sections of this book are accurate and readable because of him.

Thanks.

One

MY DECISION TO BECOME A LAWYER was irrevocably sealed when I realized my father hated the legal profession. I was a young teenager, clumsy, embarrassed by my awkwardness, frustrated with life, horrified of puberty, about to be shipped off to a military school by my father for insubordination. He was an ex-Marine who believed boys should live by the crack of the whip. I'd developed a quick tongue and an aversion to discipline, and his solution was simply to send me away. It was years before I forgave him.

He was also an industrial engineer who worked seventy hours a week for a company that made, among many other items, ladders. Because by their very nature ladders are dangerous devices, his company became a frequent target of lawsuits. And because he handled design, my father was the favorite choice to speak for the company in depositions and trials. I can't say that I blame him for hating lawyers, but I grew to admire them because they made his life so miserable. He'd spend eight hours haggling with them, then hit the martinis as soon as he walked in the door. No hellos. No hugs. No dinner. Just an hour or so of continuous bitching while he slugged down four martinis then passed out in his battered recliner. One trial lasted three weeks, and when it ended with a large verdict against the company my mother called a doctor and they hid him in a hospital for a month.

The company later went broke, and of course all blame was directed at the lawyers. Not once did I hear any talk that maybe a trace of mismanagement could in any way have contributed to the bankruptcy.

Liquor became his life, and he became depressed. He went years without a steady job, which really ticked me off because I was forced to wait tables and deliver pizza so I could claw my way through college. I think I spoke to him twice during the four years of my undergraduate studies. The day after I learned I had been accepted to law school, I proudly returned home with this great news. Mother told me later he stayed in bed for a week.

Two weeks after my triumphant visit, he was changing a lightbulb in the utility room when (I swear this is true) a ladder collapsed and he fell on his head. He lasted a year in a coma in a nursing home before someone mercifully pulled the plug.

Several days after the funeral, I suggested the possibility of a lawsuit, but Mother was just not up to it. Also, I've always suspected he was partially inebriated when he fell. And he was earning nothing, so under our tort system his life had little economic value.

My mother received a grand total of fifty thousand dollars in life insurance, and remarried badly. He's a simple sort, my stepfather, a retired postal clerk from Toledo, and they spend most of their time square dancing and traveling in a Winnebago. I keep my distance. Mother didn't offer me a dime of the money, said it was all she had to face the future with, and since I'd proven rather adept at living on nothing, she felt I didn't need any of it. I had a bright future earning money; she did not, she reasoned. I'm certain Hank, the new husband, was filling her ear full of financial advice. Our paths will cross again one day, mine and Hank's.

I will finish law school in May, a month from now, then I'll sit for the bar exam in July. I will not graduate with honors, though I'm somewhere in the top half of my class. The only smart thing I've done in three years of law school was to schedule the required and difficult courses early, so I could goof off in this, my last semester. My classes this spring are a joke—Sports Law, Art Law, Selected Readings from the Napoleonic Code and, my favorite, Legal Problems of the Elderly.

It is this last selection that has me sitting here in a rickety chair behind a flimsy folding table in a hot, damp metal building filled with an odd assortment of seniors, as they like to be called. A hand-painted sign above the only visible door majestically labels the place as the Cypress Gardens Senior Citizens Building, but other than its name the place has not the slightest hint of flowers or greenery. The walls are drab and bare except for an ancient, fading photograph of Ronald Reagan in one corner between two sad little flags—one, the Stars and Stripes, the other, the state flag of Tennessee. The building is small, somber and cheerless, obviously built at the last minute with a few spare dollars of unexpected federal money. I doodle on a legal pad, afraid to look at the crowd inching forward in their folding chairs.

There must be fifty of them out there, an equal mixture of blacks and whites, average age of at least seventy-five, some blind, a dozen or so in wheelchairs, many wearing hearing aids. We were told they meet here each day at noon for a hot meal, a few songs, an occasional visit by a desperate political candidate. After a couple of hours of socializing, they will leave for home and count the hours until they can return here. Our professor said this was the highlight of their day.

We made the painful mistake of arriving in time for lunch. They sat the four of us in one corner along with our leader, Professor Smoot, and examined us closely as we picked at neoprene chicken and icy peas. My Jell-O was yellow, and this was noticed by a bearded old goat with the name Bosco scrawled on his Hello-My-Name-Is tag stuck above his dirty shirt pocket. Bosco mumbled something about yellow Jell-O, and I quickly offered it to him, along with my chicken, but Miss Birdie Birdsong corralled him and pushed him roughly back into his seat. Miss Birdsong is about eighty but very spry for her age, and she acts as mother, dictator and bouncer of this organization. She works the crowd like a veteran ward boss, hugging and patting, schmoozing with other little blue-haired ladies, laughing in a shrill voice and all the while keeping a wary eye on Bosco, who undoubtedly is the bad boy of the bunch. She lectured him for admiring my Jell-O, but seconds later placed a full bowl of the yellow putty before his glowing eyes. He ate it with his stubby fingers.

An hour passed. Lunch proceeded as if these starving souls were feasting on seven courses with no hope of another meal. Their wobbly forks and spoons moved back and forth, up and down, in and out, as if laden with precious metals. Time was of absolutely no consequence. They yelled at each other when words stirred them. They dropped food on the floor until I couldn't bear to watch anymore. I even ate my Jell-O. Bosco, still covetous, watched my every move. Miss Birdie fluttered around the room, chirping about this and that.

Professor Smoot, an oafish egghead complete with crooked bow tie, bushy hair and red suspenders, sat with the stuffed satisfaction of a man who'd just finished a fine meal, and lovingly admired the scene before us. He's a kindly soul, in his early fifties, but with mannerisms much like Bosco and his friends, and for twenty years he's taught the kindly courses no one else wants to teach and few students want to take. Children's Rights, Law of the Disabled, Seminar on Domestic Violence, Problems of the Mentally Ill and, of course, Geezer Law, as this one is called outside his presence. He once scheduled a course to be called Rights of the Unborn Fetus, but it attracted a storm of controversy so Professor Smoot took a quick sabbatical.

He explained to us on the first day of class that the purpose of the course was to expose us to real people with real legal problems. It's his opinion that all students enter law school with a certain amount of idealism and desire to serve the public, but after three years of brutal competition we care for nothing but the right job with the right firm where we can make partner in seven years and earn big bucks. He's right about this.

The class is not a required one, and we started with eleven students. After a month of Smoot's boring lectures and constant exhortations to forsake money and work for free, we'd been whittled down to four. It's a worthless course, counts for only two hours, requires almost no work, and this is what attracted me to it. But, if there were more than a month left, I seriously doubt I could tough it out. At this point, I hate law school. And I have grave concerns about the practice of law.

This is my first confrontation with actual clients, and I'm terrified. Though the prospects sitting out there are aged and infirm, they are staring at me as if I possess great wisdom. I am, after all, almost a lawyer, and I wear a dark suit, and I have this legal pad in front of me on which I'm drawing squares and circles, and my face is fixed in an intelligent frown, so I must be capable of helping them. Seated next to me at our folding table is Booker Kane, a black guy who's my best friend in law school. He's as scared as I am. Before us on folded index cards are our written names in black felt—Booker Kane and Rudy Baylor. That's me. Next to Booker is the podium behind which Miss Birdie is screeching, and on the other side is another table with matching index cards proclaiming the presence of F. Franklin Donaldson the Fourth, a pompous ass who for three years now has been sticking initials and numerals before and after his name. Next to him is a real bitch, N. Elizabeth Erickson, quite a gal, who wears pinstripe suits, silk ties and an enormous chip on her shoulder. Many of us suspect she also wears a jockstrap.

Smoot is standing against the wall behind us. Miss Birdie is doing the announcements, hospital reports and obituaries. She's yelling into a microphone with a sound system that's working remarkably well. Four large speakers hang in the corners of the room, and her piercing voice booms around and crashes in from all directions. Hearing aids are slapped and taken out. For the moment, no one is asleep. Today there are three obituaries, and when Miss Birdie finally finishes I see a few tears in the audience. God, please don't let this happen to me. Please give me fifty more years of work and fun, then an instant death while I'm sleeping.

To our left against a wall, the pianist comes to life and smacks sheets of music on the wooden grill in front of her. Miss Birdie fancies herself as some kind of political analyst, and just as she starts railing against a proposed increase in the sales tax, the pianist attacks the keys. "America the Beautiful," I think. With pure relish, she storms through a clanging rendition of the opening refrain, and the geezers grab their hymnals and wait for the first verse. Miss Birdie does not miss a beat. Now she's the choir director. She raises her hands, then claps them to get attention, then starts flopping them all over the place with the opening note of verse one. Those who are able slowly get to their feet.

The howling fades dramatically with the second verse. The words are not as familiar and most of these poor souls can't see past their noses, so the hymnals are useless. Bosco's mouth is suddenly closed but he's humming loudly at the ceiling.

The piano stops abruptly as the sheets fall from the grill and scatter onto the floor. End of song. They stare at the pianist who, bless her heart, is snatching at the air and fumbling around her feet where the music has gathered.

"Thank you!" Miss Birdie yells into the microphone as they suddenly fall back into their seats. "Thank you. Music is a wonderful thang. Let's give thanks to God for beautiful music."

"Amen!" Bosco roars.

"Amen," another relic repeats with a nod from the back row.

"Thank you," Miss Birdie says. She turns and smiles at Booker and me. We both lean forward on our elbows and once again look at the crowd. "Now," she says dramatically, "for the program today, we are so pleased to have Professor Smoot here again with some of his very bright and handsome students." She flops her baggy hands at us and smiles with her gray and yellow teeth at Smoot, who has quietly made his way to her side. "Aren't they handsome?" she asks, waving at us. "As you know," Miss Birdie proceeds into the microphone, "Professor Smoot teaches law at Memphis State, that's where my youngest son studied, you know, but didn't graduate, and every year Professor Smoot visits us here with some of his students who'll listen to your legal problems and give advice that's always good, and always free, I might add." She turns and lays another sappy smile upon Smoot. "Professor Smoot, on behalf of our group, we say welcome back to Cypress Gardens. We thank you for your concern about the problems of senior citizens. Thank you. We love you."

She backs away from the podium and starts clapping her hands furiously and nodding eagerly at her comrades to do the same, but not a soul, not even Bosco, lifts a hand.

"He's a hit," Booker mumbles.

"At least he's loved," I mumble back. They've been sitting here now for ten minutes. It's just after lunch, and I notice a few heavy eyelids. They'll be snoring by the time Smoot finishes.

He steps to the podium, adjusts the mike, clears his throat and waits for Miss Birdie to take her seat on the front row. As she sits, she whispers angrily to a pale gentleman next to her, "You should've clapped!" He does not hear this.

"Thank you, Miss Birdie," Smoot squeaks. "Always nice to visit here at Cypress Gardens." His voice is sincere, and there's no doubt in my mind that Professor Howard L. Smoot indeed feels privileged to be here at this moment, in the center of this depressing building, before this sad little group of old folks, with the only four students who happen to remain in his class. Smoot lives for this.

He introduces us. I stand quickly with a short smile, then return to my seat and once again fix my face in an intelligent frown. Smoot talks about health care, and budget cuts, and living wills, and sales tax exemptions, and abused geezers, and co-insurance payments. They're dropping like flies out there. Social Security loopholes, pending legislation, nursing home regulations, estate planning, wonder drugs, he rambles on and on, just as he does in class. I yawn and feel drowsy myself. Bosco starts glancing at his watch every ten seconds.

Finally, Smoot gets to the wrap-up, thanks Miss Birdie and her crowd once again, promises to return year after year and takes a seat at the end of the table. Miss Birdie pats her hands together exactly twice, then gives up. No one else moves. Half of them are snoring.

Miss Birdie waves her arms at us, and says to her flock, "There they are. They're good and they're free."

Slowly and awkwardly, they advance upon us. Bosco is first in line, and it's obvious he's holding a grudge over the Jell-O, because he glares at me and goes to the other end of the table and sits in a chair before the Honorable N. Elizabeth Erickson. Something tells me he will not be the last prospective client to go elsewhere for legal advice. An elderly black man selects Booker for his lawyer and they huddle across the table. I try not to listen. Something about an ex-wife and a divorce years ago that may or may not have been officially completed. Booker takes notes like a real lawyer, and listens intently as if he knows exactly what to do.

At least Booker has a client. For a full five minutes I feel utterly stupid sitting alone as my three classmates whisper and scribble and listen compassionately and shake their heads at the problems unfolding before them.

My solitude does not go unnoticed. Finally, Miss Birdie Birdsong reaches into her purse, extracts an envelope and prances to my end of the table. "You're the one I really wanted," she whispers as she pulls her chair close to the corner of the table. She leans forward, and I lean to my left, and at this precise moment, as our heads come within inches of touching, I enter into my first conference as a legal counselor. Booker glances at me with a wicked smile.

My first conference. Last summer I clerked for a small firm downtown, twelve lawyers, and their work was strictly hourly. No contingency fees. I learned the art of billing, the first rule of which is that a lawyer spends much of his waking hours in conferences. Client conferences, phone conferences, conferences with opposing lawyers and judges and partners and insurance adjusters and clerks and paralegals, conferences over lunch, conferences at the courthouse, conference calls, settlement conferences, pretrial conferences, post-trial conferences. Name the activity, and lawyers can fabricate a conference around it.

Miss Birdie cuts her eyes about, and this is my signal to keep both my head and voice low, because whatever it is she wants to confer over is serious as hell. And this suits me just fine, because I don't want a soul to hear the lame and naive advice I am destined to provide in response to her forthcoming problem.

"Read this," she says, and I take the envelope and open it. Hallelujah! It's a will! The Last Will and Testament of Colleen Janiece Barrow Birdsong. Smoot told us that more than half of these clients would want us to review and maybe update their wills, and this is fine with us because we were required last year to take a full course called Wills and Estates and we feel somewhat proficient in spotting problems. Wills are fairly simple documents, and can be prepared without defect by the greenest of lawyers.

This one's typed and official in appearance, and as I scan it I learn from the first two paragraphs that Miss Birdie is a widow and has two children and a full complement of grandchildren. The third paragraph stops me cold, and I glance at her as I read it. Then I read it again. She's smiling smugly. The language directs her executor to give unto each of her children the sum of two million dollars, with a million in trust for each of her grandchildren. I count, slowly, eight grandchildren. That's at least twelve million dollars.

"Keep reading," she whispers as if she can actually hear the calculator rattling in my brain. Booker's client, the old black man, is crying now, and it has something to do with a romance gone bad years ago and children who've neglected him. I try not to listen, but it's impossible. Booker is scribbling with a fury and trying to ignore the tears. Bosco laughs loudly at the other end of the table.

Paragraph five of the will leaves three million dollars to a church and two million to a college. Then there's a list of charities, beginning with the Diabetes Association and ending with the Memphis Zoo, and beside each is a sum of money the least of which is fifty thousand dollars. I keep frowning, do a little quick math and determine that Miss Birdie has a net worth of at least twenty million.

Suddenly, there are many problems with this will. First, and foremost, it's not nearly as thick as it should be. Miss Birdie is rich, and rich people do not use thin, simple wills. They use thick, dense wills with trusts and trustees and generation-skipping transfers and all sorts of gadgets and devices designed and implemented by expensive tax lawyers in big firms.

"Who prepared this?" I ask. The envelope is blank and there's no indication of who drafted the will.

"My former lawyer, dead now."

It's a good thing he's dead. He committed malpractice when he prepared this one.

So, this pretty little lady with the gray and yellow teeth and rather melodious voice is worth twenty million dollars. And, evidently, she has no lawyer. I glance at her, then return to the will. She doesn't dress rich, doesn't wear diamonds or gold, spends neither time nor money on her hair. The dress is cotton drip-dry and the burgundy blazer is worn and could've come from Sears. I've seen a few rich old ladies in my time, and they're normally fairly easy to spot.

The will is almost two years old. "When did your lawyer die?" I ask ever so sweetly now. Our heads are still huddled low and our noses are just inches apart.

"Last year. Cancer."

"And you don't have a lawyer now?"

"I wouldn't be here talking to you if I had a lawyer, now, would I, Rudy? There's nothing complicated about a will, so I figured you could handle it."

Greed is a funny thing. I have a job starting July 1 with Brodnax and Speer, a stuffy little sweatshop of a firm with fifteen lawyers who do little else but represent insurance companies in litigation. It was not the job I wanted, but as things developed Brodnax and Speer extended an offer of employment when all others failed to do so. I figure I'll put in a few years, learn the ropes and move on to something better.

Wouldn't those fellows at Brodnax and Speer be impressed if I walked in the first day and brought with me a client worth at least twenty million? I'd be an instant rainmaker, a bright young star with a golden touch. I might even ask for a larger office.

"Of course I can handle it," I say lamely. "It's just that, you know, there's a lot of money here, and I—"

"Shhhhh," she hisses fiercely as she leans even closer. "Don't mention the money." Her eyes dart in all directions as if thieves are lurking behind her. "I just refuse to talk about it," she insists.

"Okay. Fine with me. But I think that maybe you should consider talking to a tax lawyer about this."

"That's what my old lawyer said, but I don't want to. A lawyer is a lawyer as far as I'm concerned, and a will is a will."

"True, but you could save a ton of money in taxes if you plan your estate."

She shakes her head as if I'm a complete idiot. "I won't save a dime."

"Well, excuse me, but I think that maybe you can."

She places a brown-spotted hand on my wrist, and whispers, "Rudy, let me explain. Taxes mean nothing to me, because, you see, I'll be dead. Right?"

"Uh, right, I guess. But what about your heirs?"

"That's why I'm here. I'm mad at my heirs, and I want to cut 'em out of my will. Both of my children, and some of the grandchildren. Cut, cut, cut. They get nothing, you understand. Zero. Not a penny, not a stick of furniture. Nothing."

Her eyes are suddenly hard and the rows of wrinkles are pinched tightly around her mouth. She squeezes my wrist but doesn't realize it. For a second, Miss Birdie is not only angry but hurt.

At the other end of the table, an argument erupts between Bosco and N. Elizabeth Erickson. He's loud and railing against Medicaid and Medicare and Republicans in general, and she's pointing to a sheet of paper and attempting to explain why certain doctor bills are not covered. Smoot slowly gets to his feet and walks to the end of the table to inquire if he might be of assistance.

Booker's client is trying desperately to regain his composure, but the tears are dropping from his cheeks and Booker is becoming unnerved. He's assuring the old gentleman that, yes indeed, he, Booker Kane, will check into the matter and make things right. The air conditioner kicks in and drowns out some of the chatter. The plates and cups have been cleared from the tables, and all sorts of games are in progress—Chinese checkers, Rook, bridge and a Milton Bradley board game with dice. Fortunately, the majority of these people have come for lunch and socializing, not for legal advice.

"Why do you want to cut them out?" I ask.

She releases my wrist and rubs her eyes. "Well, it's very personal, and I really don't want to go into it."

"Fair enough. Who gets the money?" I ask, and I'm suddenly intoxicated by the power just bestowed upon me to draft the magic words that will make millionaires out of ordinary people. My smile to her is so warm and so fake I hope she is not offended.

"I'm not sure," she says wistfully, and glances about as if this is a game. "I'm just not sure who to give it to."

Well, how about a million for me? Texaco will sue me any day now for four hundred dollars. We've broken off negotiations and I've heard from their attorney. My landlord is threatening eviction because I haven't paid rent in two months. And I'm sitting here chatting with the richest person I've ever met, a person who probably can't live much longer and is pondering rather delightfully who should get how much.

She hands me a piece of paper with four names printed neatly in a narrow column, and says, "These are the grandchildren I want to protect, the ones who still love me." She cups her hand over her mouth and moves toward my ear. "Give each one a million dollars."

My hand shakes as I scrawl on my pad. Wham! Just like that, I've created four millionaires. "What about the rest?" I ask in a low whisper.

She jerks backward, sits erectly and says, "Not a dime. They don't call me, never send gifts or cards. Cut 'em out."

If I had a grandmother worth twenty million dollars I'd send flowers once a week, cards every other day, chocolates whenever it rained and champagne whenever it didn't. I'd call her once in the morning and twice before bedtime. I'd take her to church every Sunday and sit with her, hand in hand, during the service, then off to brunch we'd go and then to an auction or a play or an art show or wherever in the hell Granny wanted to go. I'd take care of my grandmother.

And I was thinking of doing the same for Miss Birdie.

"Okay," I say solemnly as if I've done this many times. "And nothing for your two children?"

"That's what I said. Absolutely nothing."

"What, may I ask, have they done to you?"

She exhales heavily as if frustrated by this, and she rolls her eyes around as if she hates to tell me, but then she lurches forward on both elbows to tell me anyway. "Well," she whispers, "Randolph, the oldest, he's almost sixty, just married for the third time to a little tramp who's always asking about the money. Whatever I leave to him she'll end up with, and I'd rather give it to you, Rudy, than to my own son. Or to Professor Snoot, or to anyone but Randolph. Know what I mean?"

My heart stops. Inches, just inches, from striking paydirt with my first client. To hell with Brodnax and Speer and all those conferences awaiting me.

"You can't leave it to me, Miss Birdie," I say, and offer her my sweetest smile. My eyes, and probably my lips and mouth and nose as well, beg for her to say Yes! Dammit! It's my money and I'll leave it to whomever I want, and if I want you, Rudy, to have it, then dammit! It's yours!

Instead, she says, "Everything else goes to the Reverend Kenneth Chandler. Do you know him? He's on television all the time now, out of Dallas, and he's doing all sorts of wonderful things around the world with our donations, building homes, feeding babies, teaching from the Bible. I want him to have it."

"A television evangelist?"

"Oh, he's much more than an evangelist. He's a teacher and statesman and counselor, eats dinner with heads of state, you know, plus he's cute as a bug. Got this head full of curly gray hair, premature, but he wouldn't dare touch it up, you know."

"Of course not. But—"

"He called me the other night. Can you believe it? That voice on television is as smooth as silk, but over the phone it's downright seductive. Know what I mean?"

"Yes, I think I do. Why did he call you?"

"Well, last month, when I sent my pledge for March, I wrote him a short note, said I was thinking of redoing my will now that my kids have abandoned me and all, and that I was thinking of leaving some money for his ministries. Not three days later he called, just full of himself, so cute and vibrant on the phone, and wanted to know how much I might be thinking of leaving him and his ministries. I shot him a ballpark figure, and he's been calling ever since. Said he would even fly out in his own Learjet to meet me if I so desired."

I struggle for words. Smoot has Bosco by the arm and is attempting to pacify him and sit him once again before N. Elizabeth Erickson, who at the moment has lost the chip on her shoulder and is obviously embarrassed by her first client and ready to crawl under the table. She cuts her eyes around, and I flash her a quick grin so she knows I'm watching. Next to her, F. Franklin Donaldson the Fourth is locked in a deep consultation with an elderly couple. They are discussing a document which appears to be a will. I'm smug in the knowledge that the will I'm holding is worth far more than the one he's frowning over.

I decide to change the subject. "Uh, Miss Birdie, you said you had two children. Randolph and—"

"Yes, Delbert. Forget him too. I haven't heard from him in three years. Lives in Florida. Cut, cut, cut."

I slash with my pen and Delbert loses his millions.

"I need to see about Bosco," she says abruptly, and

jumps to her feet. "He's such a pitiful little fella. No family, no friends except for us."

"We're not finished," I say.

She leans down and again our faces are inches apart. "Yes we are, Rudy. Just do as I say. A million each to those four, and all the rest to Kenneth Chandler. Everything else in the will stays the same; executor, bond, trustees, all stays the same. It's simple, Rudy. I do it all the time. Professor Smoot says y'all will be back in two weeks with everything all typed up real nice and neat. Is that so?"

"I guess."

"Good. See you then, Rudy." She flutters to the end of the table and puts her arm around Bosco, who is immediately calm and innocent again.

I study the will and take notes from it. It's comforting to know that Smoot and the other professors will be available to guide and assist, and that I have two weeks to collect my senses and figure out what to do. I don't have to do this, I tell myself. This delightful little woman with twenty million needs more advice than I can give her. She needs a will that she can't possibly understand, but one the IRS will certainly take heed of. I don't feel stupid, just inadequate. After three years of studying the law, I'm very much aware of how little I know.

Booker's client is trying gallantly to control his emotions, and his lawyer has run out of things to say. Booker continues to take notes and grunts yes or no every few seconds. I can't wait to tell him about Miss Birdie and her fortune.

I glance at the dwindling crowd, and in the second row I notice a couple who appear to be staring at me. At the moment, I'm the only available lawyer, and they seem to be undecided about whether to try their luck with me. The woman's holding a bulky wad of papers secured by rubber bands. She mumbles something under her breath, and her husband shakes his head as if he'd rather wait for one of the other bright young legal eagles.

Slowly, they stand and make their way to my end of the table. They both stare at me as they approach. I smile. Welcome to my office.

"Hi there," I say with a smile and an outstretched hand. He shakes it limply, then I offer it to her. "I'm Rudy Baylor."

She takes Miss Birdie's chair. He sits across the table and keeps his distance.

"I'm Dot and he's Buddy," she says, nodding at Buddy, ignoring my hand.

"Dot and Buddy," I repeat, and start taking notes. "What is your last name?" I ask with all the warmth of a seasoned counselor.

"Black. Dot and Buddy Black. It's really Marvarine and Willis Black, but everybody just calls us Dot and Buddy." Dot's hair is all teased and permed and frosted silver on top. It appears clean. She's wearing cheap white sneakers, brown socks and oversized jeans. She is a thin, wiry woman with a hard edge.

"Address?" I ask.

"Eight sixty-three Squire, in Granger."

"Are you employed?"

Buddy has yet to open his mouth, and I get the impression Dot has been doing the talking for many years now. "I'm on Social Security Disability," she says. "I'm only fifty-eight, but I've got a bad heart. Buddy draws a pension, a small one."

Buddy just looks at me. He wears thick glasses with plastic stems that barely reach his ears. His cheeks are red and plump. His hair is bushy and gray with a brown tint to it. I doubt if it's been washed in a week. His shirt is a black-and-red-plaid number, even dirtier than his hair.

"How old is Mr. Black?" I ask her, uncertain as to whether Mr. Black would tell me if I asked him.

"It's Buddy, okay? Dot and Buddy. None of this Mister business, okay? He's sixty-two. Can I tell you something?"

I nod quickly. Buddy glances at Booker across the table.

"He ain't right," she whispers with a slight nod in Buddy's general direction. I look at him. He looks at us. "War injury," she says. "Korea. You know those metal detectors at the airport?"

I nod again.

"Well, he could walk through one buck naked and the thing would go off."

Buddy's shirt is stretched almost threadbare and its buttons are about to pop as it tries desperately to cover his protruding gut. He has at least three chins. I try to picture a naked Buddy walking through the Memphis International Airport with the alarms buzzing and security guards in a panic.

"Got a plate in his head," she adds in summation.

"That's—that's awful," I whisper back to her, then write on my pad that Mr. Buddy Black has a plate in his head. Mr. Black turns to his left and glares at Booker's client three feet away.

Suddenly, she lurches forward. "Something else," she says.

I lean slightly toward her in anticipation. "Yes?"

"He has a problem with alkeehall."

"You don't say."

"But it all goes back to the war injury," she adds helpfully. And just like that, this woman I met three minutes ago has reduced her husband to an alcoholic imbecile.

"Mind if I smoke?" she asks as she tugs at her purse.

"Is it allowed in here?" I ask, looking and hoping for a No Smoking sign. I don't see one.

"Oh sure." She sticks a cigarette between her cracked lips and lights it, then yanks it out and blows a cloud of smoke directly at Buddy, who doesn't move an inch.

"What can I do for you folks?" I ask, looking at the bundle of papers with wide rubber bands wrapped tightly around it. I slide Miss Birdie's will under my legal pad. My first client is a multimillionaire, and my next clients are pensioners. My fledgling career has come crashing back to earth.

"We don't have much money," she says quietly as if this is a big secret and she's embarrassed to reveal it. I smile compassionately. Regardless of what they own, they're much wealthier than I, and I doubt if they're about to be sued.

"And we need a lawyer," she adds as she takes the papers and snaps off the rubber bands.

"What's the problem?"

"Well, we're gettin' a royal screwin' by an insurance company."

"What type of policy?" I ask. She shoves the paperwork toward me, then wipes her hands as if she's rid of it and the burden has now been passed to a miracle worker. A smudged, creased and well-worn policy of some sort is on the top of the pile. Dot blows another cloud and for a moment I can barely see Buddy.

"It's a medical policy," she says. "We bought it five years ago, Great Benefit Life, when our boys were seventeen. Now Donny Ray is dying of leukemia, and the crooks won't pay for his treatment."

"Great Benefit?"

"Right."

"Never heard of them," I say confidently as I scan the declaration page of the policy, as if I've handled many of these lawsuits and personally know everything about every insurance company. Two dependents are listed, Donny

Ray and Ronny Ray Black. They have the same birth dates.

"Well, pardon my French, but they're a bunch of sumbitches."

"Most insurance companies are," I add thoughtfully, and Dot smiles at this. I have won her confidence. "So you purchased this policy five years ago?"

"Something like that. Never missed a premium, and never used the damned thing until Donny Ray got sick."

I'm a student, an uninsured one. There are no policies covering me or my life, health or auto. I can't even afford a new tire for the left rear of my ragged little Toyota.

"And, uh, you say he's dying?"

She nods with the cigarette between her lips. "Acute leukemia. Caught it eight months ago. Doctors gave him a year, but he won't make it because he couldn't get his bone marrow transplant. Now it's probably too late."

She pronounces "marrow" in one syllable: "mare."

"A transplant?" I say, confused.

"Don't you know nothin' about leukemia?"

"Uh, not really."

She clicks her teeth and rolls her eyes around as if I'm a complete idiot, then inserts the cigarette for a painful drag. When the smoke is sufficiently exhaled, she says, "My boys are identical twins, you see. So Ron, we call him Ron because he don't like Ronny Ray, is a perfect match for Donny Ray's bone mare transplant. Doctors said so. Problem is, the transplant costs somewhere around a hundred-fifty thousand dollars. We ain't got it, you see. The insurance company's supposed to pay it because it's covered in the policy right there. Sumbitches said no. So Donny Ray's dying because of them."

She has an amazing way of getting to the core of this.

We have been ignoring Buddy, but he's been listening. He slowly removes his thick glasses and dabs his eyes with the hairy back of his left hand. Great. Buddy's crying, Bosco's whimpering at the far end. And Booker's client had been struck again with guilt or remorse or some sort of grief and is sobbing into his hands. Smoot is standing by a window watching us, no doubt wondering what manner of advice we're dispensing to evoke such sorrow.

"Where does he live?" I ask, just searching for a question the answer to which will allow me to write for a few seconds on my pad and ignore the tears.

"He's never left home. Lives with us. That's another reason the insurance company turned us down, said since he's an adult he's no longer covered."

I pick through the papers and glance at letters to and from Great Benefit. "Does the policy terminate his coverage when he becomes an adult?"

She shakes her head and smiles tightly. "Nope. Ain't in the policy, Rudy. I've read it a dozen times, and there's no such thing. Even read all the fine print."

"Are you sure?" I ask, again glancing at the policy.

"I'm positive. I've been reading that damned thing for almost a year."

"Who sold it to you? Who's the agent?"

"Some little goofy twerp who knocked on our door and talked us into it. Name was Ott or something like that, just a slick little crook who talked real fast. I've tried to find him, but evidently he's skipped town."

I pick a letter from the pile and read it. It's from a senior claims examiner in Cleveland, written several months after the first letter I looked at, and it rather abruptly denies coverage on the grounds that Donny's leukemia was a preexisting condition, and therefore not covered. If Donny in fact has had leukemia for less than a year, then he was diagnosed four years after the policy was issued by Great Benefit. "Says here coverage was denied because of a preexisting condition."

"They've used every excuse in the book, Rudy. Just take all those papers there and read them carefully. Exclusions, exemptions, preexisting conditions, fine print, they've tried everything."

"Is there an exclusion for bone marrow transplants?"

"Hell no. Our doctor even looked at the policy and said Great Benefit ought to pay because bone mare transplants are just routine treatment now."

Booker's client wipes his face with both hands, stands and excuses himself. He thanks Booker and Booker thanks him. The old man takes a chair near a heated contest of Chinese checkers. Miss Birdie finally frees N. Elizabeth Erickson of Bosco and his problems. Smoot paces behind us.

The next letter is also from Great Benefit, and at first looks like all the rest. It is quick, nasty and to the point. It says: "Dear Mrs. Black: On seven prior occasions this company has denied your claim in writing. We now deny it for the eighth and final time. You must be stupid, stupid, stupid!" It was signed by the Senior Claims Supervisor, and I rub the engraved logo at the top in disbelief. Last fall I took a course called Insurance Law, and I remember being shocked at the egregious behavior of certain companies in bad-faith cases. Our instructor had been a visiting Communist who hated insurance companies, hated all corporations in fact, and had relished the study of wrongful denials of legitimate claims by insurers. It was his belief that tens of thousands of bad-faith cases exist in this country and are never brought to justice. He'd written books about bad-faith litigation, and even had statistics to prove his point that many people simply accept the denial of their claims without serious inquiry.

I read the letter again while touching the fancy Great Benefit Life logo across the top.

"And you never missed a premium?" I ask Dot.

"No sir. Not a single one."

"I'll need to see Donny's medical records."

"I've got most of them at home. He ain't seen a doctor much lately. We just can't afford it."

"Do you know the exact date he was diagnosed with leukemia?"

"No, but it was in August of last year. He was in the hospital for the first round of chemo. Then these crooks informed us they wouldn't cover any more treatment, so the hospital shut us out. Said they couldn't afford to give us a transplant. Just cost too damned much. I can't blame them, really."

Buddy is inspecting Booker's next client, a frail little woman who also has a pile of paperwork. Dot fumbles with her pack of Salems and finally sticks another one in her mouth.

If Donny's illness is in fact leukemia, and he's had it for only eight months, then there's no way it could be excluded as a preexisting condition. If there's no exemption or exclusion for leukemia, Great Benefit must pay. Right? This makes sense to me, seems awfully clear in my mind, and since the law is rarely clear and seldom makes sense, I know there must be something fatal awaiting me deep in the depths of Dot's pile of rejections.

"I don't really understand this," I say, still staring at the Stupid Letter.

Dot blasts a dense cloud of blue fog at her husband, and the smoke boils around his head. I think his eyes are dry, but I'm not certain. She smacks her sticky lips and says, "It's simple, Rudy. They're a bunch of crooks. They think we're just simple, ignorant trash with no money to fight 'em. I worked in a blue jean factory for thirty years, joined the union, you know, and we fought the company every day. Same thing here. Big corporation running roughshod over little people."

In addition to hating lawyers, my father also frequently spewed forth venom on the subject of labor unions. Naturally, I matured into a fervent defender of the working masses. "This letter is incredible," I say to her.

"Which one?"

"The one from Mr. Krokit, in which he says you're stupid, stupid, stupid."

"That son of a bitch. I wish he'd bring his ass down here and call me stupid to my face. Yankee bastard."

Buddy waves at the smoke in his face and grunts something. I glance at him in hopes that he may try to speak, but he lets it pass. For the first time I notice the left side of his head is a tad flatter than the right, and the thought of him tiptoeing bare-assed through the airport again flashes before my eyes. I fold the Stupid Letter and place it on top of the pile.

"It will take a few hours to review all this," I say.

"Well, you need to hurry. Donny Ray ain't got long. He weighs a hundred and ten pounds now, down from a hundred and sixty. He's so sick some days he can barely walk. I wish you could see him."

I have no desire to see Donny Ray. "Yeah, maybe later." I'll review the policy and the letters, and Donny's medicals, then I'll consult with Smoot and write a nice two-page letter to the Blacks in which I'll explain with great wisdom that they should have the case reviewed by a real lawyer, and not just any real lawyer, but one who specializes in suing insurance companies for bad faith. And I'll throw in a few names of such lawyers, along with their phone numbers, then I'll be finished with this worthless course, and finished with Smoot and his passion for Geezer Law.

Graduation is thirty-eight days away.

"I'll need to keep all this," I explain to Dot as I organize her mess and gather her rubber bands. "I'll be back here in two weeks with an advisement letter."

"Why does it take two weeks?"

"Well, I, uh, I'll have to do some research, you know, consult with my professors, look up some stuff. Can you send me Donny's medical records?"

"Sure. But I wish you'd hurry."

"I'll do my best, Dot."

"Do you think we've got a case?"

Though a mere student of the law, I've already learned a great deal of double-talk. "Can't say at this point. Looks promising, though. But it'll take further review and careful research. It's possible."

"What the hell does that mean?"

"Well, uh, it means I think you've got a good claim, but I'll need to review all this stuff before I know for sure."

"What kind of lawyer are you?"

"I'm a law student."

This seems to puzzle her. She curls her lips tightly around the white filter and glares at me. Buddy grunts for the second time. Smoot, thankfully, appears from behind, and asks, "How's it going here?"

Dot glares first at his bow tie, then at his wild hair.

"Just fine," I say. "We're finishing up."

"Very well," he says, as if time is up and more clients must be tended to. He eases away.

"I'll see you folks in a couple of weeks," I say warmly with a fake smile.

Dot stubs her cigarette in an ashtray, and leans closer again. Her lip is suddenly quivering and her eyes are wet. She gently touches my wrist and looks helplessly at me. "Please hurry, Rudy. We need help. My boy is dying."

We stare at each other forever, and I finally nod and mumble something. These poor people have just entrusted the life of their son to me, a third-year law student at Memphis State. They honestly believe I can take this pile of rubble they've shoved in front of me, pick up the phone, make a few calls, write a few letters, huff and puff, threaten this and that and, Presto!, Great Benefit will fall to its knees and throw money at Donny Ray. And they expect this to happen quickly.

They stand and awkwardly retreat from my table. I am almost certain that somewhere in the policy is a perfect little exclusion, barely readable and certainly indecipherable, but nonetheless placed there by skilled legal craftsmen who've been collecting fat retainers and delightfully breeding small print for decades.

With Buddy in tow, Dot zigzags through folding chairs and serious Rook players and stops at the coffeepot, where she fills a paper cup with decaf and lights another cigarette. They huddle there in the rear of the room, sipping coffee and watching me from sixty feet away. I flip through the policy, thirty pages of scarcely readable fine print, and take notes. I try to ignore them.

The crowd has thinned and people are slowly leaving. I'm tired of being a lawyer, had enough for one day, and I hope I get no more customers. My ignorance of the law is shocking, and I shudder to think that in a few short months I will be standing in courtrooms around this city arguing with other lawyers before judges and juries. I'm not ready to be turned loose upon society with the power to sue.

Law school is nothing but three years of wasted stress. We spend countless hours digging for information we'll never need. We are bombarded with lectures that are instantly forgotten. We memorize cases and statutes which will be reversed and amended tomorrow. If I'd spent fifty hours a week for the past three years training under a good lawyer, then I would be a good lawyer. Instead, I'm a nervous third-year student afraid of the simplest of legal problems and terrified of my impending bar exam.

There is movement before me, and I glance up in time to see a chubby old fella with a massive hearing aid shuffling in my direction.

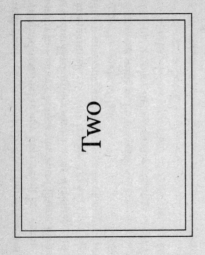

TWO

AN HOUR LATER, THE LANGUID BATTLES over Chinese checkers and gin rummy peter out, and the last of the geezers leaves the building. A janitor waits near the door as Smoot gathers us around him for a postgame summary. We take turns briefly summarizing our new clients' various problems. We're tired and anxious to leave this place.

Smoot offers a few suggestions, nothing creative or original, and dismisses us with the promise that we will discuss these real legal problems of the elderly in class next week. I can't wait.

Booker and I leave in his car, an aged Pontiac too large to be stylish but in much better shape than my crumbling Toyota. Booker has two small children and a wife who teaches school part-time, so he's hovering somewhere just above the poverty line. He studies hard and makes good grades, and because of this he caught the attention of an affluent black firm downtown, a pretty classy outfit known for its expertise in civil rights litigation. His starting salary is forty thousand a year, which is six more than Brodnax and Speer offered me.

"I hate law school," I say as we leave the parking lot of the Cypress Gardens Senior Citizens Building.

"You're normal," Booker replies. Booker does not hate anything or anybody, and even at times claims to be challenged by the study of law.

"Why do we want to be lawyers?"

"Serve the public, fight injustice, change society, you know, the usual. Don't you listen to Professor Smoot?"

"Let's go get a beer."

"It's not yet three o'clock, Rudy," Booker drinks little, and I drink even less because it's an expensive habit and right now I must save to buy food.

"Just kidding," I say. He drives in the general direction of the law school. Today is Thursday, which means tomorrow I will be burdened with Sports Law and the Napoleonic Code, two courses equally as worthless as Geezer Law and requiring even less work. But there is a bar exam looming, and when I think about it my hands tremble slightly. If I flunk the bar exam, those nice but stiff and unsmiling fellas at Brodnax and Speer will most certainly ask me to leave, which means I'll work for about a month then hit the streets. Flunking the bar exam is unthinkable —it would lead me to unemployment, bankruptcy, disgrace, starvation. So why do I think about it every hour of every day? "Just take me to the library," I say. "I think I'll work on these cases, then hit the bar review."

"Good idea."

"I hate the library."

"Everyone hates the library, Rudy. It's designed to be hated. Its primary purpose is to be hated by law students. You're just normal."

"Thanks."

"That first old lady, Miss Birdie, she got money?"

"How'd you know?"

"I thought I overheard something."

"Yeah. She's loaded. She needs a new will. She's neglected by her children and grandchildren, so, of course, she wants to cut them out."

"How much?"

"Twenty million or so."

Booker glances at me with a great deal of suspicion. "That's what she says," I add.

"So who gets the money?"

"A sexy TV preacher with his own Learjet."

"No."

"I swear."

Booker chews on this for two blocks of heavy traffic. "Look, Rudy, no offense, you're a great guy and all, good student, bright, but do you feel comfortable drafting a will for an estate worth that much money?"

"No. Do you?"

"Of course not. So what'll you do?"

"Maybe she'll die in her sleep."

"I don't think so. She's too feisty. She'll outlive us."

"I'll dump it on Smoot. Maybe get one of the tax professors to help me. Or maybe I'll just tell Miss Birdie that I can't help her, that she needs to pay a high-powered tax lawyer five grand to draft it. I really don't care. I've got my own problems."

"Texaco?"

"Yeah. They're coming after me. My landlord too."

"I wish I could help," Booker says, and I know he means it. If he could spare the money, he'd gladly loan it to me.

"I'll survive until July 1. Then I'll be a big-shot mouthpiece for Brodnax and Speer and my days of poverty will be over. How in the world, dear Booker, can I possibly spend thirty-four thousand dollars a year?"

"Sounds impossible. You'll be rich."

"I mean, hell, I've lived on tips and nickels for seven years. What will I do with all the money?"

"Buy another suit?"

"Why? I already have two."

"Perhaps some shoes?"

"That's it. That's what I'll do. I'll buy shoes, Booker. Shoes and ties, and maybe some food that doesn't come in a can, and perhaps a fresh pack of Jockey shorts."

At least twice a month for three years now, Booker and his wife have invited me to dinner. Her name is Charlene, a Memphis girl, and she does wonders with food on a lean budget. They're friends, but I'm sure they feel sorry for me. Booker grins, then looks away. He's tired of this joking about things that are unpleasant.

He pulls into the parking lot across Central Avenue from the Memphis State Law School. "I have to run some errands," he says.

"Sure. Thanks for the ride."

"I'll be back around six. Let's study for the bar."

"Sure. I'll be downstairs."

I slam the door and jog across Central.

IN A DARK and private corner in the basement of the library, behind stacks of cracked and ancient law books and hidden from view, I find my favorite study carrel sitting all alone, just waiting for me as it has for many months now. It's officially reserved in my name. The corner is windowless and at times damp and cold, ar   r this reason few people venture near here. I've spen   urs in this, my private little burrow, briefing cases and studying for exams. And for the past weeks, I've sat here for many aching hours wondering what happened to her and asking myself at what point I let her get away. I torment myself here. The flat desktop is surrounded on three sides by panels, and I've memorized the contour of the wood grain on each small wall. I can cry without getting caught. I can even curse at a low decibel, and no one will hear.

Many times during the glorious affair, Sara joined me here, and we studied together with our chairs sitting snugly side by side. We could giggle and laugh, and no one cared. We could kiss and touch, and no one saw. At this moment, in the depths of this depression and sorrow, I can almost smell her perfume.

I really should find another place in this sprawling labyrinth to study. Now, when I stare at the panels around me, I see her face and remember the feel of her legs, and I'm immediately overcome with a deadening heartache that paralyzes me. She was here, just weeks ago! And now someone else is touching those legs.

I take the Blacks' stack of papers and walk upstairs to the insurance section of the library. My movements are slow but my eyes dart quickly in all directions. Sara doesn't come here much anymore, but I've seen her a couple of times.

I spread Dot's papers on an abandoned table between the stacks, and read once again the Stupid Letter. It is shocking and mean, and obviously written by someone convinced that Dot and Buddy would never show it to a lawyer. I read it again, and become aware that the heartache has begun to subside—it comes and goes, and I'm learning to deal with it.

Sara Plankmore is also a third-year law student, and she's the only girl I've ever loved. She dumped me four months ago for an Ivy Leaguer, a local blueblood. She told me they were old friends from high school, and they somehow bumped into each other during Christmas break. The romance was rekindled, and she hated to do it to me, but life goes on. There's a strong rumor floating around these halls that she's pregnant. I actually vomited when I first heard about it.

I examine the Blacks' policy with Great Benefit, and take pages of notes. It reads like Sanskrit. I organize the letters and claim forms and medical reports. Sara has disappeared for the moment, and I've become lost in a disputed insurance claim that stinks more and more.

The policy was purchased for eighteen dollars a week from the Great Benefit Life Insurance Company of Cleveland, Ohio. I study the debit book, a little journal used to record the weekly payments. It appears as though the agent, one Bobby Ott, actually visited the Blacks every week.

My little table is covered with neat stacks of papers, and I read everything Dot gave me. I keep thinking about Max Leuberg, the visiting Communist professor, and his passionate hatred of insurance companies. They rule our country, he said over and over. They control the banking industry. They own the real estate. They catch a virus and Wall Street has diarrhea for a week. And when interest rates fall and their investment earnings plummet, then they run to Congress and demand tort reform. Lawsuits are killing us, they scream. Those filthy trial lawyers are filing frivolous lawsuits and convincing ignorant juries to dole out huge awards, and we've got to stop it or we'll go broke. Leuberg would get so angry he'd throw books at the wall. We loved him.

And he's still teaching here. I think he goes back to Wisconsin at the end of this semester, and if I find the courage I just might ask him to review the Black case against Great Benefit. He claims he's assisted in several landmark bad-faith cases up north in which juries returned huge punitive awards against insurers.

I begin writing a summary of the case. I start with the date the policy was issued, then chronologically list each significant event. Great Benefit, in writing, denied coverage eight times. The eighth was, of course, the Stupid Letter. I can hear Max Leuberg whistling and laughing when he reads this letter. I smell blood.

I HOPE Professor Leuberg smells it too. I find his office tucked away between two storage rooms on the third floor of the law school. The door is covered with flyers for gay rights marches and boycotts and endangered species rallies, the sorts of causes that draw little interest in Memphis. It's half open, and I hear him barking into the phone. I hold my breath, and knock lightly.

"Come in!" he shouts, and I slowly ease through the door. He waves at the only chair. It's filled with books and files and magazines. The entire office is a landfill. Clutter, debris, newspapers, bottles. The bookshelves bulge and sag. Graffiti posters cover the walls. Odd scraps of paper lay like puddles on the floor. Time and organization mean nothing to Max Leuberg.

He's a thin, short man of sixty with wild, bushy hair the color of straw and hands that are never still. He wears faded jeans, environmentally provocative sweatshirts and old sneakers. If it's cold, he'll sometimes wear socks. He's so damned hyper he makes me nervous.

He slams the phone down. "Baker!"

"Baylor. Rudy Baylor. Insurance, last semester."

"Sure! Sure! I remember. Have a seat." He waves again at the chair.

"No thanks."

He squirms and shuffles a stack of papers on his desk. "So what's up, Baylor?" Max is adored by the students because he always takes time to listen.

"Well, uh, have you got a minute?" I would normally be more formal and say "Sir" or something like that, but Max hates formalities. He insisted we call him Max.

"Yeah, sure. What's on your mind?"

"Well, I'm taking a class under Professor Smoot," I ex-plain, then go on with a quick summary of my visit to the geezers' lunch and of Dot and Buddy and their fight with Great Benefit. He seems to hang on every word.

"Have you ever heard of Great Benefit?" I ask.

"Yeah. It's a big outfit that sells a lot of cheap insurance to rural whites and blacks. Very sleazy."

"I've never heard of them."

"You wouldn't. They don't advertise. Their agents knock on doors and collect premiums each week. We're talking about the scratch-and-sniff armpit of the industry. Let me see the policy."

I hand it to him, and he flips pages. "What are their grounds for denial?" he asks without looking at me.

"Everything. First they denied just on principal. Then they said leukemia wasn't covered. Then they said the leukemia was a preexisting condition. Then they said the kid was an adult and thus not covered under his parents' policy. They've been quite creative, actually."

"Were all the premiums paid?"

"According to Mrs. Black they were."

"The bastards." He flips more pages, smiling wickedly. Max loves this. "And you've reviewed the entire file?"

"Yeah. I've read everything the client gave me."

He tosses the policy onto the desk. "Definitely worth looking into," he says. "But keep in mind the client rarely gives you everything up front." I hand him the Stupid Letter. As he reads it, another nasty little smile breaks across his face. He reads it again, and finally glances at me. "Incredible."

"I thought so too," I add like a veteran watchdog of the insurance industry.

"Where's the rest of the file?" he asks.

I place the entire pile of papers on his desk. "This is

everything Mrs. Black gave me. She said her son is dying because they can't afford treatment. Said he weighs a hundred and ten pounds, and won't live long."

His hands become still. "Bastards," he says again, almost to himself. "Stinkin' bastards."

I agree completely, but say nothing. I notice another pair of sneakers parked in a corner—very old Nikes. He explained to us in class that he at one time wore Converse, but is now boycotting the company because of a recycling policy. He wages his own personal little war against corporate America, and buys nothing if the manufacturer has in the slightest way miffed him. He refuses to insure his life, health or assets, but rumor has it his family is wealthy and thus he can afford to venture about uninsured. I, on the other hand, for obvious reasons, live in the world of the uninsured.

Most of my professors are stuffy academics who wear ties to class and lecture with their coats buttoned. Max hasn't worn a tie in decades. And he doesn't lecture. He performs. I hate to see him leave this place.

His hands jump back to life again. "I'd like to review this tonight," he says without looking at me.

"No problem. Can I stop by in the morning?"

"Sure. Anytime."

His phone rings and he snatches it up. I smile and back through the door with a great deal of relief. I'll meet with him in the morning, listen to his advice, then type a two-page report to the Blacks in which I'll repeat whatever he tells me.

Now, if I can only find some bright soul to do the research for Miss Birdie. I have a few prospects, a couple of tax professors, and I might try them tomorrow. I walk down the stairs and enter the student lounge next to the library. It's the only place in the building where smoking is permitted, and a permanent blue fog hangs just below the lights. There is one television and an assortment of abused sofas and chairs. Class pictures adorn the walls—framed collections of studious faces long ago sent into the trenches of legal warfare. When the room is empty, I often stare at these, my predecessors, and wonder how many have been disbarred and how many wish they'd never seen this place and how few actually enjoy suing and defending. One wall is reserved for notices and bulletins and want-ads of an amazing variety, and behind it is a row of soft-drink and food dispensers. I partake of many meals here. Machine food is underrated.

Huddled to one side I see the Honorable F. Franklin Donaldson the Fourth gossiping with three of his buddies, all prickish sorts who write for the Law Review and frown upon those of us who don't. He notices me, and seems interested in something. He smiles as I walk by, which is unusual, because his face is forever fixed in a frozen scowl.

"Say, Rudy, you're going with Brodnax and Speer, aren't you?" he calls out loudly. The television is off. His buddies stare at me. Two female students on a sofa perk up and look in my direction.

"Yeah. What about it?" I ask. F. Franklin the Fourth has a job with a firm rich in heritage, money and pretentiousness, a firm vastly superior to Brodnax and Speer. His sidekicks at this moment are W. Harper Whittenson, an arrogant little snot who will, thankfully, leave Memphis and practice with a mega-firm in Dallas; J. Townsend Gross, who has accepted a position with another huge firm; and James Straybeck, a sometimes friendly sort who's suffered three years of law school without an initial to place before his name or numerals to stick after it. With such a short name, his future as a big-firm lawyer is in jeopardy. I doubt if he'll make it.

F. Franklin the Fourth takes a step in my direction. He's all smiles. "Well, tell us what's happening."

"What's happening?" I have no idea what he's talking about.

"Yeah, you know, about the merger."

I keep a straight face. "What merger?"

"You haven't heard?"

"Heard what?"

F. Franklin the Fourth glances at his three buddies, and they all seem to be amused. His smile widens as he looks at me. "Come on, Rudy, the merger of Brodnax and Speer and Tinley Britt."

I stand very still and try to think of something intelligent or clever to say. But, for the moment, words fail me. Obviously, I know nothing about the merger, and, obviously, this asshole knows something. Brodnax and Speer is a small outfit, fifteen lawyers, and I'm the only recruit they've hired from my class. When we came to terms two months ago, there was no mention of merger plans.

Tinley Britt, on the other hand, is the largest, stuffiest, most prestigious and wealthiest firm in the state. At last count, a hundred and twenty lawyers called it home. Many are from Ivy League schools. Many have federal clerkships on their pedigrees. It's a powerful firm that represents rich corporations and governmental entities, and has an office in Washington, where it lobbies with the elite. It's a bastion of hardball conservative politics. A former U.S. senator is a partner. Its associates work eighty hours a week, and they all dress in navy and black with white button-down shirts and striped ties. Their haircuts are short and no facial hair is permitted. You can spot a Tinley Britt lawyer by the way he struts and dresses. The firm is filled with nothing but Waspy male preppies all from the right schools and right fraternities, and thus the rest of the Memphis legal community has forever dubbed it Trent & Brent.

J. Townsend Gross has his hands in his pockets and is sneering at me. He's number two in our class, and wears the right amount of starch in his Polo shirts, and drives a BMW, and so he was immediately attracted to Trent & Brent.

My knees are weak because I know Trent & Brent would never want me. If Brodnax and Speer has in fact merged with this behemoth, I fear that perhaps I've been lost in the shuffle.

"I haven't heard," I say feebly. The girls on the sofa are watching intently. There is silence.

"You mean, they haven't told you?" F. Franklin the Fourth asks in disbelief. "Jack here heard it around noon today," he says, nodding at his comrade J. Townsend Gross.

"It's true," J. Townsend says. "But the firm name is unchanged."

The firm name, other than Trent & Brent, is Tinley, Britt, Crawford, Mize and St. John. Mercifully, years back someone opted for the abbreviated version. By stating that the firm name remains the same, J. Townsend has informed this small audience that Brodnax and Speer is so small and so insignificant that it can be swallowed whole by Tinley Britt without so much as a light belch.

"So it's still Trent & Brent?" I say to J. Townsend, who snorts at this overworked nickname.

"I can't believe they wouldn't tell you," F. Franklin the Fourth continues.

I shrug as if this is nothing, and walk to the door. "Perhaps you're worrying too much about it, Frankie." They exchange confident smirks as if they've accomplished whatever they set out to accomplish, and I leave the lounge. I enter the library and the clerk behind the front desk motions for me.

"Here's a message," he says as he hands me a scrap of paper. It's a note to call Loyd Beck, the managing partner of Brodnax and Speer, the man who hired me.

The pay phones are in the lounge, but I'm in no mood to see F. Franklin the Fourth and his band of cutthroats again. "Can I borrow your phone?" I ask the desk clerk, a second-year student who acts as if he owns the library.

"Pay phones are in the lounge," he says, pointing, as if I've studied law here for three years now and still don't know the location of the student lounge.

"I just came from there. They're all busy."

He frowns and looks around. "All right, make it quick." I punch the numbers for Brodnax and Speer. It's almost six, and the secretaries leave at five. On the ninth ring, a male voice says simply, "Hello."

I turn my back to the front of the library and try to hide in the reserve shelves. "Hello, this is Rudy Baylor. I'm at the law school, and I have a note to call Loyd Beck. Says it's urgent." The note says nothing about being urgent, but at this moment I'm rather jumpy.

"Rudy Baylor? In reference to what?"

"I'm the guy you all just hired. Who is this?"

"Oh, yeah. Baylor. This is Carson Bell. Uh, Loyd's in a meeting and can't be disturbed right now. Try back in an hour."

I met Carson Bell briefly when they gave me the tour of the place, and I remember him as a typically harried litigator, friendly for a second then back to work. "Uh, Mr. Bell, I think I really need to talk to Mr. Beck."

"I'm sorry, but you can't right now. Okay?"

"I've heard a rumor about a merger with Trent, uh, with Tinley Britt. Is it true?"

"Look, Rudy, I'm busy and I can't talk right now. Call back in an hour and Loyd will handle you."

Handle me? "Do I still have a position?" I ask in fear and some measure of desperation.

"Call back in an hour," he says irritably, and then slams down the phone.

I scribble a message on a scrap of paper and hand it to the desk clerk. "Do you know Booker Kane?" I ask.

"Yeah."

"Good. He'll be here in a few minutes. Give him this message. Tell him I'll be back in an hour or so."

He grunts but takes the message. I leave the library, ease by the lounge and pray that no one sees me, then leave the building and run to the parking lot, where my Toyota awaits me. I hope the engine will start. One of my darkest secrets is that I still owe a finance company almost three hundred dollars on this pitiful wreck. I've even lied to Booker. He thinks it's paid for.

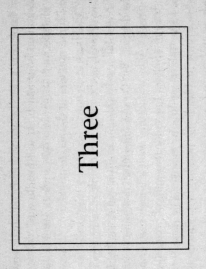

Three

I T'S NO SECRET THAT THERE ARE TOO MANY lawyers in Memphis. They told us this when we started law school, said the profession was terribly overcrowded not just here but everywhere, that some of us would kill ourselves for three years, fight to pass the bar and still not be able to find employment. So, as a favor, they told us at first-year orientation that they would flunk out at least a third of our class. This, they did.

I can name at least ten people who'll graduate with me next month and after graduation they'll have plenty of time to study for the bar because they have yet to find work. Seven years of college, and unemployed. I can also think of several dozen of my classmates who will go to work as assistant public defenders and assistant city prosecutors and low-paid clerks for underpaid judges, the jobs they didn't tell us about when we started law school.

So, in many ways, I've been quite proud of my position with Brodnax and Speer, a real law firm. Yes, I've been rather smug at times around lesser talents, some of whom are still scrambling around and begging for interviews.

That arrogance, however, has suddenly vanished. There is a knot in my stomach as I drive toward downtown. There's no place for me in a firm such as Trent & Brent. The Toyota sputters and spits, as usual, but at least it's moving.

I try to analyze the merger. A couple of years ago Trent & Brent swallowed a thirty-man firm, and it was big news around town. But I can't remember if jobs were lost in the process. Why would they want a fifteen-man firm like Brodnax and Speer? I'm suddenly aware of precisely how little I know about my future employer. Old man Brodnax died years ago, and his beefy face has been immortalized in a hideous bronze bust sitting by the front door of the offices. Speer is his son-in-law, though long since divorced from his daughter. I met Speer briefly, and he was nice enough. They told me during the second or third interview that their biggest clients were a couple of insurance companies, and that eighty percent of their practice was defending car wrecks.

Perhaps Trent & Brent needed a little muscle in their car wreck defense division. Who knows.

Traffic is thick on Poplar, but most of it is running the other way. I can see the tall buildings downtown. Surely Loyd Beck and Carson Bell and the rest of those fellas at Brodnax and Speer would not agree to hire me, make all sorts of commitments and plans, then cut my throat for the sake of money. They wouldn't merge with Trent & Brent and not protect their own people, would they?

For the past year, those of my classmates who will graduate with me next month have scoured this city looking for work. There cannot possibly be another job available. Not even the slightest morsel of employment could have slipped through the cracks.

Though the parking lots are emptying and there are plenty of spaces, I park illegally across the street from the eight-story building where Brodnax and Speer operates. Two blocks away is a bank building, the tallest downtown, and of course Trent & Brent leases the top half. From their lofty perch, they are able to gaze down with disdain upon the rest of the city. I hate them.

I dash across the street and enter the dirty lobby of the Powers Building. Two elevators are to the left, but to the right I notice a familiar face. It's Richard Spain, an associate with Brodnax and Speer, a really nice guy who took me to lunch during my first visit here. He's sitting on a narrow marble bench, staring blankly at the floor.

"Richard," I say as I walk over. "It's me, Rudy Baylor."

He doesn't move, just keeps staring. I sit beside him. The elevators are directly in front of us, thirty feet away.

"What's the matter, Richard?" I ask. He's in a daze. "Richard, are you all right?" The small lobby is empty for the moment, and things are quiet.

Slowly, he turns his head to me and his mouth drops slightly open. "They fired me," he says quietly. His eyes are red, and he's either been crying or drinking.

I take a deep breath. "Who?" I ask in a low-pitched voice, certain of the answer.

"They fired me," he says again.

"Richard, please talk to me. What's happening here? Who's been fired?"

"They fired all of us associates," he says slowly. "Beck called us into the conference room, said the partners had agreed to sell out to Tinley Britt, and that there was no room for the associates. Just like that. Gave us an hour to clean out our desks and leave the building." His head nods oddly from shoulder to shoulder when he says this, and he stares at the elevator doors.

"Just like that," I say.

"I guess you're wondering about your job," Richard says, still staring across the lobby.

"It has crossed my mind."

"These bastards don't care about you."

I, of course, had already determined this. "Why would they fire you guys?" I ask, my voice barely audible. Honestly, I don't care why they fired the associates. But I try to sound sincere.

"Trent & Brent wanted our clients," he says. "To get the clients, they had to buy the partners. We, the associates, just got in the way."

"I'm sorry," I say.

"Me too. Your name came up during the meeting. Somebody asked about you because you're the only incoming associate. Beck said he was trying to call you with the bad news. You got the ax too, Rudy. I'm sorry."

My head drops a few inches as I study the floor. My hands are sweaty.

"Do you know how much money I made last year?" he asks.

"How much?"

"Eighty thousand. I've slaved here for six years, worked seventy hours a week, ignored my family, shed blood for good old Brodnax and Speer, you know, and then these bastards tell me I've got an hour to clean out my desk and leave my office. They even had a security guard watch me pack my stuff. Eighty thousand bucks they paid me, and I billed twenty-five hundred hours at a hundred and fifty, so that's three hundred and seventy-five thousand I grossed for them last year. They reward me with eighty, give me a gold watch, tell me how great I am, maybe I'll make partner in a couple of years, you know, one big happy family. Then along comes Trent & Brent with their millions, and I'm out of work. And you're out of work too, pal. Do you know that? Do you realize you've just lost your first job before you even started?"

I can think of no response to this.

He gently lays his head on his left shoulder, and ignores me. "Eighty thousand. Pretty good money, don't you think, Rudy?"

"Yeah." Sounds like a small fortune to me.

"No way to find another job making that much money, you know? Impossible in this city. Nobody's hiring. Too many damned lawyers."

No kidding.

He wipes his eyes with his fingers, then slowly rises to his feet. "I gotta tell my wife," he mumbles to himself as he walks hunchbacked across the lobby, out of the building and disappears down the sidewalk.

I take the elevator to the fourth floor, and exit into a small foyer. Through a set of double glass doors I see a large, uniformed security guard standing near the front reception desk. He sneers at me as I enter the Brodnax and Speer suite.

"Can I help you?" he growls.

"I'm looking for Loyd Beck," I say, trying to peek around him for a glance down the hallway. He moves slightly to block my view.

"And who are you?"

"Rudy Baylor."

He leans over and picks up an envelope from the desk. "This is for you," he says. My name is handwritten in red ink. I unfold a short letter. My hands shake as I read it.

A voice squawks on his radio, and he backs away slowly. "Read the letter and leave," he says, then disappears down the hall.

The letter is a single paragraph, Loyd Beck to me, breaking the news gently and wishing me well. The merger was "sudden and unexpected."

I toss the letter on the floor and look for something else to throw. All's quiet in the back. I'm sure they're hunkered down behind locked doors, just waiting for me and the other misfits to clear out. There's a bust on a concrete pedestal by the door, a bad work of sculpture in bronze of old man Brodnax's fat face, and I spit on it as I walk by. It doesn't flinch. So I sort of shove it as I open the door. The pedestal rocks and the head falls off.

"Hey!" a voice booms from behind, and just as the bust crashes into the plate glass wall, I see the guard rushing toward me.

For a microsecond I give thought to stopping and apologizing, but then I dash through the foyer and yank open the door to the stairs. He yells at me again. I race downward, my feet pumping furiously. He's too old and too bulky to catch me.

The lobby is empty as I enter it from a door near the elevators. I calmly walk through the door, onto the sidewalk.

IT'S ALMOST SEVEN, and almost dark when I stop at a convenience store six blocks away. A hand-painted sign advertises a six-pack of cheap lite beer for three bucks. I need a six-pack of cheap lite beer.

Loyd Beck hired me two months ago, said my grades were good enough, my writing was sound, my interviews went well, that the guys around the office were unanimous in their opinion that I would fit in. Everything was lovely. Bright future with good old Brodnax and Speer.

Then Trent & Brent waves a few bucks, and the partners hit the back door. These greedy bastards make three hundred thousand a year, and want more.

I step inside and buy the beer. After taxes, I have four dollars and some change in my pocket. My bank account is not much healthier.

I sit in my car next to the phone booth and drain the first can. I have eaten nothing since my delicious lunch a few hours ago with Dot and Buddy and Bosco and Miss

Birdie. Maybe I should've eaten extra Jell-O, like Bosco. The cold beer hits my empty stomach, and there is an immediate buzz.

The cans are emptied quickly. The hours pass as I drive the streets of Memphis.

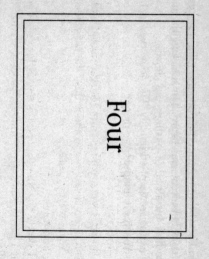

Four

M Y APARTMENT IS A GRUNGY TWO-room efficiency on the second floor of a decaying brick building called The Hampton; two seventy-five per month, seldom paid on time. It's a block off a busy street, a mile from campus. I've given much thought lately to simply skipping out in the middle of the night, then trying to negotiate some monthly payout over the next twelve months. Until now, these plans always included the element of a job and monthly paycheck from Brodnax and Speer. The Hampton is filled with students, deadbeats like myself, and the landlord is accustomed to haggling over arrearages.

The parking lot is dark and still when I arrive, just before two. I park near the Dumpster, and as I crawl from my car and shut the door, there is a sudden movement not far away. A man is quickly getting out of his car, slamming the door, coming straight for me. I freeze on the sidewalk. All is dark and quiet.

"Are you Rudy Baylor?" he asks, in my face. He's a

regular cowboy—pointed-toe boots, tight Levi's, denim shirt, neat haircut and beard. He smacks gum and looks like he's not afraid of pushing and shoving.

"Who are you?" I ask.

"You Rudy Baylor? Yes or no?"

"Yes."

He jerks some papers from his rear pocket and thrusts them in my face. "Sorry about this," he says sincerely.

"What is it?" I ask.

"Summons."

I slowly take the papers. It's too dark to read any of it, but I get the message. "You're a process server," I say in defeat.

"Yep."

"Texaco?"

"Yep. And The Hampton. You're being evicted."

If I were sober I might be shocked to be holding an eviction notice. But I've been stunned enough for one day. I glance at the dark, gloomy building with litter in the grass and weeds in the sidewalk, and I wonder how this pathetic place got the best of me.

He takes a step back. "It's all in there," he explains. "Court date, lawyers' names, etc. You can probably work this out with a few phone calls. None of my business though. Just doing my job."

What a job. Sneaking around in the shadows, jumping on unsuspecting people, shoving papers in their faces, leaving a few words of free legal advice, then slithering off to terrorize someone else.

As he's walking away, he stops and says, "Oh, listen. I'm an ex-cop, and I keep a scanner in my car. Had this weird call a few hours ago. Some guy named Rudy Baylor trashed a law office downtown. Description fits you. Same make and model on the car. Don't suppose it fits?"

"And if it does?"

"None of my business, you know. But the cops are looking for you. Destruction of private property."

"You mean, they'll arrest me?"

"Yep. I'd find another place to sleep tonight."

He ducks into his car, a BMW. I watch as he drives away.

BOOKER MEETS ME on the front porch of his neat duplex. He's wearing a paisley bathrobe over his pajamas. No slippers, just bare feet. Booker may be only another impoverished law student counting the days until employment, but he's serious about fashion. There's not much hanging in his closet, but his wardrobe is carefully selected. "What the hell's going on?" he asks tensely, his eyes still puffy. I called him from a pay phone at the Junior Food Mart around the corner.

"I'm sorry," I say as we step into the den. I can see Charlene in the tiny kitchen, also in her paisley bathrobe, hair pulled back, eyes puffy, making coffee or something. I can hear a kid yelling somewhere in the back. It's almost three in the morning, and I've wakened the whole bunch.

"Have a seat," Booker says, taking my arm and gently shoving me onto the sofa. "You've been drinking."

"I'm drunk, Booker."

"Any particular reason?" He's standing before me, much like an angry father.

"It's a long story."

"You mentioned the police."

Charlene sets a cup of hot coffee on the table next to me. "You okay, Rudy?" she asks with the sweetest voice.

"Great," I answer like a true smartass.

"Go check the kids," Booker says to her, and she disappears.

"I'm sorry," I say again. Booker sits on the edge of the coffee table, very close to me, and waits.

I ignore the coffee. My head is pounding. I unload my version of events since he and I left each other early yesterday afternoon. My tongue is thick and ponderous, so I take my time and try to concentrate on my narrative. Charlene eases into the nearest chair, and listens with great concern. "I'm sorry," I whisper to her.

"It's okay, Rudy. It's okay."

Charlene's father is a minister, somewhere in rural Tennessee, and she has no patience for drunkenness or slovenly conduct. The few drinks Booker and I have shared together in law school have been on the sly.

"You drank two six-packs?" he asks with disbelief.

Charlene leaves to check on the child who's begun squalling again from the back. I conclude with the process server, the lawsuit, the eviction. It's just been a helluva day.

"I gotta find a job, Booker," I say, gulping coffee.

"You got bigger problems right now. We take the bar in three months, then we face the screening committee. An arrest and conviction for this stunt could ruin you."

I hadn't thought about this. My head is splitting now, really pounding. "Could I have a sandwich?" I feel sick. I had a bag of pretzels with the second six-pack, but that's been it since lunch with Bosco and Miss Birdie.

Charlene hears this in the kitchen. "How about some bacon and eggs?"

"Fine, Charlene. Thanks."

Booker is deep in thought. "I'll call Marvin Shankle in a few hours. He can call his brother, maybe pull some strings with the police. We have to prevent the arrest."

"Sounds good to me." Marvin Shankle is the most prominent black lawyer in Memphis, Booker's future boss. "While you're at it, ask him if he's got any job openings."

"Right. You want to go to work in a black civil rights firm."

"Right now I'd take a job with a Korean divorce firm. No offense, Booker. I have to get a job. I'm looking at bankruptcy, man. There might be other creditors out there, just lurking in the bushes waiting to jump on me with papers. I can't take it." I slowly lie down on the sofa. Charlene's frying bacon and the heavy aroma drifts through the tiny den.

"Where are the papers?" Booker asks.

"In the car."

He leaves the room and returns in a minute. He sits in a chair nearby and studies the Texaco suit and the eviction notice. Charlene buzzes around the kitchen, brings me more coffee and aspirin. It's three-thirty in the morning. The kids are finally quiet. I feel safe and warm, even loved.

My head is spinning slowly as I close my eyes and drift away.

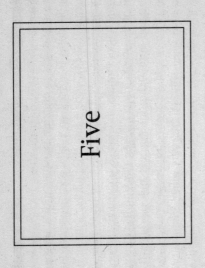

Five

L IKE A SNAKE CREEPING THROUGH THE undergrowth, I sneak into the law school well past noon and hours after both of my scheduled classes have broken up. Sports Law and Selected Readings from the Napoleonic Code, what a joke. I hide in my little pit in the remote corner of the library's basement floor.

Booker woke me on the sofa with the hopeful news that he'd talked to Marvin Shankle and the wheels were turning downtown. A certain captain or such was being called, and Mr. Shankle was optimistic the matter could be worked out. Mr. Shankle's brother is a judge in one of the criminal divisions, and if the charges couldn't get dismissed then other strings would be pulled. But there is still no word on whether the cops are looking for me. Booker would make some more calls and keep me posted.

Booker already has an office in the Shankle firm. He's clerked there for two years, working part-time and learning more than any five of the rest of us. He calls a secretary between classes, works diligently with his appointment book, tells me about this client and that one. He'll make a great lawyer.

It's impossible to organize thoughts with a hangover. I scribble notes to myself on a legal pad, important things, like, now that I've made it into this building without being spotted, what next? I'll wait a couple of hours here while the law school empties. It's Friday afternoon, the slowest time of the week. Then I'll ease down to the Placement Office and corner the director and spill my guts. If I'm lucky, there might be some obscure government agency which has been spurned by every other graduate and is still offering twenty thousand a year for a bright legal mind. Or maybe a small company has suddenly found the need for another in-house lawyer. At this point, there aren't many maybes left.

There's a legend in Memphis by the name of Jonathan Lake, a graduate of this law school who also could not find employment with the big firms downtown. Happened about twenty years ago. Lake was jilted by the established firms, so he rented some space, hung out a shingle, declared himself ready to sue. He starved for a few months, then crashed his motorcycle one night and woke up with a broken leg at St. Peter's, the charity hospital. Not long afterward, the bed next to him was occupied by a guy who'd also crashed a motorcycle. This guy was all broken up and badly burned. His girlfriend was burned even worse, and died a couple of days later. Lake and this guy got to be friends. Lake signed up both cases. As things evolved, the driver of the Jaguar that ran the stop sign and hit the motorcycle upon which Lake's new clients were riding just happened to be the senior partner for the third-largest law firm downtown. And he was the same guy who'd interviewed Lake six months earlier. And he was drunk when he ran the stop sign.

Lake sued with a vengeance. The drunk senior partner

had tons of insurance, which the company immediately began throwing at Lake. Everybody wanted a quick settlement. Six months after passing the bar exam, Jonathan Lake settled the cases for two point six million. Cash, no long-term payouts. Just up-front cash.

Legend holds that the biker told Lake while they were both laid up in the hospital that since Lake was so young and just out of school he could have half of whatever he recovered. Lake remembered this. The biker kept his word. Lake walked away with one point three, according to legend.

Me, I'd be off to the Caribbean with my one point three, sailing my own ketch and sipping rum punch.

Not Lake. He built an office, filled it with secretaries and paralegals and runners and investigators, and got serious about the business of litigation. He put in eighteen-hour days and was not afraid to sue anybody for any wrong. He studied hard, trained himself and quickly became the hottest trial lawyer in Tennessee.

Twenty years later, Jonathan Lake still works eighteen hours a day, owns a firm with eleven associates, no partners, tries more big cases than any lawyer around and makes, according to the legend, somewhere in the neighborhood of three million dollars a year.

And he likes to splash it around. Three million bucks a year is hard to hide in Memphis, so Jonathan Lake is always hot news. And his legend grows. Each year an unknown number of students enter this law school because of Jonathan Lake. They have the dream. And a few graduates leave this place without jobs because they want nothing more than a cubbyhole downtown with their name on the door. They want to starve and scratch, just like Lake.

I suspect they ride motorcycles too. Maybe that's where I'm headed. Maybe there's hope. Me and Lake.

I CATCH MAX LEUBERG at a bad time. He's on the phone, talking with his hands and cursing like a drunken sailor. Something about a lawsuit in St. Paul in which he's supposed to testify. I pretend to scribble notes, look at the floor, try not to listen as he stomps around behind his desk, tugging at the phone line.

He hangs up. "You got 'em by the neck, okay," he says rapidly to me as he reaches for something amid the wreckage of his desk.

"Who?"

"Great Benefit. I read the entire file last night. Typical debit insurance scam." He lifts an expandable file from a corner and falls into his chair with it. "Do you know what debit insurance is?"

I think I do, but I'm afraid he'll want specifics. "Not really."

"Blacks call it 'streetsurance.' Cheap little policies sold door to door to low-income people. The agents who sell the policies come around every week or so and collect the premiums, and they make a debit in the payment books kept by the insureds. They prey on the uneducated, and when claims are made on the policies the companies routinely turn them down. Sorry, no coverage for this reason or that. They're extremely creative when conjuring up reasons to deny."

"Don't they get sued?"

"Not very often. Studies have shown that only about one in thirty bad-faith denials ends up in court. The companies know this, of course, it's something they factor in. Keep in mind, they go after the lower classes, people afraid of lawyers and the legal system."

"What happens when they get sued?" I ask. He waves his hand at a bug or fly and two sheets of something lift from his desk and drift to the floor.

He cracks his knuckles violently. "Generally, not much.

There have been some large punitive awards around the country. I've been involved with two or three myself. But juries are reluctant to make millionaires out of simple sorts who buy cheap insurance. Think about it. Here's a plaintiff with, say, five thousand dollars in legitimate medical bills, clearly covered by the policy. But the insurance company says no. And the company is worth, say, two hundred million. At trial, the plaintiff's lawyer asks the jury for the five thousand, and also a few million to punish the corporate wrongdoer. It rarely works. They'll give the five, throw in ten thousand punitive, and the company wins again."

"But Donny Ray Black is dying. And he's dying because he can't get the bone marrow transplant he's entitled to under the policy. Am I right?"

Leuberg gives me a wicked smile. "You are indeed. Assuming his parents have told you everything. Always a shaky assumption."

"But if everything's right there?" I ask, pointing to the file.

He shrugs and nods and smiles again. "Then it's a good case. Not a great one, but a good one."

"I don't understand."

"Simple, Rudy. This is Tennessee. Land of the five-figure verdicts. Nobody gets punitive damages here. The juries are extremely conservative. Per capita income is pretty low, so the jurors have great difficulty making rich people out of their neighbors. Memphis is an especially tough place to get a decent verdict."

I'll bet Jonathan Lake could get a verdict. And maybe he'd give me a small slice if I brought him the case. In spite of the hangover, the wheels are turning upstairs.

"So what do I do?" I ask.

"Sue the bastards."

"I'm not exactly licensed."

"Not you. Send these folks to some hotshot trial lawyer downtown. Make a few phone calls on their behalf, talk to the lawyer. Write a two-page report for Smoot and you'll be done with it." He jumps to his feet as the phone rings, and shoves the file across the desk to me. "There's a list in here of three dozen bad-faith cases you should read, just in case you're interested."

"Thanks," I say.

He waves me off. As I leave his office, Max Leuberg is yelling into his phone.

LAW SCHOOL has taught me to hate research. I've lived in this place for three years now, and at least half of these painful hours have been spent digging through old worn books searching for ancient cases to support primitive legal theories no sane lawyer has thought about in decades. They love to send you on treasure hunts around here. The professors, almost all of whom are teaching because they can't function in the real world, think it's good training for us to track down obscure cases to put in meaningless briefs so that we can get good grades which will enable us to enter the legal profession as well-educated young lawyers.

This was especially true for the first two years of law school. Now it's not so bad. And maybe the training has a method to its madness. I've heard thousands of stories about the big firms and their practice of enslaving green recruits to the library for two years to write briefs and trial memos.

All clocks stop when one does legal research with a hangover. The headache worsens. The hands continue to shake. Booker finds me late Friday in my little pit with a dozen open books scattered on my desk. Leuberg's list of must-read cases. "How do you feel?" he asks.

Booker has on a coat and tie, and he's no doubt been at

the office, taking calls and using the Dictaphone like a real lawyer.

"I'm okay."

He kneels beside me and stares at the pile of books. "What's this?" he asks.

"It's not the bar exam. Just a little research for Smoot's class."

"You've never researched for Smoot's class."

"I know. I'm feeling guilty."

Booker stands and leans on the side of my carrel. "Two things," he says, almost in a whisper. "Mr. Shankle thinks the little incident at Brodnax and Speer has been taken care of. He's made some phone calls, and has been assured that the so-called victims do not wish to press charges."

"Good," I say. "Thanks, Booker."

"Don't mention it. I think it's safe for you to venture out now. That is, if you can tear yourself away from your research."

"I'll try."

"Second. I had a long talk with Mr. Shankle. Just left his office. And, well, there's nothing available right now. He's hired three new associates, me and two others from Washington, and he's not sure where they're gonna fit. He's looking for more office space right now."

"You didn't have to do that, Booker."

"No. I wanted to. It's nothing. Mr. Shankle promised to put out some feelers, shake the bushes, you know. He knows a lot of people."

I'm touched almost beyond words. Twenty-four hours ago I had the promise of a good job with a nice check. Now I've got people I haven't met pulling in favors and trying to locate the tiniest scrap of employment.

"Thanks," I say, biting my lip and staring at my fingers.

He glances at his watch. "Gotta run. You wanna study for the bar in the morning?"

"Sure."

"I'll call you." He pats me on the shoulder and disappears.

AT EXACTLY ten minutes before five, I walk up the stairs to the main floor and leave the library. I'm looking for cops now, not afraid to face Sara Plankmore, not even worried about more process servers. And I'm virtually unafraid of unpleasant confrontations with various of my fellow students. They're all gone. It's Friday, and the law school is deserted.

The Placement Office is on the main floor, near the front of the building, where the administrating occurs. I glance at the bulletin board in the hallway, but I keep walking. It's normally filled with dozens of notices of potential job openings—big firms, medium firms, sole practitioners, private companies, government agencies. A quick look tells me what I already know. There is not a single notice on the board. There is no job market at this time of the year.

Madeline Skinner has run Placement here for decades. She's rumored to be retiring, but another rumor says that she threatens it every year to squeeze something out of the dean. She's sixty and looks seventy, a skinny woman with short gray hair, layers of wrinkles around the eyes and a continuous cigarette in the tray on her desk. Four packs a day is the rumor, which is kind of funny because this is now an official nonsmoking facility but no one has mustered the courage to tell Madeline. She has enormous clout because she brings in the folks who offer the jobs. If there were no jobs, there would be no law school.

And she's very good at what she does. She knows the right people at the right firms. She's found jobs for many of the very people who are now recruiting for their firms, and she's brutal. If a Memphis State grad is in charge of recruiting for a big firm, and the big firm gets long on Ivy Leaguers and short on our people, then Madeline has been known to call the president of the university and lodge an unofficial complaint. The president has been known to visit the big firms downtown, have lunch with the partners and remedy the imbalance. Madeline knows every job opening in Memphis, and she knows precisely who fills each position.

But her job's getting tougher. Too many people with law degrees. And this is not the Ivy League.

She's standing by the watercooler, watching the door, as if she's waiting for me. "Hello, Rudy," she says in a gravelly voice. She is alone, everyone else is gone. She has a cup of water in one hand and a skinny cigarette in the other.

"Hi," I say with a smile as if I'm the happiest guy in the world.

She points with the cup to her office door. "Let's talk in here."

"Sure," I say as I follow her inside. She closes the door and nods at a chair. I sit where I'm told, and she perches herself on the edge of her chair across the desk.

"Rough day, huh," she says, as if she knows everything that's happened in the last twenty-four hours.

"I've had better."

"I talked to Loyd Beck this morning," she says slowly. I was hoping he was dead.

"And what did he say?" I ask, trying to be arrogant.

"Well, I heard about the merger last night, and I was concerned about you. You're the only grad we placed with Brodnax and Speer, so I was quite anxious to see what happened to you."

"And?"

"That merger happened fast, golden opportunity, etc."

"That's the same 'spill I got."

"Then I asked him when they first notified you about the merger, and he gave me some double-talk about how this partner or that partner had tried to call you a couple of times but the phone was disconnected."

"It was disconnected for four days."

"Anyway, I asked him if he could fax me a copy of any written correspondence between Brodnax and Speer and you, Rudy Baylor, regarding the merger and your role after it took place."

"There's none."

"I know. He admitted as much. Bottom line is that they did nothing until the merger was over."

"That's right. Nothing." There's something cozy about having Madeline on my side.

"So I explained to him in great detail how he had screwed one of our grads, and we got into one huge catfight on the phone."

I can't help but smile. I know who won the catfight.

She continues, "Beck swears they wanted to keep you. I'm not sure I believe it, but I explained that they should've discussed this with you long before now. You're a student now, almost a graduate, damned near an associate, not a piece of property. I said I knew he ran a sweatshop, but I explained that slavery is over. He cannot simply take you or leave you, transfer you or keep you or protect you or waste you."

Atta girl. My thoughts exactly.

"We finished the fight, and I met with the dean. The dean called Donald Hucek, the managing partner at Tinley Britt. They swapped a few phone calls, and Hucek came back with the same spin—Beck wanted to keep you but you didn't meet the Tinley Britt standards for new associates. The dean was suspicious, so Hucek said he'd take a look at your résumé and transcripts."

"There's no place for me at Trent & Brent," I say, like a man with many options.

"Hucek feels the same way. Said Tinley Britt would rather pass."

"Good," I say, because I can think of nothing clever. She knows better. She knows I'm sitting here suffering.

"We have little clout with Tinley Britt. They've hired only five of our grads in the past three years. They've become so big that they can't be leaned on. Frankly, I wouldn't want to work there."

She's trying to console me, make me feel as if a good thing has happened to me. Who needs Trent & Brent and their beginning salaries of fifty thousand bucks a year?

"So what's left?" I ask.

"Not much," she says quickly. "In fact, nothing." She glances at some notes. "I've called everybody I know. There was an assistant public defender's job, part-time, twelve thousand a year, but it was filled two days ago. I put Hall Pasterini in it. You know Hall? Bless his heart. Finally got a job."

I suppose people are blessing my heart right now.

"And there are a couple of good prospects for in-house counsel with small companies, but both require the bar exam first."

The bar exam is in July. Virtually every firm takes its new associates in immediately after graduation, pays them, preps them for the exam, and they hit the ground running when they pass it.

She places her notes on the desk. "I'll keep digging, okay. Maybe something will turn up."

"What should I do?"

"Start knocking on doors. There are three thousand lawyers in this city, most are either sole practitioners or in two- or three-man firms. They don't deal with Placement here, so we don't know them. Go find them. I'd start with the small groups, two, three, maybe four lawyers together, and talk them into a job. Offer to work on their fish files, do their collections——"

"Fish files?" I ask.

"Yeah. Every lawyer has a bunch of fish files. They keep them in a corner and the longer they sit the worse they smell. They're the cases lawyers wish they'd never taken. The things they don't teach you in law school.

"Can I ask a question?"

"Sure. Anything."

"This advice you're giving me right now, about knocking on doors, how many times have you repeated this in the past three months?"

She smiles briefly, then consults a printout. "We have about fifteen graduates still looking for work."

"So they're out there scouring the streets as we speak."

"Probably. It's hard to tell, really. Some have other plans which they don't always share with me."

It's after five, and she wants to go. "Thanks, Mrs. Skinner. For everything. It's nice to know someone cares."

"I'll keep looking, I promise. Check back next week."

"I will. Thanks."

I return unnoticed to my study carrel.

Six

T HE BIRDSONG HOUSE IS IN MIDTOWN, an older, affluent area in the city, only a couple of miles from the law school. The street is lined with ancient oaks and appears secluded. Some of the homes are quite handsome, with manicured lawns and luxury cars glistening in the driveways. Still others seem almost abandoned, and peer hauntingly through dense growth of unpruned trees and wild shrubbery. Still others are somewhere in between. Miss Birdie's is a white-stone turn-of-the-century Victorian with a sweeping porch that disappears around one end. It needs paint, a new roof and some yard work. The windows are dingy and the gutters are choked with leaves, but it's obvious someone lives here and tries to keep it up. The drive is lined with disorderly hedges. I park behind a dirty Cadillac, probably ten years old.

The porch planks squeak as I step to the front door, looking in all directions for a large dog with pointed teeth. It's late, almost dark, and there are no lights on the porch. The heavy wooden door is wide open, and through the screen I can see the shape of a small foyer. I can't find a button for the doorbell, so I very gently tap on the screen door. It rattles loosely. I hold my breath—no barking dogs.

No noise, no movement. I tap a bit louder.

"Who is it?" a familiar voice calls out.

"Miss Birdie?"

A figure moves through the foyer, a light switches on, and there she is, wearing the same cotton dress she wore yesterday at the Cypress Gardens Senior Citizens Building. She squints through the door.

"It's me. Rudy Baylor. The law student you talked to yesterday."

"Rudy!" She is thrilled to see me. I'm slightly embarrassed for a second, then I am suddenly sad. She lives alone in this monstrous house, and she's convinced her family has abandoned her. The highlight of her day is taking care of those deserted old people who gather for lunch and a song or two. Miss Birdie Birdsong is a very lonely person.

She hurriedly unlocks the screen door. "Come in, come in," she repeats without the slightest hint of curiosity. She takes me by the elbow and ushers me through the foyer and down a hallway, hitting light switches along the way. The walls are covered with dozens of old family portraits. The rugs are dusty and threadbare. The smell is moldy and musty, an old house in need of serious cleaning and refurbishing.

"So nice of you to stop by," she says sweetly, still squeezing my arm. "Didn't you have fun with us yesterday?"

"Yes ma'am."

"Won't you come back and visit us again?"

"Can't wait."

She parks me at the kitchen table. "Coffee or tea?" she

asks, bouncing toward the cabinets and swatting at light switches.

"Coffee," I say, looking around the room.

"How about instant?"

"That's fine." After three years of law school, I can't tell instant coffee from real.

"Cream or sugar?" she asks, reaching into the refrigerator.

"Just black."

She gets the water on and the cups lined up, and she takes a seat across from me at the table. She's grinning from ear to ear. I've made her day.

"I'm just delighted to see you," she says for the third or fourth time.

"You have a lovely home, Miss Birdie," I say, inhaling the musty air.

"Oh, thank you. Thomas and I bought it fifty years ago."

The pots and pans, sink and faucets, stove and toaster are all at least forty years old. The refrigerator is probably of early sixties' vintage.

"Thomas died eleven years ago. We raised our two sons in this house, but I'd rather not talk about them." Her cheery face is somber for a second, but she's quickly smiling again.

"Sure. Of course not."

"Let's talk about you," she says. It's a subject I'd rather avoid.

"Sure. Why not?" I'm braced for the questions.

"Where are you from?"

"I was born here, but I grew up in Knoxville."

"How nice. And where did you go to college?"

"Austin Peay."

"Austin who?"

"Austin Peay. It's a small school in Clarksville. State-supported."

"How nice."

"It's really a fine school, plus I like Memphis." There are two other reasons, actually. Memphis State admitted me, and I could afford it.

"How nice. Why did you choose Memphis State for law school?"

"How nice. When do you graduate?"

"Just a few weeks."

"Then you'll be a real lawyer, how nice. Where will you go to work?"

"Well, I'm not sure. I've been thinking a lot lately of just hanging out my shingle, you know, running my own office. I'm an independent type, and I'm not sure I can work for anyone else. I'd like to practice law my own way."

She just stares at me. The smile is gone. The eyes are frozen on mine. She's puzzled. "That's just wonderful," she finally says, then jumps up to fix the coffee.

If this sweet little lady is worth millions, she's doing a marvelous job of hiding it. I study the room. The table under my elbows has aluminum legs and a worn Formica top. Every dish and appliance and utensil and furnishing was purchased decades ago. She lives in a somewhat neglected house and drives an old car. Apparently, there are no maids or servants. No fancy little dogs.

"How nice," she says again as she places the two cups on the table. There is no steam rising from them. My cup is slightly warm. The coffee tastes weak, bland and stale.

"Good coffee," I say, smacking my lips.

"Thanks. And so you're just gonna start your own little law office?"

"I'm thinking about it. It'll be tough, you know, for a while. But if I work hard, treat people fairly, then I won't have to worry about attracting clients."

She grins sincerely and slowly shakes her head. "Why, that's just wonderful, Rudy. How courageous. I think the profession needs more young people like you."

I'm in the last thing this profession needs—another hungry young vulture roaming the streets, scavenging for litigation, trying to make something happen so I can squeeze a few bucks out of broke clients.

"You may wonder why I'm here," I say, sipping the coffee.

"I'm so glad you came."

"Yes, well, it's great to see you again. But I wanted to talk about your will. I had trouble sleeping last night because I was worried about your estate."

Her eyes become moist. She's touched by this.

"A few things are particularly troublesome," I explain now with my best lawyerly frown. I remove a pen from my pocket and hold it as if I'm ready for action. "First, and please forgive me for saying this, but it really troubles me to see you or any client take such harsh measures against family. I think this is something we should discuss at length." Her lips tighten, but she says nothing. "Second, and again please forgive me, but I couldn't live with myself as a lawyer if I didn't mention this, I have a real problem drafting a will or any instrument which conveys the bulk of an estate to a TV personality."

"He's a man of God," she says emphatically, quickly defending the honor of the Reverend Kenneth Chandler.

"I know. Fine. But why give him everything, Miss Birdie? Why not twenty-five percent, you know, something reasonable?"

"He has a lot of overhead. And his jet is getting old. He told me all about it."

"Okay, but the Lord doesn't expect you to finance the reverend's ministry, does he?"

"What the Lord tells me is private, thank you."

"Of course it is. My point is this, and I'm sure you know it, but a lot of these guys have fallen hard, Miss Birdie. They've been caught with women other than their wives. They've been caught blowing millions on lavish lifestyles —homes, cars, vacations, fancy suits. A lot of them are crooks."

"He's not a crook."

"Didn't say he was."

"What are you implying?"

"Nothing," I say, then take a long sip. She's not angry, but it wouldn't take much. "I'm here as your lawyer, Miss Birdie, that's all. You asked me to prepare a will for you, and it's my duty to be concerned about everything in the will. I take this responsibility seriously."

The mass of wrinkles around her mouth relax and her eyes soften again. "How nice," she says.

I suppose many old rich people like Miss Birdie, especially those who suffered through the Depression and made the money themselves, would guard their fortunes fiercely with accountants and lawyers and unfriendly bankers. But not Miss Birdie. She's as naive and trusting as a poor widow on a pension. "He needs the money," she says, taking a sip and eyeing me rather suspiciously.

"Can we talk about the money?"

"Why do you lawyers always want to talk about the money?"

"For a very good reason, Miss Birdie. If you're not careful, the government will get a big chunk of your estate. Certain things can be done with the money now, some careful estate planning, and a lot of the taxes can be avoided."

This frustrates her. "All that legal gobbledygook."

"That's what I'm here for, Miss Birdie."

"I suppose you want your name in the will somewhere," she says, still burdened with the law.

"Of course not," I say, trying to appear shocked but also trying to hide my surprise at getting caught.

"The lawyers are always trying to put their names in my wills."

"I'm sorry, Miss Birdie. There are a lot of crooked lawyers."

"That's what Reverend Chandler said."

"I'm sure he did. Look, I don't wanna know all the specifics, but could you tell me if the money is in real estate, stocks, bonds, cash or other investments? It's very important for estate planning purposes to know where the money is."

"It's all in one place."

"Okay. Where?"

"Atlanta."

"Atlanta?"

"Yes. It's a long story, Rudy."

"Why don't you tell me?"

Unlike our conference yesterday at Cypress Gardens, Miss Birdie is not pressed for time now. She has no other responsibilities. Bosco is not around. There is no lunch cleanup to supervise, no board games to referee.

So she slowly spins her coffee cup and ponders all of this as she stares at the table. "No one really knows about it," she says very softly, her dentures clicking once or twice. "At least no one in Memphis."

"Why not?" I ask, a bit too anxiously perhaps.

"My children don't know about it."

"The money?" I ask in disbelief.

"Oh, they know about some of it. Thomas worked hard and we saved a lot. When he died eleven years ago he left me close to a hundred thousand dollars in savings. My sons, and especially their wives, are convinced it's now worth five times that much. But they don't know about

Atlanta. Can I get you some more coffee?" She's already on her feet.

"Sure." She takes my cup to the counter, dumps in slightly more than a half a teaspoon of coffee, more luke-warm water, then returns to the table. I stir it as if I'm anticipating an exotic cappuccino.

Our eyes meet, and I'm all sympathy. "Look, Miss Birdie. If this is too painful, then perhaps we can skip around it. You know, just hit the high points."

"It's a fortune. Why should it be painful?"

Well, that's exactly what I was thinking. "Fine. Just tell me, in general terms, how the money is invested. I'm particularly concerned with real estate." This is true. Cash and other liquid investments are generally liquidated first to pay taxes. Real estate is used as a last resort. So my questions are prompted by more than just sheer curiosity.

"I've never told anyone about the money," she says, still in a very soft voice.

"But you told me yesterday that you had talked about it with Kenneth Chandler."

There's a long pause as she rotates her cup on the Formica. "Yes, I guess I did. But I'm not sure I told him everything. I might've lied just a bit. And I'm sure I didn't tell him where it came from."

"Okay. Where did it come from?"

"My second husband."

"Your second husband?"

"Yeah, Tony."

"Thomas and Tony?"

"Yeah. About two years after Thomas died, I married Tony. He was from Atlanta, sort of passing through Memphis when we met. We lived together off and on for five years, fought all the time, then he left and went home. He was a deadbeat who was after my money."

"I'm confused. I thought you said the money came from Tony."

"It did, except he didn't know it. It's a long story. There were some inheritances and stuff, things Tony didn't know about and I didn't know about. He had a rich brother who was crazy, whole family was, really, and just before Tony died he inherited a fortune from his crazy brother. I mean, two days before Tony kicked the bucket, his brother died in Florida. Tony died with no will, nothing but a wife. Me. And so they contacted me from Atlanta, this big law firm did, and told me that I, under Georgia law, was now worth a lot of money."

"How much money?"

"A helluva lot more than Thomas left me. Anyway, I've never told anyone about it. Until now. You won't tell, will you, Rudy?"

"Miss Birdie, as your lawyer I cannot tell. I am sworn to silence. It's called the attorney-client privilege."

"How nice."

"Why didn't you tell your last lawyer about the money?" I ask.

"Oh him. Didn't really trust him. I just gave him the amounts for the gifts, but didn't really tell him how much. Once he figured out I was loaded, he wanted me to put him in the will somewhere."

"But you never told him everything?"

"Never."

"You didn't tell him how much?"

"Nope."

If I calculated correctly, her old will contained gifts totaling at least twenty million. So the lawyer knew of at least that much, since he prepared the will. The obvious question here is exactly how much does this precious little woman have?

"Are you gonna tell me how much?"

"Maybe tomorrow, Rudy. Maybe tomorrow."

We leave the kitchen and head for the rear patio. She has a new water fountain by the rosebushes she wants to show me. I admire it with rapt attention.

It's clear to me now. Miss Birdie is a rich old woman, but she doesn't want anyone to know it, especially her family. She's always lived a comfortable life, and now arouses no suspicion as an eighty-year-old widow living off her more than adequate savings.

We sit on ornamental iron benches and sip cold coffee in the darkness until I finally string together enough excuses to permit myself an escape.

TO SUPPORT this affluent lifestyle of mine, I have worked for the past three years as a bartender and waiter at Yogi's, a student hangout just off campus. It's known for its juicy onionburgers and for green beer on St. Patrick's. It's a rowdy place where lunch to closing is one prolonged happy hour. Pitchers of watery lite beer are one dollar during "Monday Night Football"; two bucks during any other event.

It's owned by Prince Thomas, a ponytailed rumhead with a massive body and even larger ego. Prince is one of the city's better acts, a real entrepreneur who likes his picture in the paper and his face on the late news. He organizes pub crawls and wet tee shirt contests. He's petitioned the city to allow joints such as his to stay open all night. The city has in turn sued him for various sins. He loves it. Name the vice, and he'll organize a group and try to legalize it.

Prince runs a loose ship at Yogi's. We, the employees, keep our own hours, handle our own tips, run the show without a lot of supervision. Not that it's complicated. Keep enough beer in the front and enough ground beef in the kitchen and the place runs with surprising precision.

Prince prefers to handle the front. He likes to greet the pretty little coeds and show them to their booths. He'll flirt with them and in general make a fool of himself. He likes to sit at a table near the big-screen and take bets on the games. He's a big man with thick arms, and occasionally he'll break up a fight.

There's a darker side to Prince. He's rumored to be involved in the skin business. The topless clubs are a booming industry in this city, and his alleged partners have criminal records. It's been in the papers. He's been to trial twice for gambling, for being a bookie, but both juries were hopelessly deadlocked. After working for him for three years, I'm convinced of two things: First, Prince skims most of the cash from the receipts at Yogi's. I figure it's at least two thousand a week, a hundred thousand a year. Second, Prince is using Yogi's as a front for his own little corrupt empire. He launders cash through it, and makes it show a loss each year for tax purposes. He has an office down below, a rather secure, windowless room where he meets with his cronies.

I couldn't care less. He's been good to me. I make five bucks an hour, and I work about twenty hours a week. Our customers are students, thus the tips are small. I can shift hours during exams. At least five students a day come here looking for work, so I feel lucky to have the job.

And for whatever else it might be, Yogi's is a great student hangout. Prince decorated it years ago in blues and grays, Memphis State colors, and there are team pennants and framed photos of sports stars all over the walls. Tigers everywhere. It's a short walk from campus, and the kids flock here for hours of talking, laughing, flirting.

He's watching a game tonight. The baseball season is young, but Prince is already convinced the Braves are in the Series. He'll bet on anything, but his favorite is the Braves. It makes no difference who they're playing or where, who's pitching or who's hurt, Prince will take the Braves heads up.

I tend the main bar tonight, and my principal job in this capacity is to make sure his glass of rum and tonic does not run dry. He squeals as Dave Justice hits a massive home run. Then he collects some cash from a fraternity boy. The wager was who would hit the first home run—Dave Justice or Barry Bonds. I've seen him bet on whether the first pitch to the second batter in the third inning would be a ball or a strike.

It's a good thing I'm not waiting tables tonight. My head is still aching, and I need to move as little as possible. Plus, I can sneak an occasional beer from the cooler, the good stuff in the green bottles, Heineken and Moosehead. Prince expects his bartenders to nip a little.

I'm gonna miss this job. Or will I?

A front booth fills with law students, familiar faces I'd rather avoid. They're my peers, third-year students, probably all with jobs.

It's okay to be a bartender and a waiter when you're still a lowly student, in fact there's a bit of prestige in working at Yogi's. But the prestige will suddenly vanish in about a month, when I graduate. Then I'll become something much worse than a struggling student. I'll become a casualty, a statistic, another law student who's fallen through the cracks of the legal profession.

Seven

I HONESTLY CAN'T REMEMBER THE CRITE-ria I formulated and then used to select the Law Offices of Aubrey H. Long and Associates as my first possible quarry, but I think it had something to do with their nice, somewhat dignified ad in the yellow pages. The ad contained a grainy black-and-white photo of Mr. Long. Lawyers are getting as bad as chiropractors about plaster-ing their faces everywhere. He appeared to be an earnest fellow, about forty, nice smile, as opposed to most of the mug shots in the Attorney Section. His firm has four law-yers, specializes in car wrecks, seeks justice on all ave-nues, likes injuries and insurance cases, fights for its cli-ents and takes nothing until something is recovered.

What the hell. I have to start somewhere. I find the address downtown in a small, square, really ugly brick building with free parking next to it. The free parking was mentioned in the yellow pages. A bell jingles as I push open the door. A chunky little woman behind a littered desk greets me with something between a sneer and a scowl. I've made her stop typing.

"May I help you?" she asks, her fat fingers hovering just inches from the keys.

Damn, this is hard. I cajole myself into a smile. "Yes, I was wondering if by chance I could see Mr. Long."

"He's in federal court," she says as two fingers hit the keys. A small word is produced. Not just any court, but federal court! Federal means the big leagues, so when any ham-and-egg lawyer like Aubrey Long has a case in federal court, he damned sure wants everyone to know. His secretary is told to broadcast it. "May I help you?" she repeats.

I have decided that I will be brutally honest. Fraud and chicanery can wait, but not for long. "Yes, my name is Rudy Baylor. I'm a third-year law student at Memphis State, about to graduate, and I wanted to, well, I was sort of looking for work."

It becomes a full-blown sneer. She takes her hands away from the keyboard, swivels her chair to face me, then begins shaking her head slightly. "We're not hiring," she says with a certain satisfaction, as if she's the foreman down at the refinery.

"I see. Could I just leave a résumé, along with a letter for Mr. Long?"

She takes the papers from me gingerly, as if they're drenched with urine, and drops them onto her desk. "I'll put them with all the others."

I'm actually able to force a chuckle and a grin. "Lots of us out here, huh?"

"About one a day, I'd say."

"Oh well. Sorry to bother you."

"No problem," she grunts, already returning to her typewriter. She starts pecking furiously as I turn to leave the building.

I have lots of letters and lots of résumés. I spent the weekend organizing my paperwork and plotting my attack. Right now, I'm long on strategy and short on optimism. I figure I'll do this for a month, hit two or three small firms a day, five days a week, until I graduate, then, who knows. Booker has persuaded Marvin Shankle to scour the halls of justice in search of a job, and Madeline Skinner is probably on the phone right now demanding that someone hire me.

Maybe something will work.

My second prospect is a three-man firm two blocks from the first. I've actually planned this so I can move quickly from one rejection to the next. No wasted time here.

According to the legal directory, Nunley Ross & Perry is a firm of general practice, three guys in their early forties with no associates and no paralegals. They appear to do a lot of real estate, something I can't stand, but this is not the time to be particular. They're on the third floor of a modern concrete building. The elevator is hot and slow.

The reception area is surprisingly nice, with an oriental rug over faux hardwood flooring. Copies of *People* and *Us* litter a glass coffee table. The secretary hangs up the phone and smiles. "Good morning. Can I help you?"

"Yes. I'd like to see Mr. Nunley."

Still smiling, she glances down at a thick appointment book in the middle of her clean desk. "Do you have an appointment?" she asks, knowing damned well that I don't.

"No."

"I see. Mr. Nunley is quite busy at the moment."

Since I worked in a law office last summer, I knew perfectly well that Mr. Nunley would be quite busy. It's standard procedure. No lawyer in the world will admit or have his secretary admit that he is anything less than swamped.

Could be worse. He could be in federal court this
morning.

Roderick Nunley is the senior partner in this outfit, a
graduate of Memphis State, according to the legal directory. I've tried to plan my attack to include as many fellow
alumni as possible.

"I'll be happy to wait," I say with a smile. She smiles.
We all smile. A door opens down the brief hallway, and a
coatless man with his sleeves rolled up walks toward us.
He glances up, sees me, and suddenly we're close to each
other. He hands a file to the smiling secretary.

"Good morning," he says. "What can I do for you?" His
voice is loud. A real friendly sort.

She starts to say something, but I beat her to it. "I need
to talk to Mr. Nunley," I say.

"That's me," he says, thrusting his right hand at me.
"Rod Nunley."

"I'm Rudy Baylor," I say, taking his hand, shaking it
firmly. "I'm a third-year student at Memphis State, about
to graduate, and I wanted to talk to you about a job."

We're still shaking hands, and there's no noticeable
limp to his grasp when I mention employment. "Yeah," he
says. "A job, huh?" He glances down at her, as if to say
"How did you allow this to happen?"

"Yes sir. If I could just have ten minutes. I know you're
quite busy."

"Yeah, well, you know, got a deposition in just a few
minutes, then off to court." He's on his heels, glancing at
me, then at her, then at his watch. But at the core he's a
good guy, a soft touch. Maybe one day not long ago he
was standing on this side of the canyon. I plead with my
eyes, and hold the thin file with my résumé and letter out
to him.

"Yeah, well, sure, come on in. But just for a minute."
"I'll buzz you in ten minutes," she says quickly, trying

to make amends. Like all busy lawyers, he glances at his watch, studies it for a second, then tells her gravely, "Yeah, ten minutes max. And call Blanche, tell her I might be running a few minutes late."

They've rallied quite nicely, the two of them. They'll accommodate me, but they've quickly orchestrated my swift departure.

"Follow me, Rudy," he says with a smile. I'm glued to his back as we walk down the hall.

His office is a square room with a wall of bookcases behind the desk and a pretty serious Ego Wall facing the door. I quickly scan the numerous framed certificates—perfect attendance at the Rotary Club, Boy Scout volunteer, lawyer of the month, at least two college degrees, a photo of Rod with a red-faced politician, Chamber of Commerce member. This guy will frame anything.

I can hear the clock ticking as we sit across his huge, Catalog America–style desk. "Sorry to barge in like this," I begin, "but I really need a job."

"When do you graduate?" he asks, leaning forward on his elbows.

"Next month. I know this is late in the game, but there's a good reason." And then I tell him the story of my job with Brodnax and Speer. When I come to the part about Tinley Britt, I play heavy on what I hope is his dislike for big firms. It's a natural rivalry, the little guys like my pal Rod here, the ham-and-egg street lawyers, versus the silk stocking boys in the tall buildings downtown. I fudge a little when I explain that Tinley Britt wanted to talk to me about a job, then drive home the self-serving point that there's simply no way I could ever work for a big firm. Just not in my blood. I'm too independent. I want to represent people, not big corporations.

This takes less than five minutes.

He's a good listener, somewhat nervous with the phone

lines buzzing in the background. He knows he's not gonna hire me, so he's just passing time, waiting for my ten minutes to pass. "What a cheap shot," he says sympathetically when I finish my narrative.

"Probably for the best," I say, like the sacrificial lamb.

"But I'm ready to go to work. I'll finish in the top third of my class. I really enjoy real estate, and I've taken two property courses. Good grades in both."

"We do a lot of real estate," he says smugly, as if it's just the most profitable labor in the world. "And litigation," he adds, even more smugly. He's little more than an office practitioner, a paper shuffler, probably very good at what he does and able to make a nice living at it. But he wants me to think he's also an accomplished courtroom brawler, a litigating fool. He says this because it's simply what lawyers do, part of the routine. I haven't met many, but I've yet to meet one who didn't want me to think he could kick some ass in the courtroom.

My time is running out. "I've worked my way through school. All seven years. Not a penny from family."

"What type of work?"

"Anything. Right now I work at Yogi's, waiting tables, tending bar."

"You're a bartender?"

"Yes sir. Among other things."

He's holding my résumé. "You're single," he says slowly. It says so right there in black and white.

"Yes sir."

"Any serious romance?"

It's really none of his business, but I'm in no position.

"No sir."

"Not a queer, are you?"

"No, of course not," and we share a quick, heterosexual moment of humor. Just a couple of very straight white guys.

He leans back and his face is suddenly serious, as if important business is now at hand. "We haven't hired a new associate in several years. Just curious, what are the big boys downtown paying now for fresh recruits?"

There's a reason for this question. Regardless of my answer, he will profess shock and disbelief at such exorbitant salaries in the tall buildings. That, of course, will lay the groundwork for any discussion we have about money.

Lying will do no good. He probably has a good idea of the salary range. Lawyers love gossip.

"Tinley Britt insists on paying the most, as you know. I've heard it's up to fifty thousand."

His head is shaking before I finish. "No kiddin'," he says, floored. "No kiddin'."

"I'm not that expensive," I announce quickly. I've decided to sell myself cheaply to anyone willing to offer. My overhead is low, and if I can get my foot in the door, work hard for a couple of years, then maybe something else will come along.

"What did you have in mind?" he asks, as if his mighty little firm could run with the big boys and anything less might be degrading.

"I'll work for half. Twenty-five thousand. I'll put in eighty-hour weeks, handle all the fish files, do all the grunt work. You and Mr. Ross and Mr. Perry can give me all the files you wish you'd never taken, and I'll have them closed in six months. Promise. I'll earn my salary the first twelve months, and if I don't, then I'll leave."

Rod's lips actually part and I can see his teeth. His eyes are dancing at the thought of shoveling the manure from his office and dumping it on someone else. A loud buzzer discharges from his phone, followed by her voice. "Mr. Nunley, they're waiting on you in the deposition."

I glance at my watch. Eight minutes.

He glances at his. A frown, then to me he says, "Interesting proposal. Lemme think about it. I'll have to get with my partners. We meet every Thursday morning for review." He's on his feet. "I'll bring it up then. We haven't thought about this, actually." He's around the desk, ready to escort me out.

"It'll work, Mr. Nunley. Twenty-five thousand is a bargain." I'm backpedaling toward the door.

He appears to be stunned for a second. "Oh, it's not the money," he says, as if he and his partners wouldn't dare consider paying less than Tinley Britt. "It's just that we're running along pretty smoothly right now. Making lots of money, you know. Everybody's happy. Haven't thought of expanding." He opens the door, waits for me to leave. "We'll be in touch."

He follows me closely to the front, then instructs the secretary to make sure she has my phone number. He gives me a tight handshake, wishes me the best, promises to call soon and seconds later I'm on the street.

It takes a moment or two to collect my thoughts. I just offered to prostitute my education and training for something far less than the best, and it landed me on the sidewalk in a matter of minutes.

As things developed, my brief interview with Roderick Nunley would be one of my more productive outings.

It's almost ten. In thirty minutes I have Selected Readings from the Napoleonic Code, a class I need to attend because I've skipped it for a week. I could skip it for the next three weeks and no one would care. There's no final exam.

I'm moving freely around the law school these days, no longer ashamed to show my face. With a matter of days to go, most of the third-year students are abandoning the place. Law school starts with a barrage of intense work and pressurized exams, but it ends with a few scattered volleys of soft quizzes and throwaway papers. All of us are spending more time studying for the bar exam than worrying about our final classes.

Most of us are preparing to enter the state of employment.

MADELINE SKINNER has taken up my cause as if it's her own. And she's suffering almost as much as me because we're both having no luck. There's a state senator from Memphis whose office in Nashville might need a staff attorney to draft legislation—thirty thousand with benefits, but it requires a law license and two years' experience. A small company wants a lawyer with an undergraduate degree in accounting. I studied history.

"The Shelby County Welfare Department may have an opening in August for a staff lawyer." She's shuffling papers on her desk, trying desperately to find something.

"A welfare lawyer?" I repeat.

"Sounds glamorous, doesn't it?"

"What's the pay?"

"Eighteen thousand."

"What kind of work?"

"Tracking down deadbeat fathers, trying to collect support. Paternity cases, the usual."

"Sounds dangerous."

"It's a job."

"So what do I do until August?"

"Study for the bar exam."

"Right, and if I study real hard and pass the exam, then I get to go to work for the Welfare Department at minimum wage."

"Look, Rudy—"

"I'm sorry. It's been a bad day."

I promise to return tomorrow for what will no doubt be a repeat of this conversation.

Eight

BOOKER FOUND THE FORMS SOMEwhere in the depths of the Shankle firm. He said there was an associate tucked away in the basement who occasionally handled bankruptcies, and he was able to pilfer the necessary paperwork.

They're fairly straightforward. Listing of assets on one page, a quick and easy task in my case. A listing of liabilities on another page. Spaces for employment info, pending litigation, etc. It's what's known as a Chapter 7, straight bankruptcy, where the assets are wiped out to cover the debts, which are also wiped out.

I'm no longer employed at Yogi's. I work, but I now get paid in cash, no records. Nothing to garnish or attach. No obligation to share my meager wages with Texaco. I discussed my predicament with Prince, told him how bad things were, blamed it on tuition and credit cards, and he just loved the idea of paying me in cash and screwing the government. He's a firm disciple of cash-and-no-taxes economics.

Prince offered to make me a loan to bail myself out, but

it wouldn't work. He thinks I'll soon be making big money as a wealthy young lawyer, and I didn't have the heart to tell him that I may be with him for a while.

Nor did I tell him how hefty the loan would be. Texaco has sued me for $612.88, a sum which includes court costs and attorneys' fees. My landlord has sued me for $809, ditto on costs and fees. But the real wolves are just getting near. They're writing the dirty letters, just now threatening to send in the lawyers.

I have a MasterCard and a Visa, each issued by different banks here in Memphis. Between Thanksgiving and Christmas of last year, during a blissful little period of time in which I was assured of a good job in a few months, and while I was vainly in love with Sara, I set about to purchase for her a couple of charming gifts for the holidays. I wanted expensive things of enduring quality. With the MasterCard I purchased a gold and diamond tennis bracelet for seventeen hundred dollars, and with the Visa I bought my dearest a set of antique silver earrings. Cost me eleven hundred dollars. The day before she told me she never wanted to see me again, I went to a designer food store and bought a bottle of Dom Pérignon, a half pound of foie gras, some caviar, some fine cheeses and a few other goodies for our Christmas feast. Cost me three hundred dollars, but what the hell, life is short.

The insidious banks which issued the cards had inexplicably raised my lines of available credit just weeks before the holiday season. I was suddenly able to spend at will, and with graduation and work only months away, I knew I would be able to plod along making the small, required monthly payments until summertime. So I spent and spent, with dreams of the good life with Sara.

I hate myself for it now, but I actually put pen to paper and calculated everything. It was workable.

The foie gras rotted when I left it on top of the refrigerator one night during a nasty bout with cheap beer. For Christmas lunch, I dined alone in my darkened apartment on cheese and champagne. The caviar went untouched. I sat on my unlevel sofa and stared at the jewelry lying on the floor across from me. As I nibbled on large chunks of Brie and sipped the Dom, I looked at the Christmas gifts to my beloved, and wept.

At some unknown point between Christmas and New Year's, I pulled myself together and made arrangements to return the expensive items to the stores from whence they came. I toyed with the idea of throwing them off a bridge, like Billy Joe, or pulling a similar dramatic stunt. Given my current emotional state, though, I knew I'd better stay away from bridges.

It was the day after New Year's. I returned to my apartment after a long walk and jog, and realized that I'd been burglarized. The door had been jimmied. The thieves took my old TV and stereo, a jar of quarters on my dresser and, of course, the jewelry I'd purchased for Sara.

I called the cops and filled out the reports. I showed them the credit card receipts. The sergeant just shook his head and told me to contact my insurance company.

I ate over three thousand dollars in plastic purchases. The time has come to settle up.

I'M SCHEDULED to be evicted tomorrow. The Bankruptcy Code has a marvelous provision which grants an automatic stay in all legal proceedings against a debtor. That's why you see big rich corporations, including my pal Texaco, run into bankruptcy court when they need temporary protection. My landlord can't touch me tomorrow; can't even call me on the phone and give me a tongue lashing.

I step off the elevator and take a deep breath. The hallway is packed with lawyers. There are three full-time bankruptcy judges and their courtrooms are on this floor. They schedule dozens of hearings each day, and each hearing involves a group of lawyers; one for the debtor, and several for the creditors. It's a zoo. I hear dozens of important conferences as I shuffle along, lawyers haggling over unpaid medical bills and how much the pickup truck is worth. I enter the clerk's office and wait ten minutes while the lawyers in front of me take their time filing their petitions. They know the assistant clerks real well, and there's a lot of flirting and mindless chitchat. Gee, I'd love to be an important bankruptcy lawyer so the gals here would call me Fred or Sonny.

A professor told us last year that bankruptcy was the growth area of the future, what with uncertain economic times and all, job cutbacks, corporate downsizing, he had it all figured out. This was from a man who'd never billed an hour in private practice.

But it sure looks lucrative today. Bankruptcy petitions are being filed left and right. Everybody's going broke.

I hand my paperwork to a harried clerk, a cute girl with a mouthful of gum. She glances at the petition, and studies me carefully. I'm wearing a denim shirt and khakis.

"Are you a lawyer?" she asks rather loudly, and I see people looking at me.

"No."

"Are you the debtor?" she asks, even louder, gum smacking.

"Yes," I answer quickly. A debtor who's not a lawyer can file his own petition, though you'll never see this advertised anywhere.

She nods approvingly and stamps the petition. "Filing fee is eighty dollars please."

I hand her four twenties. She takes the cash and looks at it suspiciously. My petition does not list a checking account because I closed it yesterday, effectively eliminating an asset with a value of $11.84. My other listed assets are: one very used Toyota—$500; miscellaneous furniture and furnishings—$150; CD collection $200; law books—$125; clothing—$150. All of these assets are considered personal and thus exempted from the proceedings I have just commenced. I get to keep them all, but I'm required to continue paying for the Toyota.

"Cash, huh?" she says, then starts to give me a receipt.

"I don't have a bank account," I almost yell at her, for the benefit of those who've been listening and might want the rest of the story.

She glares at me, and I glare at her. She returns to her busywork and within a minute she slides me a copy of the petition along with a receipt. I notice the date, time and courtroom of my initial hearing.

I almost make it to the door before I get stopped. A stout young man with a sweaty face and black beard gently touches my arm. "Excuse me, sir," he says. I stop and look at him. He's sticking a business card in my hand. "Robbie Molk, attorney. Couldn't help but hear you over there. Thought you might need some help with your BK."

BK is cool lawyer jive for bankruptcy.

I look at the card, then at his pockmarked face. I've actually heard of Molk. I've seen his ads in the classified section of the newspaper. He advertises Chapter 7's for a hundred and fifty dollars down, and here he is, hanging around the clerk's office like a vulture, just waiting to pounce on some broke schmuck who might be good for a hundred and fifty bucks.

I politely take his card. "No thanks," I say, trying to be nice. "I can handle it."

"Lots of ways to screw it up," he says rapidly, and I'm sure he's used this line a thousand times. "A seven can be tricky. I do a thousand of them a year. Two hundred down, and I take the ball and run. Got a full office and staff."

Now it's two hundred dollars. I guess if you get to meet him in person he tacks on another fifty. It would be very easy at this point to rebuke him, but something tells me Molk is the type who cannot be humiliated.

"No thanks," I say, and push by him.

The ride down is slow and painful. The elevator is packed with lawyers, all badly dressed with battered briefcases and scuffed shoes. They're still jabbering about exemptions and what's unsecured and what's not. Impossible lawyer talk. Terribly important discussions. They can't seem to turn it off.

As we're about to stop on the ground floor, it hits me. I have no idea what I'll be doing a year from now, and it's not only probable but very likely that I'll be riding this elevator, engaging in these banal debates with these same people. In all likelihood, I'll be just like them, loose on the streets, trying to squeeze fees out of people who can't pay, hanging around courtrooms looking for business.

I'm dizzy with this terrible thought. The elevator is hot and airless. I think I'll be sick. It stops, and they rush forward into the lobby and scatter, still talking and dealing.

The fresh air clears my head as I stroll along the Mid-America Mall, a pedestrian walkway with a contrived trolley to carry the winos to and fro. Used to be called Main Street, and is still home to a huge number of lawyers. The courthouses are within a few blocks of here. I pass the tall buildings of downtown, wondering what's happening up there in countless firms: associates scrambling about, working eighteen-hour days because the next guy is working twenty; junior partners conferencing with each other about firm strategy; senior partners holding forth in their richly decorated corner offices as teams of younger lawyers wait for their instruction.

This is honestly what I wanted when I started law school. I wanted the pressure and power which emanate from working with smart, highly motivated people, all of whom are under stress and strain and deadline. The firm I clerked for last summer was small, only twelve lawyers, but there were lots of secretaries and paralegals and other clerks, and at times I found the chaos exhilarating. I was a very small part of the team, and I longed to one day be the captain.

I buy an ice cream from a street vendor and sit on a bench in Court Square. The pigeons watch me. Looming above is the First Federal Building, the tallest building in Memphis, and home of Trent & Brent. I would kill to work there. It's easy for me and my buddies to cuss Trent & Brent. We cuss them because we're not good enough for them. We hate them because they wouldn't look at us, couldn't be bothered to give us an interview.

I guess there's a Trent & Brent in every city, in every field. I didn't make it and I don't belong, so I'll just go through life hating them.

Speaking of firms. I figure that since I'm downtown, I'll spend a few hours knocking on doors. I have a list of lawyers who either work by themselves or have clustered with one or two other general practitioners. About the only encouraging factor in entering a field so horribly overcrowded is that there are so many doors to knock on. There is hope, I keep telling myself, that at the perfect moment I'll find an office no one has found before, and latch onto some badgered lawyer in dire need of a rookie to do his grunt work. Or her grunt work. I don't care.

I walk a few blocks to the Sterick Building, the first tall building in Memphis, and now the home of hundreds of lawyers. I chat with a few secretaries and hand over my résumés. I'm amazed at the number of law offices that employ moody and even rude receptionists. Long before we get around to the issue of employment, I'm often treated like a beggar. A couple have snatched my résumés and shoved them in a drawer. I'm tempted to present myself as a potential client, the grieving husband of a young woman who's just been killed by a large truck, a truck covered with lots of insurance. And a drunk driver behind the wheel. An Exxon truck, perhaps. It'd be hilarious to watch these snappy bitches spring from their seats, grinning wildly, rushing to get me some coffee.

I go from office to office, smiling when I'd love to be growling, repeating the same lines to the same women. "Yes, my name is Rudy Baylor, and I'm a third-year law student at Memphis State. I'd like to speak to Mr. Whoever about a job."

"A what?" they often ask. And I continue smiling as I hand over the résumé and ask again to see Mr. Bigshot. Mr. Bigshot is always too busy, so they brush me aside with the promise that someone will get back to me.

THE GRANGER SECTION of Memphis is north of downtown. Its rows of cramped brick houses on shaded streets provide irrefutable evidence of a suburb thrown together when the Second War ended and the Boomers began building. They took good jobs in nearby factories. They planted trees in the front lawns and built patios over the rear ones. With time, the mobile Boomers moved east and built nicer homes, and Granger slowly became a mixture of retired pensioners and lower-class whites and blacks.

The home of Dot and Buddy Black looks just like a thousand others. It sits on a flat plot of no more than eighty by a hundred feet. Something has happened to the obligatory shade tree in the front yard. An old Chevrolet sits in the one-car garage. The grass and shrubs are neatly trimmed.

To the left, the neighbor is in the process of rebuilding a hot rod, parts and tires strewn all the way to the street. To the right, the neighbor has fenced in the entire front yard, chain link with weeds a foot high growing in it. Two Dobermans patrol the dirt path just inside the fence.

I park in their drive behind the Chevrolet, and the Dobermans, not five feet away, snarl at me.

It's mid-afternoon and the temperature is pushing ninety. The windows and doors are open. I peek through the front door, a screen, and tap lightly.

I do not enjoy being here because I have no desire to see Donny Ray Black. I suspect he's just as sick and just as emaciated as his mother described, and I have a weak stomach.

She comes to the door, menthol in hand, and glares at me through the screen.

"It's me, Mrs. Black. Rudy Baylor. We met last week at Cypress Gardens."

Door-to-door salesmen must be a nuisance in Granger, because she glares at me with a blank face. She takes a step closer, and sticks the cigarette between her lips.

"Remember? I'm handling your case against Great Benefit."

"I thought you was a Jehovah's Witness."

"Well, I'm not, Mrs. Black."

"Name's Dot. I thought I told you that."

"Okay, Dot."

"Damned people drive us crazy. Them and the Mormons. Get the Boy Scouts on Saturday mornin' sellin' doughnuts before sunrise. What do you want?"

"Well, if you have a minute, I'd like to talk about your case."

"What about it?"

"I'd like to go over a few things."

"Thought we'd already done that."

"We need to talk some more."

She blows smoke through the screen, and slowly un-hooks the door. I enter a tiny living room and follow her into the kitchen. The house is humid and sticky, the smell of stale tobacco everywhere.

"Something to drink?" she asks.

"No thanks." I take a seat at the table. Dot pours a generic diet cola over ice and leans with her back to the counter. Buddy is nowhere to be seen. I assume Donny Ray is in a bedroom.

"Where's Buddy?" I ask merrily, as if he's an old friend I sorely miss.

She nods at the window overlooking the rear lawn. "See that old car out there?"

In a corner, overgrown with vines and shrubbery, next to a dilapidated storage shed and under a maple tree, is an old Ford Fairlane. It's white with two doors, both of which are open. A cat is resting on the hood.

"He's sitting in his car," she explains.

The car is surrounded by weeds, and appears to be tireless. Nothing around it has been disturbed in decades.

"Where's he going?" I ask, and she actually smiles.

She sips her cola loudly. "Buddy, he ain't goin' no-where. We bought that car new in 1964. He sits in it every day, all day, just Buddy and the cats."

There's a certain logic to this. Buddy out there, alone, no cigarette fog clogging his system, no worries about Donny Ray. "Why?" I ask. It's obvious she doesn't mind talking about it.

"Buddy ain't right. I told you that last week."

How could I forget.

"How's Donny Ray?" I ask.

She shrugs and moves to a seat across the flimsy dinette

table from me. "Good days and bad. You wanna meet him?"

"Maybe later."

"He stays in his bed most of the time. But he can walk around a little. Maybe I'll get him up before you leave."

"Yeah. Maybe. Look, I've done a lot of work on your case. I mean, I've spent hours and hours going through all of your records. And I've spent days in the library researching the law, and, and, well, frankly, I think you folks should sue the hell out of Great Benefit."

"I thought we'd already decided this," she says with a hard stare. Dot has an unforgiving face, no doubt the result of an arduous life with that nut out there in the Fairlane.

"Maybe so, but I needed to research it. It's my advice that you sue, and do so immediately."

"What're you waiting for?"

"But don't expect a quick solution. You're going up against a big corporation. They have lots of lawyers who can stall and delay. It's what they do for a living."

"How long will it take?"

"Could take months, maybe years. We might file suit, and force them to settle quickly. Or they may force us to go to trial, then appeal. There's no way to predict."

"He'll be dead in a few months."

"Can I ask you something?"

She blows and nods in perfect harmony.

"Great Benefit first denied this claim last August, right after Donny Ray was diagnosed. Why'd you wait until now to see a lawyer?" I'm using the term "lawyer" very loosely.

"I ain't proud of it, okay? I thought the insurance company would come through and pay the claim, you know, take care of his bills and treatment. I kept writing them, they kept writing me back. I don't know. Just dumb, I guess. We'd paid the premiums so regular over the years, never was late on a one. Just figured they'd honor the policy. Plus, I ain't ever used a lawyer, you know. No divorce or anything like that. God knows I should have." She turns sadly and looks through the window, gazing forlornly at the Fairlane and all the sorrow therein. "He drinks a pint of gin in the mornin', and a pint in the afternoon. And I don't really care. It makes him happy, keeps him outta the house, and it ain't like the drinking keeps him from being productive, know what I mean?"

We're both looking at the figure slumped low in the front seat. The overgrowth and maple tree shade the car.

"Do you buy it for him?" I ask, as if it matters.

"Oh no. He pays a kid next door to go buy it and sneak it to him. Thinks I don't know."

There's movement in the back of the house. There's no air conditioner to muffle sounds. Someone coughs. I start talking. "Look, Dot, I'd like to handle this case for you. I know I'm just a rookie, a kid almost out of law school, but I've already spent hours on this, and I know it like no one else."

She has a blank, almost hopeless look. One lawyer's as good as the next. She'll trust me as much as she'll trust the next guy, which is not saying much. How strange. With all the money spent by lawyers on cutthroat advertising, the silly low-budget TV ads and sleazy billboards and fire-sale prices in the classifieds, there are still people like Dot Black who don't know a trial stud from a third-year law student.

I'm counting on her naïveté. "I'll probably have to associate another lawyer, just to put his name on everything until I pass the bar exam and get admitted, you know."

This doesn't seem to register.

"How much will it cost?" she asks with no small amount of suspicion.

I give her a really warm smile. "Not a dime. I'll take it

on a contingency. I get a third of whatever we recover. No recovery, no fee. Nothing down." Surely she's seen this drill advertised somewhere, but she appears clueless.

"How much?"

"We sue for millions," I say dramatically, and she's hooked. I don't think there's a greedy bone in this broken woman's body. Any dreams she had of the good life vanished so long ago she can't remember them. But she likes the idea of sticking it to Great Benefit and making them suffer.

"And you get a third of it?"

"I don't expect to recover millions, but whatever we get, I take only a third. And that's a third after Donny Ray's medicals are first paid out. You have nothing to lose."

She slaps the table with her left palm. "Then do it. I don't care what you get, just do it. Do it now, okay? Tomorrow."

Folded neatly in my pocket is a contract for legal services, one I found in a form book in the library. I should at this point whip it out and sign her up, but I can't make myself do it. Ethically I cannot sign agreements to represent people until I'm admitted to the bar and have a license to practice. I think Dot will stick to her word.

I start glancing at my watch, just like a real lawyer. "Lemme get to work," I say.

"Don't you want to meet Donny Ray?"

"Maybe next time."

"I don't blame you. Nothin' but skin and bones."

"I'll come back in a few days when I can stay longer. We have lots to talk about, and I'll need to ask him a few questions."

"Just hurry, okay."

We chat a few more minutes, talk about Cypress Gardens and all the festivities there. She and Buddy go once a week, if she can keep him sober until noon. It's the only time they leave the house together.

She wants to talk, and I want to leave. She follows me outside, examines my dirty and dented Toyota, says bad things about imported products, especially those from Japan, and barks at the Dobermans.

She's standing by the mailbox as I drive away, smoking and watching me disappear.

FOR A FRESH NEW BANKRUPT, I can still spend money foolishly. I pay eight dollars for a potted geranium, and take it to Miss Birdie. She loves flowers, she says, and she's lonely, of course, and I think it's a nice gesture. Just a little sunshine in an old woman's life.

My timing is good. She's on all fours in the flower bed beside the house, next to the driveway that runs to a detached garage in the backyard. The concrete is heavily lined with flowers and shrubs and vines and decorative saplings. The rear lawn is heavily shaded with trees as old as she. There's a brick patio with flower boxes filled with vividly colored bouquets.

She actually hugs me as I present this small gift. She rips off her gardening gloves, drops them in the flowers and leads me to the rear of the house. She has just the spot for the geranium. She'll plant it tomorrow. Would I like coffee?

"Just water," I say. The taste of her diluted instant brew is still fresh in my memory. She makes me sit in an ornamental chair on the deck as she wipes mud and dirt on her apron.

"Ice water?" she asks, plainly thrilled with the prospect of serving me something to drink.

"Sure," I say, and she skips through the door into the kitchen. The backyard has an odd symmetry to its overgrowth. It runs for at least fifty yards before yielding to a thick hedgerow. I can see a roof beyond, through the trees. There are lively little pockets of organized growth, small beds of assorted flowers that she or someone obviously spends time with. There's a fountain on a brick platform along the fence, but there's no water circulating. There's an old hammock hanging between two trees, its shredded cord and canvas twisting in the breeze. The grass is free of weeds but needs clipping.

The garage catches my attention. It has two closed, retractable doors. There's a storage room to one side with covered windows. Above it, there appears to be a small apartment with a set of wooden stairs twisting around the corner and apparently up the back. There are two large windows facing the house, one with a broken pane. Ivy is consuming the outer walls, and appears to be making its way through the cracked window.

There's a certain quaintness about the place.

Miss Birdie bounces through the double french doors with two tall glasses of ice water. "What do you think of my garden?" she asks, taking the seat nearest me.

"It's beautiful, Miss Birdie. So peaceful."

"This is my life," she says, waving her hands expansively, sloshing her water on my feet without realizing it. "This is what I do with my time. I love it."

"It's very pretty. Do you do all the work?"

"Oh, most of it. I pay a kid to cut the grass once a week, thirty dollars, can you believe it? Used to get it for five." She slurps the water, smacks her lips.

"Is that a little apartment up there?" I ask, pointing above the garage.

"Used to be. One of my grandsons lived here for a while. I fixed it up, put in a bathroom, small kitchen, it was real nice. He was in school in Memphis State."

"How long did he live there?"

"Not long. I really don't want to talk about him."

He must be one of those to be chopped from her will.

When you spend much of your time knocking on law office doors, begging for work and getting stiff-armed by bitchy secretaries, you lose your inhibitions. You develop a thick skin. Rejection comes easy, because you learn quickly that the worst thing that can happen is to hear the word "No."

"Don't suppose you'd be interested in renting it now?" I venture forth with little hesitation and absolutely no fear of being turned down.

Her glass stops in midair, and she stares at the apartment as if she's just discovered it. "To who?" she asks.

"I'd love to live there. It's very charming, and it has to be quiet."

"Deathly."

"Just for a little while, though. You know, until I start work and get on my feet."

"You, Rudy?" she asks in disbelief.

"I love it," I say with a semi-phony smile. "It's perfect for me. I'm single, live very quietly, can't afford to pay much in rent. It's perfect."

"How much can you pay?" she asks crisply, suddenly much like a lawyer grilling a broke client.

This catches me off guard. "Oh, I don't know. You're the landlord. How much is the rent?"

She rolls her head around, looking wildly at the trees. "How about four, no three hundred dollars a month?"

It's obvious Miss Birdie's never been a landlord before. She's pulling numbers out of the air. Lucky she didn't start with eight hundred a month. "I think we should look at it first," I say cautiously.

She's on her feet. "It's kinda junky, you know. Been using it for storage for ten years. But we can clean it up. Plumbing works, I think." She takes my hand and leads me across the grass. "We'll have to get the water turned on. Not sure about the heating and air. Has some furniture, but not much, old things I've discarded."

She starts up the creaky steps. "Do you need furniture?"

"Not much." The handrail is wobbly and the entire building seems to shake.

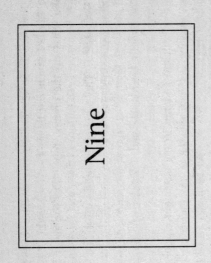

Nine

YOU MAKE ENEMIES IN LAW SCHOOL. The competition can be vicious. People learn how to cheat and backstab; it's training for the real world. We had a fistfight here in my first year when two third-year students started screaming at each other during a mock trial competition. They expelled them, then readmitted them. This school needs the tuition money.

There are quite a few people here I truly dislike, one or two I detest. I try not to hate people.

But at the moment I hate the little snot who did this to me. They publish in this city a record of all sorts of legal and financial transactions. It's called *The Daily Report*, and includes, among the filings for divorce and a dozen other vital categories, a listing of yesterday's bankruptcy activities. My pal or group of pals thought it would be cute to lift my name from yesterday's sorrows, blow up a cutout from under Chapter 7 Petitions and scatter this little tidbit all around the law school. It reads: "Baylor, Rudy L., student; Assets: $1,125 (exempt); Secured Debts: $285 to Wheels and Deals Finance Company; Unsecured Debts: $5,136.88; Pending Actions: (1) Collection of past due account by Texaco, (2) Eviction from The Hampton; Employer: None; Attorney, Pro Se."

Pro Se means I can't afford a lawyer and I'm doing it on my own. The student clerk at the front desk of the library handed me a copy as soon as I walked in this morning, said he'd seen them lying all over the school, even tacked to the bulletin boards. He said, "Wonder who thinks this is funny?"

I thanked him and ran to my basement corner, once again ducking between the stacks, evading contact with familiar faces. Classes will be over soon and I'll be out of here, away from these people I can't stand.

I'M SCHEDULED to visit with Professor Smoot this morning, and I arrive ten minutes late. He doesn't care. His office has the mandatory clutter of a scholar too bright to be organized. His bow tie is crooked, his smile is genuine.

We first talk about the Blacks and their dispute with Great Benefit. I hand him a three-page summary of their case, along with my ingenious conclusions and suggested courses of action. He reads it carefully while I study the wadded balls of paper under his desk. He's very impressed, and says so over and over. It's my advice to the Blacks that they contact a trial lawyer and pursue a bad-faith action against Great Benefit. Smoot wholeheartedly agrees. Little does he know.

All I want from him is a passing grade, nothing else. Next we talk about Miss Birdie Birdsong. I tell him she is quite comfortable and wants to remake her will. I keep the details to myself. I present to him a five-page document, the revised last will and testament for Miss Birdie, and he scans it quickly. Says it looks fine without seeing anything in it. Legal Problems of the Elderly has no final exam, no papers to be submitted. You attend class, visit the geezers, do the case summaries. Smoot gives you an A.

Smoot has known Miss Birdie for several years. Evidently she's been the queen of Cypress Gardens for a while, and he's seen her twice a year on visits there with his students. She's never been inclined to take advantage of the free legal advice before, he says, pondering and tugging at the bow tie. Says he's surprised to learn she's wealthy.

He'd really be surprised to learn she's about to be my landlord.

Max Leuberg's office is around the corner from Smoot's. He left a message for me at the front desk of the library, said he needed to see me. Max is leaving when classes are over. He's been on loan for two years from Wisconsin, and it's time for him to go. I'll probably miss Max a little when both of us are gone from here, but right now it's hard to imagine any lingering feelings of sentiment for anything or anybody connected with this law school.

Max's office is filled with cardboard liquor boxes. He's packing to move, and I've never seen such a mess. We reminisce for a few awkward moments, a desperate effort to make law school sound provocative. I've never seen him subdued before. It's almost as if he's genuinely sad to be leaving. He points to a stack of papers in a Wild Turkey box. "That's for you. It's a bunch of recent materials I've used in bad-faith cases. Take it. Might come in handy."

I haven't quite finished the last batch of research materials he laid on me. "Thanks, Max," I say, looking at the red turkey.

"Have you filed suit yet?" he asks.

"Uh, no. Not yet."

"You need to. Find a lawyer downtown with a good trial

record. Someone with bad-faith experience. I've been thinking about this case a lot, and it grows on you. Lots of jury appeal. I can see a jury getting mad here, wanting to punish the insurance company. Someone needs to take this case and run with it."

I'm running like hell.

He bounces from his seat and stretches his arms. "What kinda firm are you going with?" he asks, on his toes, performing some yoga expansion on his calves. "Because this is a great case for you to work on. I'm just thinking, you know. Maybe you should take it to your firm, let them sign it up, then do the grunt work yourself. Surely there's somebody in your firm with trial experience. You can call me if you want. I'll be in Detroit all summer working on a huge case against Allstate, but I'm interested, okay? I think this might be a big case, a landmark. I'd love to see you pop these boys."

"What's Allstate done?" I ask, steering matters away from my firm.

He breaks into a wide grin, clasps his hands together on top of his head, just can't believe it. "Incredible," he says, then launches into a windy narrative about a gorgeous case. I wish I hadn't asked.

In my limited experience of hanging around lawyers, I've learned that they all suffer the same afflictions. One of the most obnoxious habits is the telling of war stories. If they've had a great trial, they want you to know it. If they have a great case that's destined to make them rich, they must share it with other like minds. Max is losing sleep with visions of bankrupting Allstate.

"But anyway," he says, drifting back to reality, "I might be able to help with this one. I'm not coming back next fall, but my phone number and address are in the box. Call me if you need me."

I pick up the Wild Turkey box. It's heavy and the bottom flaps sag. "Thanks," I say, facing him. "I really appreciate this."

"I wanna help, Rudy. There's nothing more thrilling than nailing an insurance company. Believe me."

"I'll give it my best shot. Thanks."

The phone rings and he attacks it. I ease from his office with my bulky load.

MISS BIRDIE and I strike an odd deal. She's not much of a negotiator, and she obviously doesn't need the money. I get her down to a hundred and fifty dollars a month rent, utilities included. She also throws in enough furniture to fill the four rooms.

In addition to the money, she receives from me a commitment to assist with various chores around the place, primarily lawn and garden work. I'll mow the grass, so she can save thirty dollars a week. I'll trim hedges, rake leaves, weed-pull the usual. There was some vague and unfinished talk of weed-pulling, but I didn't take it seriously.

It's a good deal for me, and I'm proud of my business-like approach to it. The apartment is worth at least three hundred and fifty dollars per month, so I saved two hundred in cash. I figure I can get by working five hours a week, twenty hours a month. Not a bad deal under the circumstances. After three years of life in the library, I need the fresh air and exercise. No one will know I'm a yard boy. Plus, it'll keep me close to Miss Birdie, my client.

It's an oral lease, from month to month, so if it doesn't work out then I'll move on.

Not very long ago, I looked at some nice apartments, fit for an up-and-coming lawyer. They wanted seven hundred a month for two bedrooms, less than a thousand square feet. And I was perfectly willing to pay it. A lot has changed.

Now I'm moving into a rather spartan afterthought, designed by Miss Birdie, then neglected by her for ten years. There's a modest den with orange shag carpeting and pale green walls. There's a bedroom, a small efficiency kitchen and a separate dining area. The ceilings are vaulted from all directions, in every room, giving a rather claustrophobic effect to my little attic.

It's perfect for me. As long as Miss Birdie keeps her distance, then it'll work fine. She made me promise there'd be no wild parties, loud music, loose women, booze, drugs, dogs or cats. She cleaned the place herself; scrubbed the floors and walls, moved as much junk as she could. She literally clung to my side as I trudged up the steps with my sparse belongings. I'm sure she felt sorry for me.

As soon as I finished hauling the last box up the stairs and before I had a chance to unpack anything, she insisted we drink coffee on the patio.

We sat on the patio for about ten minutes, just long enough for me to stop sweating, when she declared it was time to hit the flower beds. I pulled weeds until my back cramped. She was an active partner for a few minutes, then took to standing behind me, pointing.

I'M ABLE TO ESCAPE the yard work only by retreating to the safety of Yogi's. I'm scheduled to tend bar until closing, sometime after 1 A.M.

The place is full tonight, and much to my dismay there are a bunch of my peers grouped around two long tables in a front corner. It's the final meeting of one of the various legal fraternities, one I was not asked to join. It's called The Barristers, a group of Law Review types, important students who take themselves much too seriously. They try to be secretive and exclusive, with obscure initiation rites chanted in Latin and other such foolishness. Almost all are headed for either big firms or federal judicial clerkships. A couple have been accepted to tax school at NYU. It's a pompous clique.

They quickly get drunk as I draw pitcher after pitcher of beer. The loudest is a little squirrel named Jacob Staples, a promising young lawyer who began law school three years ago, already having mastered the art of dirty tricks. Staples has found more ways to cheat than any person in the history of this law school. He's stolen exams, hidden research books, filched outlines from the rest of us, lied to professors to delay papers and briefs. He'll make a million bucks soon. I suspect Staples is the one who copied my newsbrief from *The Daily Report* and plastered it around the law school. Sounds just like him.

Though I try to ignore them, I catch an occasional stare. I hear the word "bankruptcy" several times.

But I stay busy, occasionally sipping beer from a coffee mug. Prince is in the opposite corner, watching television and keeping a wary eye on The Barristers. Tonight he's watching greyhound racing from a track in Florida, and betting on every race. His gambling and drinking buddy tonight is his lawyer, Bruiser Stone, an enormously fat and broad man with long, thick gray hair and sagging goatee. He weighs at least 350, and together they look like two bears sitting on rocks, chomping peanuts.

Bruiser Stone is a lawyer with highly questionable ethics. He and Prince go way back, old high school buddies from South Memphis, and they've done many shady deals together. They count their cash when no one is around. They bribe politicians and police. Prince is the front man, Bruiser does the thinking. And when Prince gets caught, Bruiser is on the front page screaming about injustices. Bruiser is very effective in the courtroom, primarily because he's known to offer significant sums of cash to jurors. Prince has no fear of guilty verdicts.

Bruiser has four or five lawyers in his firm. I cannot

imagine the depths of desperation which would force me to ask him for a job. I cannot think of anything worse than to tell people I work for Bruiser Stone.

Prince could arrange it for me. He'd love to do the favor, show how much clout he's got.

I can't believe I'm even thinking about it.

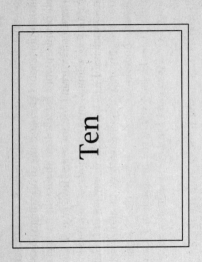

Ten

U NDER PRESSURE FROM THE FOUR OF us, Smoot relents and says we can return to Cypress Gardens on our own, without going as a group and suffering through another lunch. Booker and I sneak in one day during "America the Beautiful," and sit in the back while Miss Birdie gives 'em all a pep talk about vitamins and proper exercise. She finally sees us, and insists that we walk to the podium for formal introductions.

After the program breaks up, Booker slides into a far corner, where he meets with his clients and dispenses advice he wants no one else to hear. Since I've already met with Dot, and since Miss Birdie and I have spent hours sparring over her will, there's not much left for me to do. Mr. DeWayne Deweese, my third client from our previous visit, is in the hospital, and I've mailed him a thoroughly useless summary of my suggestions to aid him in his own private little war against the Veterans Administration.

Miss Birdie's will is incomplete and unsigned. She's

been very touchy about it in recent days. I'm not sure she wants to change it. She says she hasn't heard from the Reverend Kenneth Chandler, so she might not leave him her fortune. I've tried to encourage this.

We've had a few conversations about her money. She likes to wait until I'm buried up to my ass in mulch and potting soil, my nose dripping with sweat and moist with peat, then, hovering over me, ask some off-the-wall question like "Can Delbert's wife sue my estate if I leave him nothing?" Or, "Why can't I just give the money away right now?"

I'll stop, extract myself from beneath the flowers, wipe my face and try to think of an intelligent answer. Usually, by this time she's changed the subject and wants to know why the azaleas over there are not growing.

I've broached the subject a few times over coffee on the patio, but she gets nervous and agitated. She has a healthy suspicion of lawyers.

I've been able to verify a few facts. She was in fact married a second time, to a Mr. Anthony Murdine. Their marriage lasted almost five years until he died in Atlanta four years ago. Apparently, Mr. Murdine left a sizable estate when he passed on, and apparently it was surrounded by a great deal of controversy because the court in De Kalb County, Georgia, ordered the file sealed. That's as far as I've gotten. I plan to talk to some of the lawyers involved in his estate.

Miss Birdie wants to talk, to conference. It makes her feel important in front of her people. We sit at a table near the piano, away from the others. We huddle, our heads just inches apart. You'd think we hadn't seen each other in a month.

"I need to know what to do with your will, Miss Birdie," I say. "And before I can properly draft it, I need to know a little about the money."

She darts her eyes around as if everyone is listening. In fact, most of these poor souls couldn't hear us if we were screaming at each other. She dips low, hand over mouth. "None of it's in real estate, okay. Money markets, mutual funds, municipal bonds."

I'm surprised to hear her rattle off these types of investments with obvious familiarity. The money must actually be there.

"Who handles it?" I ask. The question is unnecessary. It makes no difference to the will or to her estate who manages her money. My curiosity is eating at me.

"A firm in Atlanta."

"A law firm?" I ask, scared.

"Oh no. I wouldn't trust lawyers with it. A trust company. The money is all in trust. I get the income until I die, then I give it away. That's the way the judge set things up."

"How much income?" I ask, completely out of control.

"Now, that's really not any of your business, is it, Rudy?"

No, it's not. I've been slapped on the hand, but in the finest legal tradition, I try and cover my ass. "Well, it could be important, you know. For tax purposes."

"I didn't ask you to do my taxes, did I? I have an accountant for that. I simply asked you to do redo my will, and, my, it sure seems over your head."

Bosco walks to the other end of the table, and grins at us. Most of his teeth are missing. She politely asks him to go play Parcheesi for a few minutes. She is remarkably kind and gentle with these people.

"I'll prepare your will any way you want it, Miss Birdie," I say sternly. "But you'll have to make up your mind."

She sits straight, exhales with great drama and clenches her dentures together. "Lemme think about it."

"Fine. But just remember. There are many things in your current will that you don't like. If something happens to you, then—"

"I know, I know," she interrupts, hands going everywhere. "Don't lecture me. I've done twenty wills in the past twenty years. I know all about them."

Bosco's crying over by the kitchen, and she races off to comfort him. Booker mercifully finishes his consultations. His last client is the old man he spent so much time with during our original visit. It's obvious this fella isn't too happy with Booker's summary of his mess, and I hear Booker say at one point as he's trying to get away, "Look, it's free. What do you expect?"

We pay our respects to Miss Birdie, and make a quick exit. Legal Problems of the Elderly is now history. In a few days our classes will end.

After three years of hating law school, we are suddenly about to be liberated. I heard a lawyer say once that it takes a few years for the pain and misery of law school to fade, and, as with most things in life, you're left with the good memories. He seemed to be downright melancholy as he reminisced about the glory days of his legal education.

I cannot fathom the moment in my life when I'll look back on the past three years and declare that it was enjoyable after all. I might one day be able to piece together some bright little memories of times spent with friends, of hanging out with Booker, of tending bar at Yogi's, of other things and events which escape me now. And I'm sure Booker and I will laugh about these dear old folks here at Cypress Gardens and the trust they placed in us.

It might be funny one day.

I suggest we get a beer at Yogi's. I'll treat. It's two o'clock and it's raining, the perfect time to huddle around a table and blow an afternoon. It may be our last chance.

Booker really wants to, but he is expected at the office in an hour. Marvin Shankle has him working on a brief that's due in court on Monday. He'll spend the entire weekend buried in the library.

Shankle works seven days a week. His firm pioneered much of the civil rights litigation in Memphis, and now he's reaping vast rewards. There are twenty-two lawyers, all black, half female, all trying to keep the brutal work schedule required by Marvin Shankle. The secretaries work in shifts so there's always at least three available twenty-four hours a day. Booker idolizes Shankle, and I know that within a matter of weeks he too will be working on Sundays.

I FEEL LIKE A BANK ROBBER riding around the suburbs, casing the branches and deciding which will be the easiest to hit. I find the firm I'm looking for in a modern glass and stone building with four floors. It's in East Memphis, along a busy corridor that runs west to downtown and the river. This is where the white flight landed.

The firm has four lawyers, all in their mid-thirties, all alumni of Memphis State. I've heard that they were friends in law school, went to work for big firms around the city, grew dissatisfied with the pressure, then reassembled themselves here in a quieter practice. I saw their ad in the yellow pages, a full-page spread, rumored to cost four thousand a month. They do everything, from divorce to real estate to zoning, but of course the boldest print in the ad announces their expertise in PERSONAL INJURY.

Regardless of what a lawyer does, more often than not he or she will profess great know-how in the field of personal injury. Because for the vast majority of lawyers who don't have clients they can bill by the hour forever, the only hope of serious money is representing people who've been hurt or killed. It's easy money, for the most part.

Take a guy who's injured in a car wreck where the other driver is at fault and has insurance. He's got a week in the hospital, a broken leg, lost salary. If the lawyer can get to him before the insurance adjuster, then his claim can be settled for fifty thousand dollars. The lawyer spends some time shuffling paper, but probably is not forced to file suit. He invests thirty hours max, and takes a fee of around fifteen thousand. That's five hundred dollars an hour.

Great work if you can get it. That's why almost every lawyer in the Memphis yellow pages cries out for victims of injuries. No trial experience is necessary—ninety-nine percent of the cases are settled. The trick is getting the cases signed up.

I don't care how they advertise. My only concern is whether or not I can talk them into employment. I sit in my car for a few moments as the rain beats against the windshield. I'd rather be bullwhipped than enter the office, smile warmly at the receptionist, chatter away like a door-to-door salesman and unveil my latest ploy to get past her and see one of her bosses.

I cannot believe I'm doing this.

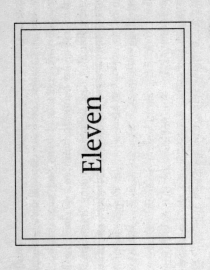

Eleven

MY EXCUSE FOR SKIPPING THE GRADU-
ation ceremony is that I have some interviews
with law firms. Promising interviews, I assure
Booker, but he knows better. Booker knows I'm doing
nothing but knocking on doors and air-dropping résumés
over the city.

Booker is the only person who cares if I wear a cap and
gown and take part in the exercises. He's disappointed
that I'm not attending. My mother and Hank are camping
somewhere in Maine, watching the foliage turn green. I
talked to her a month ago, and she has no clue as to when
I'll finish law school.

I've heard the ceremony is quite tedious, lots of
speeches from long-winded old judges who implore the
graduates to love the law, treat it as an honorable profession, respect it as a jealous mistress, rebuild the image so
tarnished by those who've gone before us. Ad nauseum.
I'd rather sit at Yogi's and watch Prince gamble on goat
races.

Booker will be there with his family. Charlene and the

kids. His parents, her parents, several grandparents, aunts, uncles, cousins. The Kane clan will be a formidable group. There will be lots of tears and photographs. He was the first in his family to finish college, and the fact that he's finishing law school is causing immeasurable pride. I'm tempted to hide in the audience just so I can watch his parents when he receives his degree. I'd probably cry along with them.

I don't know if the Sara Plankmore family will take part in the festivities, but I'm not running that risk. I cannot stand the idea of seeing her smiling for the camera with her fiancé, S. Todd Wilcox, giving her a hug. She'd be wearing a bully gown, so it would be impossible to tell if she's showing. I'd have to stare, though. Try as I might, there'd be no way for me to keep my eyes off her midsection.

It's best if I skip graduation. Madeline Skinner confided in me two days ago that every other graduate has found a job of some sort. Many took less than they wanted. At least fifteen are hitting the streets on their own, opening small offices and declaring themselves ready to sue. They've borrowed money from parents and uncles, and they rented little rooms with cheap furniture. She's got the statistics. She knows where everybody's going. There's no way I'd sit there in my black cap and gown with a hundred and twenty of my peers, all of us knowing that I, Rudy Baylor, am the sole remaining unemployed schmuck in the class. I might as well wear a pink robe with a neon cap. Forget it.

I picked up my diploma yesterday.

GRADUATION STARTS at 2 P.M., and at precisely that hour I enter the law offices of Jonathan Lake. This will be an encore performance, my first. I was here a month ago, feebly handing over a résumé to the receptionist. This visit will be different. Now I have a plan.

I've done a bit of research on the Lake firm, as it's commonly known. Since Mr. Lake does not believe in sharing much of his wealth, he is the sole partner. He has twelve lawyers working for him, seven known as trial associates, and the other five are younger, garden-variety associates. The seven trial associates are skilled courtroom advocates. Each has a secretary, a paralegal, and even the paralegal has a secretary. This is known as a trial unit. Each trial unit works autonomously from the others, with only Jonathan Lake occasionally stepping in to do the quarterbacking. He takes the cases he wants, usually the ones with the greatest potential for large verdicts. He loves to sue obstetricians in bad baby cases, and recently made a fortune in asbestos litigation.

Each trial associate handles his own staff, can hire and fire, and is also responsible for generating new cases. I've heard that almost eighty percent of the firm's business comes in as referrals from other lawyers, street hacks and real estate types who stumble onto an occasional injured client. The income of a trial associate is determined by several factors, including how much new business he generates.

Barry X. Lancaster is a rising young star in the firm, a freshly anointed trial associate who hit a doctor in Arkansas for two million last Christmas. He's thirty-four, divorced, lives at the office, studied law at Memphis State. I've done my homework. He is also advertising for a paralegal. Saw it in *The Daily Record*. If I can't get my start as a lawyer, what's wrong with being a paralegal? It'll make a great story one day, after I'm successful and have my own big firm; young Rudy couldn't buy a job, so he started in the mail room at Jonathan Lake. Now look at him.

I have a two o'clock appointment with Barry X. The

receptionist gives me the double take, but lets it pass. I doubt if she recognizes me from my first visit. A thousand people have come and gone since then. I hide behind a magazine on a leather sofa and admire the Persian rugs and hardwood floors and exposed twelve-inch beams above. These offices are in an old warehouse near the medical district of Memphis. Lake reportedly spent three million dollars renovating and decorating this monument to himself. I've seen it laid out in two different magazines.

Within minutes I'm led by a secretary through a maze of foyers and walkways to an office on an upper level. Below is an open library with no walls or boundaries, just row after row of books. A solitary scholar sits at a long table, treatises stacked around him, lost in a flood of conflicting theories.

The office of Barry X. is long and narrow, with brick walls and creaky floors. It's adorned with antiques and accessories. We shake hands and take our seats. He's lean and fit, and I remember from the magazine spread the photos of the gym Mr. Lake installed for his firm. There's also a sauna and a steam room.

Barry's quite busy, no doubt needing to be in a strategy session with his trial unit, preparing for a major case. His phone is situated so I can see the lights blinking furiously. His hands are quiet and still, but he can't help but glance at his watch.

"Tell me about your case," he says after a brief moment of preliminaries. "Something about an insurance claim denied." He's already suspicious because I'm wearing a coat and tie, not your average-looking client.

"Well, I'm actually here looking for a job," I say boldly. All he can do is ask me to leave. What's to lose?

He grimaces and snatches at a piece of paper. Damned secretary has screwed up again.

"I saw your ad for a paralegal in *The Daily Record*."

"So you're a paralegal?" he snaps.

"I could be."

"What the hell does that mean?"

"I've had three years of law school."

He studies me for about five seconds, then shakes his head, glances at his watch. "I'm really busy. My secretary will take your application."

I suddenly jump to my feet and lean forward on his desk. "Look, here's the deal," I say dramatically as he looks up, startled. I then rush through my standard routine about being bright and motivated and in the top third of my class, and how I had a job with Brodnax and Speer. Got the shaft. I blast away with both barrels. Tinley Britt, my hatred of big firms. My labor is cheap. Anything to get going. Really need a job, mister. I rattle on without interruption for a minute or two, then return to my seat.

He stews for a bit, chews a fingernail. I can't tell if he's angry or thrilled.

"You know what pisses me off?" he finally says, obviously somewhat less than thrilled.

"Yeah, people like me lying to the people up front so I can get back here and make my pitch for a job. That's exactly what pisses you off. I don't blame you. I'd be pissed too, but then I'd get over it, you know. I'd say, look, this guy is about to be a lawyer, but instead of paying him forty grand, I can hire him to do grunt work at, say twenty-four thousand."

"Twenty-one."

"I'll take it," I say. "I'll start tomorrow at twenty-one. And I'll work a whole year at twenty-one. I promise I won't leave for twelve months, regardless of whether I pass the bar. I put in sixty, seventy hours a week for twelve months. No vacation. You have my word. I'll sign a contract."

"We require five years' experience before we'll look at a paralegal. This is high-powered stuff."

"I'll learn it quick. I clerked last summer for a defense firm downtown, nothing but litigation."

There's something unfair here, and he's just figured it out. I walked in with my guns loaded, and he's been ambushed. It's obvious that I've done this several times, because I have such rapid responses to anything he says. I don't exactly feel sorry for him. He can always order me out.

"I'll run it by Mr. Lake," he says, conceding a little. "He has pretty strict rules about personnel. I don't have the authority to hire a paralegal who doesn't meet our specs."

"Sure," I say sadly. Kicked in the face again. I've actually become quite good at this. I've learned that lawyers, regardless of how busy they are, have an inherent sympathy for a fresh new graduate who can't find work. Limited sympathy.

"Maybe he'll say yes, and if he does, then the job's yours." He offers this to ease me down gently.

"There's something else," I say, rallying. "I do have a case. A very good one."

This causes him to be extremely suspicious. "What kind of case?" he asks.

"Insurance bad faith."

"You the client?"

"Nope. I'm the lawyer. I sort of stumbled across it."

"What's it worth?"

I hand him a two-page summary of the Black case, heavily modified and sensationalized. I've worked on this synopsis for a while now, fine-tuning it every time some lawyer read it and turned me down.

Barry X. reads it carefully, with more concentration than I've seen from anyone yet. He reads it a second time as I admire his aged-brick walls and dream of an office like this.

"Not bad," he says when he's finished. There's a gleam in his eye, and I think he's more excited than he lets on. "Lemme guess. You want a job, and a piece of the action."

"Nope. Just the job. The case is yours. I'd like to work on it, and I'll need to handle the client. But the fee is yours."

"Part of the fee. Mr. Lake gets most of it," he says with a grin.

Whatever. I honestly don't care how they split the money. I only want a job. The thought of working for Jonathan Lake in this opulent setting makes me dizzy.

I've decided to keep Miss Birdie for myself. As a client, she's not that attractive because she spends nothing on lawyers. She'll probably live to be a hundred and twenty, so there's no benefit in using her as a trump card. I'm sure there are highly skilled lawyers who could show her all sorts of ways to pay them, but this would not appeal to the Lake firm. These guys litigate. They're not interested in drafting wills and probating estates.

I stand again. I've taken enough of Barry's time. "Look," I say as sincerely as possible, "I know you're busy. I'm completely legitimate. You can check me out at the law school. Call Madeline Skinner if you want."

"Mad Madeline. She's still there?"

"Yes, and right now she's my best friend. She'll vouch for me."

"Sure. I'll get back with you as soon as possible." Sure you will.

I get lost twice trying to find the front door. No one's watching me, so I take my time, admiring the large offices scattered around the building. At one point, I stop at the edge of the library and gaze up at three levels of walkways and narrow promenades. No two offices are even remotely similar. Conference rooms are stuck here and there. Secretaries and clerks and flunkies move quietly about on the heartpine floors.

I'd work here for a lot less than twenty-one thousand a year.

I PARK QUIETLY behind the long Cadillac, and ease from my car without a sound. I'm in no mood to repot mums. I step softly around the house and am greeted by a tall stack of huge white plastic bags. Dozens of them. Pine bark mulch, by the ton. Each bag weighs one hundred pounds. I now recall something Miss Birdie said a few days ago about remulching all the flower beds, but I had no idea.

I dart for the steps leading to my apartment, and as I bound for the top I hear her calling, "Rudy. Rudy dear, let's have some coffee." She's standing by the monument of pine bark, grinning broadly at me with her gray and yellow teeth. She is truly happy I'm home. It's almost dark and she likes to sip coffee on the patio as the sun disappears.

"Of course," I say, folding my jacket over the rail and ripping off my tie.

"How are you, dear?" she sings upward. She started this "Dear" business about a week ago. It's dear this and dear that.

"Just fine. Tired. My back is bothering me," I've been hinting about a bad back for several days, and so far she hasn't taken the bait.

I take my familiar chair while she mixes her dreadful brew in the kitchen. It's late afternoon, the shadows are falling across the back lawn. I count the bags of mulch. Eight across, four deep, eight high. That's 256 bags. At 100 pounds each, that's a total of 25,600 pounds. Of mulch. To be spread. By me.

We sip our coffee, very small sips for me, and she wants to know everything I've done today. I lie and tell her I've been talking to some lawyers about some lawsuits, then I studied for the bar exam. Same thing tomorrow. Busy, busy, busy, you know, with lawyer stuff. Certainly no time to lift and carry a ton of mulch.

Both of us are sort of facing the white bags, but neither wants to look at them. I avoid eye contact.

"When do you start working as a lawyer?" she asks.

"Not sure," I say, then explain for the tenth time how I will study hard for the next few weeks, just bury myself in the books at law school, and hope I pass the bar exam. Can't practice till I pass the exam.

"How nice," she says, drifting away for a moment. "We really need to get started with that mulch," she adds, nodding and rolling her eyes wildly at it.

I can't think of anything to say for a moment, then, "Sure is a lot."

"Oh, it won't be bad. I'll help."

That means she'll point with her spade and maintain an endless line of chatter.

"Yeah, well, maybe tomorrow. It's late and I've had a rough day."

She thinks about this for a second. "I was hoping we could start this afternoon," she says. "I'll help."

"Well, I haven't had dinner," I say.

"I'll make you a sandwich," she offers quickly. A sandwich to Miss Birdie is a transparent slice of processed turkey between two thin slices of no-fat white bread. Not a drop of mustard or mayo. No thought of lettuce or cheese. It would take four to knock off the slightest of hunger pains.

She stands and heads for the kitchen as the phone rings. I have yet to receive a separate line into my apartment, though she's been promising one for two weeks.

Right now I have an extension, which means there is no privacy on the phone. She has asked me to restrict my calls because she needs complete access to it. It seldom rings.

"It's for you, Rudy," she calls from the kitchen. "Some lawyer."

It's Barry X. He says he's talked it over with Jonathan Lake, and it's okay if we pursue another conversation. He asks if I can come to his office now, at this moment, he says he works all night. And he wants me to bring the file. He wants to see the entire file on my bad-faith case.

As we talk, I watch Miss Birdie prepare with great care a turkey sandwich. Just as she slices it in two, I hang up.

"Gotta run, Miss Birdie," I say breathlessly. "Something's come up. Gotta meet with this lawyer about a big case."

"But what about—"

"Sorry. I'll get to it tomorrow." I leave her standing there, a half a sandwich in each hand, face sagging as if she just can't believe I won't dine with her.

BARRY MEETS ME at the front door, which is locked, though there are still many people at work inside. I follow him to his office, my step a little quicker than it's been in days. I can't help but admire the rugs and bookshelves and artwork and think to myself that I'm about to be a part of this. Me, a member of the Lake firm, the biggest trial lawyers around.

He offers me an egg roll, the remnants of his dinner. Says he eats three meals a day at his desk. I remember that he's divorced, and now understand why. I'm not hungry.

He clicks on his Dictaphone and places the microphone on the edge of the desk nearest me. "We'll record this. I'll get my secretary to type it tomorrow. Is that okay?"

"Sure," I say. Anything.

"I'll hire you as a paralegal for twelve months. Your salary will be twenty-one thousand a year, payable in twelve equal installments on the fifteenth of each month. You won't be eligible for health insurance or other fringes until you've been here for a year. At the end of twelve months, we'll evaluate our relationship, and at that time explore the possibility of hiring you as a lawyer, not a paralegal."

"Sure. Fine."

"You'll have an office, and we're in the process of hiring a secretary who'll assist you. Minimum of sixty hours a week, starting at eight in the morning and going until whenever. No lawyer in this firm works less than sixty hours a week."

"No problem." I'll work ninety. It'll keep me away from Miss Birdie and her pine bark mulch.

He checks his notes carefully. "And we will become counsel of record for the, uh, what's the name of your case?"

"Black. *Black versus Great Benefit.*"

"Okay. We'll represent the Blacks against Great Benefit Life Insurance Company. You'll work on the file, but be entitled to none of the fees, if any."

"That's right."

"Can you think of anything else?" he says, speaking toward the microphone.

"When do I start?"

"Now. I'd like to go over the case tonight, if you have the time."

"Sure."

"Anything else?"

I swallow hard. "I filed for bankruptcy earlier this month. It's a long story."

"Aren't they all? Seven or thirteen?"

"Straight seven."

"Then it won't affect your paycheck. Also, you study for the bar on your own time, okay?"

"Fine."

He turns off the Dictaphone, and again offers me an egg roll. I decline. I follow him down a spiral staircase to a small library.

"It's easy to get lost here," he says.

"It's incredible," I say, marveling at the maze of rooms and passageways.

We sit at a table and begin to spread the Black file before us. He's impressed with my organization. He asks for certain documents. They're all at my fingertips. He wants dates and names. I have them memorized. I make copies of everything—one copy for his file, one for mine.

I have everything but a signed contract for legal services with the Blacks. He seems surprised by this, and I explain how I came to represent them.

We'll need to get a contract, he says more than once.

I LEAVE after ten o'clock. I catch myself smiling in the rearview mirror as I drive across town. I'll call Booker first thing in the morning with the good news. Then I'll take some flowers to Madeline Skinner and say thanks.

It may be a lowly job, but there's no place to go but up. Give me a year, and I'll be making more money than Sara Plankmore and S. Todd and N. Elizabeth and F. Franklin and a hundred other assholes I've been hiding from for the past month. Just give me some time.

I stop by Yogi's and have a drink with Prince. I tell him the wonderful news, and he gives me a drunken bear hug. Says he hates to see me go. I tell him I'd like to hang around for a month or so, maybe work weekends until the bar exam is over. Anything is fine with Prince.

I sit alone in a booth in the rear, sipping a cool one and

surveying the sparse crowd. I'm not ashamed anymore. For the first time in weeks I am not burdened with humiliation. I'm ready for action now, ready to get on with this career. I dream of facing Loyd Beck in a courtroom one day.

Twelve

AS I'VE WADED THROUGH THE CASES and materials given to me by Max Leuberg, I have continually been astonished at the lengths to which wealthy insurance companies have gone to screw little people. No dollar is too trivial to connive for. No scheme is too challenging to activate. I've also been amazed at how few policyholders actually file suit. Most never consult a lawyer. They are shown layers of language in the appendices and addenda and convinced that they only thought they were insured. One study estimates that less than five percent of bad-faith denials are ever seen by a lawyer. The people who buy these policies are not educated. They are often as fearful of the lawyers as they are of the insurance companies. The idea of walking into a courtroom and testifying before a judge and jury is enough to silence them.

Barry Lancaster and I spend the better part of two days plowing through the Black file. He's handled several bad-faith cases over the years, with varying degrees of success. He says repeatedly that juries are so damned conservative in Memphis that it's hard to get a just verdict. I've heard this for three years. For a Southern city, Memphis is a tough union town. Union towns usually produce good verdicts for plaintiffs. But for some unknown reason, it rarely happens here. Jonathan Lake has had a handful of million-dollar verdicts, but now prefers to try cases in other states.

I have yet to meet Mr. Lake. He's in a big trial somewhere, and unconcerned about meeting his newest employee.

My temporary office is in a small library on a ledge overlooking the second floor. There are three round tables, eight stacks of books, all relating to medical malpractice. During my first full day on the job, Barry showed me a nice room just down the hall from him and explained this would be mine in a couple of weeks. Needs some paint and there's something wrong with the electrical wiring. What do you expect from a warehouse? he has asked me more than once.

I haven't actually met anyone else in the firm, and I'm sure this is because I'm a lowly paralegal, not a lawyer. I'm nothing new or special. Paralegals come and go.

These are very busy people, and there's not much camaraderie. Barry says little about the other lawyers in the building, and I get the distinct impression that each little trial unit is pretty much on its own. I also get the feeling that handling lawsuits under the supervision of Jonathan Lake is edgy business.

Barry arrives at the office before eight each morning, and I'm determined to meet him at the front door until I get a key to this place. Evidently, Mr. Lake is very particular about who has access to the building. It's a long story about his phones getting bugged years ago while engaged in a vicious lawsuit with an insurance company. Barry told me the story when I first broached the subject of a key. Might take weeks, he said. And a polygraph.

He parked me on the ledge, gave me my instructions and left for his office. During the first two days, he checked on me every two hours or so. I copied everything in the Black file. Without his knowledge, I also ran a complete copy of the file for my records. I took this copy home at the end of the second day, tucking it away nicely in my sleek new attaché case, a gift from Prince.

Using Barry's guidelines, I drafted a rather severe letter to Great Benefit, in which I laid out all the relevant facts and pertinent misdeeds on its behalf. When his secretary finished typing it, it ran for four pages. He performed radical surgery on it, and sent me back to my corner. He's very intense and takes great pride in his ability to concentrate.

During a break on my third day, I finally mustered the courage to ask his secretary about the paperwork relevant to my employment. She was busy, but said she'd look into it.

At the end of the third day, Barry and I left his office just after nine. We had completed the letter to Great Benefit, a three-page masterpiece to be sent by certified mail, return receipt. He never talks about life outside the office. I suggested we go have a beer and a sandwich, but he quickly stiff-armed me.

I drove to Yogi's for a late snack. The place was packed with drunk frat boys, and Prince himself was tending bar. And not happy about it. I took over and told him to go play bouncer. He was delighted.

He went instead to his favorite table, where his lawyer, Bruiser Stone, was chain-smoking Camels and taking bets on a boxing match. Bruiser was in the paper again this morning, denying any knowledge of anything. The cops found a dead body in a waste Dumpster behind a topless joint two years ago. The deceased was a local thug who owned a piece of the porno business in town, and evidently wanted to branch out into the bouncing boob trade. He stepped onto the wrong turf with the wrong deal, and was decapitated. Bruiser wouldn't do a thing like that, but the cops seem reasonably confident that he knows precisely who did.

He's been in here a lot lately, drinking heavily, whispering to Prince.

Thank God I have a real job. I'd almost resigned myself to asking Bruiser for work.

TODAY IS FRIDAY, my fourth day as an employee of the Lake firm. I have told a handful of people that I work for the Lake firm, and it's very pleasant, the way it rolls off my tongue. It has a satisfying ring to it. The Lake firm. No one has to ask about the firm. Just mention its name, and people see the magnificent old warehouse and they know it's the home of the great Jonathan Lake and his gang of kick-ass lawyers.

Booker almost cried. He bought steaks and a bottle of nonalcoholic wine. Charlene cooked and we celebrated until midnight.

I hadn't planned on waking before seven this morning, but there is a loud whacking noise against my apartment door. It's Miss Birdie, rattling the doorknob now, calling, "Rudy! Rudy!"

I unbolt the door, and she barges in. "Rudy. Are you awake?" She's looking at me in the small kitchen. I'm wearing gym shorts and a tee shirt, nothing indecent. My eyes are barely open, hair sticking out in all directions. I'm awake, but barely.

The sun is hardly up, but she's already dirty with soil on her apron and mud on her shoes. "Good morning," I say, trying hard not to sound irritated.

She grins, yellow and gray. "Did I wake you?" she chirps.

"No, I was just getting up."

"Good. We have work to do."

"Work? But—"

"Yes, Rudy. You've ignored the mulch long enough, now it's time to get busy. It'll rot if we don't hurry."

I blink my eyes and try to focus. "Today is Friday," I mumble with some uncertainty.

"No. It's Saturday," she snaps.

We stare at each other for a few seconds, then I glance at my watch, a habit I've picked up after only three days on the job. "It's Friday, Miss Birdie. Friday. I have to work today."

"It's Saturday," she repeats stubbornly.

We stare some more. She glances at my gym shorts. I study her muddy shoes.

"Look, Miss Birdie," I say warmly, "I know today is Friday, and I'm expected at the office in an hour and a half. We'll do the mulch this weekend." Of course I'm trying to placate her. I had planned to man my desk tomorrow morning.

"It'll rot."

"Not before tomorrow." Does mulch really rot in the bag? I don't think so.

"I wanted to do the roses tomorrow."

"Well, why don't you work on the roses today while I'm at the office, then tomorrow we'll do the mulch."

She chews on this for a moment, and is suddenly pitiful. Her shoulders sink and her face saddens. It's hard to tell whether she's embarrassed. "Do you promise?" she asks meekly.

"I promise."

"You said you'd do the yard work if I'd lower the rent."

"Yes, I know." How could I forget? She's reminded me of this a dozen times already.

"Well, okay," she says as if she's gotten exactly what she came for. Then she waddles out the door and down the steps, mumbling all the way. I quietly close the door, wondering at what hour she'll come and fetch me in the morning.

I dress and drive to the office, where a half-dozen cars are already parked and the warehouse is partially lit. It's not yet seven. I wait in my car until another one pulls into the lot, and I time my approach perfectly so that I catch a middle-aged man at the front door. He's holding a briefcase and balancing a tall paper cup of coffee while fumbling for his keys.

He seems startled by me. This is not a high-crime area, but it's still midtown Memphis and people are jumpy.

"Good morning," I say warmly.

"Mornin'," he grunts. "Can I help you?"

"Yes sir. I'm Barry Lancaster's new paralegal, just reporting for work."

"Name?"

"Rudy Baylor."

His hands become still for a moment and he frowns hard. His bottom lip curls and protrudes and he shakes his head. "Doesn't ring a bell. I'm the business manager. Nobody's said a word to me."

"He hired me four days ago, I swear."

He sticks the key in the door with a fearful glance over his shoulder. The guy thinks I'm a thief or a killer. I'm wearing a coat and tie, and look quite nice.

"Sorry. But Mr. Lake has very strict rules about security. No one gets in before hours unless they're on the payroll." He almost jumps inside the door. "Tell Barry to buzz me this morning," he says, then slams the door in my face.

I'm not going to hang around the front steps like a panhandler waiting for the next payrolled person to come along. I drive a few blocks to a deli, where I buy a morning paper, roll and coffee. I kill an hour breathing cigarette smoke and hearing the gossip, then return to the parking lot, which now has even more cars in it. Nice cars. Elegant German cars and other glossy imports. I carefully select a space next to a Chevrolet.

The front receptionist has seen me come and go a few times, but pretends I'm a complete stranger. I'm not about to inform her that I am now an employee, same as she. She calls Barry, who greenlights my entrance into the maze.

He's due in court at nine, motions in a product liability case, so he's moving quickly. I'm determined to discuss the addition of my name to the firm payroll, but the timing is bad. It can wait a day or two. He's stuffing files into a bulky briefcase, and for a moment I'm taken with the idea of assisting him in court this morning.

He has other plans. "I want you to go see the Blacks, and come back with a signed contract. It needs to be done now." He really emphasizes the word "now," so I know precisely where I'm headed.

He hands me a thin file. "Contract's in there. I prepared it last night. Look it over. It needs to be signed by all three Blacks—Dot, Buddy and Donny Ray, since he's an adult."

I nod confidently, but I'd rather be beaten than spend the morning with the Blacks. I'll finally meet Donny Ray, a meeting I thought I could postpone forever. "And after that?" I ask.

"I'll be in court all day. Come find me in Judge Anderson's courtroom." His phone rings and he sort of waves me away, as if my time is up now.

□ □ □ □ □

THE IDEA of me collecting all the Blacks around the kitchen table for a group signing is not appealing. I'd be forced to sit and watch as Dot stalked through the backyard to the wrecked Fairlane, bitching every step of the way then coaxing and cajoling old Buddy away from his cats and gin. She'd probably pull him from the car by his ear. It could be nasty. And I'd have to sit nervously as she disappeared into the rear of the house to prepare Donny Ray, then hold my breath as he came to meet me, his lawyer.

To avoid as much of this as possible, I stop at a pay phone at a Gulf station and call Dot. What a shame. The Lake firm has the finest electronic gadgetry available, and I'm forced to use a pay phone. Thank goodness Dot answers. I cannot imagine a phone chat with Buddy. I doubt if he has a car phone in his Fairlane.

As always, she's suspicious, but agrees to meet with me for a few moments. I don't exactly instruct her to assemble the clan, but I stress the need to have everyone's signature. And, typically, I tell her I'm in a great hurry. Off to court, you know. Judges are waiting.

The same dogs snarl at me from behind the chain-link next door as I park in the Black driveway. Dot is standing on the cluttered porch, cigarette cocked with filter tip just inches from her lips, a bluish fog drifting lazily from above her head across the front lawn. She's been waiting and smoking for a while.

I force a wide, phony grin and offer all sorts of greetings. The wrinkles around her mouth barely crack. I follow her through the cramped and muggy den, past the torn sofa sitting under a collection of old portraits of the Blacks as a happy lot, over the worn shag carpeting with small throw rugs to hide the holes, into the kitchen, where no one is waiting.

"Coffee?" she asks, pointing to my spot at the kitchen table.

"No, thanks. Just some water."

She fills a plastic glass with tap water, no ice, and places it before me. Slowly, we both look through the window.

"I can't get him to come in," she says without a trace of frustration. I guess some days Buddy will come in, some days he won't.

"Why not?" I ask, as if his behavior can be rationalized.

She just shrugs. "You need Donny Ray too, right?"

"Yes."

She eases from the kitchen, leaving me with my warm water and view of Buddy. He's actually hard to see because the windshield hasn't been washed in decades and a horde of mangy cats romps around the hood. He's wearing a cap of some sort, probably with wool earflaps, and he slowly lifts the bottle to his lips. It appears to be in a brown paper bag. He takes a leisurely nip.

I hear Dot speaking softly to her son. They're shuffling through the den, then they're in the kitchen. I stand to meet Donny Ray Black.

He's definitely about to die, whatever the cause. He's horribly gaunt and emaciated, hollow-cheeked, skin as bleached as chalk. He was small-framed before this affliction struck, and now he's stooped at the waist and no taller than his mother. His hair and eyebrows are jet black, in graphic contrast to his pasty skin. But he smiles and sticks out a bony hand, which I shake as firmly as I dare.

Dot has been clutching him around the waist, and she gently eases him into a chair. He's wearing baggy jeans and a plain white tee shirt that drapes and sags loosely over his skeleton.

"Nice to meet you," I say, trying to avoid his sunken eyes.

"Mom's said nice things about you," he replies. His voice is weak and raspy, but his words are clear. I never thought about Dot saying kind things about me. He cups his chin in both hands, as if his head won't stay up by itself. "She says you're suing those bastards at Great Benefit, gonna make 'em pay." His words are more desperate than angry.

"That's right," I say. I open the file and produce a copy of the demand letter Barry X. mailed to Great Benefit. I hand it to Dot, who is standing behind Donny Ray. "We filed this," I explain, very much the efficient lawyer. Filed, as opposed to mailed. Sounds better, like we're really on the move now. "We don't expect them to respond in a satisfactory manner, so we'll be suing in a matter of days. Probably ask for at least a million."

Dot glances at the letter, then places it on the table. I had expected a barrage of questions about why I haven't filed suit already. I was afraid it could get contentious. But she gently rubs Donny Ray's shoulders, and stares forlornly through the window. She'll watch her words because she doesn't want to upset him.

Donny Ray is facing the window. "Is Daddy comin' in?" he asked.

"Said he won't," she answers.

I pull the contract from the file, and hand it to Dot. "This must be signed before we can file suit. It's a contract between you, the clients, and my law firm. A contract for legal representation."

She holds it warily. It's only two pages. "What's in it?"

"Oh, the usual. It's pretty standard language. You guys hire us as your lawyers, we handle the case, take care of the expenses, and we get a third of any recovery."

"Then why does it take two pages of small print?" she asks as she pulls a cigarette from a pack on the table.

"Don't light that!" Donny snaps over his shoulder. He looks at me, and says, "No wonder I'm dying."

Without hesitation, she sticks the cigarette between her lips and keeps looking at the document. She doesn't light it. "And all three of us have to sign it?"

"That's right."

"Well, he said he ain't comin' in," she said.

"Then take it out there to him," Donny Ray says angrily. "Just get a pen and go out there and make him sign the damned thing."

"I hadn't thought of that," she says.

"We've done it before." Donny Ray lowers his head and scratches his scalp. The sharp words have winded him.

"I guess I could," she says, still hesitant.

"Just go, dammit!" he says, and Dot scratches around in a drawer until she finds a pen. Donny Ray raises his head and rests it on his hands. His hands are supported by wrists as thin as broom handles.

"Be back in a minute," Dot says, as though she's running errands down the street and worried about her boy. She walks slowly across the brick patio and into the weeds. A cat on the hood sees her coming and dives under the car.

"A few months ago," Donny Ray says, then takes a long pause. His breathing is labored and his head rocks slightly. "A few months ago we had to have his signature notarized, and he wouldn't leave. She found a notary willing to make a house call for twenty dollars, but when she got here he wouldn't come in. So Mom and the notary go out there to the car, high-stepping through the weeds. You see that big orange cat on top of the car?"

"Uh-huh."

"We call her Claws. She's sort of the watchcat around here. Anyway, when the notary reached in to get the papers from Buddy, who of course was soused and barely conscious, Claws jumped from the car and attacked the notary. Cost us sixty bucks for the doctor's visit. And a new pair of panty hose. Have you ever seen anybody with acute leukemia?"

"No. Not until now."

"I weigh a hundred and ten pounds. Eleven months ago I weighed a hundred and sixty. The leukemia was detected in plenty of time to be treated. I'm lucky enough to have an identical twin, and the bone marrow's an identical match. The transplant would've saved my life, but we couldn't afford it. We had insurance, but you know the rest of the story. I guess you know all this, right?"

"Yes. I'm very familiar with your case, Donny Ray."

"Good," he says, relieved. We watch Dot shoo away the cats. Claws, perched on top of the car, pretends to be asleep. Claws wants no part of Dot Black. The doors are open, and Dot sticks the contract inside. We can hear her penetrating voice.

"I know you think they're crazy," he says, reading my mind. "But they're good people who've had some bad breaks. Be patient with them."

"They're nice folks."

"I'm eighty percent gone, okay. Eighty percent. If I'd received the transplant, hell even six months ago, then I would've had a ninety percent chance of being cured. Ninety percent. Funny how doctors use numbers to tell us we'll live or die. Now it's too late." He suddenly gasps for breath, clenching his fists and shuddering all over. His face turns a light shade of pink as he desperately sucks in air, and for a second I feel as if I need to help. He beats his chest with both fists, and I'm afraid his whole body is about to cave in.

He catches his breath finally, and snorts rapidly through his nose. It is precisely at this moment that I begin to hate Great Benefit Life Insurance Company.

I'm not ashamed to look at him anymore. He's my client, and he's counting on me. I'll take him, warts and all.

His breathing is as normal as possible, and his eyes are red and moist. I can't tell if he's crying or just recovering from the seizure. "I'm sorry," he whispers.

Claws hisses loud enough for us to hear, and we look just in time to see her flying through the air and landing in the weeds. Evidently, the watchcat was a bit too interested in my contract, and Dot knocked the hell out of her. Dot is saying something ugly to her husband, who's hunkered even lower behind the wheel. She reaches in, snatches the paperwork, then storms toward us, cats diving for cover in all directions.

"Eighty percent gone, okay?" Donny Ray says hoarsely. "So I won't be around much longer. Whatever you get out of this case, please take care of them with it. They've had a hard life."

I'm touched by this to the point of being unable to respond.

Dot opens the door and slides the contract across the table. The first page is ripped slightly at the bottom and the second has a smudge on it. I hope it's not cat poop. "There," she says. Mission accomplished. Buddy has indeed signed it, a signature that's absolutely illegible.

I point here and there. Donny Ray and his mother sign, and the deal is sealed. We chat a few minutes as I start glancing at my watch.

When I leave them, Dot is seated next to Donny Ray, gently stroking his arm and telling him that things will get better.

Thirteen

I HAD BEEN PREPARED TO EXPLAIN TO Barry X. that I wouldn't be able to work on Saturday, what with more pressing demands around the house and all. And I had been prepared to suggest a few hours on Sunday afternoon, if he needed me. But I worried for nothing. Barry is leaving town for the weekend, and since I wouldn't dare try to enter the office without his assistance, the issue quickly became moot.

For some reason, Miss Birdie does not rattle my door before sunrise, choosing instead to busy herself in front of the garage, below my window, with all manner of tool preparation. She drops rakes and shovels. She chips crud off the inside of the wheelbarrow with an unwieldly pickax. She sharpens two flat hoes, singing and yodeling all the while. I finally come down just after seven, and she acts surprised to see me. "Why good morning, Rudy. And how are you?"

"Fine, Miss Birdie. You?"

"Wonderful, just wonderful. Isn't it a lovely day?"

The day has hardly begun, and it's still too early to

measure its loveliness. It is, if anything, rather sticky for such an early hour. The insufferable heat of the Memphis summer cannot be far away.

She allows me one cup of instant coffee and a piece of toast before she starts rumbling about the mulch. I spring into action, much to her delight. Under her guidance, I manhandle the first hundred-pound bag into the wheelbarrow and follow her around the house and down the drive and across the front lawn to a scrawny little flower bed near the street. She holds her coffee in gloved hands and points to the precise spot where the mulch should go. I am quite winded by the trek, especially the last leg across the damp grass, but I rip the bag open with gusto and begin moving mulch with a pitchfork.

My tee shirt is soaked when I finish the first bag fifteen minutes later. She follows me and the wheelbarrow back to the edge of the patio, where we reload. She actually points to the exact bag she wants next, and we haul it to a spot near the mailbox.

We spread five bags in the first hour. Five hundred pounds of mulch. And I am suffering. The temperature hits eighty at nine o'clock. I talk her into a water break at nine-thirty, and find it difficult to stand after sitting for ten minutes. A legitimate backache seizes me sometime thereafter, but I bite my tongue and allow myself only a fair amount of grimacing. She doesn't notice.

I'm not a lazy person, and at one point during college, not too long ago, I was in excellent physical condition. I jogged and played intramural sports, but then law school happened and I've had little time for such activities during the past three years. I feel like a soft little wimp after a few hours of hard labor.

For lunch she feeds me two of her tasteless turkey sandwiches and an apple. I eat very slowly on the patio, under the fan. My back aches, my legs are numb, my hands actually shake as I nibble like a rabbit.

As I wait for her to finish in the kitchen, I stare across the small green patch of lawn, around the monument of mulch, to my apartment sitting innocently above the garage. I'd been so proud of myself when I negotiated the paltry sum of one hundred and fifty dollars per month as rent, but how clever had I really been? Who got the best end of this deal? I remember feeling slightly ashamed of myself for taking advantage of this sweet little woman. Now I'd like to stuff her in an empty mulch bag.

According to an ancient thermometer nailed to the garage, the temperature at 1 P.M. is ninety-three degrees. At two, my back finally locks up, and I explain to Miss Birdie that I have to rest. She looks at me sadly, then slowly turns and studies the undiminished heap of white bags. We've barely made a dent. "Well, I guess. If you must."

"Just an hour," I plead.

She relents, but by three-thirty I am once again pushing the wheelbarrow with Miss Birdie at my heels.

After eight hours of harsh labor, I have disposed of exactly seventy-nine bags of mulch, less than a third of the shipment she'd ordered.

Shortly after lunch, I dropped the first hint that I was expected at Yogi's by six. This was a lie, of course. I am scheduled to tend bar from eight to closing. But she'd never know the difference, and I am determined to liberate myself from the mulch before dark. At five, I simply quit. I tell her I've had enough, my back is aching, I have to go to work and I pull myself up the stairs as she watches sadly from below. She can evict me, for all I care.

THE MAJESTIC SOUND of rolling thunder wakes me late Sunday morning, and I lie stiffly on the sheets as a heavy rain pounds my roof. My head is in fine shape—I stopped drinking last night when I went on duty. But the rest of my body is fixed in concrete, unable to move. The slightest shift causes excruciating pain. It hurts to breathe.

At some point during yesterday's arduous ordeal, Miss Birdie asked me if I'd like to worship with her this morning. Church attendance was not a condition in my lease, but why not, I thought. If this lonely old lady wants me to go to church with her, it's the least I can do. I certainly couldn't be harmed by it.

Then I asked her what church she attends. Abundance Tabernacle in Dallas, she answered. Live via satellite, she worships with the Reverend Kenneth Chandler, and in the privacy of her own home.

I begged off. She appeared to be hurt, but rallied quickly.

When I was a small boy, long before my father succumbed to alcohol and sent me away to a military school, I attended church occasionally with my mother. He went with us a time or two, but did nothing but gripe, so Mother and I preferred that he stay home and read the paper. It was a little Methodist church with a friendly pastor, the Reverend Howie, who told funny stories and made everyone feel loved. I remember how content my mother was whenever we listened to his sermons. There were plenty of kids in Sunday School, and I didn't object to being scrubbed and starched on Sunday morning and led off to church.

My mother once had minor surgery and was in the hospital for three days. Of course, the ladies in the church knew the most intimate details of the operation, and for three days our house was flooded with casseroles, cakes, pies, breads, pots and dishes filled with more food than my father and I could eat in a year. The ladies organized a sitting for us. They took turns supervising the food, cleaning the kitchen, greeting even more guests who brought even more casseroles. For the three days my mother was in the hospital, and for three days after she returned home, we had at least one of the ladies living with us, guarding the food, it seemed to me.

My father hated the ordeal. For one, he couldn't sneak around and drink, not with a houseful of church ladies. I think they knew that he liked to nip at the bottle, and since they had managed to barge into the house, they were determined to catch him. And he was expected to be the gracious host, something my father simply couldn't do. After the first twenty-four hours, he spent most of his time at the hospital, but not exactly doting over his ailing wife. He stayed in the visitors lounge, where he watched TV and sipped spiked colas.

I have fond memories of it. Our house had never felt such warmth, never seen so much delicious food. The ladies fussed over me as if my mother had died, and I relished the attention. They were the aunts and grandmothers I'd never known.

Shortly after my mother recuperated, Reverend Howie got himself run off for an indiscretion I never fully understood, and the church split wide open. Someone insulted my mother, and that was the end of church for us. I think she and Hank, the new husband, attend sporadically.

I missed the church for a while, then grew into the habit of not attending. My friends there would occasionally invite me back, but before long I was too cool to go to church. A girlfriend in college took me to mass a few times, on Saturday evening of all times, but I'm too much of a Protestant to understand all the rituals.

Miss Birdie timidly mentioned the possibility of yard work this afternoon. I explained that it was the Sabbath, God's holy day, and I just didn't believe in labor on Sunday.

She couldn't think of a thing to say.

Fourteen

THE RAIN IS INTERMITTENT FOR THREE days, effectively suspending my work as a yard boy. After dark on Tuesday, I am hiding in my apartment, studying for the bar exam, when the phone rings. It's Dot Black, and I know something is wrong. She wouldn't call me otherwise.

"I just got a phone call," she says, "from a Mr. Barry Lancaster. Said he was my lawyer."

"That's true, Dot. He's a big-shot lawyer with my firm. He works with me." I guess Barry is just checking a few details.

"Well, that ain't what he said. He called to see if me and Donny Ray can come down to his office tomorrow, said he needed to get some things signed. I asked about you. He said you ain't working there. I want to know what's going on."

So do I. I stutter for a second, say something about a misunderstanding. A thick knot hits deep in my stomach. "It's a big firm, Dot, and I'm new, you know. He probably just forgot about me."

"No. He knows who you are. He said you used to work there, but not anymore. This is pretty confusing, you know?"

I know. I fall into a chair and try to think clearly. It's almost nine o'clock. "Look, Dot, sit tight. Let me call Mr. Lancaster and find out what he's up to. I'll call you back in a minute."

"I want to know what's going on. Have you sued those bastards yet?"

"I'll call you back in just a minute, okay? Bye now." I hang up the phone, then quickly punch the number for the Lake firm. I'm hit with the rotten feeling that I've been here before.

The late receptionist routes me to Barry X. I decide to be cordial, play along, see what he says.

"Barry, it's me, Rudy. Did you see my research?"

"Yeah, looks great." He sounds tired. "Listen, Rudy, we may have a slight problem with your position."

The knot claws its way into my throat. My heart freezes. My lungs skip a breath. "Oh yeah?" I manage to say.

"Yeah. Looks bad. I met with Jonathan Lake late this afternoon, and he's not going to approve you."

"Why not?"

"He doesn't like the idea of a lawyer filling the position of a paralegal. And now that I think about it, it's not such a good idea after all. You see, Mr. Lake thinks, and I concur, that the natural tendency for a lawyer in that position would be to try and force his way into the next associate's slot. And we don't operate that way. It's bad business."

I close my eyes and want to cry. "I don't understand," I say.

"I'm sorry. I tried my best, but he simply wouldn't give. He runs this place with an iron fist, and he has a certain way of doing things. To be honest, he really chewed my ass good for even thinking about hiring you."

"I want to talk to Jonathan Lake," I say as firmly as possible.

"No way. He's too busy, plus he just wouldn't do it. And he's not going to change his mind."

"You son of a bitch."

"Look, Rudy, we—"

"You son of a bitch!" I'm shouting into the phone, and it feels good.

"Take it easy, Rudy."

"Is Lake in the office now?" I demand.

"Probably. But he won't—"

"I'll be there in five minutes," I yell, and slam the phone down.

Ten minutes later, I squeal tires and slam on brakes and come to a stop in front of the warehouse. There are three cars in the lot, lights are on in the building. Barry is not waiting for me.

I pound on the front door but nobody appears. I know they can hear me in there, but they're too cowardly to come out. They'll probably call the cops if I don't quit.

But I can't quit. I walk to the north side and pound on another door, then the same for an emergency exit around back. I stand under Barry's office window and yell at him. His lights are on, but he ignores me. I go back to the front door and beat on it some more.

A uniformed security guard steps from the shadows and grabs my shoulder. My knees buckle with fright. I look up at him. He's at least six-six, black with a black cap.

"You need to leave, son," he says gently in a deep voice.

"Go on now, before I call the police."

I shake his hand off my shoulder and walk away.

□ □ □
  □ □

I SIT FOR A LONG TIME in the darkness on the battered sofa Miss Birdie loaned me, and try to put things into some perspective. I'm largely unsuccessful in doing so. I drink two warm beers. I curse and I cry. I plot revenge. I even think of killing Jonathan Lake and Barry X. Sleazy bastards conspired to steal my case. What do I tell the Blacks now? How do I explain this to them?

I walk the floor, waiting for sunrise. I actually laughed last night when I thought of retrieving my list of firms and knocking on doors again. I cringed with the prospect of calling Madeline Skinner. "It's me again, Madeline. I'm back."

I finally fall asleep on the sofa, and someone wakes me just after nine. It is not Miss Birdie. It's two cops in plainclothes. They flash their badges through the open door, and I invite them in. I'm wearing gym shorts and a tee shirt. My eyes are burning so I rub them and try and figure out why I suddenly have attracted the police.

They could be twins, both about thirty, not much older than myself. They're wearing jeans and sneakers and black mustaches and act like a couple of B actors from television. "Can we sit down?" one asks as he pulls a chair from under the table and sits down. His partner does the same, and they are quickly in position.

"Sure," I say like a real smartass. "Have a seat."

"Join us," one says.

"Why not?" I sit at the end, between them. They both lean forward, still acting. "Now what the hell's going on?" I ask.

"You know Jonathan Lake?"

"Yes."

"You know where his office is?"

"Yes."

"Did you go there last night?"

"Yes."

"What time?"

"Between nine and ten."

"What was your purpose in going there?"

"It's a long story."

"We have hours."

"I wanted to talk to Jonathan Lake."

"Did you?"

"No."

"Why not?"

"Doors were locked. I couldn't get in the building."

"Did you try to break in?"

"Nope."

"Are you sure?"

"Yep."

"Did you return to the building after midnight?"

"Nope."

"Are you sure?"

"Yep. Ask the security guard."

With this, they glance at each other. Something here has hit the mark. "Did you see the security guard?"

"Yep. He asked me to leave, so I left."

"Can you describe him?"

"Yep."

"Then do it."

"Big black guy, probably six-six. Uniform, cap, gun, the works. Ask him, he'll tell you I left when he told me to leave."

"We can't ask him." They glance at each other again.

"Why not?" I ask. Something awful is coming.

"Because he's dead." They both watch me intently as I react to this. I'm genuinely shocked, as anybody would be.

"How, uh, how did he die?"

"Burned up in the fire."

"What fire?"

They clam up in unison, both nodding suspiciously as they look at the table. One pulls a notepad from his pocket like some cub reporter. "That little car out there, the Toyota, is that yours?"

"You know it is. You've got computers."

"Did you drive it to the office last night?"

"No. I pushed it over there. What fire?"

"Don't be a smartass, okay?"

"Okay. It's a deal. I won't be a smartass if you won't be a smartass."

The other chimes in. "We have a possible sighting of your car in the vicinity of the office at two this morning."

"No you don't. Not my car." It is impossible at this moment to know if these guys are telling the truth. "What fire?" I ask again.

"The Lake firm was burned last night. Completely destroyed."

"To the ground," the other adds helpfully.

"And you guys are from the arson squad," I say, still stunned but at the same time really pissed because they think I was involved in it. "And Barry Lancaster told you that I'd make a wonderful suspect for torching the place, right?"

"We do arson. We also do homicide."

"How many were killed?"

"Just the guard. First call came in at three this morning, so the building was deserted. Evidently the guard got trapped somehow when the roof fell in."

I almost wish Jonathan Lake had been with the guard, then I think of those beautiful offices with the paintings and rugs.

"You're wasting your time," I say, angrier at the thought of being a suspect.

"Mr. Lancaster said you were pretty upset when you went to the office last night."

"True. But not mad enough to torch the place. You guys are wasting your time. I swear."

"He said you'd just been fired, and you wanted to confront Mr. Lake."

"True, true, true. All of the above. But that hardly proves I had a motive to burn his offices. Get real."

"A murder committed in the course of an arson can carry the death penalty."

"No kiddin'! I'm with you. Go find the murderer and let's fry his ass. Just leave me out of it."

I guess my anger is pretty convincing because they retreat at the same time. One pulls a folded piece of paper from his front shirt pocket. "Gotta report here, couple of months ago, where you were wanted for destruction of private property. Something about some broken glass in a law office downtown."

"See, your computers do work."

"Pretty bizarre behavior for a lawyer."

"I've seen worse. And I'm not a lawyer. I'm a paralegal, or something like that. Just finished law school. And the charges were dropped, which I'm sure is written somewhere conspicuously on your little printout there. And if you guys think that my breaking some glass in April is somehow related to last night's fire, then the real arsonist can relax. He's safe. He'll never get caught."

At this, one jumps up and is quickly joined by the other. "You'd better talk to a lawyer," one says, pointing down at me. "Right now you're the prime suspect."

"Yeah, yeah. Like I said, if I'm the prime suspect, then the real killer is a lucky soul. You boys are not close."

They slam the door and disappear. I wait half an hour, then get into my car. I drive a few blocks and carefully maneuver myself close to the warehouse. I park, walk another block and duck into a convenience store. I can see the smoldering remains two blocks away. Only one wall is standing. Dozens of people mill about, the lawyers and secretaries pointing this way and that, the firemen tromping around in their bulky boots. Yellow crime scene tape is being strung by the police. The smell of burned wood is pungent, and a grayish cloud hangs low over the entire neighborhood.

The building had wooden floors, ceilings, and, with few exceptions, the walls were pine too. Add to the mix the tremendous number of books scattered throughout the building and the tons of paper necessarily stored about, and it's easy to understand how it was incinerated. What's puzzling is the fact that there was an extensive fire sprinkling system throughout the warehouse. Painted pipes ran everywhere, often woven into the decorative scheme.

FOR OBVIOUS REASONS, Prince is not a morning person. He usually locks up Yogi's around 2 A.M., then stumbles into the backseat of his Cadillac. Firestone, his lifelong driver and alleged bodyguard, takes him home. A couple of times Firestone himself has been too drunk to drive, and I took them both home.

Prince is usually in his office by eleven because Yogi's does a brisk lunch business. I find him there at noon, at his desk, shuffling paper and dealing with his daily hangover. He eats painkillers and drinks mineral water until the magic hour of five, then slides into his soothing world of rum and tonic.

Prince's office is a windowless room under the kitchen, very much out of sight and accessible only by quick footwork through three unmarked doors and down a hidden staircase. It's a perfect square with every inch of the walls covered with photos of Prince shaking hands with local pols and other photogenic types. There are also lots of framed and laminated newspaper clippings of Prince being suspected, accused, indicted, arrested, tried and, always, found innocent. He loves to see himself in print.

He's in a foul mood, as usual. I've learned over the years to avoid him until he's had his third drink, usually about 6 P.M. So I'm six hours early. He motions for me to come in, and I close the door behind me.

"What's wrong?" he grunts. His eyes are bloodshot. He's always reminded me of Wolfman Jack with his long dark hair, flowing beard, open shirt, hairy neck.

"I'm in a bit of a bind," I say.

"What else is new?"

I tell him about last night—the loss of job, the fire, the cops. Everything. I place particular emphasis on the fact that there's a dead body and that the cops are very concerned about it. Rightfully so. I can't imagine being the favorite suspect, but the cops sure seem to think so.

"So Lake got torched," he reflects aloud. He seems pleased. A good arson job is just the sort of thing that would amuse Prince and brighten his morning. "I never particularly liked him."

"He's not dead. He's just temporarily out of business. He'll be back." And this is a major cause of my concern. Jonathan Lake spends a lot of money on a lot of politicians. He cultivates relationships so he can call in favors. If he's convinced I was involved in the fire, or if he simply wants a temporary scapegoat, then the cops will come after me with a vengeance.

"You swear you didn't do it?"

"Come on, Prince."

He ponders this, strokes his beard, and I can immediately tell he's delighted to suddenly be in the middle of it. It's crime, death, intrigue, politics, a regular slice of life in the gutter. If it only had some topless dancers and a few payoffs to the police, then Prince would be yanking out the good booze to celebrate.

"You better talk to a lawyer," he says, still stroking his whiskers. This, sadly, is the real reason I'm here. I thought about calling Booker, but I've troubled him enough. And he's currently laboring with the same disability that afflicts me, to wit, we haven't passed the bar and we're really not lawyers.

"I can't afford a lawyer," I say, then wait for the next line in this script. If there were an alternative at the moment, I would happily lunge for it.

"Lemme handle it," he says. "I'll call Bruiser."

I nod and say, "Thanks. Do you think he'll help?"

Prince grins and spreads his arms expansively. "Bruiser will do anything I ask him, okay?"

"Sure," I say meekly. He picks up a phone and punches the number. I listen as he growls his way past a couple of people, then gets Bruiser on the line. He speaks in the rapid, clipped phrases of a man who knows his phones are wired. Prince spits out the following: "Bruiser, Prince here. Yeah, yeah. Need to see you pretty quick. . . . A little matter regarding one of my employees. . . . Yeah, yeah. No, at your place. Thirty minutes. Sure." And he hangs up.

I pity the poor FBI technician trying to extract incriminating data from that conversation.

Firestone pulls the Cadillac to the rear door, and Prince and I jump in the backseat. The car is black and the windows are deeply tinted. He lives in darkness. In three years I've never known him to engage in any outdoor activities. He vacations in Las Vegas, never leaving the casinos.

I listen to what quickly becomes a tedious recitation of Bruiser's greatest legal triumphs, almost all of which involve Prince. Oddly, I begin to relax. I'm in good hands.

Bruiser went to law school at night, and finished when he was twenty-two, still a record, Prince believes. They were best of friends as children, and in high school they gambled a little, drank a lot, chased girls, fought boys. Tough Memphis neighborhood on the south side. They could write a book. Bruiser went to college, Prince got himself a beer truck. One thing led to another.

The law offices are in a short, red-bricked strip shopping center with a cleaner's at one end and a video rental at the other. Bruiser invests wisely, Prince explains, and owns the entire unit. Across the street is an all-night pancake house and next to it is Club Amber, a gawdy topless joint with Vegas-style neon. This is an industrial section of town, near the airport.

Except for the words LAW OFFICE painted in black on a glass door in the center of the strip, there is nothing to indicate which profession is practiced here. A secretary with tight jeans and sticky red lips greets us with a toothy grin, but we do not slow. I follow Prince through the front area. "She used to work across the street," he mumbles. I hope it was the pancake house but I doubt it.

Bruiser's office is remarkably similar to Prince's—no windows, no chance of sunlight, large and square and gawdy, photos of important but unknown people clutching Bruiser and grinning at us. One wall is reserved for firearms, all sorts of rifles and muskets and awards for sharpshooting. Behind Bruiser's massive leather swivel chair is a large, elevated aquarium with what appear to be miniature sharks gliding through the murky waters.

He's on the phone, and so he waves at us to take our seats across from his long and wide desk. We sit, and Prince can't wait to inform me. "Those are real sharks in there," he says, pointing to the wall above Bruiser's head. Live sharks in a lawyer's office. Get it. It's a joke. Prince snickers.

I glance at Bruiser and try to avoid eye contact. The phone looks tiny next to his enormous head. His long, half-gray hair falls in shaggy layers to his shoulders. His goatee, completely gray, is thick and long and the phone is almost lost in it. His eyes are dark and quick, surrounded by rolls of swarthy skin. I've often thought he must be of Mediterranean extraction.

Although I've served Bruiser a thousand drinks, I've never actually engaged in conversation with him. I've never wanted to. And I don't want to now, but, obviously, my options are limited.

He snarls a few brief remarks, and hangs up the phone. Prince makes quick introductions, and Bruiser assures us that he knows me well. "Sure, I've known Rudy for a long time," he says. "What's the problem?"

Prince looks at me, and I go through the routine.

"Saw it on the news this morning," Bruiser injects when my narrative reaches the part about the fire. "Already had five calls about it. Doesn't take much to get the lawyers gossiping."

I smile and nod because I feel I'm supposed to, then get to the part about the cops. I finish without further interruption, and wait for words of counsel and advice from my lawyer.

"A paralegal?" he says, obviously perplexed.

"I was desperate."

"So where do you work now?"

"I don't know. I'm much more concerned about being arrested at the moment."

This makes Bruiser smile. "I'll take care of that," he says smugly. Prince has assured me repeatedly that Bruiser knows more cops than the mayor himself. "Just let me make some phone calls."

"He needs to lay low, doesn't he?" Prince asks, as if I'm an escaped felon.

"Yeah. Keep low." For some reason, I'm struck with the certainty that this advice has been uttered many times in this office. "How much do you know about arson?" he asks me.

"Nothing. They didn't teach it in law school."

"Well, I've handled a few arson cases. It can take days before they know whether or not it's arson. Old building like that, anything could've happened. If it's arson, they won't make any arrests for a few days."

"I really don't want to be arrested, you know. Especially since I'm innocent. I don't need the press." I say this with a glance at the wall plastered with his newspaper stories.

"Don't blame you there," he actually says with a straight face. "When do you take the bar exam?"

"July."

"Then what?"

"I don't know. I'll look around."

My buddy Prince suddenly charges into the conversation. "Can't you use him around here, Bruiser? Hell, you got a bunch of lawyers. What's one more? He's a top student, works hard, bright. I can vouch for him. The boy needs a job."

I slowly turn and look at Prince, who smiles at me as if he's Santa Claus. "This'll be a great place to work," he says right jolly like. "You'll learn what *real* lawyers do." He laughs and slaps me on the knee.

We both look at Bruiser, whose eyes are darting as his mind races wildly, with excuses. "Uh, sure. I'm always looking for good legal talent."

"See there," Prince says.

"In fact, two of my associates just left to form their own firm. So, I've got two empty offices."

"See there," Prince says again. "I told you things would work out."

"But it ain't exactly a salaried position," Bruiser says, warming to the idea. "No sir. I don't operate that way. I expect my associates to pay for themselves, to generate their own fees."

I'm too stunned to speak. Prince and I did not discuss the topic of my employment. I hadn't wanted his assistance. I don't really want Bruiser Stone as my boss. But I can't insult the man either, not with the cops poking around, making not so vague references about the death penalty. I'm unable to muster the strength to tell Bruiser that he's sleazy enough to represent me, but too sleazy to employ me.

"How does that work?" I ask.

"It's very simple, and it works, at least on my end. And keep in mind that in twenty years I've tried everything. I've had a bunch of partners and I've had dozens of associates. The only system that works is one where the associate is required to generate enough fees to cover his salary. Can you do that?"

"I can try," I say, all shrugs and uncertainty.

"Sure you can," Prince adds helpfully.

"You draw a thousand dollars a month, and you keep one third of the fees you generate. Your one third is applied against the draw. One third goes into my office fund, which covers overhead, secretarial, stuff like that. The other one third comes to me. If you don't cover your draw each month, then you owe me the balance. I keep a running total until you hit a big month. Understand?"

I ponder this ridiculous scheme for a few seconds. The only thing worse than being unemployed is having a job in which you lose money and your debts become cumulative each month. I can think of several very pointed and unanswerable questions, and I start to ask one when Prince says, "Sounds fair to me. Helluva deal." He slaps me on the knee again. "You can make some real money."

"It's the only way I operate," Bruiser says for the second or third time.

"How much do your associates make?" I ask, not expecting the truth.

The long wrinkles squeeze together across his forehead. He's deep in thought. "It varies. Depends on how much you hustle. One guy made close to eighty last year, one guy made twenty."

"And you made three hundred thousand," Prince says with a hearty laugh.

"I wish."

Bruiser is watching me closely. He's offering me the only possible job left in the city of Memphis, and he seems to know I'm not anxious to take it.

"When can I start?" I ask in an awkward attempt at eagerness.

"Right now."

"But the bar exam——"

"Don't worry about it. You can start generating fees today. I'll show you how to do it."

"You're gonna learn a lot," Prince joins in, almost beside himself with satisfaction.

"I'll pay you a thousand bucks today," Bruiser says, like the last of the big spenders. "Get you started. I'll show you the office, sort of get you plugged in."

"Great," I say with a forced smile. It is utterly impossible at this moment to pursue any other course of action. I shouldn't even be here, but I'm scared and need help. Left unsaid at this moment is the matter of how much I will owe Bruiser for his services. He is not the kind of good-hearted soul who might do an occasional favor for the poor.

I feel a bit ill. Maybe it's the lack of sleep, the shock of being awakened by the police. Maybe it's sitting here in this office, watching live sharks swim about, getting myself hustled by two of the biggest hustlers in the city.

Not long ago I was a bright, fresh-faced, third-year law

student with a promising job with a real firm, anxious to join the profession, work hard, get myself active in the local bar association, start the career, do all the things my friends would do. And now I sit here, so vulnerable and weak that I agree to whore myself out for a shaky thousand dollars a month.

Bruiser takes an urgent phone call, probably a topless dancer in jail for solicitation, and we ease from our seats. He whispers over the phone that he wants me to return this afternoon.

Prince is so proud he's about to bust. Just like that, he's saved me from the death penalty and found me a job. Try as I might, I cannot be cheerful as Firestone weaves through traffic and speeds us back to Yogi's.

Fifteen

I DECIDE TO HIDE IN THE LAW SCHOOL. I spend a couple of hours lurking between the tiers in the basement, retrieving and perusing case after case on insurance bad faith. I kill time.

I drive slowly in the general direction of the airport and arrive at Bruiser's at three-thirty. The neighborhood is worse than it seemed just hours earlier. The street has five lanes for traffic and is lined with light industries and freight terminals and dark little bars and clubs where the workingmen unwind. It's somewhere near the final approach to the airport, and jets scream by overhead.

Bruiser's strip is labeled Greenway Plaza, and as I sit in my car in the littered lot I notice, in addition to the cleaners and video rental, a liquor store and a small coffee shop. Though it's difficult to tell because of the blackened windows and sealed doors, it appears as if the law offices occupy six or seven contiguous bays in the center of the strip. I grit my teeth, and pull open the door.

The denim-clad secretary is visible on the other side of a chest-high partition. She has bleached hair and a remarkable figure, the curves and grooves of which are magnificently displayed.

I explain my presence to her. I expect to be rebuffed and asked to leave, but she is civil. In a sultry and intelligent voice, quite unbimbolike, she asks me to fill out the necessary employment forms. I'm stunned to learn that this firm, the Law Offices of J. Lyman Stone, offers comprehensive health insurance to its employees. I carefully read the fine print because I half-expect Bruiser to hide little clauses that further sink his claws into my flesh.

But there are no surprises. I ask her if I may see Bruiser, and she asks me to wait. I take a seat in a row of plastic chairs along the wall. The reception area is designed on the same lines as a welfare office—well-worn tile floor, thin layer of dirt on said floor, cheap seats, flimsy paneled walls, amazing assortment of torn magazines. She, Dru, the secretary, is typing away and answering the phone at the same time. It rings a lot, and she is very efficient, often able to continue typing rapidly while chatting with clients.

She eventually sends me back to see my new boss. Bruiser is at his desk, poring over my employment forms like an accountant. I'm surprised at his interest in the details. He welcomes me back, goes over the financial terms of our arrangement, then slides a contract in front of me. It's customized with my name in the blanks. I read it, then sign it. There's a thirty-day walkout clause in case either of us wishes to terminate my employment. I'm quite thankful for it, but I sense he placed it there for a very good reason.

I explain my recent bankruptcy. Tomorrow, I'm scheduled to be in court for my first meeting with my creditors. It's called a Debtor's Examination, and the lawyers for the folks I've stiffed are entitled to poke around in my dirty laundry. They can ask virtually any question they want about my finances, and about my life in general. It will be a low-key affair. In fact, there's a good chance there will be no one there to grill me.

Because of the hearing, it's to my advantage to remain unemployed for a few days. I ask Bruiser to hold the forms there, and to postpone the first month's salary until after the hearing. This has a fraudulent ring to it, and Bruiser likes it. No problem.

He takes me on a quick tour of the place. It's just as I figured—a little sweatshop of rooms stuck here and there as the firm expanded from one bay to the next, walls being knocked out as things progressed. We fade deeper and deeper into the maze. He introduces me to two harried women in a small room crowded with computers and printers. I doubt if they ever danced on tables. "I think we have six girls now," he says as we move on. A secretary is simply a girl.

He introduces me to a couple of the lawyers, nice enough guys, badly dressed and working in cramped offices. "We're down to five lawyers," he explains as we enter the library. "Used to have seven, but that's too many headaches. I prefer four or five. The more I hire, the more I referee. Same with the girls."

The library is a long, narrow room with books from floor to ceiling, in no apparent order. A long table in the center is covered with open volumes and wadded-up legal paper. "Some of these guys are pigs," he mumbles to himself. "So what do you think of my little spread?"

"It's fine," I say. And I'm not lying. I'm relieved to see that law is actually practiced here. Bruiser may be a well-connected thug with shady deals and crooked investments, but he is still a lawyer. His offices hum with the busy noise of legitimate commerce.

"Not as fancy as the big boys downtown," he says, not apologizing. "But it's all paid for. Bought it fifteen years ago. Your office is over here." He points and we leave the library. Two doors down, next to a soft-drink machine, is a well-used room with a desk, some chairs, file cabinets and pictures of horses on the walls. On the desk is a phone, a dictating machine, a stack of legal pads. Everything is neat. The smell of disinfectant lingers as if it's been cleaned in the past hour.

He hands me a ring with two keys on it. "This is for the front door, this is for your office. You're free to come and go at all hours. Just be careful at night. This is not the best part of town."

"We need to talk," I say, taking the keys.

He glances at his watch. "For how long?"

"Give me thirty minutes. It's urgent."

He shrugs, and I follow him back to his office, where he settles his wide rear into his leather chair. "What's up?" he asks, all business, taking a designer pen from his pocket and addressing the obligatory legal pad. He starts scribbling before I start talking.

I give him a rapid, fact-filled summary of the Black case that takes ten minutes. In doing so, I fill in the gaps of my termination from the Lake firm. I explain how Barry Lancaster used me so he could steal the case, and this leads to my strong-arm maneuver with Bruiser. "We have to file suit today," I tell him gravely. "Because Lancaster technically owns the case. I think he'll file soon."

Bruiser glares at me with his black eyes. I think I've caught his attention. The idea of beating the Lake firm to the courthouse appeals to him. "What about the clients?" he asks. "They've signed up with Lake."

"Yeah. But I'm on my way to see them. They'll listen to me." I pull from my briefcase a rough draft of a lawsuit against Great Benefit, one that Barry and I had spent hours on. Bruiser reads it carefully.

I then hand him a termination letter I've typed to

Barry X. Lancaster, to be signed by all three Blacks. He reads it slowly.

"This is good work, Rudy," he says, and I feel like an accomplished shyster. "Lemme guess. You file the lawsuit this afternoon, then take a copy of it to the Blacks. Show it to them, then get them to sign the letter of termination."

"Right. I just need your name and signature on the lawsuit. I'll do all the work and keep you posted."

"That'll effectively screw the Lake firm, won't it?" he says, pondering and tugging at a wayward whisker. "I like it. What's the lawsuit worth?"

"Probably whatever the jury says. I doubt if it'll be settled out of court."

"And you're gonna try it?"

"I might need a little help. I figure it's a year or two away."

"I'll introduce you to Deck Shifflet, one of my associates. He used to work for a big insurance company and reviews a lot of policies for me."

"Great."

"His office is just down the hall from yours. Get this thing redrafted, put my name on it and we'll get it filed today. Just be damned sure the clients go along with us."

"The clients are with us," I assure him with images of Buddy stroking his cats and swatting horseflies in the Fairlane, of Dot sitting on the front porch smoking and watching the mailbox as if a check from Great Benefit will arrive at any moment, of Donny Ray holding his head up with his hands.

"Changing the subject a bit," I say, clearing my throat. "Any word from the cops?"

"Nothing to it," he says smugly, as if the master fixer has once again performed his magic. "I talked to some people I know, and they're not even sure it's arson. Could take days."

"So they won't be arresting me in the middle of the night."

"Nope. They promised me they'd call me if they want you. I assured them you'd turn yourself in, post bond, etcetera. But it won't get that far. Relax."

I do in fact relax. I trust Bruiser Stone to be able to squeeze promises out of the police.

"Thanks," I say.

FIVE MINUTES before closing, I walk into the office of the Circuit Clerk and file my four-page lawsuit against Great Benefit Life Insurance Company and Bobby Ott, the missing agent who sold the policy. My clients, the Blacks, seek actual damages of two hundred thousand dollars, and punitive damages of ten million. I have no idea of the net worth of Great Benefit, and it will be a long time before I find out. I pulled the ten million from the air because it has a nice ring to it. Trial lawyers do this all the time.

Of course, my name is nowhere to be seen. Plaintiff's counsel of record is J. Lyman Stone, and his garish signature adorns the last page, giving the entire pleading the weight of authority. I hand the deputy clerk a firm check for the filing fee, and we're in business.

Great Benefit has been officially sued!

I race across town to North Memphis into the Granger section, where I find my clients much as I had left them a few days ago. Buddy's outside. Dot fetches Donny Ray from his room. The three of us sit around the table while they admire their copy of the lawsuit. They're very impressed with the big numbers. Dot keeps repeating the sum of ten million, as if she holds the winning lottery number.

I am eventually forced to explain what happened with those awful folks at the Lake firm. A conflict of strategy.

They weren't moving fast enough to suit me. They didn't like my hard-charging approach to the case. And on and on.

They really don't care. The lawsuit has been filed, and they have proof. They can read it all they want. They want to know what will happen next, how soon might they know something? What are the chances of a quick settlement? These questions knock the wind out of me. I know it will take much too long, and I feel cruel concealing this.

I cajole them into signing a letter addressed to Barry X. Lancaster, their old lawyer. It tersely fires him. There's also a new contract with the firm of J. Lyman Stone. I talk real fast as I explain this new batch of paperwork. From the same seats at the kitchen table, Donny Ray and I watch as Dot stomps through the weeds again and quarrels with her husband to get his signatures.

I leave them in better spirits than when I found them. They're taking a fair amount of satisfaction in the fact that they've sued this company they've hated for so long. They've finally fought back: they've been stepped on, and they've convinced me that they've been wronged. Now, they've joined the millions of other Americans who file suit each year. It makes them feel somewhat patriotic.

I SIT in my hot little car in rush hour traffic, and think about the insanity of the past twenty-four hours. I've just signed a quicksand employment contract. A thousand dollars a month is such a paltry sum, yet it frightens me. It's not a salary, but a loan, and I have no idea how Bruiser plans for me to immediately start generating fees. If I collect on the Black case, it'll be many months away. I'll continue to work at Yogi's for a while. Prince still pays me in cash—five bucks an hour plus dinner and a few beers.

There are firms in this town that expect their new asso-

THE RAINMAKER

173

ciates to wear nice suits every day, to drive a presentable vehicle, to live in a respectable house, even to hang out at the fashionable country clubs. Of course, they pay them a helluva lot more than Bruiser's paying me, but they also weigh them down with a lot of unnecessary societal burdens.

Not me. Not my firm. I can wear anything, drive anything, hang out anywhere, and no one will ever say a word. In fact, I wonder what I'll say the first time one of the guys in the office wants to dart across the street for a quick table dance or two.

Suddenly, I'm my own man. A wonderful feeling of independence comes over me as the traffic inches forward. I can survive! I'll put in some hard time with Bruiser, and probably learn much more about law than I would with the boys in the buildings downtown. I'll endure the snubs and quips and put-downs from others about working in such a seedy outfit. I can handle it. It'll make me tough. I was a bit haughty not long ago when I was safe and secure with old Brodnax and Speer, and then with Lake, so I'll eat a little crow.

It's dark when I park at Greenway Plaza. Most of the cars are gone. Across the street, the bright lights of Club Amber have attracted the usual crowd of pickup trucks and corporate rental cars. The neon swirls around the roof of the entire building and illuminates the area.

The skin business has exploded in Memphis, and it's difficult to explain. This is a very conservative town with lots of churches, the heart of the Bible Belt. The people who seek elective office here are quick to embrace strict moral standards, and they're usually rewarded accordingly by the voters. I cannot imagine a candidate being soft on the skin trade and getting elected.

I watch a carload of businessmen unload and stagger into Club Amber. It's an American with four of his Japanese friends, no doubt about to top off a long day of deal-making with a few drinks and a pleasant review of the latest developments in American silicon.

The music is already loud. The parking lot is filling fast. I walk quickly to the front door of the firm and unlock it. The offices are empty. Hell, they're probably across the street. I got the distinct impression this afternoon that the firm of J. Lyman Stone is not a place for workaholics.

All the doors are closed and I presume locked. No one trusts anyone around here. I certainly plan to lock mine.

I'll stay here for a few hours. I need to call Booker and update him on my latest adventures. We've been neglecting our studies for the bar exam. For three years we've been able to prod and motivate each other. The bar exam is looming like a date with a firing squad.

Sixteen

I SURVIVE THE NIGHT WITHOUT AN ARREST, but with little sleep as well. At some point between five and six, I surrender to the muddled thoughts racing wildly through my mind, and get out of bed. I haven't slept four hours in the last forty-eight.

The phone number is listed, and I punch the numbers at five minutes before six. I'm on my second cup of coffee. It rings ten times before a sleepy voice says, "Hello."

"Barry Lancaster please," I say.

"Speaking."

"Barry, Rudy Baylor here."

He clears his throat and I can see him lurching up from his bed. "What's up?" he asks, his voice much sharper.

"Sorry to call so early, but I just wanted to mention a couple of things."

"Like what?"

"Like the Blacks filed suit yesterday against Great Benefit. I'll send you a copy as soon as you boys get yourselves a new office. They've also signed a release, so you've been terminated. No need to worry about them again."

"How'd you file suit?"

"That's really none of your business."

"The hell it's not."

"I'll send a copy of the lawsuit, you'll figure it out. You're a bright guy. Do you have a new address yet, or does the old one still work?"

"Righto. Anyway, I'd appreciate it if you'd leave me out of this arson business. I had nothing to do with the fire, and if you insist on implicating me, then I'll be forced to sue your thieving ass."

"I'm petrified."

"I can tell. Just stop throwing my name around." I hang up before he can respond. I watch the phone for five minutes, but he doesn't call. What a coward.

I'm very anxious to see how the fire plays in the morning paper, so I shower, dress and leave quickly under the cover of darkness. There's little traffic as I head south toward the airport, toward Greenway Plaza, a place that's beginning to feel like home. I park in the same spot I left seven hours ago. Club Amber is dark and quiet, the lot littered with trash and beer cans.

The slender bay next to the bay which I think houses my office is rented by a stocky German woman named Trudy who runs a cheap coffee shop. I met her last night when I walked over for a sandwich. She told me she opened at six for coffee and doughnuts.

She's pouring coffee as I enter. We chat for a moment as she toasts my bagel and pours my coffee. There are already a dozen men cramped around the small tables, and Trudy has things on her mind. For starters, the doughnut man is late.

I get a paper and sit at a table by the window as the sun is rising. On the front page of the Metro section is a large photo of Mr. Lake's warehouse in full blaze. A brief article gives a history of the building, says that it was completely destroyed, and that Mr. Lake himself estimates the loss at three million dollars. "The renovation has been a five-year love affair," he is quoted as saying. "I'm devastated."

Weep some more, old boy. I scan it quickly and do not see the word "arson" used. Then I read it carefully. The police are tight-lipped—the matter still under investigation, too early to speculate, no comment. The usual cop-speak.

I didn't expect to see my name kicked about as a possible suspect, but I'm relieved nonetheless.

I'M IN MY OFFICE, trying to seem busy and wondering how in the world I'm supposed to generate a thousand dollars in fees over the next thirty days, when Bruiser barges in. He slides a piece of paper across my desk. I grab it.

"It's a copy of a police report," he growls, already heading for the door.

"About me?" I ask, horrified.

"Hell no! It's an accident report. Car wreck last night at the corner of Airways and Shelby, just a few blocks from here. Maybe a drunk driver involved. Looks like he ran a red light." He pauses and glares at me.

"Do we represent one of the—"

"Not yet! That's what you're for. Go get the case. Check it out. Sign it up. Investigate it. Looks like there might be some good injuries."

I'm thoroughly confused, and he leaves me that way. The door slams and I can hear him growling his way down the hall.

The accident report is filled with information: names of drivers and passengers, addresses, telephone numbers, injuries, damage to vehicles, eyewitness accounts. There's a diagram of how the cop thinks it happened, and another one showing how he found the vehicles. Both drivers were injured and taken to the hospital, and the one who ran the red light apparently had been drinking.

Interesting reading, but what do I do now? The wreck happened at ten minutes after ten last night, and Bruiser somehow got his grubby hands on it first thing this morning. I read it again, then stare at it for a long time.

"Come in," I say.

A knock on the door jolts me from my confused state.

It cracks slowly and a slight little man sticks his head through. "Rudy?" he says, his voice high and nervous.

"Yes, come in."

He slides through the narrow gap and sort of sneaks to the chair across my desk. "I'm Deck Shifflet," he says, sitting without offering a handshake or a smile. "Bruiser said you had a case you wanted to talk about." He glances over his shoulder, as if someone may have entered the room behind him and is now listening.

"Nice to meet you," I say. It's hard to tell if Deck is forty or fifty. Most of his hair is gone, and the few remaining streaks are heavily oiled and slicked across his wide scalp. The patches around his ears are thin and mostly gray. He wears square, wire-rimmed glasses that are quite thick and dirty. It's also difficult to tell if his head is extra large or his body is undersized, but the two don't fit. His forehead is divided into two round halves that meet pretty much in the center, where a deep crease joins them then plummets to his nose.

Poor Deck is one of the most unattractive men I've ever seen. His face bears the ravages of teenage acne. His chin is virtually nonexistent. When he talks his nose wrinkles and his upper lip rises to reveal four large upper teeth, all the same size.

The collar of his double-pocketed and stained white

shirt is frayed. The knot on his plain red knit tie is as big as my fist.

"Yes," I say, trying not to look at the two huge eyes studying me from behind those glasses. "It's an insurance case. Are you one of the associates here?"

The nose and lip crunch together. The teeth shine at me. "Sort of. Not really. You see, I'm not a lawyer, yet. Been to law school and all, but I haven't passed the bar."

Ah, a kindred spirit. "Oh, really," I say. "When did you finish law school?"

"Five years ago. You see, I'm having a little trouble with the bar exam. I've sat for it six times."

This is not something I want to hear. "Wow," I mumble. I honestly didn't know a person could take the bar that many times. "Sorry to hear it."

"When do you take it?" he asks, glancing nervously around the room. He's sitting on the edge of his chair as if he might need to bolt at any moment. The thumb and index finger of his right hand pull at the skin on the back of his left hand.

"July. Pretty rough, huh?"

"Yeah, pretty rough. I'd say. I haven't taken it in a year. Don't know if I'll ever try again."

"Where'd you go to law school?" I ask him this because he makes me very nervous. I'm not sure I want to talk about the Black case. How does he figure in? What's his cut going to be?

"In California," he says with the most violent facial twitch I've ever seen. Eyes open and close. Eyebrows dance. Lips flutter. "Night school. I was married at the time, working fifty hours a week. Didn't have much time to study. Took five years to finish. Wife left me. Moved out here." His words trail off as his sentences get shorter, and for a few seconds he leaves me hanging.

"Yeah, well, how long have you worked for Bruiser?"

"Almost three years. He treats me like the rest of the associates. I find the cases, work them up, give him his cut. Everybody's happy. He usually asks me to review insurance cases when they come in. I worked for Pacific Mutual for eighteen years. Got sick of it. Went to law school." The words fade again.

I watch and wait. "What happens if you have to go to court?"

He grins sheepishly like he's such a joker. "Well, I've gone a few times myself, actually. Haven't got caught yet. So many lawyers here, you know, it's impossible to keep up with us. If we have a trial, I'll get Bruiser to go. Maybe one of the other associates."

"Bruiser said there were five lawyers in the firm."

"Yeah. Me, Bruiser, Nicklass, Toxer and Ridge. I wouldn't call it a firm, though. It's every man for himself. You'll learn. You find your own cases and clients, and you keep a third of the gross."

I'm taken with his frankness, so I press. "Is it a good deal for the associates?"

"Depends on what you want," he says, jerking around as if Bruiser might be listening. "There's a lot of competition out there. Suits me fine because I can make forty thousand a year practicing law without a license. Don't tell anyone, though."

I wouldn't dream of it.

"How do you fit in with me and my insurance case?" I ask.

"Oh that. Bruiser'll pay me if there's a settlement. I help him with his files, but I'm the only one he'll trust. No one else here is allowed to touch his files. He's fired lawyers before who tried to butt in. Me, I'm harmless. I have to stay here, at least until I pass the bar exam."

"What are the other lawyers like?"

"Okay. They come and go. He doesn't hire the top

graduates, you know. He gets young guys off the streets. They work for a year or two, develop some clients and contacts, then they open their own shop. Lawyers are always moving."

Tell me about it.

"Can I ask you something?" I say against my better judgment. -

"Sure."

I hand the accident report to him, and he skims it quickly. "Bruiser gave it to you, right?"

"Yeah, just a few minutes ago. What does he expect me to do?"

"Get the case. Find the guy who got run over, sign him up with the law firm of J. Lyman Stone, then put the case together."

"How do I find him?"

"Well, looks like he's in the hospital. That's usually the best place to find them."

"You go to the hospitals?"

"Sure. I go all the time. You see, Bruiser has some contacts at Main Precinct. Some very good contacts, guys he grew up with. They feed him these accident reports almost every morning. He'll dole them out around the office, and he expects us to go get the cases. Doesn't take a rocket scientist."

"Which hospital?"

His saucerlike eyes roll and he shakes his head in disgust. "What'd they teach you in law school?"

"Not much, but they certainly didn't teach us how to chase ambulances."

"Then you'd better learn quick. If not, you'll starve. Look, you see this home phone number here for the injured driver. You simply call the number, tell whoever answers that you're with Memphis Fire Department Rescue Division, or something like that, and you need to speak to the injured driver, whatever his name is. He can't come to the phone because he's in the hospital, right? Which hospital? You need it for your computer. They'll tell you. Works every time. Use your imagination. People are gullible."

I feel sick. "Then what?"

"Then you go to the hospital and talk to such and such. Hey, look, you're just a rookie, okay. I'm sorry. Tell you what I'll do. Let's grab a sandwich, eat in the car and we'll go to the hospital and sign this boy up."

I really don't want to. I'd really like to walk out of this place and never return. But at the moment I have nothing else to do. "Okay," I say with great hesitation.

He jumps to his feet. "Meet me up front. I'll call and find out which hospital."

THE HOSPITAL is St. Peter's Charity Hospital, a zoo of a place where most trauma patients are taken. It's owned by the city and provides, among many other things, indigent care for countless patients.

Deck knows it well. We zip across town in his ragged minivan, the only asset he was awarded from the divorce, a divorce caused by years of alcohol abuse. He's clean now, a proud member of Alcoholics Anonymous, and he's stopped smoking too. He does like to gamble, though, he admits gravely, and the new casinos sprouting up just across the state line in Mississippi have him worried.

The ex-wife and two kids are still in California.

I get all these details in less than ten minutes as I chew on a hot dog. Deck drives with one hand, eats with the other, and twitches, jerks, grimaces and talks across half of Memphis with a glob of chicken salad stuck to the corner of his mouth. I cannot bear to look.

We actually park in the lot reserved for doctors because Deck has a parking card that identifies him as a physician.

The guard seems to be familiar with him, and waves us through.

Deck leads me straight to the information desk in the main lobby, a lobby packed with people. Within seconds he has the room number of Dan Van Landel, our prospect. Deck is pigeon-toed and has a slight limp, but I have trouble keeping up with him as he hikes to the elevators. "Don't act like a lawyer," he whispers under his breath as we wait in a crowd of nurses.

How could anyone suspect Deck of being a lawyer? We ride in silence to the eighth floor, and exit with a flood of people. Deck, sadly, has done this many times.

Despite the odd shape of his large head, and his gimpy gait and all his other striking features, no one notices us. We shuffle along a crowded corridor until it intersects with another at a busy nurses' station. Deck knows exactly how to find Room 886. We veer to the left, walk past nurses and technicians and a doctor studying a chart. Gurneys without sheets line one wall. The tiled floor is worn and needs scrubbing. Four doors down on the left, and we enter, without knocking, a semiprivate room. It's semidark. The first bed is occupied by a man with the sheets pulled tightly to his chin. He's watching a soap opera on a tiny TV that swings over his bed.

He glances at us with horror, as if we've come to take a kidney, and I hate myself for being here. We have no business violating the privacy of these people in such a ruthless manner.

Deck, on the other hand, does not miss a step. It's hard to believe that this brazen impostor is the same little weasel who slinked into my office less than an hour ago. Then he was afraid of his shadow. Now he seems utterly fearless.

We take a few steps and walk to the gap in a foldaway partition. Deck hesitates slightly to see if anyone is with

Dan Van Landel. He is alone, and Deck pushes forward.

"Good afternoon, Mr. Van Landel," he says sincerely.

Van Landel is in his late twenties, though his age is difficult to estimate because there are bandages on his face. One eye is swollen almost completely shut, the other has a laceration under it. An arm is broken, a leg is in traction.

He is awake, so mercifully we don't have to touch him or yell at him. I stand at the foot of the bed, near the entrance, hoping mightily that no nurse or doctor or family member shows up and catches us doing this.

Deck leans closer. "Can you hear me, Mr. Van Landel?" he asks with the compassion of a priest.

Van Landel is pretty well strapped to the bed, so he can't move. I'm sure he would like to sit up or make some adjustment, but we've got him pinned down. I cannot imagine the shock he must be in. One moment he's lying here gazing at the ceiling, probably still groggy and in pain, then in a split-second he's looking into one of the oddest faces he's ever seen.

He blinks his eyes rapidly, trying to focus. "Who are you?" he grunts through clenched teeth. Clenched because they're wired.

This is not fair.

Deck smiles at these words and delivers the four shining teeth. "Deck Shifflet, law firm of Lyman Stone." He says this with remarkable assurance, as if he's *supposed* to be here. "You haven't talked to any insurance company, have you?"

Just like that, Deck establishes the bad guys. It's certainly not us. It's the insurance boys. He takes a giant stride in gaining confidence. Us versus them.

"No," Van Landel grunts.

"Good. Don't talk to them. They're just out to screw you," Deck says, inching closer, already dispensing advice.

"We've looked over the accident report. Clear case of running a red light. We're gonna go out in about an hour," he says, looking importantly at his watch, "and photograph the site, talk to witnesses, you know, the works. We have to do it quick before the insurance company investigators get to the witnesses. They've been known to bribe them for false testimony, you know, crap like that. We need to move fast, but we need your authorization. Do you have a lawyer?"

I hold my breath. If Van Landel says that his brother is a lawyer, then I'm out the door.

"No," he says.

Deck moves in for the kill. "Well, like I said, we need to move fast. My firm handles more car wrecks than anybody in Memphis, and we get huge settlements. Insurance companies are afraid of us. And we don't charge a dime. We take the usual one third of any recovery." As he's delivering the closer, he's slowly pulling a contract from the center of a legal pad. It's a quickie contract—one page, three paragraphs, just enough to hook him. Deck waves it in his face in such a way that Van Landel has to take it. He holds it with his good arm, tries to read it.

Bless his heart. He's just gone through the worst night of his life, lucky to be alive, and now, bleary-eyed and punch-drunk, he's supposed to peruse a legal document and make an intelligent decision.

"Can you wait for my wife?" he asks, almost pleading.

Are we about to get caught? I clutch the bed railing, and in doing so inadvertently hit a cable which jerks a pulley that yanks his leg up another inch. "Ahhh!" he groans.

"Sorry," I say quickly, jerking my hands away. Deck looks at me if he could slaughter me, then regains control.

"Where is your wife?" he asks.

"Ahhh!" the poor guy groans again.

"Sorry," I repeat because I can't help it. My nerves are shot.

Van Landel watches me fearfully. I keep both hands deep in my pockets.

"She'll be back in a little while," he says, pain evident with every syllable.

Deck has an answer for everything. "I'll talk to her later, in my office. I need to get a ton of information from her." Deck deftly slides his legal pad under the contract so the signing will be smoother, and he uncaps a pen.

Van Landel mumbles something, then takes the pen and scribbles his name. Deck slides the contract into the legal pad, and hands a business card to the new client. It identifies him as a paralegal for the firm of J. Lyman Stone.

"Now, a couple of things," Deck says. His tone is so authoritative. "Don't talk to anyone except your doctor. There will be insurance people bugging you, in fact, they'll probably be here today trying to get you to sign forms and things. They might even offer you a settlement. Do not, under any circumstances, say a word to these people. Do not, under any circumstances, sign anything until I first review it. You have my number. Call me twenty-four hours a day. On the back is the number for Rudy Baylor here, and you can call him anytime. We'll handle the case together. Any questions?"

"Good," Deck says before he can grunt or groan. "Rudy here will be back in the morning with some paperwork. Have your wife call us this afternoon. It's very important that we talk to her." He pats Van Landel on his good leg. It's time for us to go, before he changes his mind. "We're gonna get you a bunch of money," Deck assures him.

We say our good-byes as we backtrack and make a quick exit. Once in the hallway, Deck proudly says, "And that's how it's done, Rudy. Piece of cake."

We dodge a woman in a wheelchair and we stop for a patient being taken away on a gurney. The hall is crawling with people. "What if the guy had a lawyer?" I ask, beginning to breathe normally again.

"There's nothing to lose, Rudy. That's what you must remember. We came here with nothing. If he ran us out of his room, for whatever reason, what have we lost?"

A little dignity, some self-respect. His reasoning is completely logical. I say nothing. My stride is long and quick, and I try not to watch him jerk and shuffle. "You see, Rudy, in law school they don't teach you what you need to know. It's all books and theories and these lofty notions of the practice of law as a profession, like between gentleman, you know. It's an honorable calling, governed by pages of written ethics."

"What's wrong with ethics?"

"Oh, nothing, I guess. I mean, I believe a lawyer should fight for his client, refrain from stealing money, try not to lie, you know, the basics."

Deck on Ethics. We spent hours probing ethical and moral dilemmas, and, wham, just like that, Deck has reduced the Canons of Ethics to the Big Three: Fight for your client, don't steal, try not to lie.

We take a sudden left and enter a newer hallway. St. Peter's is a maze of additions and annexes. Deck is in a lecturing mood. "But what they don't teach you in law school can get you hurt. Take that guy back there, Van Landel. I get the feeling you were nervous about being in his room."

"I was. Yes."

"You shouldn't be."

"But it's unethical to solicit cases. It's blatant ambulance chasing."

"Right. But who cares? Better us than the next guy. I promise you that within the next twenty-four hours another lawyer will contact Van Landel and try to sign him up. It's simply the way it's done, Rudy. It's competition, the marketplace. There are lots of lawyers out there."

As if I don't know this. "Will the guy stick?" I ask.

"Probably. We've been lucky so far. We hit him at the right time. It's usually fifty-fifty going in, but once they sign on the dotted line, then it's eighty-twenty they'll stick with us. You need to call him in a couple of hours, talk to his wife, offer to come back here tonight and discuss the case with them."

"Me?"

"Sure. It's easy. I've got some files you can go through. Doesn't take a brain surgeon."

"But I'm not sure—"

"Look, Rudy, take it easy. Don't be afraid of this place. He's our client now, okay. You have the right to visit him, and there's nothing anybody can do. They can't throw you out. Relax."

WE DRINK COFFEE from plastic cups in a grill on the third floor. Deck prefers this small cafeteria because it's near the orthopedic wing, and because it's the result of a recent renovation and few lawyers know about it. The lawyers, he explains in a hushed tone as he examines each patient, are known to hang out in hospital cafeterias, where they prey on injured folks. He says this with a certain scorn for such behavior. Irony is lost on Deck.

Part of my job as a young associate for the law firm of J. Lyman Stone will be to hang out here and graze these pastures. There is also a large cafeteria on the main floor of Cumberland Hospital, two blocks away. And the VA Hospital has three cafeterias. Deck, of course, knows where they are, and he shares this knowledge.

He advises me to start off with St. Peter's because it has the largest trauma unit. He draws a map on a napkin showing me the locations of other potential hot spots—the main cafeteria, a grill near maternity on the second floor, a coffee shop near the front lobby. Nighttime is good, he says, still studying the prey, because the patients often get bored in their rooms and, assuming they're able, like to wheel down for a snack. Not too many years ago, one of Bruiser's lawyers was trolling in the main cafeteria at one in the morning when he hooked a kid who'd been burned. The case settled a year later for two million. Problem was, the kid had fired Bruiser and hired another lawyer.

"It got away," Deck says like a defeated fisherman.

Seventeen

MISS BIRDIE RETIRES TO BED AFTER the "M°A°S°H" reruns go off at eleven. She's invited me several times to sit with her after dinner and watch television, but so far I've been able to find the right excuses.

I sit on the steps outside my apartment and wait for her house to become dark. I can see her silhouette moving from one door to the next, checking locks, pulling shades.

I suppose old people grow accustomed to loneliness, though no one expects to spend his or her last years in solitude, absent from loved ones. When she was younger, I'm sure she looked ahead with the confidence that these years would be spent surrounded by her grandchildren. Her own kids would be nearby, stopping by daily to check on Mom, bringing flowers and cookies and gifts. Miss Birdie did not plan to spend her last years alone, in an old house with fading memories.

She rarely talks about her children or grandchildren. There are a few photographs sitting around, but, judging by the fashions, they are quite dated. I've been here for a few weeks, and I'm not aware of a single contact she's had with her family.

I feel guilty because I don't sit with her at night, but I have my reasons. She watches one stupid sitcom after another, and I can't bear them. I know this because she talks about them constantly. Plus, I need to be studying for the bar exam.

There's another good reason I'm keeping my distance. Miss Birdie has been hinting rather strongly that the house needs painting, that if she can ever get the mulch finished then she'll have time for the next project.

I drafted and mailed a letter today to a lawyer in Atlanta, signed my name as a paralegal to J. Lyman Stone, and in it made a few inquiries about the estate of one Anthony L. Murdine, the last husband of Miss Birdie. I'm slowly digging, without much luck.

Her bedroom light goes off, and I ease down the rickety steps and tiptoe barefoot across the wet lawn to a shredded hammock swinging precariously between two small trees. I swung in it for an hour the other night without injury. Through the trees, the hammock has a splendid view of the full moon. I rock gently. The night is warm.

I've been in a funk since the Van Landel episode today at the hospital. I started law school less than three years ago with typical noble aspirations of one day using my license to better society in some small way, to engage in an honorable profession governed by ethical canons I thought all lawyers would strive to uphold. I really believed this. I knew I couldn't change the world, but I dreamed of working in a high-pressure environment filled with sharp-witted people who adhered to a set of lofty standards. I wanted to work hard and grow in my profession, and in doing so attract clients not by slick advertising but by reputation. And along the way, as my skills and fees increased, I would be able to take on unpopular cases and clients without the burden of getting paid. These dreams are not unusual for beginning law students.

To the credit of the law school, we spent hours studying and debating ethics. Great emphasis was placed on the subject, so much so that we assumed the profession was zealous about enforcing a rigid set of guidelines. Now I'm depressed by the truth. For the past month, I've had one real lawyer after another throw darts in my balloon. I've been reduced to a poacher in hospital cafeterias, for a thousand bucks a month. I'm sickened and saddened by what I've become, and I'm staggered by the speed at which I've fallen.

My best friend in college was Craig Balter. We roomed together for two years. I was in his wedding last year. Craig had one goal when we started college, and that was to teach high school history. He was very bright and college was too easy for him. We had long discussions about what to do with our lives. I thought he was shortchanging himself by wanting to teach, and he'd get angry when I compared my future profession with his. I was headed for big money and success on a high level. He was headed for the classroom, where his salary was subject to factors out of his control.

Craig got a master's and married a schoolteacher. He's now teaching ninth-grade history and social studies. She's pregnant and teaching kindergarten. They have a nice home in the country with a few acres and a garden, and they are the happiest people I know. Their joint income is probably around fifty thousand a year.

But Craig doesn't care about money. He's doing exactly what he always wanted to do. I, on the other hand, have no idea what I'm doing. Craig's job is immensely rewarding because he's affecting young minds. He can envision the results of his labors. I, on the other hand, will go to the office tomorrow in hopes that by hook or crook I'll seize upon some unsuspecting client wallowing in some degree of misery. If lawyers earned the same salaries as schoolteachers, they'd immediately close nine law schools out of ten.

Things must improve. But before they do, there are still at least two more possible disasters. First, I could be arrested or otherwise embarrassed for the Lake fire, and second, I could flunk the bar exam.

Thoughts of both keep me tottering in the hammock until the early morning hours.

BRUISER'S AT THE OFFICE early, red-eyed and hung over but decked out in his lawyer's finest—expensive wool suit, nicely starched white cotton shirt, rich silk tie. His flowing mane appears to have received an extra laundering this morning. It has a clean shine.

He's on his way to court to argue pretrial motions in a drug-trafficking case, and he's all nerves and action. I've been summoned to stand before his desk and receive my instructions.

"Good work on Van Landel," he says, awash in papers and files. Dru is buzzing around behind him, just out of harm's way. The sharks watch her hungrily. "I talked to the insurance company a few minutes ago. Plenty of coverage. Liability looks clear. How bad's the boy hurt?"

I spent a nerve-racking hour last night at the hospital with Dan Van Landel and his wife. They had lots of questions, the principal concern being how much they might get. I had few solid answers, but performed admirably with legalspeak. So far, they're sticking. "Broken leg, arm, ribs, plenty of lacerations. His doctor says he'll spend ten days in the hospital."

Bruiser smiles at this. "Stay on it. Do the investigating. Listen to Deck. This could be a nice settlement."

Nice for Bruiser, but I won't share in the rewards. This case will not count as fee origination for me.

"The cops want to take your statement about the fire," he tosses out while reaching for a file. "Talked to them last night. They'll do it here, in this office, with me present."

He says this as if it's already planned and I have no choice. "And if I refuse?" I ask.

"Then they'll probably take you downtown for questioning. If you have nothing to hide, I suggest you give them the statement. I'll be here. You can consult with me. Talk to them, and after that they'll leave you alone."

"So they think it's arson?"

"They're reasonably sure."

"What do they want from me?"

"Where you were, what you were doing, times, places, alibis, stuff like that."

"I can't answer everything, but I can tell the truth." Bruiser smiles. "Then the truth shall set you free."

"Let me write that down."

"Let's do it at two this afternoon."

I nod affirmatively but say nothing. It's odd that in this state of vulnerability I have complete trust in Bruiser Stone, a man I would never trust otherwise.

"I need some time off, Bruiser," I say.

His hands freeze in midair and he stares at me. Dru, in a corner picking through a file cabinet, stops and looks. One of the sharks seems to have heard me.

"You just started," Bruiser says.

"Yeah, I know. But the bar exam is just around the corner. I'm really behind with my studies."

He cocks his head to one side and strokes his goatee. Bruiser has really harsh eyes when he's drinking and having fun. Now they're like lasers. "How much time?"

"Well, I'd like to come in each morning and work till

noon or so. Then, you know, depending on my trial calendar and schedule of appointments, sneak off to the library and study." My attempt at humor falls incredibly flat.

"You could study with Deck," Bruiser says with a sudden smile. It's a joke, so I laugh goofily. "Tell you what you do," he says, serious again. "You work till noon, then you pack your books and hang out in the cafeteria at St. Peter's. Study like hell, okay, but also keep your eyes open. I want you to pass the bar, but I'm much more concerned about new cases right now. Take a cellular phone so I can reach you at all times. Fair enough?"

Why did I do this? I kick myself in the rear for mentioning the bar exam. "Sure," I say with a frown.

Last night in the hammock I thought that maybe with a little luck I might be able to avoid St. Peter's. Now I'm being stationed there.

THE SAME TWO COPS who came to my apartment present themselves to Bruiser for his permission to interrogate me. The four of us sit around a small round table in the corner of his office. Two tape recorders are placed in the center, both are turned on.

It quickly becomes boring. I repeat the same story I told these two clowns the first time we met, and they waste an enormous amount of time rehashing each tiny little aspect of it. They try to force me into discrepancies on thoroughly insignificant details—"thought you said you were wearing a navy shirt, now you're saying it was blue" —but I'm telling the absolute truth. There are no lies to cover, and after an hour they seem to realize that I'm not their man.

Bruiser gets irritated and tells them more than once to move forward. They obey him, for a while. I honestly think these two cops are afraid of Bruiser.

They finally leave, and Bruiser says that'll be the end of

it. I'm not really a suspect anymore, they're just covering their tails. He'll talk to their lieutenant in the morning and get the book closed on me.

I thank him. He hands me a tiny phone that folds into the palm of my hand. "Keep this with you at all times," he says. "Especially when you're studying for the bar. I might need you in a hurry." The tiny device suddenly grows much heavier. Through it I'll be subject to his whim around the clock.

He dispatches me to my office.

I RETURN TO THE GRILL, near the orthopedic wing with a solemn resolve to hide in a corner, study my materials, keep the damned cellular phone handy, but to ignore those around me.

The food is not terrible. After seven years of college cuisine, anything tastes fine. I dine on a pimento cheese sandwich and chips. I spread my bar review course on a table in the corner, my back to the wall.

I eat first, devouring the sandwich while examining the other diners. Most wear medical garb of some variety—doctors in their scrubs, nurses in their whites, technicians in their lab jackets. They sit in small groups and discuss the ins and outs of ailments and treatments I've never heard of. For people who are supposed to be concerned with health and nutrition, they eat the worst junk foods possible. Fries, burgers, nachos, pizza. I watch a group of young doctors huddled over their dinner, and wonder what they would think if they knew there was a lawyer in their midst, one studying for the bar so he could one day sue them.

I doubt if they'd care. I have as much right to this place as they do.

No one notices me. An occasional patient either limps

through on crutches or is wheeled in by an orderly. I can spot no other lawyers sitting around, ready to pounce.

I pay for my first cup of coffee at 6 P.M., and soon lose myself in a painful review of contracts and real estate, two subjects that revive the horror of my first year in law school. I plow ahead. I have procrastinated to this point, and there's no tomorrow. An hour passes before I go for a refill. The crowd has thinned, and I spot two casualties sitting near each other on the other side of the room. Both have lots of plaster and gauze. Deck would be in their faces. But not me.

After a while and much to my surprise, I decide that I like it here. It's quiet and no one knows me. It's ideal for studying. The coffee's not bad and refills are half-price. I'm away from Miss Birdie and thus unconcerned about manual labor. My boss expects me to be here, and though I'm supposed to be scouting for game, he'll never know the difference. Surely I don't have a quota. I can't be expected to sign up X number of cases a week.

The phone emits a sickly beep. It's Bruiser, just checking in. Any luck? No, I say, looking across the room at the two wonderful torts comparing injuries from their wheelchairs. He says he talked to the lieutenant and things look good. He's confident they'll pursue other leads, other suspects. Happy fishing! he says with a laugh, and is gone, no doubt headed for Yogi's and a few stiff ones with Prince.

I study for another hour, then leave my table and go to the eighth floor to check on Dan Van Landel. He's in pain but willing to talk. I deliver the good news that we've contacted the other driver's insurance company, and there's a nice policy waiting for us. His case has it all, I explain, repeating what Deck had told me earlier; clear liability (a drunk driver no less!), lots of insurance coverage and good injuries. Good, meaning some well-busted bones that might easily evolve into the magical condition of *permanent injury*.

Dan manages a pleasant smile. He's already counting his money. He has yet to deal with Bruiser at pie-splitting time.

I say good-bye and promise to see him tomorrow. Since I've been assigned to hospital duty, I'll be able to visit all of my clients. Talk about service!

THE GRILL is crowded again when I return and assume my position in the corner. I left my books scattered on the table, and one plainly labels itself as the *Elton Bar Review*. This has caught the attention of a group of young doctors sitting at the next table, and they eye me suspiciously as I take my seat. They are instantly silent, so I know they've been discussing my materials at length. They soon leave. I get more coffee and lose myself in the wonders of federal trial procedure.

The crowd thins to a handful. I'm drinking decaf now, and amazed at the materials I've plowed through in the past four hours. Bruiser calls again at nine forty-five. Sounds like he's in a bar somewhere. He wants me in his office at nine tomorrow to discuss a point of law he needs briefed for his current drug trial of the month. I'll be there, I say.

I'd hate to know my lawyer was being inspired with legal theories to use in my defense while chugging drinks in a topless club.

But Bruiser is my lawyer.

At ten, I am alone in the grill. It's open all night, so the cashier ignores me. I'm deep into the language governing pretrial conferences when I hear the delicate sneeze of a young woman. I look up, and two tables away is a patient in a wheelchair, the only other person seated in the grill. Her right leg is in a cast from the knee down and extends out so that I see the bottom of the white plaster. It appears to be fresh, from what I know about plaster at this point in my career.

She's very young, and extremely pretty. I can't help but stare for a few seconds before looking down at my notes. Then I stare some more. Her hair is dark and pulled back loosely behind her neck. Her eyes are brown and appear to be moist. She has strong facial features that are striking in spite of an obvious bruise on her left jaw. A nasty bruise, the type usually left by a fist. She wears a standard white hospital gown, and under it she appears to be almost frail.

An old man in a pink jacket, one of the innumerable kindly souls who act as volunteers at St. Peter's, gently places a plastic glass of orange juice on the table in front of her. "There you are, Kelly," he says like the perfect grandfather.

"Thanks," she answers with a quick smile.

"Thirty minutes, you say?" he asks.

She nods and bites her lower lip. "Thirty minutes," she tells him.

"Anything else I can do?"

"No. Thanks."

He pats her on the shoulder, and leaves the grill.

We are alone. I try not to stare, but it's impossible not to. I look down at my materials as long as I can bear it, then up slowly until my eyes can see her. She does not face me directly, but looks away at almost a ninety-degree angle. She lifts her drink, and I notice the bandages on both wrists. She has yet to see me. In fact, I realize she would see no one if the room was full. Kelly's in her own little world.

Looks like a broken ankle. The bruise on the face would satisfy Deck's requirement of a multiple, though there appears to be no laceration. The injured wrists are puzzling. As pretty as she is, I'm not tempted to practice my solicitation techniques. She looks very sad and I don't want to add to her misery. There's a thin wedding band on her left ring finger. She can't be more than eighteen.

I try to concentrate on the law for at least five uninterrupted minutes, but I see her dab her eyes with a paper napkin. Her head tilts slightly to the right as the tears flow. She sniffles quietly.

I realize quickly that the tears have nothing to do with the pain of a broken ankle. They're not caused by physical injuries.

My sleazy lawyer's imagination runs wild. Perhaps there was a car wreck and her husband was killed and she was injured. She's too young to have children and her family lives far away, and she sits here grieving over her dead husband. Could be a helluva case.

I shake off these terrible thoughts and try to concentrate on the book before me. She keeps sniffling and crying silently. A few customers come and go, but no one joins Kelly and me at the tables. I drain my coffee cup, quietly ease from my chair and walk directly in front of her on my way to the counter. I glance at her, she glances at me, our eyes meet for a second and I almost crash into a metal chair. My hands are a bit jumpy as I pay for the coffee. I take a deep breath, and stop at her table.

She slowly raises her beautiful wet eyes. I swallow hard and say, "Look, I'm not one to meddle, but is there anything I can do? Are you in pain?" I ask this as I nod at her cast.

"No," she says, barely audible. And then a stunning little smile. "But thanks."

"Sure," I say. I look at my table, less than twenty feet away. "I'm over there, studying for the bar exam, if you need anything." I shrug as if I'm not sure what to do, but I'm a wonderful, caring klutz anyway and so please forgive me if I've stepped out of bounds. But I care. And I'm available.

"Thanks," she says again.

I ease into my chair, now having established that I am a quasi-legitimate person who's studying thick books in hopes of soon joining a noble profession. Surely, she's remotely impressed. I plunge into my studies, oblivious to her suffering.

Minutes pass. I flip a page and look at her at the same time. She's looking at me, and my heart skips a beat. I totally ignore her for as long as I can bear, then I look up. She's lost again, deep in her suffering. She squeezes the napkin. The tears stream down her cheeks.

My heart breaks just watching her suffer like this. I'd love to sit next to her, maybe place my arm around her, and talk about things. If she's married, then where the hell is her husband? She glances my way, but I don't think she sees me.

Her escort in the pink jacket arrives promptly at ten-thirty, and she quickly tries to compose herself. He pats her gently on the head, offers soothing words I cannot hear, wheels her around with tenderness. As she's leaving, she very deliberately looks at me. And she gives me a long, teary smile.

I'm tempted to follow at a distance, to find her room, but I control myself. Later, I think about finding her man in pink and pressing him for details. But I don't. I try to forget about her. She's just a kid.

THE NEXT NIGHT I arrive at the grill and assume the same table. I listen to the same busy chatter from the same hurried people. I visit the Van Landels and deflect their endless questions. I watch for other sharks feeding in these murky waters, and I ignore a few obvious clients just waiting to be hustled. I study for hours. My concentration is keen and my motivation has never been more intense.

And I watch the clock. As ten approaches, I lose my edge and start gazing about. I try to remain calm and studious, but I find myself jumping whenever a new customer enters the grill. Two nurses are eating at one table, a lone technician reads a book at another.

She rolls in five minutes after the hour, the same elderly gent pushing her carefully to the spot she wants. She picks the same table as last night, and smiles at me as he maneuvers her chair. "Orange juice," she says. Her hair is still pulled back, but, if I'm not mistaken, she is wearing a trace of mascara and a bit of eyeliner. She's also wearing a pale red lipstick, and the effect is dramatic. I was not aware last night that her face was completely clean. Tonight, with just a little makeup, she is exceptionally beautiful. Her eyes are clear, radiant, free of sadness.

He places her orange juice before her, and says the identical words he said last night. "There you are, Kelly. Thirty minutes, you say?"

"Make it forty-five," she says.

"As you wish," he says, then ambles away.

She sips the juice and looks vacantly at the top of the table. I've spent a lot of time today thinking about Kelly, and I've long since decided my course of action. I wait a few minutes, pretend she's not there while making a fuss over the *Elton Bar Review*, then slowly rise as if it's time for a coffee break.

I stop at her table, and say, "You're doing much better tonight."

She was waiting for me to say something like this. "I feel much better," she says, showing that smile and perfect teeth. A gorgeous face, even with that hideous bruise.

"Can I get you something?"

"I'd like a Coke. This juice is bitter."

"Sure," I say, and walk away, thrilled beyond words. At the self-serve machine I prepare two large soft drinks, pay for them and set them on her table. I look at the empty chair across from her as if I'm thoroughly confused.

"Please sit down," she says.

"Are you sure?"

"Please. I'm tired of talking to nurses."

I take my seat and lean on my elbows. "My name's Rudy Baylor," I say. "And you're Kelly somebody."

"Kelly Riker. Nice to meet you."

"Nice to meet you." She is pleasant enough to look at from twenty feet, but now that I can stare at her without embarrassment from four feet away it's impossible not to gape. Her eyes are a soft brown with a mischievous twinkle. She is exquisite.

"Sorry if I bothered you last night," I say, anxious to get the conversation going. There are many things I want to know.

"You didn't bother me. I'm sorry I made such a spectacle of myself."

"Why do you come here?" I ask, as if she's the stranger and I belong here.

"Gets me out of the room. What about you?"

"I'm studying for the bar exam, and this is a quiet place."

"So you're gonna be a lawyer?"

"Sure. I finished law school a few weeks ago, got a job with a firm. As soon as I pass the bar exam I'll be ready to go."

She drinks from the straw and grimaces slightly as she shifts her weight. "Pretty bad break, huh?" I ask, nodding at her leg.

"It's my ankle. They put a pin in it."

"How'd it happen?" This is the obvious next question, and I assumed the answer would be perfectly easy for her.

It's not. She hesitates, and the eyes instantly water. "A domestic accident," she says as if she's rehearsed this vague explanation.

What the hell does that mean? A domestic accident?

Did she fall down the stairs?

"Oh," I say as if everything's perfectly clear. I'm worried about the wrists because they're both bandaged, not plastered. They do not appear to be broken or sprained. Lacerated, perhaps.

"It's a long story," she mumbles between sips, and looks away.

"How long have you been here?" I ask.

"A couple of days. They're waiting to see if the pin is straight. If not, they'll have to do it again." She pauses and plays with the straw. "Isn't this an odd place to study?" she asks.

"Not really. It's quiet. There's plenty of coffee. Open all night. You're wearing a wedding band." This fact has bothered me more than anything else.

She looks at it as if she's not sure it's still on her finger. "Yeah," she says, then stares at her straw. The band is by itself, no diamond to accompany it.

"So where's your husband?"

"You ask a lot of questions."

"I'm a lawyer, or almost one. It's the way we're trained."

"Why do you want to know?"

"Because it's odd that you're here alone in the hospital, obviously injured in some way, and he's not around."

"He was here earlier."

"Now he's home with the kids?"

"We don't have kids. Do you?"

"No. No wife, no children."

"How old are you?"

"You ask a lot of questions," I say with a smile. Her eyes are sparkling. "Twenty-five. How old are you?"

She thinks about this for a second. "Nineteen."

"That's awfully young to be married."

"It wasn't by choice."

"Oh, sorry."

"It's not your fault. I got pregnant when I was barely eighteen, got married shortly thereafter, miscarried a week after I got married, and life's been downhill since. There, does that satisfy your curiosity?"

"No. Yes. I'm sorry. What do you want to talk about?"

"College. Where did you go to college?"

"Austin Peay. Law school at Memphis State."

"I always wanted to go to college, but it didn't work out. Are you from Memphis?"

"I was born here, but I grew up in Knoxville. What about you?"

"A small town an hour from here. We left there when I got pregnant. My family was humiliated. His family is trash. It was time to leave."

There's some heavy family stuff prowling just beneath the surface here, and I'd like to stay away from it. She's brought up her pregnancy twice, and both times it could've been avoided. But she's lonely, and she wants to talk.

"So you moved to Memphis?"

"We ran to Memphis, got married by a justice of the peace, a real classy ceremony, then I lost the baby."

"What does your husband do?"

"Drives a forklift. Drinks a lot. He's a washed-up jock who still dreams of playing major league baseball."

I didn't ask for all this. I take it he was a high school athletic stud, she was the cutest cheerleader, the perfect all-American couple, Mr. and Miss Podunk High, most handsome, most beautiful, most athletic, most likely to succeed until they get caught one night without a condom. Disaster strikes. For some reason they decide against an abortion. Maybe they finish high school, maybe they don't. Disgraced, they flee Podunk for the anonymity of the big city. After the miscarriage, the romance wears off and they wake up to the reality that life has arrived.

He still dreams of fame and fortune in the big leagues. She longs for the careless years so recently gone, and dreams of the college she'll never see.

"I'm sorry," she says. "I shouldn't have said that."

"You're young enough to go to college," I say.

She chortles at my optimism, as if this dream buried itself long ago. "I didn't finish high school."

Now, what am I supposed to say to this? Some trite little bootstrap speech, get a GED, go to night school, you can do it if you really want.

"Do you work?" I ask instead.

"Off and on. What kind of lawyer do you want to be?"

"I enjoy trial work. I'd like to spend my career in courtrooms."

"Representing criminals?"

"Maybe. They're entitled to their day in court, and they have a right to a good defense."

"Murderers?"

"Yeah, but most can't pay for a private lawyer."

"Rapists and child molesters?"

I frown and pause for a second. "No."

"Men who beat their wives?"

"No, never." I'm serious about this, plus I'm suspicious about her injuries. She approves of my preference in clients.

"Criminal work is a rare specialty," I explain. "I'll probably do more civil litigation."

"Lawsuits and stuff."

"Yeah, that's it. Non-criminal litigation."

"Divorces?"

"I'd rather avoid them. It's really nasty work."

She's working hard at keeping the conversation on my side of the table, away from her past and certainly her present. This is fine with me. Those tears can appear instantaneously, and I don't want to ruin this conversation. I want it to last.

She wants to know about my college experience—the studying, partying, things like fraternities, dorm life, exams, professors, road trips. She's watched a lot of movies, and has a romanticized image of a perfect four years on a quaint campus with leaves turning yellow and red in the fall, of students dressed in sweaters rooting for the football team, of new friendships that last a lifetime. This poor kid barely made it out of Podunk, but she had wonderful dreams. Her grammar is perfect, her vocabulary broader than mine. She reluctantly confesses that she would've finished first or second in her graduating class, had it not been for the teenaged romance with Cliff, Mr. Riker.

Without much effort, I bolster the glory days of my undergraduate studies, skipping over such essential facts as the forty hours a week I worked delivering pizzas so I could remain a student.

She wants to know about my firm, and I'm in the middle of an incredible reimaging of J. Lyman and his offices when the phone rings two tables away. I excuse myself by telling her it's the office calling.

It's Bruiser, at Yogi's, drunk, with Prince. They are amused by the fact that I'm sitting where I'm sitting while they're drinking and betting on whatever ESPN happens to be broadcasting. Sounds like a riot in the background. "How's the fishing?" Bruiser yells into the phone.

I smile at Kelly, who's undoubtedly impressed by this call, and explain as quietly as I can that I'm talking to a prospect this very instant. Bruiser roars with laughter, then hands the phone to Prince, who's the drunker of the two. He tells a lawyer joke with absolutely no punch line, something about ambulance chasing. Then he launches into an I-told-you-so speech about getting me hooked with Bruiser, who'd teach me more law than fifty professors. This takes a while, and before long Kelly's volunteer arrives for the ride back to her room.

I take a few steps toward her table, cover the phone with my hand and say, "I enjoyed meeting you."

She smiles and says, "Thanks for the drink, and the conversation."

"Tomorrow night?" I ask, with Prince screaming in my ear.

"Maybe." Very deliberately, she winks at me, and my knees tremble.

Evidently, her escort in pink has been around this place long enough to spot a hustler. He frowns at me and whisks her away. She'll be back.

I punch a button on the phone and cut off Prince in mid-sentence. If they call back, I won't answer. If they remember it later, which is extremely doubtful, I'll blame it on Sony.

Eighteen

DECK LOVES A CHALLENGE, ESPECIALLY when it involves the gathering of dirt through hushed phone conversations with unnamed moles. I give him the bare details about Kelly and Cliff Riker, and in less than an hour he slips into my office with a proud grin.

He reads from his notes. "Kelly Riker was admitted to St. Peter's three days ago, at midnight I might add, with assorted injuries. The police had been called to her apartment by unidentified neighbors who reported a rather fierce domestic squabble. Cops found her beat to hell and lying on a sofa in the den. Cliff Riker was obviously intoxicated, highly agitated and initially wanted to give the cops some of what he'd been dishing out to his wife. He was wielding an aluminum softball bat, evidently his weapon of choice. He was quickly subdued, placed under arrest, charged with assault, taken away. She was transported by ambulance to the hospital. She gave a brief statement to the police, to the effect that he came home drunk after a softball game, some silly argument erupted, they fought, he won. She said he struck her twice on the ankle with the bat, and twice in the face with his fist."

I lost sleep last night thinking about Kelly Riker and her brown eyes and tanned legs, and the thought of her being attacked in such a manner makes me sick. Deck's watching my reaction, so I try to keep a poker face. "Her wrists are bandaged," I say, and Deck proudly flips the page. He has another report from another source, this one buried deep in the files of Rescue, Memphis Fire Department. "Kind of sketchy on the wrists. At some point during the assault, he pinned her wrists to the floor and tried to force intercourse. Evidently, he was not in the mood he thought he was, probably too much beer. She was nude when the cops found her, covered only with a blanket. She couldn't run because her ankle was splintered."

"What happened to him?"

"Spent the night in jail. Bailed out by his family. Due in court in a week, but nothing will happen."

"Why not?"

"Odds are she'll drop the charges, they'll kiss and make up, and she'll hold her breath until he does it again."

"How do you know—"

"Because it's happened before. Eight months ago, cops get the same call, same fight, same everything except she was luckier. Just a few bruises. Evidently, the bat was not handy. Cops separate them, do a little on-the-spot counseling, they're just kids, right, newlyweds, and they kiss and make up. Then, three months ago the bat is introduced into battle, and she spends a week at St. Peter's with broken ribs. The matter gets turned over to the Domestic Abuse Section of Memphis P.D., and they push hard for a severe punishment. But she loves the old boy, and refuses to testify against him. Everything's dropped. Happens all the time."

It takes a moment for this to sink in. I suspected trouble at home, but nothing this horrible. How can a man take an aluminum bat and beat his wife with it? How can Cliff Riker punch such a beautiful face?

"Happens all the time," Deck repeats himself, perfectly reading my mind.

"Anything else?" I ask.

"No. Just don't get too close."

"Thanks," I say, feeling dizzy and weak. "Thanks."

He eases to his feet. "Don't mention it."

IT'S NO SURPRISE that Booker has been studying for the bar exam much more than I. And, typically, he's worried about me. He's scheduled a marathon review for this afternoon in a conference room at the Shankle firm.

I arrive, as instructed by Booker, promptly at noon. The offices are modern and busy, and the oddest thing about the place is that everyone is black. I've seen my share of law offices in the past month, and I can recall only one black secretary and no black lawyers. Here, there's not a white face to be seen.

Booker gives me a quick tour. Even though it's lunch, the place is hopping. Word processors, copiers, faxes, phones, voices—there's a veritable racket in the hallways. The secretaries eat hurriedly at their desks, desks invariably covered with tall stacks of pending work. The lawyers and paralegals are nice enough, but need to be on their way. And there's a strict dress code for everyone—dark suits, white shirts for the men, plain dresses for the women—no bright colors, no pants.

Comparisons with the firm of J. Lyman Stone before my eyes, and I cut them off.

Booker explains that Marvin Shankle runs a tight ship. He dresses sharp, is thoroughly professional in all aspects, and maintains a wicked work schedule. He expects nothing less from his partners and staff.

The conference room is in a quiet corner. I'm in charge of lunch, and I unpack some sandwiches I picked up at Yogi's. Free sandwiches. We chat for five minutes at the most about family and law school friends. He asks a few questions about my job, but he knows to keep his distance. I've already told him everything. Almost everything. I prefer that he doesn't know about my new outpost at St. Peter's or my activities there.

Booker's become such a damned lawyer! He glances at his watch after the allotted time for small talk, then launches into the splendid afternoon he has planned for us. We'll work nonstop for six hours, taking coffee and rest room breaks only, and at 6 P.M. sharp we're outta here because someone else has reserved the room.

From twelve-fifteen to one-thirty we review federal income taxation. Booker does most of the talking because he's always had a better grasp for tax. We're working from bar review materials, and tax is as dense now as it was in the fall of last year.

At one-thirty he lets me use the rest room and get some coffee, and from then until two-thirty I take the ball and run with the federal rules of evidence. Thrilling stuff. Booker's high-octane vigor is contagious, and we blitz through some tedious material.

Flunking the bar exam is a nightmare for any young associate, but I sense that it would be especially disastrous for Booker. Frankly, it wouldn't be the end of the world for me. It would crush my ego, but I'd rally. I'd study harder and take it again in six months. Bruiser wouldn't care as long as I snare a few clients each month. One good burn case and Bruiser wouldn't expect me to take the exam again.

But Booker might be in trouble. I suspect Mr. Marvin Shankle would make his life miserable if he flunks it the first time. If he flunks it twice, he's probably history.

At precisely two-thirty, Marvin Shankle enters the conference room and Booker introduces me. He's in his early fifties, very fit and trim. His hair is slightly gray around the ears. His voice is soft but his eyes are intense. I think Marvin Shankle can see around corners. He's a legend in Southern legal circles, and it's an honor to meet him.

Booker has arranged a lecture. For almost an hour we listen intently as Shankle covers the basics of civil rights litigation and employment discrimination. We take notes, ask a few questions, but mainly we just listen.

Then he's off to a meeting, and we spend the next half hour by ourselves, blitzing through antitrust law and monopolies. At four, another lecture.

Our next speaker is Tyrone Kipler, a Harvard-educated partner whose speciality is the Constitution. He starts slow, and picks up some steam only after Booker jumps in and peppers him with questions. I catch myself lurking in the shrubbery at night, jumping out like a madman with a Ruthian-sized baseball bat and beating the hell out of Cliff Riker. To stay awake, I walk around the table, gulping coffee, trying to concentrate.

By the end of the hour, Kipler is animated and feisty, and we're drilling him with questions. He stops in mid-sentence, looks wildly at his watch and says he has to go. A judge is waiting somewhere. We thank him for his time, and he races away.

"We have one hour," Booker says. It's five minutes after five. "What shall we do?"

"Let's grab a beer."

"Sorry. It's real property law or ethics."

I need the ethics, but I'm tired and in no mood to be reminded of how grave my sins are. "Let's do property."

Booker bounces across the room and grabs the books.

□
□ □
□

IT'S ALMOST EIGHT before I drag myself through the maze of corridors deep in the heart of St. Peter's and find my favorite table occupied by a doctor and a nurse. I get coffee and sit nearby. The nurse is very attractive and quite distraught, and judging by their whispers I'd say the affair is on the rocks. He's sixty with hair transplants and a new chin. She's thirty, and evidently will not be elevated to the position of wife. Just mistress for now. Serious whispers.

I'm in no mood to study. I've had enough for one day, but I'm motivated only by the fact that Booker is still at the office, working and preparing for the exam.

The lovers abruptly leave after a few minutes. She's in tears. He's cold and heartless. I ease into my chair at my table and spread my notes, try to study.

And I wait.

Kelly arrives a few minutes after ten, but she has a new guy pushing her wheelchair. She glances coldly at me, and points to a table in the center of the room. He parks her there. I look at him. He looks at me.

I assume it's Cliff. He's about my height, no more than six-one, with a stocky frame and the beginnings of a beer belly. His shoulders are wide, though, and his biceps bulge through a tee shirt that's much too tight and worn specifically to flaunt his arms. Tight jeans. Hair that's brown and curly and too long to be stylish. Lots of growth on his forearms and face. Cliff was the kid who was shaving in the eighth grade.

He has greenish eyes and a handsome face that looks much older than nineteen. He steps around the ankle that he broke with a softball bat, and walks to the counter for drinks. She knows I'm staring at her. She very deliberately glances around the room, then at the last moment gives me a quick wink. I almost spill my coffee.

It doesn't take much of an imagination to hear the

words that have been passed between these two lately. Threats, apologies, pleas, more threats. It appears as though they're having a rough time of it tonight. Both faces are stern. They sip their drinks in silence. There's an occasional word or two, but they're like two puppy lovers in the midst of their weekly pouting session. A short sentence here, an even shorter reply there. They look at each other only when necessary, a lot of hard stares at the floor and the walls. I hide behind a book.

She's positioned herself so that she can glance at me without getting caught. His back is almost squarely to me. He looks around every now and then, but his movements are telegraphed. I can scratch my hair and pore over my studies long before he lays eyes on me.

After ten minutes of virtual silence, she says something that draws a hot response. I wish I could hear. He's suddenly shaking and snarling words at her. She dishes it right back. The volume increases and I quickly discern that they're discussing whether or not she'll testify against him in court. Seems she hasn't made up her mind. Seems this really bothers Cliff. He has a short fuse, no surprise for a macho redneck, and she's telling him not to yell. He glances around, and tries to lower his voice. I can't hear what he says.

After provoking him, she calms him, though he's still very unhappy. He simmers as they ignore each other for a spell.

Then she does it again. She mumbles something, and his back stiffens. His hands shake, his words are filled with foul language. They quarrel for a minute before she stops talking and ignores him. Cliff doesn't take to being ignored, so he gets louder. She tells him to be quiet, they're in public. He gets even louder, talking about what he'll do if she doesn't drop everything, and how he might go to jail, and on and on.

She says something I can't hear, and he suddenly slaps his tall cup and bolts to his feet. The soda flies across half the room, spraying carbonated foam on the other tables and the floor. It drenches her. She gasps, closes her eyes, starts crying. He can be heard stomping and cursing down the hall.

I instinctively get to my feet, but she is quick to shake her head. I sit down. The cashier has watched this and arrives with a hand towel. She gives it to Kelly, who wipes Coke from her face and arms.

"I'm sorry," she says to the cashier.

Her gown is soaked. She fights back tears as she wipes her cast and legs. I'm nearby but I can't help. I assume she's afraid he might return and catch us talking.

There are many places in this hospital where one can sit and have a Coke or a coffee, but she brought him here because she wanted me to see him. I'm almost certain she provoked him so I could witness his temper.

We look at each other for a long time as she methodically wipes her face and arms. Tears stream down her face, and she dabs at them. She possesses that inexplicable feminine ability to produce tears while appearing not to cry. She's not sobbing or bawling. Her lips are not quivering. Her hands are not shaking. She just sits there, in another world, staring at me with glazed eyes, touching her skin with a white towel.

Time passes, but I lose track of it. A crippled janitor arrives and mops around her. Three nurses rush in with loud talk and laughter until they see her, then they're suddenly quiet. They stare, whisper and occasionally look at me.

He's been gone long enough to assume he's not coming back, and the idea of being a gentleman is exciting. The nurses leave, and Kelly slowly wiggles an index finger at me. It's now okay for me to approach.

"I'm sorry," she says as I crouch near her.

"It's okay."

And then she utters words I will never forget. "Will you take me to my room?"

In another setting, these words might have profound consequences, and for an instant my mind drifts away to an exotic beach where the two young lovers finally decide to have a go at it.

Her room, of course, is a semiprivate cubicle with a door that's subject to being opened by a multitude of people. Even lawyers can barge in.

I carefully weave Kelly and her wheelchair around the tables and into the hallway. "Fifth floor," she says over her shoulder. I'm in no hurry. I'm very proud of myself for being so chivalrous. I like the fact that men look twice at her as we roll along the corridor.

We're alone for a few seconds in the elevator. I kneel beside her. "Are you okay?" I ask.

She's not crying now. Her eyes are still moist and a shade red, but she's under control. She nods quickly and says, "Thanks." And then she takes my hand and squeezes it firmly. "Thanks so much."

The elevator jerks and stops. A doctor steps in, and she quickly lets go of my hand. I stand behind the wheelchair, like a devoted husband. I want to hold hands again.

It's almost eleven, according to the clock on the wall at the fifth floor. Except for a few nurses and orderlies, the hallway is quiet and deserted. A nurse at the station looks twice at me as we roll by. Mrs. Riker left with one man, and now she's back with another.

We make a left turn and she points to her door. To my surprise and delight, she has a private room with her own window and bath. The lights are on.

I'm not sure how mobile she really is, but at this moment she's completely helpless. "You have to help me," she says. And she says it only once. I carefully bend over her, and she wraps her arms around my neck. She squeezes and presses harder than necessary, but no complaints. The gown is stained with soda, but I'm not particularly concerned. She's a snug fit, up close to me, and I quickly discern that she's not wearing a bra. I squeeze her tighter to me.

I gently lift her from the chair, an easy task because she doesn't weigh more than a hundred and ten, cast and all. We maneuver up to the bed, taking as long as possible, making a fuss over her fragile leg, adjusting her just right as I very slowly ease her onto the bed. We reluctantly let go of each other. Our faces are just inches apart when the same nurse romps in, her rubber soles squishing on the tiled floor.

"What happened?" she exclaims, pointing at the stained gown.

We're still untangling and trying to separate. "Oh, that. Just an accident," Kelly explains.

The nurse never stops moving. She reaches into a drawer under the television and pulls out a folded gown. "Well, you need to change," she says, tossing it onto the bed beside Kelly. "And you need a sponge bath." She stops for a second, jerks her head toward me and says, "Get him to help you."

I take a deep breath and feel faint.

"I can do it," Kelly says, placing the gown on the table next to the bed.

"Visiting hours are over, hon," she says to me. "You kids need to wrap it up." She squishes out of the room. I close the door and return to the side of her bed. We study each other.

"Where's the sponge?" I ask, and we both laugh. She has big dimples that form perfectly at the corners of her smile.

"Sit up here," she says, patting the edge of the bed. I sit next to her with my feet hanging off. We are not touching. She pulls a white sheet up to her armpits, as if to hide the stains.

I'm quite aware of how this looks. A battered wife is a married woman until she gets a divorce. Or until she kills the bastard.

"So what do you think of Cliff?" she asks.

"You wanted me to see him, didn't you?"

"I guess."

"He should be shot."

"That's rather severe for a little tantrum, isn't it?"

I pause for a moment and look away. I've decided that I will not play games with her. Since we're talking, then we're going to be honest.

What am I doing here?

"No, Kelly, it's not severe. Any man who beats his wife with an aluminum bat needs to be shot." I watch her closely as I say this, and she doesn't flinch.

"How do you know?" she asks.

"The paper trail. Police reports, ambulance reports, hospital records. How long do you wait before he decides to hit you in the head with his bat? That could kill you, you know. Coupla good shots to the skull—"

"Stop it! Don't tell me how it feels." She looks at the wall, and when she looks back at me the tears have started again. "You don't know what you're talking about."

"Then tell me."

"If I wanted to discuss it, I would've brought it up. You have no right to go digging around in my life."

"File for divorce. I'll bring the papers tomorrow. Do it now, while you're in the hospital being treated for the last beating. What better proof? It'll sail through. In three months, you'll be a free woman."

She shakes her head as if I'm a total fool. I probably am.

"You don't understand."

"I'm sure I don't. But I can see the big picture. If you don't get rid of this jerk you might be dead in a month. I have the names and phone numbers of three support groups for abused women."

"Abused?"

"Right. Abused. You're abused, Kelly. Don't you know that? That pin in your ankle means you're abused. That purple spot on your cheek is clear evidence that your husband beats you. You can get help. File for divorce and get help."

She thinks about this for a second. The room is quiet. "Divorce won't work. I've already tried it."

"When?"

"A few months ago. You don't know? I'm sure there's a record of it in the courthouse. What happened to the paper trail?"

"What happened to the divorce?"

"I dismissed it."

"Why?"

"Because I got tired of getting slapped around. He was going to kill me if I didn't dismiss it. He says he loves me."

"That's very clear. Can I ask you something? Do you have a father or brother?"

"Why?"

"Because if my daughter got beat up by her husband, I'd break his neck."

"My father doesn't know. My parents are still seething over my pregnancy. They'll never get over it. They despised Cliff from the moment he set foot in our house, and when the scandal broke they went into seclusion. I haven't talked to them since I left home."

"No brother?"

"No. No one to watch over me. Until now."

This hits hard, and it takes a while for me to absorb it.

"I'll do whatever you want," I say. "But you have to file for divorce."

She wipes tears with her fingers, and I hand her a tissue from the table. "I can't file for divorce."

"Why not?"

"He'll kill me. He tells me so all the time. See, when I filed before, I had this really rotten lawyer, found him in the yellow pages or someplace like that. I figured they were all the same. And he thought it would be cute to get the deputy to serve the divorce papers on Cliff while he was at work, in front of his little gang, his drinking buddies and softball team. Cliff, of course, was humiliated. That was my first visit to the hospital. I dismissed the divorce a week later, and he still threatens me all the time. He'll kill me."

The fear and terror are plainly visible in her eyes. She shifts slightly, frowning as if a sharp pain has hit her ankle. She groans, and says, "Can you put a pillow under it?"

I jump from the bed. "Sure." She points to two thick cushions in the chair.

"One of those," she says. This, of course, means that the sheet will be removed. I help with this.

She pauses for a second, looks around, says, "Hand me the gown too."

I take a jittery step to the table, and hand her the fresh gown. "Need some help?" I ask.

"No, just turn around." As she says this, she's already tugging at the old gown, pulling it over her head. I turn around very slowly.

She takes her time. Just for the hell of it, she tosses the stained gown onto the floor beside me. She's back there, less than five feet away, completely naked except for a pair of panties and a plaster cast. I honestly believe I could turn around and stare at her, and she wouldn't mind. I'm dizzy with this thought.

I close my eyes and ask myself, What am I doing here?

"Rudy, would you get me the sponge?" she coos. "It's in the bathroom. Run some warm water over it. And a towel, please."

I turn around. She's sitting in the middle of the bed clutching the thin sheet to her chest. The fresh gown has not been touched.

I can't help but stare. "In there," she nods. I take a few steps into the small bathroom, where I find the sponge. As I soak it in water, I watch her in the mirror above the sink. Through a crack in the door, I can see her back. All of it. The skin is smooth and tanned, but there's an ugly bruise between her shoulders.

I decide that I'll be in charge of this bath. She wants me to, I can tell. She's hurt and vulnerable. She likes to flirt, and she wants me to see her body. I'm all tingles and shakes.

Then, voices. The nurse is back. She's buzzing around the room when I reenter. She stops and grins at me, as if she almost caught us.

"Time's up," she says. "It's almost eleven-thirty. This isn't a hotel." She pulls the sponge from my hand. "I'll do this. Now you get out of here."

I just stand there, smiling at Kelly and dreaming of touching those legs. The nurse firmly grabs my elbow and ushers me to the door. "Now go on," she scolds in mock frustration.

AT THREE in the morning I sneak down to the hammock, where I rock absently in the still night, watching the stars flicker through the limbs and leaves, recalling every delightful move she made, hearing her troubled voice, dreaming of those legs.

It has fallen upon me to protect her, there's no one else. She expects me to rescue her, then to put her back together. It's obvious to both of us what will happen then.

I can feel her clutching my neck, pressing close to me for those few precious seconds. I can feel the feather-weight of her entire body resting naturally in my arms.

She wants me to see her, to rub her flesh with a warm sponge. I know she wants this. And, tonight, I intend to do it.

I watch the sun rise through the trees, then fall asleep counting the hours until I see her again.

Nineteen

I'M SITTING IN MY OFFICE STUDYING FOR the bar exam because I have nothing else to do. I realize I'm not supposed to be doing anything else because I'm not a lawyer yet, and won't be until I pass the bar exam.

It's difficult to concentrate. Why am I falling in love with a married woman just days before the exam? My mind should be as sharp as possible, free of clutter and distractions, finely tuned and focused on one goal.

She's a loser, I've convinced myself. She's a broken girl with scars, many of which could be permanent. And he's dangerous. The idea of another man touching his cute little cheerleader would surely set him off.

I ponder these things with my feet on my desk, hands clasped behind my head, gazing dreamily into a fog, when the door suddenly bursts open and Bruiser charges through. "What are you doing?" he barks.

"Studying," I answer, jerking myself into position.

"Thought you were going to study in the afternoons." It's ten-thirty now. He's pacing in front of my desk.

"Look, Bruiser, today is Friday. The exam starts next Wednesday. I'm scared."

"Then go study at the hospital. And pick up a case. I haven't seen a new one in three days."

"It's hard to study and hustle at the same time."

"Deck does it."

"Yeah, Deck the eternal scholar."

"Just got a call from Leo F. Drummond. Ring a bell?"

"No. Should it?"

"He's a senior partner at Tinley Britt. Marvelous trial lawyer, all sorts of commercial litigation. Rarely loses. Really fine lawyer, big firm."

"I know all about Trent & Brent."

"Well, you're about to know them even better. They represent Great Benefit. Drummond is lead counsel."

I would guess that there are at least a hundred firms in this city that represent insurance companies. And there must be a thousand insurance companies. What are the odds of the company I hate the most, Great Benefit, retaining the firm I curse every day of my life, Trent & Brent?

Oddly, I take it well. I'm not really surprised.

I suddenly realize why Bruiser is pacing and talking so fast. He's worried. Because of me, he's filed a ten-million-dollar lawsuit against a big company that's represented by a lawyer who intimidates him. This is amusing. I never dreamed Bruiser Stone was afraid of anything.

"What did he say?"

"Hello. Just checking in. He tells me the case has been assigned to Harvey Hale, who, son of a gun, was his roommate at Yale thirty years ago when they studied law together, and who, by the way, if you don't know, was a superb insurance defense lawyer before his heart attack and before his doctor told him to change careers. Got himself elected to the bench, where he can't shake the defense notion that a just and fair verdict is one under ten thousand dollars."

"Sorry I asked."

"So we have Leo F. Drummond and his considerable staff, and they have their favorite judge. You got your work cut out for you."

"Me? What about you?"

"Oh, I'll be around. But this is your baby. They'll drown you with paperwork." He walks to the door. "Remember, they get paid by the hour. The more paper they produce, the more hours they bill." He laughs at me and slams the door, seemingly happy that I'm about to be roughed up by the big boys.

I've been abandoned. There are over a hundred lawyers at Trent & Brent, and I suddenly feel very lonely.

DECK AND I eat a bowl of soup at Trudy's. Her small lunch crowd is strictly blue collar. The place smells of grease, sweat and fried meats. It's Deck's favorite lunch spot because he's picked up a few cases here, mostly on-the-job injuries. One settled for thirty thousand. He took a third of twenty-five percent, or twenty-five hundred dollars.

There are a few bars in the area he also frequents, he confesses, low over the soup. He'll take off his tie, try to look like one of the boys, and drink a soda. He listens to the workers as they lubricate themselves after work. He might tell me where the good bars are, the good grazing spots, as he likes to call them. Deck's full of advice for chasing cases and finding clients.

And, yes, he's even gone to the skin clubs occasionally, but only to be with his clientele. You just have to circulate, he says more than once. He likes the casinos down in Mississippi, and is of the farsighted opinion that they are undesirable places because poor people go there and gamble with grocery money. But there could be opportunity. Crime will rise. Divorces and bankruptcies are bound to increase as more people gamble. Folks will need lawyers. There's a lot of potential suffering out there, and he's wise to it. He's on to something.

He'll keep me posted.

I EAT ANOTHER FINE MEAL at St. Peter's, in the Gauze Grill, as this place is known. I overheard a group of interns call it that. Pasta salad from a plastic bowl. I study sporadically, and watch the clock.

At ten, the elderly gentleman in the pink jacket arrives, but he is alone. He pauses, looks around, sees me and walks over, stern-faced and obviously not happy doing whatever he's doing.

"Are you Mr. Baylor?" he asks properly. He's holding an envelope, and when I nod affirmatively, he places it on the table. "It's from Mrs. Riker," he says, bending just slightly at the waist, then walks away.

The envelope is letter-sized, plain and white. I open it and remove a blank get-well card. It reads:

Dear Rudy:

My doctor released me this morning, so I'm home now. Thanks for everything. Say a prayer for us. You are wonderful.

She signed her name, then added a postscript: "Please don't call or write, or try to see me. It will only cause trouble. Thanks again."

She knew I'd be here waiting faithfully. With all the lust-filled thoughts swirling through my brain during the past twenty-four hours, it never occurred to me that she might be leaving. I was certain we'd meet tonight.

I walk aimlessly along the endless corridors, trying to

collect myself. I am determined to see her again. She needs me, because there's no one else to help her.

At a pay phone, I find a listing for Cliff Riker and punch the numbers. A recorded message informs me that the line has been disconnected.

Twenty

WE ARRIVE AT THE HOTEL MEZZANINE early Wednesday morning and are efficiently herded into a ballroom larger than a football field. We are registered and catalogued, the fees having long since been paid. There's a little nervous chatter, but not much socializing. We're all scared to death.

Of the two hundred or so people taking the bar exam this outing, at least half finished at Memphis State last month. These are my friends and enemies. Booker takes a seat at a table far away from me. We've decided not to sit together. Sara Plankmore Wilcox and S. Todd are in a corner on the other side of the room. They were married last Saturday. Nice honeymoon. He's a handsome guy with the preppy grooming and cocky air of a blueblood. I hope he flunks the exam. Sara too.

I can feel the competition here, very much like the first few weeks of law school when we were terribly concerned with each other's initial progress. I nod at a few acquaintances, silently hoping they flunk the exam because they're silently hoping I collapse too. Such is the nature of the profession.

Once we're all properly seated at folding tables spaced generously apart, we are given ten minutes' worth of instruction. Then the exams are passed out at exactly 8 A.M.

The exam begins with a section called Multi-State, an endless series of tricky multiple-choice questions covering that body of law common to all states. It's absolutely impossible to tell how well I'm prepared. The morning drags along. Lunch is a quiet hotel buffet with Booker, not a word spoken about the exam.

Dinner is a turkey sandwich on the patio with Miss Birdie. I'm in bed by nine.

THE EXAM ENDS at 5 P.M. Friday, with a whimper. We're too exhausted to celebrate. They gather our papers for the last time, and tell us we can leave. There's talk of a cold drink somewhere, for old times' sake, and six of us meet at Yogi's for a few rounds. Prince is gone tonight and there's no sign of Bruiser, which is quite a relief because I'd hate my friends to see me in the presence of my boss. There'd be a lot of questions about our practice. Give me a year, and I'll have a better job.

We learned after the first semester in law school that it's best never to discuss exams. If notes are compared afterward, you become painfully aware of things you missed.

We eat pizza, drink a few beers, but are too tired to do any damage. Booker tells me on the way home that the exam has made him physically ill. He's certain he blew it.

I SLEEP for twelve hours. I have promised Miss Birdie that I will tend to my chores this day, assuming it's not raining, and my apartment is filled with bright sunlight when I finally awake. It's hot, humid, muggy, the typical

Memphis July. After three days of straining my eyes and imagination and memory in a windowless room, I'm ready for a little sweat and dirt. I leave the house without being seen, and twenty minutes later I park in the Blacks' driveway.

Donny Ray is waiting on the front porch, dressed in jeans, sneakers, dark socks, white tee shirt, and wearing a regular-sized baseball cap which over his shrunken face looks much too large. He walks with a cane, but needs a firm hand under his fragile arm for stability. Dot and I shuffle him along the narrow sidewalk and carefully fold him into the front seat of my car. She's relieved to get him out of the house for a few hours, his first time out in months, she tells me. Now she's left with only Buddy and the cats.

Donny Ray sits with his cane between his legs, resting his chin on it, as we drive across town. After he thanks me once, he doesn't say much.

He finished high school three years ago at the age of nineteen, his twin, Ron, having graduated a year earlier. He never attempted college. For two years he worked as a clerk in a convenience store, but quit after a robbery. His employment history is sketchy, but he has never left home. From the records I've studied so far, Donny Ray has never earned more than minimum wage.

Ron, on the other hand, scratched his way through UTEP and is now in grad school in Houston. He, too, is single, never married, and seldom returns to Memphis. The boys were never close, Dot said. Donny Ray stayed indoors and read books and built model airplanes. Ron rode bikes and once joined a street gang of twelve-year-olds. They were good boys, Dot assured me. The file is thoroughly documented with clear and sufficient evidence that Ron's bone marrow would be a perfect match for Donny Ray's transplant.

We bounce along in my ragged little car. He stares straight ahead, the bill of the cap resting low on his forehead, speaking only when spoken to. We park beside Miss Birdie's Cadillac, and I explain that this rather nice old house in this exclusive section of town is where I live. I can't tell if he's impressed, but I doubt it. I help him around the mulch to a shady spot on the patio.

Miss Birdie knows I'm bringing him over, and she's waiting eagerly with fresh lemonade. Introductions are made, and she quickly takes control of the visit. Cookies? Brownies? Something to read? She props pillows around him on the bench, chirping happily the entire time. She has a heart of gold. I explained to her that I met Donny Ray's parents at Cypress Gardens, so she feels especially close to him. One of her flock.

Once he's properly situated in a cool spot, safely away from any sunlight that would blister his chalky skin, Miss Birdie declares it's time to start working. She dramatically pauses and surveys the backyard, scratches her chin as if deeply in thought, then slowly allows her gaze to descend upon the mulch. She gives a few orders, for Donny Ray's benefit, and I hop to it.

I'm soon soaked with sweat, but this time I enjoy every minute of it. Miss Birdie fusses about the humidity for the first hour, then decides to piddle in the flowers around the patio, where it's cooler. I can hear her talking nonstop to Donny Ray, who says little but is enjoying the fresh air. On one trip with the wheelbarrow, I notice they're playing checkers. On another, she's sitting snugly beside him, pointing to pictures in a book.

I've thought many times about asking Miss Birdie if she would be interested in helping Donny Ray. I do believe this dear woman would write a check for the transplant, if she in fact has the money. But I haven't for two reasons. First, it's too late for the transplant. And second, it would humiliate Miss Birdie if she didn't have the money. She already has enough suspicions about my interest in her money. I can't ask for any of it.

Shortly after he was diagnosed with acute leukemia, a feeble effort was made to raise funds for his treatment. Dot organized some friends and they placed Donny Ray's face on milk cartons in cafés and in convenience stores all over North Memphis. Didn't raise much, she said. They rented a local Moose Lodge and threw a big party with catfish and bluegrass, even got a local country DJ to spin records. The shindig lost twenty-eight dollars.

His first round of chemo cost four thousand dollars, two thirds of which was absorbed by St. Peter's. They scraped together the rest. Five months later, the leukemia was back in full bloom.

As I shovel and haul and sweat, I direct my mental energies into hating Great Benefit. It doesn't take a lot of work, but I'll need a lot of self-righteous zeal to sustain me once the war starts with Tinley Britt.

Lunch is a pleasant surprise. Miss Birdie has made chicken soup, not exactly what I wanted on a day like today, but a welcome change from turkey sandwiches. Donny Ray eats a half a bowl, then says he needs a nap. He'd like to try the hammock. We walk him across the lawn, and ease him into it. Though the temperature is above ninety, he asks for a blanket.

WE SIT IN THE SHADE, sip more lemonade and talk about how sad he is. I tell her a little about the case against Great Benefit, and place emphasis on the fact that I've sued them for ten million dollars. She asks a few general questions about the bar exam, then disappears into the house.

When she returns, she hands me an envelope from a lawyer in Atlanta. I recognize the name of the firm.

"Can you explain this?" she asks, standing before me, hands on hips.

The lawyer has written a letter to Miss Birdie, and along with his letter he has attached a copy of the letter I sent to him. In my letter, I explained that I now represent Miss Birdie Birdsong, that she has asked me to draft a new will and that I need information about the estate of her deceased husband. In his letter to her, he simply asks if he may divulge any information to me. He sounds quite indifferent, as if he's just following orders.

"It's all in black and white," I say. "I'm your lawyer. I'm trying to gather information."

"You didn't tell me you were going to go dig around in Atlanta."

"What's wrong with it? What's hidden over there, Miss Birdie? Why is this so secretive?"

"The judge sealed the court file," she says with a shrug, as if that's the end of it.

"What's in the court file?"

"A bunch of trash."

"Concerning you?"

"Heavens no!"

"Okay. About who?"

"Tony's family. His brother was filthy rich, down in Florida, you see, had several wives and different sets of children. Whole family was loony. They had this big fight over his wills, four wills, I think. I don't know much about it, but I heard once that when it was all over the lawyers got paid six million dollars. Some of the money filtered down to Tony, who lived just long enough to inherit it under Florida law. Tony didn't even know it, because he died too fast. Left nothing but a wife. Me. That's all I know."

It's not important how she obtained the money. But it

would be nice to know how much of it she inherited. "Do you want to talk about your will?" I ask.

"No. Later," she says, reaching for her gardening gloves. "Let's get to work."

HOURS LATER, I sit with Dot and Donny Ray on the weedy patio outside their kitchen. Buddy is in bed, thank goodness. Donny Ray is exhausted from his day at Miss Birdie's.

It's Saturday night in the suburbs, and the smell of charcoal and barbecue permeates the sweltering air. The voices of backyard chefs and their guests filter across wooden fences and neat hedgerows.

It's easier to sit and listen than it is to sit and talk. Dot prefers to smoke and drink her instant decaf coffee, occasionally passing along some useless tidbit of gossip about one of the neighbors. Or one of the neighbor's dogs. The retired man next door lost a finger last week with a jigsaw, and she mentions this no fewer than three times.

I don't care. I can sit and listen for hours. My mind is still numb from the bar exam. It doesn't take much to amuse me. And when I'm successful in forgetting the law, I always have Kelly to occupy my thoughts. I have yet to figure out a harmless way to contact her, but I will. Just give me time.

Twenty-one

T HE SHELBY COUNTY JUSTICE CENTER IS a twelve-story modern building downtown. The concept is one-stop justice. It has lots of courtrooms and offices for clerks and administrators. It houses the district attorney and the sheriff. It even has a jail.

Criminal Court has ten divisions, ten judges with different dockets in different courtrooms. The middle levels swarm with lawyers and cops and defendants and their families. It's a forbidding jungle for a novice lawyer, but Deck knows his way around. He's made a few calls.

He points to the door for Division Four, and says he'll meet me there in an hour. I enter the double doors and take a seat on the back bench. The floor is carpeted, the furnishings are depressingly modern. Lawyers are as thick as ants in the front of the room. To the right is a holding area where a dozen orange-clad arrestees await their initial appearances before the judge. A prosecutor of some variety handles a stack of files, shuffling through them for the right defendant.

On the second row from the front, I see Cliff Riker.

He's huddled with his lawyer, looking over some paperwork. His wife is not in the courtroom.

The judge appears from the back, and everyone rises. A few cases are disposed of, bonds reduced or forgotten, future dates agreed upon. The lawyers meet in brief huddles, then nod and whisper to His Honor.

Cliff's name is called, and he swaggers to a podium in front of the bench. His lawyer is beside him with the papers. The prosecutor announces to the court that the charges against Cliff Riker have been dropped for lack of evidence.

"Where's the victim?" the judge interrupts.

"She chose not to be here," the prosecutor answers.

"Why?" the judge asks.

Because she's in a wheelchair, I want to scream.

The prosecutor shrugs as if she doesn't know, and, furthermore, doesn't really care. Cliff's lawyer shrugs as if he's surprised the little lady is not here to exhibit her wounds.

The prosecutor is a busy person, with dozens of cases to work before noon. She quickly recites a summary of the facts, the arrest, the lack of evidence because the victim will not testify.

"This is the second time," the judge says, glaring at Cliff. "Why don't you divorce her before you kill her?"

"We're trying to get some help, Your Honor," Cliff says in a pitifully rehearsed voice.

"Well, get it quick. If I see these charges again, I will not dismiss them. Do you understand?"

"Yes sir," Cliff answers, as if he's deeply sorry to be such a bother. The paperwork is handed to the bench. The judge signs it while shaking his head. The charges are dismissed.

The voice of the victim once again has not been heard. She's at home with a broken ankle, but that's not what kept her away. She's hiding because she prefers not to be beaten again. I wonder what price she paid for dropping the charges.

Cliff shakes hands with his lawyer, and struts down the aisle, past my bench, out the door, free to do whatever he pleases, immune from prosecution because there's no one to help Kelly.

There's a frustrating logic to this assembly line justice. Not far away, sitting over there in orange jumpsuits and handcuffs, are rapists, murderers, drug dealers. The system barely has enough time to run these thugs through and allocate some measure of justice. How can the system be expected to care for the rights of one beaten wife?

While I was taking the bar last week, Deck was making phone calls. He found the Rikers' new address and phone number. They just moved to a large apartment complex in southeast Memphis. One bedroom, four hundred a month. Cliff works for a freight company, not far from our office, a nonunion terminal. Deck suspects he makes about seven dollars an hour. His lawyer is just another ham-and-egger, one of a million in this city.

I have told Deck the truth about Kelly. He said he thought it was important for him to know, because when Cliff blows my head off with a shotgun, he, Deck, will be around to tell why it happened.

Deck also told me to forget about her. She's nothing but trouble.

THERE'S A NOTE on my desk to immediately see Bruiser. He's alone behind his oversized desk, on the phone, the one to his right. There's another phone to his left, and three more scattered around the office. One in his car. One in his briefcase. And the one he gave me so he can reach me around the clock.

He motions for me to sit, rolls his black and red eyes as

if he's conversing with some nut and grunts an affirmative reaction into the receiver. The sharks are either asleep or hidden behind some rocks. The aquarium filter gurgles and hums.

Deck has whispered to me that Bruiser makes between three hundred and five hundred thousand dollars a year from this office. That's hard to believe, looking around the cluttered room. He keeps four associates out there beating the bushes, rustling up injury cases. (And now he's got me.) Deck was able to click off five cases last year which earned Bruiser a hundred and fifty thousand. He makes a bundle from drug cases, and has earned the reputation in the narcotics industry as a lawyer who can be trusted. But, according to Deck, Bruiser Stone's real income is from his investments. He's involved, to what extent no one knows and the federal government evidently is trying desperately to ascertain, in the topless business in Memphis and Nashville. It's a cash-rich industry, so there's no telling what he skims.

He's been divorced three times, Deck reported over a greasy sandwich at Trudy's, has three teenaged children who, not surprisingly, live with their assorted mothers, likes the company of young table dancers, drinks and gambles too much, and will never, regardless of how much cash he can clutch with his thick hands, have enough money to satisfy him.

He was arrested seven years ago on federal racketeering charges, but the government didn't stand a chance. The charges were dismissed after a year. Deck confided that he was worried about the FBI's current investigation into the Memphis underworld, an investigation that has repeatedly yielded the names of Bruiser Stone and his best friend, Prince Thomas. Deck said that Bruiser has been acting a bit unusual—drinking too much, getting angrier faster, stomping and growling around the office more than normal.

Speaking of phones. Deck is certain that the FBI has bugged every phone in our offices, including mine. And he thinks the walls are wired too. They've done it before, he said with grave authority. And be careful at Yogi's too.

He left me with this comforting thought yesterday afternoon. If I pass the bar exam, get just a little money in my pocket, I'm outta here.

Bruiser finally hangs up and wipes his tired eyes. "Take a look at this," he says, shoving a thick stack of papers at me.

"What is it?"

"Great Benefit responds. You're about to learn why it's painful to sue big corporations. They have lots of money to hire lots of lawyers who produce lots of paper. Leo F. Drummond probably clips Great Benefit for two-fifty per hour."

It's a motion to dismiss the Blacks' lawsuit, with a supporting brief that's sixty-three pages long. There's a notice to hear argument on said motion before the Honorable Harvey Hale.

Bruiser watches me calmly. "Welcome to the battle-field."

I have a nice lump in my throat. Responding in kind to this will take days. "It's impressive," I say with a dry throat. I don't know where to begin.

"Read the rules carefully. Respond to the motion. Write your brief. Do it fast. It's not as bad as it looks."

"It's not?"

"No, Rudy. It's paperwork. You'll learn. These bastards will file every motion known and many they invent, all with thick supporting briefs. And they'll want to run to court every time to have a hearing on their beloved little motions. They really don't care if they win or lose them, they're making money regardless. Plus, it delays the trial. They've got it down to a fine art, and their clients foot the bill. Problem is, they'll run you ragged in the process."

"I'm already tired."

"It's a bitch. Drummond snaps his fingers, says, 'I wanna motion to dismiss,' and three associates bury themselves in the library, and two paralegals pull up old briefs on their computers. Presto! In no time there's a fat brief, thoroughly researched. Then Drummond has to read it several times, plow through it at two-fifty an hour, maybe get a partner buddy of his to read it too. Then he has to edit and cut and modify, so the associates go back to the library and the paralegals go back to their computers. It's a rip-off, but Great Benefit has plenty of money and doesn't mind paying people like Tinley Britt."

I feel like I've challenged an army. Two phones ring at once, and Bruiser grabs the nearest. "Get busy," he says to me, then says "Yeah" into the receiver.

With both hands, I carry the bundle to my office and close the door. I read the motion to dismiss with its handsomely presented and perfectly typed brief, a brief I quickly find to be filled with persuasive arguments against almost everything I said in the lawsuit. The language is rich and clear, as devoid of dense legalese as any brief can be, remarkably well written. The positions set forth are fortified with a multitude of authorities which appear to be squarely on point. There are fancy footnotes at the bottom of most pages. There's even a table of contents, an index and a bibliography.

The only thing lacking is a prepared order for the judge to sign granting everything Great Benefit wants.

After the third reading, I collect myself and start taking notes. There might be a hole or two to poke in it. The shock and fright wear off. I summon forth my immense dislike for Great Benefit and what it's done to my client, and I roll up my sleeves.

Mr. Leo F. Drummond may be a litigating wizard, and he may have countless minions at his beck and call, but I, Rudy Baylor, have nothing else to do. I'm bright and I can work. He wants to start a paper war with me, fine. I'll smother him.

DECK'S BEEN THROUGH the bar exam six times before. He almost passed it on the third try, in California, but missed when his overall score fell two points short. He's taken it three times in Tennessee, never really coming close, he told me with remarkable candor. I'm not sure Deck wants to pass the bar. He makes forty thousand a year chasing cases for Bruiser, and he's not burdened with ethical constraints. (Not that they bother Bruiser.) Deck doesn't have to pay bar dues, worry about continuing legal education, attend seminars, appear before judges, feel guilty about pro bono work, not to mention overhead.

Deck's a leech. As long as he has a lawyer with a name he can use and an office for him to work, Deck's in business.

He knows I'm not too busy, so he's fallen into the habit of dropping by my office around eleven. We'll gossip for half an hour, then walk down to Trudy's for a cheap lunch. I'm used to him now. He's just Deck, an unpretentious little guy who wants to be my friend.

We're in a corner, doing lunch among the freight handlers at Trudy's, and Deck is talking so low I can barely hear him. At times, especially in hospital waiting rooms, he can be so bold it's uncomfortable, then at times he's as timid as a mouse. He's mumbling something he desperately wants me to hear while glancing over both shoulders as if he's about to be attacked.

"Used to be a guy who worked here in the firm, name's

David Roy, and he got close to Bruiser. They counted their money together, thick as thieves, you know. Roy got himself disbarred for co-mingling funds, so he can't be a lawyer." Deck wipes tuna salad from his lips with his fingers. "No big deal. Roy steps outta here, steps across the street and opens a skin club. It burns. He opens another, it burns. Then another. Then war breaks out in the boob business. Bruiser's too smart to get in the middle of it, but he's always on the fringes. So's your pal Prince Thomas. The war goes on for a couple years. A dead body turns up every so often. More fires. Roy and Bruiser have a bitter falling out of some sort. Last year the feds nail Roy, and it's rumored that he's gonna sing. Know what I mean."

I nod with my face as low as Deck's. No one can hear, but we get a few stares because of the way we're hunkered over our food.

"Well, yesterday, David Roy testified before the grand jury. Looks like he's cut a deal."

With this, the punch line, Deck straightens stiffly and rolls his eyes down as if I now should be able to figure out everything.

"So," I snap, still low.

He frowns, glances around warily, then descends. "There's a good chance he's singing on Bruiser. Maybe Prince Thomas. I've even heard a wild one that there's a price on his head."

"A contract!"

"Yes. Quiet."

"By whom?" Surely not my employer.

"Take a wild guess."

"Not Bruiser."

He offers me a tight-lipped, toothless, coy little smile, then says, "It wouldn't be the first time." And with this, he takes an enormous bite of his sandwich, chews it slowly while nodding at me. I wait until he swallows.

"So what are you trying to tell me?" I ask.

"Keep your options open."

"I have no options."

"You may have to make a move."

"I just got here."

"Things might get hot."

"What about you?" I ask.

"I might be making a move too."

"What about the other guys?"

"Don't worry about them, because they're not worrying about you. I'm your only friend."

These words stick with me for hours. Deck knows more than he's telling, but after a few more lunches I'll have it all. I have a strong suspicion that he is looking for a place to land if disaster strikes. I've met the other lawyers in the firm—Nicklass, Toxer and Ridge—but they keep to themselves and have little to say. Their doors are always locked. Deck doesn't like them, and I can only speculate about their feelings for him. According to Deck, Toxer and Ridge are friends and might be scheming to soon open their own little firm. Nicklass is an alcoholic who's on the ropes.

The worst scenario would be for Bruiser to get indicted and arrested and put on trial. That process would take at least a year. He'd still be able to work and operate his office. I think. They can't disbar him until he's convicted.

Relax, I keep telling myself.

And if I get tossed into the street, it's happened before. I've managed to land on my feet.

I DRIVE in the general direction of Miss Birdie's, and pass a city park. At least three softball games are in progress under lights.

I stop at a pay phone next to a car wash, and dial the

number. After the third ring, she answers, "Hello." The voice echoes through my body.

"Is Cliff there?" I say, an octave lower. If she says yes, I'll simply hang up.

"No. Who's calling?"

"Rudy," I say in a normal tone. I hold my breath, expecting to hear a click followed by a dial tone, and also expecting to hear soft, longing words. Hell, I don't know what to expect.

There's a pause, but she doesn't hang up. "I asked you not to call," she says with no trace of anger or frustration.

"I'm sorry. I couldn't help it. I'm worried about you."

"We can't do this."

"Do what?"

"Good-bye." Now I hear the click, then the dial tone.

It took a lot of guts to make the call, and now I wish I hadn't. Some people have more guts than brains. I know her husband is a demented hothead, but I don't know how far he'll go. If he's the jealous type, and I'm sure he is because he's a nineteen-year-old washed-up redneck jock who's married to a beautiful girl, then I figure he's suspicious of her every move. But would he go to the extreme of wiring their phones?

It's a long shot, but it keeps me awake.

I'VE SLEPT for less than an hour when my phone rings. It's almost 4 A.M., according to the digital clock. I fumble for the phone in the darkness.

It's Deck, highly excited and talking rapidly on his car phone. He's racing toward me, less than three blocks away. It's something big, something urgent, some wonderful disaster. Hurry up! Get dressed! I'm instructed to meet him at the curb in less than a minute.

He's waiting for me in his ragged minivan. I jump in,

and he lays rubber as we race away. I didn't get a chance to brush my teeth. "What the hell are we doing?" I ask.

"Big wreck on the river," he announces solemnly, as if he's deeply saddened by it. Just another day at the office. "Just after eleven last night, an oil barge broke free from its tug, and floated downriver until it struck a paddle wheeler which was being used for a high school prom. Maybe three hundred kids on board. The paddle wheeler goes down near Mud Island, right off the bank."

"That's awful, Deck, but what in hell are we supposed to do about it?"

"Check it out. Bruiser gets a call. Bruiser calls me. Here we are. It's a huge disaster, potentially the biggest ever in Memphis."

"And this is something to be proud of?"

"You don't understand. Bruiser is not gonna miss it."

"Fine. Let him get his fat ass in a scuba suit and dive for bodies."

"Could be a gold mine." Deck is driving rapidly across town. We ignore each other as downtown approaches. An ambulance races by us, and my pulse quickens. Another ambulance cuts in front of us.

Riverside Drive is blocked off by dozens of police cars, all with lights streaking through the night. Fire trucks and ambulances are parked bumper to bumper. A helicopter hovers in the air downriver. There are groups of people standing perfectly still, and there are others scurrying about shouting and pointing. The boom of a crane is visible near the bank.

We walk quickly around the crowd of onlookers near the edge of the water. The scene is now several hours old, and most of the urgency has worn off. They're waiting now. Many of the people are huddled together in horrified little groups sitting on the cobblestoned banks, watching and crying as the divers and paramedics search for bodies. Ministers kneel and pray with the families. Dozens of stunned kids in wet tuxedoes and torn prom dresses sit together, holding hands, staring at the water. One side of the paddle wheeler sticks ten feet above the surface, and the rescuers, many clad in black and blue wet suits and scuba gear, hang on to it. Others work from three pontoon boats roped together.

A ritual is under way here, but it takes a while to comprehend it. A police lieutenant walks slowly along a gangplank leading from a floating pier, and steps onto the cobblestones. The crowd, already subdued, becomes perfectly still. He steps to the front of a squad car as several reporters gather around him. Most of the people remain seated, clutching their blankets, lowering their heads in fervent prayers. They are the parents, families and friends. The lieutenant says, "I'm sorry, but we have identified the body of Melanie Dobbins."

His words carry through the stillness, which is broken almost instantly by gasps and groans from the family of the girl. They squeeze and sink together. Friends kneel and hug, then a woman's voice cries out.

The others turn and watch, but also breathe a collective sigh of relief. Their bad news is inevitable, but at least it's been postponed. There's still hope. I would later learn that twenty-one kids survived by being sucked into an air pocket.

The police lieutenant walks away, returns to the pier, where another body is being pulled from the water.

Then a second ritual, one not as tragic but far more disgusting, slowly unfolds. Men with somber faces ease or even try to sneak close to the grieving family. They have small white business cards which they attempt to give to family members or friends of the deceased. In the darkness, they inch closer, eyeing each other warily. They'd kill for the case. They only want a third.

All of this registers on Deck long before I realize what's happening. He nods to a spot closer to the families, but I refuse to move. He slinks away into the crowd, disappearing quickly into the darkness, off to mine his gold.

I turn my back to the river, and soon I am running through the streets of downtown Memphis.

Twenty-two

THE BOARD OF LAW EXAMINERS USES certified mail to send the results of the bar exam. In law school, you hear stories of rookies waiting, then collapsing by the mailbox. Or running wildly down the street, waving the letter like an idiot. Lots of stories, stories that seemed funny then but have lost all humor now.

Thirty days have passed and there's no letter. I used my home address because I damned sure didn't want the letter opened by anyone at Bruiser's.

Day thirty-one falls on a Saturday, a day on which I am allowed to sleep until nine before my taskmaster beats on my door with a paintbrush. The garage under my apartment suddenly needs painting, she has decided, though it looks fine to me. She lures me out of bed with the news that she's already prepared bacon and eggs, and they're getting cold, so hurry.

The work goes well. Painting produces immediate results that are quite pleasing. I can see progress. The sun is blocked by high clouds, and my pace is leisurely at best.

She announces at 6 P.M. that it's time to quit, that I've worked enough and that she has wonderful news for dinner—she will make us a vegetarian pizza!

I worked at Yogi's until one this morning, and I have no desire to go back for a while. So, typically, I have nothing to do on this Saturday night. What's worse is that I haven't thought about doing anything. Sadly, the idea of eating a vegetarian pizza with an eighty-year-old woman is appealing.

I shower and put on my khakis and sneakers. An odd smell emanates from the kitchen when I enter the house. Miss Birdie is buzzing around the kitchen. She's never made a pizza before, she tells me, as if I should be pleased to hear this.

It's not bad. The zucchini and yellow peppers are a bit crunchy, but she loaded it down with goat cheese and mushrooms. And I'm starving. We eat in the den and watch a Cary Grant-Audrey Hepburn movie. She cries through most of it.

The second movie is Bogart and Bacall, and the aches in my muscles start to set in. I'm getting sleepy. Miss Birdie, however, sits on the edge of the sofa, breathlessly absorbing every line of a movie she's watched for fifty years.

Suddenly, she jumps to her feet. "I forgot something!" she exclaims, and hurries to the kitchen, where I hear her digging through some papers. She races back to the den with a piece of paper, stops dramatically in front of me and proclaims, "Rudy! You've passed the bar!"

She's holding a single sheet of white paper which I lunge for. It's from the Tennessee Board of Law Examiners, addressed to me, of course, and in bold letters across the center of the page are the majestic words: "Congratulations. You've passed the bar exam."

I whirl around and look at Miss Birdie, and for a split

second would like to slap her for such a gross invasion of privacy. She should've told me earlier, and she damned sure had no right to open the letter. But every one of her gray and yellow teeth is showing. She has tears in her eyes, hands to her face, she's almost as thrilled as I am. My anger quickly yields to complete elation.

"When did it come?" I ask.

"Today, while you were painting. The mailman knocked on my door, asked for you but I said you were busy, and so I signed for it."

Signing for it is one thing. Opening it is another matter.

"You shouldn't have opened it," I say, but not really angrily. It's impossible to be furious at a time like this.

"I'm sorry. I thought you'd want me to. But isn't it exciting?"

Indeed it is. I float to the kitchen, grinning like a goofy idiot, taking deep breaths of unburdened air. Everything is wonderful. What a great world!

"Let's celebrate," she says with a naughty little grin.

"Anything," I say. I feel like running through the backyard, yelling at the stars.

She reaches far into a cabinet, fumbles around, smiles, then slowly extracts an odd-shaped bottle. "I save this for special occasions."

"What is it?" I say, taking the bottle. I've never seen one of these at Yogi's.

"Melon brandy. Pretty strong stuff too." She lets forth a giggle. At this moment, I'll drink anything. She finds two matching coffee cups—drinks are never served in this house—and fills them half full. The liquid is thick and gooey. The aroma reminds me of something from the dentist's office.

We toast my good fortune, clink our Bank of Tennessee cups together and take a sip. It tastes like children's cough syrup and burns like straight vodka. She smacks her lips. "We'd better sit down," she says.

After a few sips, Miss Birdie is snoring on the sofa. I mute the movie, and pour another cup. It's a potent liquor, and after the initial searing the taste buds are not as offended. I drink it on the patio, under the moon, still smiling upward in glorious thanks for this divine news.

THE EFFECTS of the melon brandy linger until well after sunrise. I shower and ease from my apartment, sneak to my car, then race down the driveway in reverse until I hit the street.

I go to a yuppie coffee bar with bagels and blends of the day. I pay for a thick Sunday paper and spread it on a table in the rear. Several items hit close to home.

For the fourth day in a row, the front page is filled with stories about the paddle wheel disaster. Forty-one kids were killed. The lawyers have already started filing suits.

The second item, this one in the Metro section, is the latest installment of an investigative series about police corruption, and more specifically the relationship between the topless business and law enforcement. Bruiser's name is mentioned several times as the lawyer for Willie McSwane, a local kingpin. And Bruiser's name is mentioned as the lawyer for Bennie Thomas, also known as Prince, a local tavern owner and former federal indictee. And Bruiser's name is mentioned as a likely federal target in his own right.

I can feel the train coming. The federal grand jury has been meeting nonstop for a month. This newspaper runs stories almost daily. Deck is increasingly nervous.

The third item is a complete surprise. On the last page of the business section is a small story with the caption 161 PASS BAR EXAM. It's a three-sentence press release from the

Board of Law Examiners, then an alphabetical listing, in very small print, of those of us who passed.

I pull the paper closer to my face, and read furiously. There I am! It's true. There's been no clerical error. I've passed the bar exam! I blitz through the names, many of whom I've known well for three years.

I search for Booker Kane, but he's not here. I check and triple check, and my shoulders sag. I place the paper on the table, and read aloud each name. There's no Booker Kane.

I almost called him last night, after Miss Birdie's memory revived itself and she handed me the wonderful news, but I just couldn't. Since I passed it, I decided to wait and let Booker call me. I figured if he didn't call within a few days, then I'd know he failed it.

Now I'm not sure what to do. I can see him, at this moment, helping Charlene dress the kids for church, trying to smile and put his best face on it, trying to convince them both that it's just a temporary setback, that he'll nail the exam next time.

But I know he's devastated. He's hurt and angry at himself for failing. He's worried about Marvin Shankle's reaction, and he's dreading tomorrow at the office.

Booker is an intensely proud man who's always believed he could achieve anything. I would love to drive over and grieve with him, but it wouldn't work.

He'll call tomorrow and congratulate me. On the surface he'll be a sport with vows to do better next time.

I read the list again, and it suddenly hits me that Sara Plankmore's name is not here. Neither is the name Sara Plankmore Wilcox. Mr. S. Todd Wilcox passed the exam, but his new bride did not.

I laugh out loud. This is mean and petty, spiteful, childish, vindictive, even hateful. But I just can't help it. She got herself pregnant so she could get herself married, and

I bet the pressure was too much. She's been sidetracked for the past three months, planning her wedding and picking out colors for her nursery. Must've neglected her studies.

Ha. Ha. Ha. I get the last laugh after all.

THE DRUNK who hit Dan Van Landel had liability insurance with a limit of one hundred thousand dollars. Deck has convinced the drunk's carrier that Van Landel's claim is worth more than the limit, and he's right about this. The carrier has agreed to fork over the limit. Bruiser was used only at the last minute, to threaten litigation and such. Deck did eighty percent of the work. I did fifteen percent at most. We quietly give Bruiser credit for the rest. But under Bruiser's firm's scheme of compensation, neither Deck nor I will share in the profits. This is because Bruiser has a clear definition of fee generation. Van Landel is his case because he heard about it first. Deck and I went to the hospital to sign it up, but that's what we're supposed to do as Bruiser's employees. If we had seen the case first, and signed it up, then we would qualify for some fees.

Bruiser calls both of us into his office and closes the door. He congratulates me on passing the bar exam. He, too, passed it on the first try, and this I'm sure makes Deck feel even more stupid. But Deck shows nothing, just sits there licking his teeth, his head cocked permanently to one side. Bruiser chats for a moment about the Van Landel settlement. He received the hundred-thousand-dollar check this morning, and the Van Landels will be in this afternoon for the disbursements. And he feels that we, perhaps, should get something out of the deal. Deck and I exchange nervous looks.

Bruiser says he's already had a good year, made more money than all of last year, and he wants to keep his people happy. Plus, it's been a very quick settlement. He, personally, has worked on it less than six hours.

Deck and I are both wondering what he did for six hours.

And so, out of the goodness of his heart, he wants to compensate us. His cut is a third, or thirty-three thousand dollars, but he's not going to keep all of it. He's going to share it with us. "I'm going to give you boys a third of my share, to be split equally."

Deck and I silently do the math. One third of thirty-three thousand dollars is eleven thousand, and half of that is fifty-five hundred.

I manage to keep a straight face and say, "Thanks, Bruiser. That's awfully generous."

"Don't mention it," he says as if these favors are a way of life for him. "Call it a gift for passing the bar."

"Thanks."

"Yeah, thanks," Deck says. We're both stunned, but we're also both thinking that Bruiser gets to keep twenty-two thousand dollars for six hours of work. That's somewhere in the neighborhood of thirty-five hundred an hour.

But I didn't expect a dime, and I suddenly feel wealthy.

"Good work, you boys. Now let's sign up some more."

We nod in unison. I'm counting and spending my fortune. Deck, no doubt, is doing the same.

"Are we ready for tomorrow?" Bruiser asks me. We argue Great Benefit's motion to dismiss at nine in the morning before the Honorable Harvey Hale. Bruiser has had one unpleasant conversation with the judge about the motion, and we're not looking forward to the hearing.

"I think so," I reply with a nervous twinge. I prepared and filed a thirty-page rebuttal brief, then Drummond and company fired back a counter-rebuttal brief. Bruiser called Hale to object, and the conversation went badly.

"I might let you handle some of the argument, so be ready," Bruiser says. I swallow hard. The twinge turns into panic.

"Get to work," he adds. "It'll be embarrassing to lose the case on a motion to dismiss."

"I'm working on it too," Deck adds helpfully.

"Good. All three of us will go to court. God knows they'll have twenty people there."

SUDDEN AFFLUENCE triggers a desire for the better things in life. Deck and I decide to forgo our usual soup and sandwich lunch at Trudy's, and dine instead at a nearby steakhouse. We order prime rib.

"He's never split money like that before," Deck says, twitching and jerking around. We're in a booth in the back of a dark dining room. No one could possibly hear us, but he's anxious nonetheless. "Something's about to go down, Rudy, I'm sure of it. Toxer and Ridge are about to walk. The feds are all over Bruiser. He's giving away money. I'm nervous, real nervous."

"Okay, but why? They can't arrest us."

"I'm not worried about being arrested. I'm worried about my job."

"I don't understand. If Bruiser is indicted and arrested, he'll be out on bond before they turn around. The office will stay in business."

This irritates him. "Listen, what if they come in with subpoenas and hacksaws. They can do that, you know. It's happened before in racketeering cases. The feds love to attack law offices, seizing files and carrying away computers. They don't care about me and you."

Honestly, I've never thought about this. I guess I looked surprised. "Of course they can put him outta business," he continues, very intense. "And they'd love to do it. You and I get caught in the crossfire, and nobody, absolutely nobody, will give a damn."

"So what're you saying?"

"Let's bolt!"

I start to ask what he means, but it's rather obvious. Deck is now my friend, but he wants much more. I've passed the bar exam, so I can provide an umbrella for him. Deck wants a partner! Before I can say anything, he's on the attack. "How much money do you have?" he asks.

"Uh, fifty-five hundred dollars."

"Me too. That's eleven thousand. If we put up two thousand each, that's four. We can rent a small office for five hundred a month, phone and utilities will run another five hundred. We can pick up a few pieces of furniture, nothing fancy. We'll operate on a shoestring for six months and see how it goes. I'll hustle the cases, you make the court appearances, we split the profits evenly. Everything's fifty-fifty—expenses, fees, profits, work, hours."

I'm on the ropes but thinking fast. "What about a secretary?"

"Don't need one," he says quickly. Deck has spent time on this. "At least, not at first. We can both cover the phone and use an answering machine. I can type. You can type. It'll work. After we make some money, then we'll get us a girl."

"How much will the overhead run?"

"Less than two thousand. Rent, phone, utilities, supplies, copies, a hundred other smaller items. But we can cut corners and operate cheaply. We watch the overhead, and we take home more money. It's very simple." He studies me as he sips iced tea, then he leans forward again. "Look, Rudy, the way I see it we just left twenty-two thousand dollars on the table. We should've walked away with the entire fee, which would cover our overhead for a year. Let's get our own show, and keep all the money."

There's an ethical prohibition against lawyers establishing partnerships with non-lawyers. I start to mention this, but realize the futility of it. Deck will think of a dozen ways around it.

"The rent sounds low," I say, just to be saying something, and also to see how much research he's done.

He squints and smiles, the beaver teeth glistening. "I've already found a spot. It's in an old building on Madison above an antique store. Four rooms, a rest room, exactly halfway between the city jail and St. Peter's."

"The perfect location! Every lawyer's dream spot. That's a rough part of town," I say.

"Why do you think the rent's so cheap?"

"Is it in good shape?"

"It's okay. We'll have to paint it."

"I'm quite a painter."

Our salads arrive, and I cram romaine lettuce into my mouth. Deck shoves his around but eats little. His mind is racing too wildly to concentrate on food.

"I've gotta make a move, Rudy. I know things I can't tell, okay. So trust me when I say Bruiser's about to fall hard. His luck's run out." He pauses and picks at a walnut. "If you don't wanna go with me, then I'm talking to Nicklass this afternoon."

Nicklass is the only one left after Toxer and Ridge, and I know Deck doesn't like him. I also strongly suspect Deck is telling the truth about Bruiser. A quick perusal of the newspaper twice a week, and you know the man's in serious trouble. Deck has been his most loyal employee for the past few years, and the fact that he's ready to run scares me.

We eat slowly in silence, both of us contemplating our

next moves. Four months ago, the idea of practicing law with someone like Deck would have been unthinkable, even laughable, yet here I am unable to create enough excuses to keep him from becoming my partner.

"You don't want me as your partner?" he says pitifully.

"I'm just thinking, Deck. Give me a minute. You've hit me over the head with this."

"I'm sorry. But we have to move fast."

"How much do you know?"

"Enough to convince me. Don't ask any more questions."

"Give me a few hours. Let me sleep on it."

"Fair enough. We're both going to court tomorrow, so let's meet early. At Trudy's. We can't talk in our office. You sleep on it and tell me in the morning."

"It's a deal."

"How many files do you have?"

I think for a second. I have a thick file on the Black case, a rather thin one on Miss Birdie and a useless workers' compensation case Bruiser dumped on me last week. "Three."

"Get them out of your office. Take them home."

"Now?"

"Now. This afternoon. And anything else you might want from your office, better remove it quickly. But don't get caught, okay?"

"Is someone watching us?"

He jerks and glances, then carefully nods his head at me, eyes rolling wildly behind the crooked glasses.

"Who?"

"Feds, I think. The office is under surveillance."

Twenty-three

BRUISER'S CASUAL LITTLE ASIDE THAT HE might let me handle some of the argument in the Black hearing keeps me awake most of the night. I don't know if it was simply the usual bluff of the wise mentor, but I worry about it more than I worry about going into business with Deck.

It's dark when I arrive at Trudy's. I'm her first customer. The coffee is brewing and the doughnuts are hot. We chat for a moment, but Trudy has things to do.

So do I. I ignore the newspapers and bury myself in my notes. From time to time I glance through the window into the empty parking lot and strain to see agents out there in unmarked vehicles, smoking filterless cigarettes, drinking stale coffee, just like in the movies. At times Deck is perfectly believable, and at times he's as nutty as he looks.

He's early too. He gets his coffee at a few minutes after seven, and eases into the chair across from me. The place is half-full now.

"Well?" he says, his first word.

"Let's try it for a year," I say. I've decided that we'll sign an agreement which will last for only one year, and it will also include a thirty-day walkout clause in the event either of us becomes dissatisfied.

His shining teeth quickly emerge and he can't hide his excitement. He sticks his right hand across the table for me to shake. This is a huge moment for Deck. I wish I felt the same way.

I've also decided that I'll try to rein him in, to shame him from racing to every disaster. By working hard and servicing our clients, we can make a nice living and hopefully grow. I'll encourage Deck to study for the bar, get his license and approach the profession with more respect.

This, of course, will have to be done gradually.

And I'm not naive. Expecting Deck to stay away from hospitals will be as easy as expecting a drunk to steer clear of bars. But at least I'll try.

"Did you remove your files?" he whispers, looking at the door where two truck drivers have just entered.

"Yes. And you?"

"I've been sneaking stuff out for a week."

I'd rather not hear any more about this. I change the conversation to the Black hearing, and Deck moves it back to our new venture. At eight, we walk down to our offices, Deck eyeing every car in the parking lot as if they're all loaded with G-men.

Bruiser has not arrived by eight-fifteen. Deck and I are arguing the points made in Drummond's briefs. Here, where the walls and phones are wired, we discuss nothing but the law.

Eight-thirty, and there's no sign of Bruiser. He specifically said he'd be here at eight to go over the file. Judge Hale's courtroom is in the Shelby County Courthouse downtown, twenty minutes away in unpredictable traffic.

Deck reluctantly calls Bruiser's condo, no answer. Dru said she expected him at eight. She tries his car phone, no answer. Maybe he'll just meet us in court, she says.

Deck and I stuff the file in my briefcase and leave the office at a quarter to nine. He knows the quickest route, he says, so he drives while I sweat. My hands are clammy and my throat is dry. If Bruiser stiffs me on this hearing, I'll never forgive him. In fact, I'll hate him forever.

"Relax," Deck says, hunched over the wheel, zipping around cars and running red lights. Even Deck can look at me and see the fright. "I'm sure Bruiser'll be there." He says this without the slightest trace of conviction. "And if he's not, then you'll do fine. It's just a motion. I mean, there's no jury in the box, you know."

"Just shut up and drive, Deck, okay. And try not to get us killed."

"Touchy, touchy."

We're downtown, in traffic, and I glance with horror at my watch. It's nine, straight up. Deck forces two pedestrians off the street, then zips through a tiny parking lot. "You see that door over there," he says, pointing at the corner of the Shelby County Courthouse, a massive structure that covers an entire city block.

"Yeah."

"Take it, go up one flight, courtroom is the third door on your right."

"You think Bruiser's there?" I ask, my voice quite frail.

"Sure," he says, lying. He slams on the brakes, hits the curb, and I jump out scrambling. "I'll be there after I park," he yells. I bound up a flight of concrete steps, through the door, up another flight, then suddenly I'm in the halls of justice.

The Shelby County Courthouse is old, stately and wonderfully preserved. The floors and walls are marble, the double doors are polished mahogany. The hallway is wide, dark, quiet, and lined with wooden benches under portraits of distinguished jurists.

I slow to a jog, then stop at the courtroom of the Honorable Harvey Hale. Circuit Court Division Eight, according to a brass sign beside the doors.

There's no sign of Bruiser outside the courtroom, and as I slowly push open the door and look inside, the first thing I don't see is his huge body. He's not here.

But the courtroom is not empty. I gaze down the red-carpeted aisle, past the rows of polished and cushioned benches, through the low swinging gate, and I see that quite a few people are waiting for me. Up high, in a black robe, in a large burgundy leather chair, and scowling down my way, is an unpleasant man I presume to be Judge Harvey Hale. A clock on the wall behind him gives the time as twelve minutes after nine. One hand holds his chin while the fingers on the other tap impatiently.

To my left, beyond the bar that separates the spectators' section from the bench, the jury box and the counsel tables, I see a group of men, all of whom are straining to see me. Amazingly, they all possess the same appearance and dress—short hair, dark suits, white shirts, striped ties, stern faces, contemptible smirks.

The room is silent. I feel like a trespasser. Even the court reporter and bailiff seem to have an attitude.

With heavy feet and rubbery knees, I walk with zero confidence to the gate in the bar. My throat is parched. The words are dry and weak. "Excuse me, sir, but I'm here for the Black hearing."

The judge's expression doesn't change. His fingers keep tapping. "And who are you?"

"Well, my name's Rudy Baylor. I work for Bruiser Stone."

"Where's Mr. Stone?" he asks.

"I'm not sure. He was supposed to meet me here."

There's a rustling of activity to my left, among the cluster of lawyers, but I don't look. Judge Hale stops his tapping, raises his chin from his hand and shakes his head in frustration. "Why am I not surprised?" he says into his microphone.

Since Deck and I are bolting, I am determined to flee with the Black case safely in tow. It's mine! No one else can have it. Judge Hale has no way of knowing at this moment that I'm the lawyer who'll be prosecuting this case, not Bruiser. As scared as I am, I decide quickly that this is the moment to establish myself.

"I suppose you want a continuance," he says.

"No sir. I'm prepared to argue the motion," I say as forcefully as possible. I ease through the gate and place the file on the table to my right.

"Are you a lawyer?" he asks.

"Well, I just passed the bar."

"But you haven't received your license?"

I don't know why this distinction hasn't hit me until now. I guess I've been so proud of myself it just slipped my mind. Plus, Bruiser was going to do the talking today, with me perhaps chiming in for a bit of practice. "No sir. We take the oath next week."

One of my enemies clears his throat loudly so that the judge will look at him. I turn and see a distinguished gentleman in a navy suit in the process of dramatically rising from his chair. "May it please the court," he says as if he's said it a million times. "For the record, my name is Leo F. Drummond of Tinley Britt, counsel for Great Benefit Life." He says this somberly, up in the direction of his lifelong friend and Yale roommate. The keeper of the record, the court reporter, has returned to her nail filing.

"And we object to this young man's appearance in this matter." He sweeps his arms toward me. His words are slow and heavy. I hate him already. "Why, he doesn't even have a license."

I hate him for his patronizing tone, and for his silly hairsplitting. This is only a motion, not a trial.

"Your Honor, I'll have my license next week," I say. My anger is greatly assisting my voice.

"That's not good enough, Your Honor," Drummond says, arms open wide, like this is such a ridiculous idea. The nerve!

"I've passed the bar exam, Your Honor."

"Big deal," Drummond snaps at me.

I look directly at him. He's standing in the midst of four other people, three of whom are sitting at his table with legal pads in front of them. The fourth sits behind them. I'm getting the collective glare.

"It is a big deal, Mr. Drummond. Go ask Shell Boykin," I say. Drummond's face tightens and there's a noticeable flinch. In fact, there's a collective flinch from the defense table.

This is a real cheap shot, but for some reason I couldn't resist. Shell Boykin is one of two students from our class privileged enough to be hired by Trent & Brent. We despised each other for three years, and we took the exam together last month. His name was not in the newspaper last Sunday. I'm sure the great firm is slightly embarrassed that one of its bright young recruits flunked the bar.

Drummond's scowl intensifies, and I smile in return. In the few brief seconds that we stand and watch each other, I learn an enormously valuable lesson. He's just a man. He might be a legendary trial lawyer with lots of notches in his belt, but he's just another man. He's not about to step across the aisle and slap me, because I'd whip his ass. He can't hurt me, and neither can his little covey of minions.

Courtrooms are level from one side to the other. My table is as large as his.

"Sit down!" His Honor growls into the microphone. "Both of you." I find a chair and take a seat. "One question, Mr. Baylor. Who will handle this case on behalf of your firm?"

"I will, Your Honor."

"And what about Mr. Stone?"

"I can't say. But this is my case, these are my clients. Mr. Stone filed it on my behalf, until I passed the bar."

"Very well. Let's proceed. On the record," he says, looking at the court reporter who's already working her machine. "This is the defendant's motion to dismiss, so Mr. Drummond goes first. I'll allow each side fifteen minutes to argue, then I'll take it under advisement. I don't want to be here all morning. Are we in agreement?"

Everybody nods. The defense table resembles wooden ducks wobbling on a carnival firing range, all heads rocking in unison. Leo Drummond strolls to a portable podium in the center of the courtroom, and begins his argument. He's slow and meticulous, and after a few minutes becomes boring. He's summarizing the major points already set forth in his lengthy brief, the gist of which is that Great Benefit is being wrongly sued because its policy does not cover bone marrow transplants. Then there's the issue of whether Donny Ray Black should be covered under the policy since he's an adult and no longer a member of the household.

Frankly, I expected more. I thought I'd witness something almost magical from the great Leo Drummond. Before yesterday, I had caught myself looking forward to this initial skirmish. I wanted to see a good brawl between Drummond, the polished advocate, and Bruiser, the courtroom brawler.

But if I weren't so nervous, I'd fall asleep. He goes past

fifteen minutes without a pause. Judge Hale is looking down, reading something, probably a magazine. Twenty minutes. Deck said he's heard that Drummond bills two-hundred fifty bucks an hour for office work, three-fifty when in court. That's well below New York and Washington standards, but it's very high for Memphis. He has good reason to talk slow and repeat himself. It pays to be thorough, even tedious, when billing at that rate.

His three associates scribble furiously on legal pads, evidently trying to write down everything their leader has to say. It's almost comical, and under better circumstances I might force a laugh out of myself. First they did the research, then they wrote the brief, then they rewrote it several times, then they responded to my brief and now they're writing down Drummond's arguments, which are taken directly from the briefs. But they're getting paid for this. Deck figures Tinley Britt bills its associates out at around one-fifty for office work, probably a bit more for hearings and trials. If Deck is right, then the three of these young clones are scrawling aimlessly for around two hundred bucks an hour each. Six hundred dollars. Plus, three-fifty for Drummond. That's almost a thousand dollars an hour for what I'm witnessing.

The fourth man, the one sitting behind the associates, is older, about the same age as Drummond. He's not scratching on a notepad, so he can't be a lawyer. He's probably a representative of Great Benefit, maybe one of their in-house lawyers.

I forget about Deck until he taps me on the shoulder with a legal pad. He's behind me, reaching across the bar. He wants to correspond. On the legal pad, he's written a note: "This guy's boring as hell. Just follow your brief. Keep it under ten minutes. No sign of Bruiser?"

I shake my head without turning around. As if Bruiser could be in the courtroom without being seen.

After thirty-one minutes, Drummond finishes his monologue. The reading glasses are perched on the tip of his nose. He's the professor lecturing the class. He struts back to his table, immensely satisfied with his brilliant logic and amazing powers of summation. His clones tip their heads in unison and whisper quick tributes to his marvelous presentation. What a bunch of asskissers! No wonder his ego is warped.

I place my legal pad on the podium and look up at Judge Hale, who, for the moment, seems awfully interested in whatever I'm about to say. I'm scared to death at this point, but there's nothing to do but press on.

This is a simple lawsuit. Great Benefit's denial has robbed my client of the only medical treatment that could save his life. The company's actions will kill Donny Ray Black. We're right and they're wrong. I'm comforted by the image of his gaunt face and withered body. It makes me mad.

Great Benefit's lawyers will be paid a ton of money to confuse the issues, to muddle the facts, to hopefully strangle the judge and later the jury with red herrings. That's their job. That's why Drummond rambled for thirty-one minutes and said nothing.

My version of the facts and the law will always run shorter. My briefs and arguments will remain clear and to the point. Surely, someone down the line will appreciate this.

I nervously begin with a few basic points about motions to dismiss in general, and Judge Hale stares down incredulously as if I'm the biggest fool he's ever listened to. His face is contorted with skepticism, but at least he keeps his mouth shut. I try to avoid his eyes.

Motions to dismiss are rarely granted in cases where there's a clear dispute between the parties. I may be nervous and awkward, but I'm confident we'll prevail.

I slog my way through my notes without revealing anything new. His Honor is soon as bored with me as he was with Drummond, and returns to his reading materials. When I finish, Drummond asks for five minutes to rebut what I've said, and his friend waves at the podium.

Drummond rambles for another eleven precious and valuable minutes, clears up whatever was on his mind but does so in such a way as to keep the rest of us in the dark, then sits.

"I'd like to see counsel in chambers," Hale says, rising and quickly disappearing behind the bench. Since I don't know where his chambers happen to be located, I stand and wait for Mr. Drummond to lead the way. He's polite as we meet near the podium, even places his arm on my shoulder and tells me what a superb job I did.

The robe is already off by the time we enter the judge's office. He's standing behind his desk, waving at two chairs. "Please come in. Have a seat." The room is dark with decorum; heavy drapes pulled together over the window, burgundy carpet, rows of heavy books in shelves from floor to ceiling.

We sit. He ponders. Then, "This lawsuit bothers me, Mr. Baylor. I wouldn't use the word frivolous, but I'm not impressed with the merits of it, to be frank. I'm really tired of these types of suits."

He pauses and looks at me as if I'm supposed to respond now. But I'm at a complete loss.

"I'm inclined to grant the motion to dismiss," he says, opening a drawer, then slowly removing several bottles of pills. He carefully lines them up on his desk as we watch. He stops and looks at me. "Maybe you can refile it in federal court, you know. Take it somewhere else. I just don't want it clogging up my docket." He counts pills, at least a dozen from four plastic cylinders.

"Excuse me while I visit the can," he says, and steps to a small door across the room, to his right. It locks loudly.

I sit in a dazed stillness, staring blankly at the pill bottles, hoping he chokes on them in there. Drummond hasn't said a word, but as if on cue rises and perches his butt on the corner of the desk. He looks down at me, all warmth and smiles.

"Look, Rudy, I'm a very expensive lawyer, from a very expensive firm," he says in a low, trusting voice, as if he's divulging secret information. "When we first get a case like this, we do some math and project the cost of defending it. We give this estimate to our client, and this is before we lift a finger. I've handled a lot of cases, and I can hit pretty close to the center of the dartboard." He shifts a bit, prepping for the punch line. "I've told Great Benefit that the cost of defending this case through a full-blown trial will run them between fifty and seventy-five thousand dollars."

He waits for me to indicate that this figure is impressive, but I just stare at his tie. The toilet flushes and rumbles in the distance.

"And so, Great Benefit has authorized me to offer you and your clients seventy-five thousand to settle."

I exhale heavily. A dozen wild thoughts race before me, the largest of which is the figure of twenty-five thousand dollars. My fee! I can see it.

Wait a minute. If his pal Harvey here is about to dismiss the case, why is he offering me this money?

And, then, it hits me—the good cop/bad cop routine. Harvey lowers the boom and scares the hell out of me, then Leo steps in with the velvet touch. I can't help but wonder how many times they've played tag-team in this office.

"No admission of liability, you understand," he says. "It's a one-time offer, good for only the next forty-eight hours, take it or leave it right now, while it's on the table. If you say no, then it's World War III."

"But why?"

"Simple economics. Great Benefit saves some money, plus they don't run the risk of some crazy verdict. They don't like to get sued, you understand? Their executives don't like to waste time in depositions and court appearances. They're a quiet bunch. They like to avoid this kind of publicity. Insurance is a cutthroat business, and they don't want their competitors to get wind of this. Lots of good reasons for them to settle quietly. Lots of good reasons for your clients to take the money and run. Most of it's tax-free, you know."

He's smooth. I could argue the merits of the case and talk about how rotten his client is, but he'd just smile and nod along with me. Water off a duck's back. Right now Leo Drummond wants me to take his money, and if I said nasty things about his wife it wouldn't faze him.

The door opens and His Honor exits his private little rest room. Leo now has a full bladder, and he excuses himself. The tag is made. The duet moves along.

"High blood pressure," Hale says to himself as he sits behind his desk and gathers his bottles. Not high enough, I want to say.

"Not much of a lawsuit, kid, I'm afraid. Maybe I can lean on Leo to make an offer of settlement. That's part of my job, you know. Other judges approach it differently, but not me. I like to get involved in settlement from day one. It moves things along. These boys might throw some money at you to keep from paying Leo a thousand bucks a minute." He laughs as if this is really funny. His face turns bloodred and he coughs.

I can almost see Leo in the rest room, ear stuck to the door, listening. It wouldn't surprise me if they have a mike in there.

I watch him hack until his eyes water. When he stops, I say, "He just offered me the cost of defense." Hale's a lousy actor. He tries to seem surprised. "How much?"

"Seventy-five thousand."

His mouth falls open. "Geez! Look, son, you're crazy if you don't take it."

"You think so?" I ask, playing along.

"Seventy-five. Jeez, that's a buncha money. That doesn't sound like Leo."

"He's a great guy."

"Take the money, son. I've been doing this for a long time, and you need to listen to me."

The door opens, and Leo rejoins us. His Honor stares at Leo, and says, "Seventy-five thousand?" You'd think the money was coming out of Hale's office budget.

"That's what my client said," Leo explains. His hands are tied. He's powerless.

They serve and volley for a while longer. I'm not thinking rationally, so I say little. I leave the room with Leo's arm around my shoulder.

I find Deck in the hallway, on the phone, and so I sit on a nearby bench and try to collect myself. They were expecting Bruiser. Would they have tag-teamed him the same way? No, I don't think so. How did they plan their ambush of me so quickly? They probably had another routine planned for him.

I'm convinced of two things: First, Hale is serious about dismissing the lawsuit. He's a sick old man who's been on the bench for a long time, and is immune from pressure. He couldn't care less if he's right or wrong. And it might be very difficult to file it again in another court. The lawsuit is in serious trouble. Second, Drummond is too anxious to settle. He's scared, and he's scared because his client is in serious trouble. He's scared, and he's scared because his client has been caught red-handed in a very nasty act.

□ □ □
□ □

DECK'S MADE eleven phone calls in the past twenty minutes, and there's no sign of Bruiser. As we speed back to the office, I replay the bizarre scene in Hale's office. Deck, ever the quick-change artist, wants to take the money and run. He makes the very good argument that no amount of money will save Donny Ray's life at this point, so we should grab what we can and make things a bit easier for Dot and Buddy.

Deck claims that he's heard many sordid tales of badly tried lawsuits in Hale's courtroom. For a sitting judge, he's unusually vocal in his support of tort reform. Hates plaintiffs, Deck says more than once. A fair trial will be hard to obtain. Let's take the money and run, Deck says.

DRU IS IN TEARS in the lobby as we enter. She's hysterical because everybody's looking for Bruiser. Her mascara runs down her cheeks as she curses and cries. This is just not like him, she says over and over. Something bad has happened.

Being a thug himself, Bruiser hangs out with dubious and dangerous people. Finding his fat body stuffed into the trunk of a car at the airport would not surprise me, and Deck allows as much. The thugs are after him.

I'm after him too. I call Yogi's to talk to Prince. He'll know where Bruiser is. I talk to Billy, the manager, a guy I know well, and after a few minutes learn that Prince seems to have vanished too. They've called everywhere, with no luck. Billy's worried and nervous. The feds just left. What's going on?

Deck goes from office to office, rallying the troops. We meet in the conference room—me, Deck, Toxer and Ridge, four secretaries and two flunkies I've never seen before. Nicklass, the other lawyer, is out of town. Everyone compares notes of their last meeting with Bruiser:

Anything suspicious? What was he supposed to do today? Who was he supposed to see? Who talked to him last? There is an atmosphere of panic in the room, an air of confusion that's not alleviated in the least by Dru's incessant bawling. She just knows something's gone wrong.

The meeting breaks up as we silently file back to our offices and lock our doors. Deck, of course, follows me. We talk aimlessly for a while, careful not to say anything we don't want overheard if in fact the place is wired. At eleven-thirty, we ease out a rear door and leave for lunch.

We will never set foot in the place again.

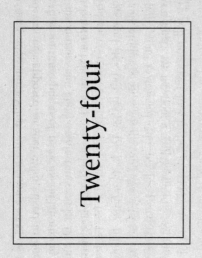

Twenty-four

I DOUBT IF I'LL EVER KNOW WHETHER Deck actually knew what was coming down, or whether he was just amazingly prophetic. He's an uncomplicated person without too many layers, and most of his thoughts are close to the surface. But there's a definite degree of weirdness, aside from appearances, that's coiled tightly within and clings to secrecy. I strongly suspect he and Bruiser were much closer than most of us knew, that the sweetheart deal on the Van Landel settlement was a result of Deck's lobbying and that Bruiser was issuing quiet warnings about his demise.

At any rate, when my phone rings at 3:20 A.M., I'm not terribly surprised. It's Deck, with the double announcement that the feds raided our offices just after midnight, and that Bruiser has skipped town. There's more. Our former offices are now locked by court order, and the feds will probably want to talk to everyone who worked in the place. And, most surprising, Prince Thomas seems to have vanished along with his lawyer and friend.

Imagine, Deck giggles into the phone, those two hogs,

with their long grayish hair and facial growths, trying to sneak through airports incognito.

Indictments are supposed to be issued later today, after the sun comes up. Deck suggests we meet at our new offices around noon, and since I have no place else to go, I agree.

I stare at the dark ceiling for half an hour, then give it up. I step barefoot through the cool wet grass and fall into the hammock. A character like Prince spawns lots of colorful rumors. He loved cash, and my first day on the job at Yogi's I was told by a waitress that eighty percent of it was never reported. The employees loved to gossip and speculate over the amounts of cash he was able to skim.

He had other ventures. A witness in a racketeering trial a couple of years ago testified that ninety percent of the income generated in a particular topless bar was in the form of cash, and that sixty percent of this was never reported. If Bruiser and Prince in fact owned one or more skin clubs, then they were mining gold.

It was rumored that Prince had a house in Mexico, bank accounts in the Caribbean, a black mistress in Jamaica, a farm in Argentina, and I can't remember the other stories. There was a mysterious door in his office, and behind it there supposedly was a small room filled with boxes of twenty- and one-hundred-dollar bills.

If he's on the run, I hope he's safe. I hope he escaped with large sums of his precious cash, and never gets caught. I don't care what he's allegedly done wrong, he's my friend.

DOT SEATS ME at the kitchen table, same chair, and serves me instant coffee, same cup. It's early, and the smell of bacon grease hangs thick in the cluttered kitchen. Buddy's out there, she says, waving her arms. I don't look.

Donny Ray is fading fast, she says, hasn't been out of bed for the past two days.

"We went to court yesterday for the first time," I explain.

"Already?"

"It wasn't a trial or anything like that. Just a preliminary motion. The insurance company is trying to get the case dismissed, and we're having a big fight over it." I try to keep it simple, but I'm not sure it registers. She looks through the dirty windows, into the backyard but certainly not at the Fairlane. Dot doesn't seem to care.

This is oddly comforting. If Judge Hale does what I think he's about to, and if we're unable to refile in another court, then this case is over. Maybe the entire family has given up. Maybe they won't scream at me when we get bounced.

I decided when I was driving over that I wouldn't mention Judge Hale and his threats. It would only complicate our discussion. There will be plenty of time to discuss this later, when we have nothing else to talk about.

"The insurance company has made an offer to settle."

"What kind of offer?"

"Some money."

"How much?"

"Seventy-five thousand dollars. They figure that's how much they'll pay their lawyers to defend the case, so they're offering it now to settle everything."

There's a noticeable reddening in her face, a tightening of her jaws. "Sumbitches think they can buy us off now, right?"

"Yes, that's what they think."

"Donny Ray don't need money. He needed a bone marrow transplant last year. Now it's too late."

"I agree."

She picks up her pack of cigarettes from the table, and

lights one. Her eyes are red and wet. I was wrong. This mother has not given up. She wants blood. "Just exactly what're we supposed to do with seventy-five thousand dollars? Donny Ray'll be dead, and it'll just be me and him." She points with her forehead in the direction of the Fairlane.

"Them sumbitches," she says.

"I agree."

"I guess you said we'll take it, didn't you?"

"Of course not. I can't settle the case without your approval. We have until tomorrow morning to make a decision." The issue of the dismissal rears up again. We'll have the right to appeal any adverse ruling by Judge Hale. It could take a year or so, but we'll have a fighting chance. Again, this is not something I want to discuss now.

We sit in silence for a long time, both of us perfectly content to think and wait. I try to arrange my thoughts. God only knows what's rattling around in her brain. Poor woman.

She stubs out her cigarette in an ashtray, and says, "We'd better talk to Donny Ray."

I follow her through the dark den and into a short hallway. Donny Ray's door is closed, and there's a NO SMOKING sign on it. She taps lightly and we enter. The room is neat and tidy, with an antiseptic smell to it. A fan blows from the corner. The screened window is open. A television is elevated at the foot of his bed, and next to it, close to his pillow, is a small table covered with bottles of fluids and pills.

Donny Ray lies stiff as a board with a sheet tucked tightly under his frail body. He smiles broadly when he sees me, and pats a spot next to him. This is where I sit. Dot assumes a position on the other side.

He tries to keep smiling as he struggles to convince me he's feeling fine, everything's better today. Just a little tired, that's all. His voice is low and strained, his words at times barely audible. He listens carefully as I recount yesterday's hearing and explain the offer to settle. Dot holds his right hand.

"Will they go higher?" he asks. It's a question Deck and I debated over lunch yesterday. Great Benefit has made the remarkable leap from zero to seventy-five thousand. We both suspect they may go as high as a hundred thousand, but I wouldn't dare be so optimistic in front of my clients.

"I doubt it," I say. "But we can try. All they can do is say no."

"How much will you get?" he asks. I explain the contract, how my third comes off the top.

He looks at his mother and says, "That's fifty thousand for you and Dad."

"What're we gonna do with fifty thousand dollars?" she asks him.

"Pay off the house. Buy a new car. Stick some away for old age."

"I don't want their damned money."

Donny Ray closes his eyes and takes a quick nap. I stare at the bottles of medication. When he wakes up, he touches my arm, tries to squeeze it and says, "Do you want to settle, Rudy? Some of the money is yours."

"No. I don't want to settle," I say with conviction. I look at him, then at her. They are listening intently. "They wouldn't offer this money if they weren't worried. I want to expose these people."

A lawyer has a duty to give his client the best possible advice without regard for his own financial circumstances. There is no doubt in my mind that I could beguile the Blacks into settling. With little effort, I could convince them that Judge Hale is about to jerk the rug from under us, that the money is now on the table but will soon be gone forever. I could paint a doomsday picture, and these people have been stepped on so much they'd readily believe it.

It would be easy. And I would walk away with twenty-five thousand dollars, a fee I have trouble comprehending at the moment. But I've overcome the temptation. I wrestled with it early this morning in the hammock, and I've made peace with myself.

It wouldn't take much to drive me from the legal profession at this point. I'll take the next step and quit before I sell out my clients.

I leave the Blacks in Donny Ray's room, hoping mightily that I don't return tomorrow with the news that our case has been dismissed.

THERE ARE AT LEAST four hospitals within walking distance of St. Peter's. There's also a med school, dental school and countless doctors' offices. The medical community in Memphis has gravitated together in a six-block area between Union and Madison. On Madison itself is an eight-story building, directly across from St. Peter's, known as the Peabody Medical Arts Building. It has an enclosed walking tunnel above Madison so the doctors can run from their offices to the hospital and back again. It houses nothing but doctors, one of whom is Dr. Eric Craggdale, an orthopedic surgeon. His office is on the third floor.

I made a series of anonymous calls to his office yesterday, and found out what I needed. I wait in the huge lobby of St. Peter's, one level above the street, and watch the parking lot around the Peabody Medical Arts Building. At twenty minutes before eleven, I watch an old Volkswagen Rabbit ease off Madison and park in the crowded lot. Kelly gets out.

She's alone, as I expected. I called her husband's place

of employment an hour ago, asked to speak to him and hung up when he came to the phone. I can barely see the top of her head as she struggles to rise from the car. She's on crutches, hobbling between rows of cars, headed into the building.

I take the escalator one floor up, then cross Madison in the glass tube walkway above it. I'm nervous, but in no hurry.

The waiting room is crowded. She's sitting with her back to the wall, flipping pages in a magazine, her broken ankle now in a walking cast. The chair to her right is empty, and I'm in it before she realizes it's me.

Her face first registers shock, then instantly breaks into a welcoming smile. She glances nervously about. No one is looking.

"Just read your magazine," I whisper as I open a *National Geographic*. She raises a copy of *Vogue* almost to eye level, and asks, "What are you doing here?"

"My back's bothering me."

She shakes her head and looks around. The lady next to her would like to stare but her neck is in a brace. Neither of us knows a soul in this room, so why should we worry?

"So who's your doctor?" she asks.

"Craggdale," I answer.

"Very funny." Kelly Riker was beautiful when she was in the hospital wearing a simple hospital gown, a bruise on her cheek and no makeup. Now it's impossible for me to take my eyes off her face. She's wearing a white cotton button-down, light starch, the type a coed would borrow from her boyfriend, and rolled-up khaki shorts. Her dark hair falls well below her shoulders.

"Is he good?" I ask.

"He's just a doctor."

"You've seen him before?"

"Don't start, Rudy. I'm not discussing it. I think you should leave." Her voice is quiet but firm.

"Well, you know, I've thought about that. In fact, I've spent a lot of time thinking about you and what I should do." I pause as a man rolls by in a wheelchair.

"And?" she says.

"And I still don't know."

"I think you should leave."

"You don't really mean that."

"Yes I do."

"No you don't. You want me to hang around, keep in touch, call every now and then, so the next time he breaks some bones you'll have someone who'll give a damn about you. That's what you want."

"There won't be a next time."

"Why not?"

"Because he's different now. He's trying to stop drinking. He's promised not to hit me again."

"And you believe him?"

"Yes, I do."

"He's promised before."

"Why don't you leave? And don't call, okay? It just makes matters worse."

"Why? Why does it make matters worse?"

She falters for a second, lowers the magazine to her lap and looks at me. "Because I think about you less as the days go by."

It's certainly nice to know she's been thinking about me. I reach into my pocket and retrieve a business card, one with my old address on it, the address that's now chained and seized by various agencies of the U.S. Government. I write my phone number on the back, and hand it to her. "It's a deal. I won't call you again. If you need me, that's my home number. If he hurts you, I want to know about it."

She takes the card. I quickly kiss her on the cheek, then leave the waiting room.

ON THE SIXTH FLOOR of the same building is a large oncology group. Dr. Walter Kord is Donny Ray's treating physician, which means at this point he's providing a few pills and other drugs, and waiting for him to die. Kord prescribed the original chemo treatment, and performed the tests that determined that Ron Black was a perfect match for his twin's bone marrow transplant. He will be a crucial witness at trial, assuming the case gets that far.

I leave a three-page letter with his receptionist. I'd like to talk to him at his convenience, and preferably without getting billed for it. As a general rule, doctors hate lawyers, and any time spent chatting with us is at great expense. But Kord and I are on the same side, and I have nothing to lose by trying to open a dialogue.

IT IS WITH GREAT TREPIDATION that I putter along this street in this rough section of the city, oblivious to traffic and trying vainly to read faded and peeling numbers above doors. The neighborhood looks as if it were once abandoned, with good reason, but is now in the process of reclaiming itself. The buildings are all two and three stories running half a block deep with brick and glass fronts. Most were built together, a few have narrow alleys between them. Many are still boarded up, a couple were burned out years ago. I pass two restaurants, one with tables on the sidewalk under a canopy but no customers, a cleaner's, a flower shop.

The Buried Treasures antique shop is on a corner, a clean-enough-looking building with the bricks painted dark gray and red awnings over the windows. It has two levels, and as my gaze rises to the second, I suspect I've found my new home.

Because I can find no other door, I enter the antique shop. In the tiny foyer, I see a stairwell with a dim light at the top.

Deck is waiting, smiling proudly. "Whatta you think?" he gushes before I have a chance to look at anything. "Four rooms, about a thousand feet, plus rest room. Not bad," he says, tapping me on the shoulder. Then he bounces forward, spinning around, arms open wide. "Thought this would be the reception area, maybe we'll use it for a secretary when we hire one. Just needs a coat of paint. All floors are hardwood," he says, stomping his foot, as if I couldn't see the floors. "Ceilings are twelve feet. Walls are plasterboard and easy to paint." He motions for me to follow. We step through an open door and into a short hallway. "One room on each side. This one here is the largest, so I thought you'd need it."

I step into my new office, and am pleasantly surprised. It's about fifteen by fifteen with a window overlooking the street. It's empty and clean, nice flooring.

"And over here is the third room. Thought we'd use it as a conference room. I'll work outta here, but I won't make a mess." He's trying hard to please, and I almost feel sorry for him. Just relax, Deck, I like the offices. Good job.

"Down there is the john. We'll need to clean and paint it, maybe get a plumber in." He backtracks to the front room. "Whatta you think?"

"It'll work, Deck. Who owns it?"

"The junk dealer downstairs. Old man and his wife. By the way, they have some stuff we might want: tables, chairs, lamps, even some old file cabinets. It's cheap, not bad-looking, sort of goes with our decorative scheme here, plus they'll allow us to pay by the month. They're kinda happy to have someone else in the building. I think they've been robbed a coupla times."

"That's comforting."

"Yeah. We gotta be careful here." He hands me a sheet of color samples from Sherwin-Williams. "I think we'd better stick with some shade of white. Less work to apply and easier on the budget. The phone company's coming tomorrow. Electricity is already on. Take a look at this." Next to the window is a card table with some papers scattered about and a small black-and-white TV in the center of it.

Deck has already been to the printer. He hands me various layouts of our new firm stationery, each with my name emblazoned in bold letters across the top, and his name in the corner as a paralegal. "Got these from a print shop down the street. Very reasonable. Takes about two days to fill the order. I'd say five hundred sheets and envelopes. See anything you like?"

"I'll study them tonight."

"When do you wanna paint?"

"Well, I guess we——"

"I figure we could knock it out in one hard day, that is if we get by with only one coat, you know. I'll get the paint and supplies this afternoon, and try to get started. Can you help tomorrow?"

"Sure."

"We need to make a few decisions. What about a fax. Do we get one now or wait? Phone guy's coming tomorrow, remember? And a copier? I say no, not right now, we can hold our originals and once a day I'll go down to the print shop. We'll need an answering machine. A good one costs eighty bucks. I'll take care of it, if you want. And we need to open a bank account. I know a branch manager at First Trust, says he'll give us thirty checks a month free and two percent interest on our money. Hard to beat. We need to get the checks ordered because we'll need to pay some bills, you know." Suddenly, he looks at his watch. "Hey, I almost forgot."

He punches a button on the television. "Indictments came down an hour ago, a hundred and something different counts against Bruiser, Bennie 'Prince' Thomas, Willie McSwane and others."

The noon report is already in progress, and the first image we see is a live shot of our former offices. Agents guard the front door, which is unchained at the moment. The reporter explains that the firm's employees are being allowed to come and go, but can't remove anything. The next shot is from outside Vixens, a topless club the feds have also seized. "Indictment says Bruiser and Thomas were involved in three clubs," Deck says. The reporter echoes this. Then there's some footage of our former boss, skulking around a courthouse corridor during an old trial. Arrest warrants have been issued, but there's no sign of either Mr. Stone or Mr. Thomas. The agent in charge of the investigation is interviewed, and it's his opinion that these two gentlemen have fled the area. An extensive search is under way.

"Run Bruiser run," Deck says.

The story is juicy enough because it involves local thugs, a flamboyant lawyer, several Memphis policemen and the skin business. But it's spiced up considerably by the element of flight. Prince and Bruiser have obviously hit the road, and this is more than the reporters can stand. There's footage of policemen being arrested, of another topless club, this time with naked dancers shown from the thighs down, of the U.S. Attorney addressing the media to announce the indictments.

Then there's a shot that breaks my heart. They've closed Yogi's, wrapped chains around the door handles and posted guards at the doors. They refer to it as the headquarters of Prince Thomas, the kingpin, and the feds seem surprised because they found no cash when they crashed in last night. "Run Prince run," I say to myself.

The related stories consume most of the noon report.

"Wonder where they are," Deck says as he turns off the TV.

We think about this in silence for a few seconds. "What's in there?" I ask, pointing to a storage box beside the card table.

"My files."

"Anything good?"

"Enough to pay the bills for two months. Some small car wrecks. Workers' comp cases. There's also a death case I took from Bruiser. Actually, I didn't take it. He gave me the file last week and asked me to review some insurance policies in it. It sort of stayed in my office, now it's here."

I suspect there are other files in the box which Deck may have lifted from Bruiser's office, but I shall not inquire.

"Do you think the feds will wanna talk to us?" I ask.

"I've been thinking about that. We don't know anything, and we didn't remove any files that would be of interest to them, so why worry?"

"I'm worried."

"Me too."

Twenty-five

I KNOW DECK'S HAVING A HARD TIME CON-
trolling his excitement these days. The idea of having
his own office and keeping half the fees without the
benefit of a law license is terribly thrilling. If I stay out of
his way, he'll have the offices in top shape within a week.
I've never seen such energy. Maybe he's a little too gung-
ho, but I'll give him a break.

However, when the phone rings for the second straight
morning before the sun is up, and I hear his voice, it's
difficult to be nice.

"Have you seen the paper?" he asks, quite chipper.

"I was sleeping."

"Sorry. You won't believe it. Bruiser and Prince are all
over the front page."

"Couldn't this wait for an hour or so, Deck?" I ask. I'm
determined to stop this rude habit of his right now. "If
you want to wake up at four, then fine. But don't call me
until seven, no, make it eight."

"Sorry. But there's more."

"What?"

"Guess who died last night?"

Now, how in hell am I supposed to know who, in all of Memphis, died last night? "I give up," I snap at the phone.

"Harvey Hale."

"Harvey Hale!"

"Yep. Croaked with a heart attack. Fell dead by his swimming pool."

"Judge Hale?"

"That's the one. Your buddy."

I sit on the edge of my bed and try to shake the fuzz from my brain. "That's hard to believe."

"Yeah, I can tell you're really distraught. There's a nice story about him on the front page, Metro, big photo, all suited up in a black robe, real distinguished. What a prick."

"How old was he?" I ask, as if it matters.

"Sixty-two. On the bench for eleven years. Quite a pedigree. It's all in the paper. You need to see it."

"Yeah, I'll do that, Deck. See you later."

.

THE PAPER seems a bit heavier this morning, and I'm sure it's because at least half of it is dedicated to the exploits of Bruiser Stone and Prince Thomas. One story follows the next. They have not been seen.

I skim the front section and go to Metro, where I'm greeted with a very dated photo of the Honorable Harvey Hale. I read the sad reflections of his colleagues, including his friend and old roommate, Leo F. Drummond.

Of particular importance is speculation as to who might replace him. The governor will appoint a successor who'll serve until the next regular election. The county is half black and half white, but only seven of the nineteen circuit court judges are black. Some people are not pleased with these numbers. Last year, when an old white judge retired, a strong effort was made to fill the vacancy with a black judge. It didn't happen.

Remarkably, the leading candidate last year was my new friend Tyrone Kipler, the Harvard-educated partner at Booker's firm who lectured us on constitutional law back when we were preparing for the bar exam. Though Judge Hale has been dead less than twelve hours, conventional wisdom, says the story, leans heavily toward Kipler as his replacement. The mayor of Memphis, who is black and vocal, is quoted as saying he and other leaders will push hard for Kipler's appointment.

The governor was out of town and unavailable for comment, but he's a Democrat and up for reelection next year. He'll fall in line this time.

AT NINE SHARP, I'm in the Circuit Clerk's office flipping through the *Black versus Great Benefit* file. I breathe a sigh of relief. His Honor Hale did not, prior to his untimely death, sign an order dismissing our case. We're still in the game.

There's a wreath on his courtroom door. How touching. I call Tinley Britt from a pay phone, ask for Leo F. Drummond and am surprised to hear his voice after a few minutes. I express my sympathy for the loss of his friend, and I tell him my clients will not accept his offer to settle. He seems surprised, but has little to say. Bless his heart, he has a lot on his mind right now.

"I think that's a mistake, Rudy," he says patiently, as if he's really on my side.

"It may be, but my clients made the decision, not me."

"Oh well, then it'll be war," he says in a sad monotone. He does not offer more money.

BOOKER AND I have talked twice on the phone since we received the results of the bar exam. As expected, he's downplaying it as a very minor and very temporary setback. As expected, he was genuinely happy for me.

He's already seated in the rear of the small diner when I enter. We greet each other as if it's been months. We order tea and gumbo without looking at the menus. Kids are fine. Charlene is wonderful.

He's buoyed by the possibility that he may pass the bar anyway. I didn't realize how close he'd come, but his overall score was only one point below the passing mark. He has appealed, and the Board of Law Examiners is reviewing his exam.

Marvin Shankle took the news of his failure hard. He'd better pass it the next time, or the firm will have to replace him. Booker can't hide the stress when he talks about Shankle.

"How's Tyrone Kipler?" I ask.

Booker thinks the appointment is in the bag. Kipler talked to the governor this morning, everything's falling into place. The only snag could be financial. As a partner in the Shankle firm, he earns between a hundred and twenty-five and a hundred and fifty thousand a year. The judge's salary is only ninety thousand. Kipler has a wife and kids, but Marvin Shankle wants him on the bench.

Booker remembers the Black case. In fact, he remembers Dot and Buddy from our first meeting at the Cypress Gardens Senior Citizens Building. I bring him up-to-date on the case. He laughs out loud when I tell him it's now sitting in Circuit Court Division Eight, just waiting for a judge to assume responsibility for it. I recount for Booker my experience in the chambers of the late Judge Hale, just three days ago, and how I was kicked back and forth by the former Yale roommates Drummond and Hale. Booker listens closely as I talk of Donny Ray and his twin and the transplant that didn't happen because of Great Benefit.

He listens with a smile. "No problem," he says more than once. "If Tyrone gets the appointment, he'll know all about the Black case."

"So you can talk to him?"

"Talk to him? I'll preach to him. He can't stand Trent & Brent, and he hates insurance companies, sues them all the time. Who do you think they prey on? Middle-class whites?"

"Everybody."

"You're right. I'll be happy to talk to Tyrone. And he'll listen."

The gumbo arrives and we add Tabasco, Booker more than I. I tell him about my new office, but not my new partner. He asks lots of questions about my old office. The entire city is buzzing over Bruiser and Prince.

I tell him everything I know, with a few embellished details.

Twenty-six

I N THIS AGE OF CONGESTED COURTROOMS and overworked judges, the late Harvey Hale left a docket remarkably well organized and free of back-log. There are a few good reasons. First, he was lazy and preferred to play golf. Second, he was quick to dismiss a plaintiff's suit if it offended his notions of protecting in-surance companies and large corporations. And because of this, most plaintiffs' lawyers avoided him.

There are ways to avoid certain judges, little tricks used by seasoned lawyers who are cozy with the filing clerks. I'll never understand why Bruiser, a twenty-year lawyer who knew the ropes, allowed me to file the Black case without taking steps to avoid Harvey Hale. That's another matter I want to discuss with him if he's ever brought home.

But Hale is gone and life is fair again. Tyrone Kipler will soon inherit a docket that's begging for action.

In response to years of criticism by laymen and lawyers alike, the rules of procedure were changed not long ago in an effort to speed up justice. Sanctions for frivolous lawsuits were increased. Mandatory deadlines for pretrial maneuvering were imposed. Judges were given more authority to ramrod litigation, and they were also encouraged to become more active in settlement negotiations. Lots of rules and laws were implemented, all in an effort to streamline the civil justice system.

Created in this mass of new regulations was a procedure commonly known as "fast-tracking," designed to bring certain cases to trial faster than others. The term "fast-tracking" was instantly added to our legal jargon. The parties involved can request that their case be fast-tracked, but this seldom happens. It's a rare defendant who'll agree to a speedy trip to the courtroom. So the judge has the authority to do it on his own volition. It's usually done when the issues are clear, the facts are sharply defined but hotly in dispute, and all that's needed is a jury's verdict.

Since *Black versus Great Benefit* is my only real case, I want it fast-tracked. I explain this to Booker over coffee one morning. Booker then explains this to Kipler. The justice system at work.

THE DAY AFTER Tyrone Kipler is appointed by the governor, he calls me to his office, the same one I visited not long ago when Harvey Hale occupied it. It's different now. Hale's books and mementos are in the process of being boxed. The dusty shelves are bare. The curtains are pulled open. Hale's desk has been removed, and we chat with each other in folding chairs.

Kipler is under forty, soft-spoken, with eyes that never blink. He's incredibly bright, and widely thought to be on his way to greatness as a federal judge somewhere. I thank him for helping me pass the bar exam.

We chat about this and that. He says kind things about Harvey Hale, but is amazed at the sparsity of his docket.

He's already reviewed every active case, and targeted a few for quick movement. He's ready for some action.

"And you think this Black case should be fast-tracked?" he asks, his words slow and careful.

"Yes sir. The issues are simple. There won't be a lot of witnesses."

"How many depositions?"

I have yet to take my first deposition. "I'm not real sure. Less than ten."

"You'll have trouble with the documents," he says. "Happens every time with insurance companies. I've sued a bunch of them, and they never give you all the paperwork. It'll take us a while to get all the documents you're entitled to."

I like the way he says "us." And there's nothing wrong with it. Among other roles, a judge is an enforcer. It's his duty to assist all parties as they try to obtain pretrial evidence to which they're entitled. Kipler does seem to be a bit partial to our side, though. But I guess there's nothing wrong with that either—Drummond had Harvey Hale on a leash for many years.

"File a motion to fast-track the case," he says, making notes on a legal pad. "The defense will refuse. We'll have a hearing. Unless I hear something very persuasive from the other side, I'll grant the motion. I'll allow four months for discovery, that should be enough time for all depositions, swapping of documents, written interrogatories, etcetera. When discovery is completed, I'll set it for a trial."

I take a deep breath and swallow hard. Sounds awfully fast to me. The image of facing Leo F. Drummond and company in open court, in front of a jury, so soon, is frightening. "We'll be ready," I say, not knowing what the next three steps are. I hope I sound a lot more confident than I feel.

We chat for a while longer, and then I leave. He tells me to call him if I have any questions.

AN HOUR LATER, I almost call him. Waiting for me when I return to my office is a bulky envelope from Tinley Britt. Leo F. Drummond, aside from grieving for his friend, has been busy. The motion machine is in high gear.

He's filed a motion for security of costs, a gentle slap in the faces of me and my clients. Since we're both poor, Drummond claims to be worried about our ability to pay costs. This *might* happen one day if we eventually lose the case and are ordered by the judge to cover the filing expenses incurred by both parties. He's also filed a motion for sanctions asking the court to impose financial penalties against both me and my clients for filing such a frivolous lawsuit.

The first motion is nothing but posturing. The second is downright nasty. Both come with long, handsome briefs properly footnoted, indexed, bibliographed.

As I read them carefully for the second time, I decide that Drummond has filed them to prove a point. Relief is rarely granted on either motion, and I think their purpose is to show me just how much paperwork the troops at Trent & Brent can produce in a short period of time, and over non-issues. Since each side has to respond to the other's motions, and since I wouldn't settle, Drummond is telling me that I'm about to be suffocated with paper.

The phones have yet to start ringing. Deck is downtown somewhere. I'm afraid to guess where he might be prowling. I have plenty of time to play the motion game. I am motivated by thoughts of my sorrowful little client and the screwing that he got. I'm the only lawyer Donny Ray has, and it will take much more than paper to slow me down.

□   □   □   □

I'VE FALLEN into the habit of calling Donny Ray each afternoon, usually around five. After the first call several weeks ago, Dot mentioned how much it meant to him, and I've tried to call each day since. We talk about a variety of things, but never his illness or the lawsuit. I try to remember something funny during the course of the day, and save it for him. I know the calls have become an important part of his waning life.

He sounds strong this afternoon, says he's been out of bed and sitting on the front porch, that he'd love to go somewhere for a few hours, get away from the house and his parents.

I pick him up at seven. We eat dinner at a neighbor-hood barbecue place. He gets a few stares, but seems oblivious. We talk about his childhood, funny stories from the earlier days of Granger when gangs of children roamed the streets. We laugh some, probably the first time in months for him. But the conversation tires him. He barely touches his food.

Just after dark, we arrive at a park near the fairgrounds where two softball games are in progress on adjacent fields. I study them both as I ease through the parking lot. I'm looking for a team in yellow shirts.

We park on a grassy incline, under a tree, far down the right field line. There is no one near us. I remove two folding lawn chairs from my trunk, borrowed from Miss Birdie's garage, and I help Donny Ray into one of them. He can walk by himself, and is determined to do so with as little assistance as possible.

It's late summer, the temperature after dark still hovers around ninety. The humidity is virtually visible. My shirt sticks to me in the center of my back. The badly weath-ered flag on the pole in centerfield does not move an inch.

The field is nice and level, the outfield turf is thick and freshly mowed. The infield is dirt, no grass. There are dugouts, bleachers, umpires, a scoreboard with lights, a concession stand between the two fields. This is the A League, highly competitive slow-pitch softball with teams consisting of very good players. They think they're good anyway.

The game is between PFX Freight, the team with the yellow shirts, and Army Surplus, the team in green with the nickname Gunners on their shirts. And it's serious business. They chatter, hustle like mad, scream encouragement to one another, occasionally ride the opposing players. They dive, slide headfirst, argue with the umpires, throw their bats when they make an out.

I played slow-pitch softball in college, but was never taken with the sport. It appears the object here is to knock the ball over the fence, nothing else matters. This happens occasionally, and the home run struts would shame Babe Ruth. Almost all of the players are in their early twenties, in reasonably good shape, extremely cocky and trimmed out with more garb than the pros use; gloves on all hands, wide wristbands, eye-black smeared across their cheeks, different gloves for fielding.

Most of these guys are still waiting to be discovered. They still have the dream.

There are several older players with larger stomachs and slower feet. They're ludicrous trying to sprint between bases and race for fly balls. You can almost hear muscles popping loose. But they're even more intense than the young guys. They have something to prove.

Donny Ray and I talk little. I buy him popcorn and a soda from the concession stand. He thanks me, and thanks me again for bringing him here.

I pay particular attention to the third baseman for PFX, a muscular player with quick feet and hands. He's fluid and intense, lots of trash-talking to the other team. The inning is over, and I watch as he walks to the fence beside his dugout, and says something to his girl. Kelly smiles, I can see the dimples and teeth from here, and Cliff laughs. He pecks her quickly on the lips, and struts off to join his team as they prepare to hit.

They appear to be a couple of lovebirds. He loves her madly and likes for his guys to see him kiss her. They can't get enough of each other.

She leans on the fence, crutches beside her, a smaller walking cast on her foot. She's alone, away from the bleachers and the other fans. She can't see me up here on the other side of the field. I'm wearing a cap just in case.

I wonder what she'd do if she recognized me. Nothing, probably, except ignore me.

I should be glad that she appears to be happy and healthy and getting along with her husband. The beatings have apparently stopped, and I'm thankful for this. The image of him knocking her around with a bat makes me ill. It's ironic, though, that the only way I'll get Kelly is if the abuse continues.

I hate myself for this thought.

Cliff's at the plate. He crushes the third pitch, sends it well over the lights in left, completely out of sight. It is truly an amazing shot, and he swaggers around the bases, yells something to Kelly as he steps on third. He's a talented athlete, much better than anyone else on the field. I cannot imagine the horror of him swinging a bat at me.

Maybe he's stopped drinking, and maybe in a sobered state he'll stop the mistreatment. Maybe it's time for me to butt out.

After an hour, Donny Ray is ready for sleep. We drive and talk about his deposition. I filed a motion today asking the court to allow me to take his evidentiary deposition, one that can be used at trial, as soon as possible. My client will soon be too weak to endure a two-hour question-and-answer session with a bunch of lawyers, so we need to hurry.

"We'd better do it pretty soon," he says softly as we pull into his driveway.

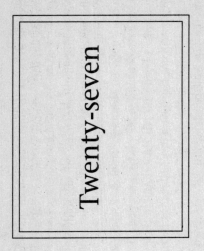

Twenty-seven

THE SETTING MIGHT BE COMICAL IF I wasn't so nervous. I'm sure the casual observer would see the humor, but no one in the courtroom is smiling. Especially me.

I'm alone at my counsel table, the piles of motions and briefs stacked neatly before me. My notes and quick references are on two legal pads, at my fingertips, strategically arranged. Deck is seated behind me, not at the table, where he might be of some benefit, but in a chair just inside the bar, at least three arm-lengths away, so it appears as if I'm alone.

I feel very isolated.

Across the narrow aisle, the table for the defense is rather heavily populated. Leo F. Drummond sits in the center, of course, facing the bench, associates surrounding him. Two on each side. Drummond is sixty years old, an alum of Yale Law, with thirty-six years of trial experience. T. Pierce Morehouse is thirty-nine, Yale Law, a Trent & Brent partner, fourteen years' experience in all courts. B. Dewey Clay Hill the Third is thirty-one, Columbia, not yet a partner, six years' trial experience. M. Alec Plunk Junior is twenty-eight, two years' experience, and is making his initial foray into the case because, I'm sure, he went to Harvard. The Honorable Tyrone Kipler, now presiding, also went to Harvard. Kipler is black. Plunk is too. Harvard-educated black lawyers are not too common in Memphis. Trent & Brent just happened to have one, and so here he is, present no doubt to try and strike a bond with His Honor. And, if things go as expected, we'll one day have a jury sitting over there. Half the registered voters in this county are black, so it's safe to assume the jury will be about fifty-fifty. M. Alec Plunk Junior will be used, it is hoped, to develop some silent harmony and trust with certain jurors.

If the jury happens to have a female Cambodian, there's no doubt in my mind that Trent & Brent will simply reach into the depths of their roster, find themselves another one and bring her to court.

The fifth member of Great Benefit's legal team is Brandon Fuller Grone, pitifully unnumeraled and inexplicably uninitialed. I can't understand why he doesn't proclaim himself B. Fuller Grone, like a real big-firm lawyer. He's twenty-seven, two years out of Memphis State, where he finished number one in his class and left a wide trail. He was a legend when I started law school, and I crammed for first-year exams by using his old outlines.

Ignoring the two years M. Alec Plunk Junior spent clerking for a federal judge, there are fifty-eight years of experience packed tightly around the defense table.

I received my law license less than a month ago. My staff has flunked the bar exam six times.

I performed all this math late last night while digging through the library at Memphis State, a place I can't seem to shake. The law firm of Rudy Baylor owns a grand total of seventeen law books, all leftovers from school, and virtually worthless.

Seated behind the lawyers are two guys with hardnosed corporate looks about them. I suspect they're executives of Great Benefit. One looks familiar. I think he was here when I argued the motion to dismiss. I didn't pay much attention then, and I'm not too terribly concerned about these guys now. I have enough on my mind.

I'm pretty tense, but if Harvey Hale were sitting up there, I'd be a wreck. In fact, I probably wouldn't be here.

However, the Honorable Tyrone Kipler is presiding. He told me on the phone yesterday, during one of our many recent conversations, that this will be his first day on the bench. He's signed some orders and performed some other routine little jobs, but this is the first argument to referee.

The day after Kipler was sworn in, Drummond filed a motion to remove the case to federal court. He's claiming that Bobby Ott, the agent who sold the policy to the Blacks, has been included as a defendant for all the wrong reasons. Ott, we think, is still a resident of Tennessee. He's a defendant. The Blacks, residents of Tennessee, are the plaintiffs. Complete diversity of citizenship between the parties must exist for federal jurisdiction to apply. Ott defeats diversity because, as we allege, he lives here, and for this reason and this reason alone, the case cannot be a federal one. Drummond filed a massive brief in support of his argument that Ott should not be a defendant.

As long as Harvey Hale was sitting, circuit court was the perfect place to seek justice. But as soon as Kipler assumed the case, then truth and fairness could be found only in federal court. The amazing thing about Drummond's motion was the timing. Kipler took it as a personal affront. I agreed with him, for what it was worth.

We're all set to argue the pending motions. In addition

to the request to remove the case, Drummond has his motion for security of costs and motion for sanctions. I took heated issue with his motion for sanctions, so I in turn filed a motion for sanctions, claiming his motion for sanctions was frivolous and mean-spirited. The battle over sanctions becomes a separate war in most lawsuits, according to Deck, and it's best not to get it started. I'm a bit wary of Deck's litigation advice. He knows his limitations. As he's fond of saying, "Anyone can cook a trout. The real art is in hooking the damned thing."

Drummond strides purposefully to the podium. We're going in chronological order, so he addresses his motion for security of costs, a very minor device. He estimates that the cost bill could run as much as a thousand bucks if this thing goes through trial, and, well, darned, he's just worried that neither me nor my clients will be able to handle this in the event we lose and are assessed with costs.

"Let me interrupt you for a second, Mr. Drummond," Judge Kipler says thoughtfully. His words are measured, his voice carries. "I have your motion, and I have your brief in support of your motion." He picks these up and sort of waves them at Drummond. "Now, you've talked for four minutes, and you've said exactly what's right here in black and white. Do you have anything new to add?"

"Well, Your Honor, I'm entitled to—"

"Yes or no, Mr. Drummond? I'm perfectly capable of reading and understanding, and you write very well I might add. But if you have nothing new to add, then why are we here?"

I'm sure this has never happened to the great Leo Drummond before, but he acts as though it's a daily occurrence. "Simply trying to aid the court, Your Honor," he says with a smile.

"Denied," Kipler says flatly. "Move along."

Drummond moves along without missing a step. "Very well, our next motion is for sanctions. We contend——"

"Denied," Kipler says.

"Beg your pardon."

"Denied."

Deck snickers behind me. All four heads at the table across from me lower in unison as this event is duly recorded. I guess they're all writing in bold letters the word DENIED.

"Each side has asked for sanctions, and I'm denying both motions," Kipler says, looking squarely at Drummond. I get my nose thumped a bit in the process.

It's serious business to cut off the debate of a lawyer who talks for three hundred and fifty bucks an hour. Drummond glares at Kipler, who is enjoying this immensely.

But Drummond is a pro with thick skin. He would never let on that a lowly circuit court judge irritates him. "Very well, moving right along, I'd like to address our request to remove this case to federal court."

"Let's do that," Kipler says. "First, why didn't you try to remove this case when Judge Hale had it?"

Drummond is ready for this. "Your Honor, the case was new and we were still investigating the involvement of the defendant Bobby Ott. Now that we've had some time, we're of the opinion that Ott has been included solely to defeat federal jurisdiction."

"So you wanted this case in federal court all along?"

"Yes sir."

"Even when Harvey Hale had it?"

"That's correct, Your Honor," Drummond says earnestly.

Kipler's face tells everyone that he doesn't believe this. Not a single person in the courtroom does either. But it's a minor detail, and Kipler has made his point.

Drummond plows ahead with his argument, completely unfazed. He's seen a hundred judges come and go, and he is remarkably unafraid of any of them. It will be many years, through many trials in many courtrooms, before I will ever feel unintimidated by the guys up there in the black robes.

He talks for about ten minutes, and is in the process of covering the precise points already set forth in his brief when Kipler interrupts. "Mr. Drummond, excuse me, but do you recall just a few minutes ago I asked if you had anything new to present to the court this morning?"

Drummond, hands frozen in place, mouth open, glares at His Honor.

"Do you recall that?" Kipler asks. "Happened less than fifteen minutes ago."

"I thought we were here to argue these motions," Drummond says crisply. The calm voice has a few cracks in it.

"Oh, we certainly are. If you have something new to add, or perhaps a confusing point to clear up, then I'd love to hear it. But you're simply rehashing what I'm holding here in my hand."

I glance to my left and catch a glimpse of some awfully grave faces. Their hero is getting ravaged. It's not pretty.

It hits me that the guys across the aisle are taking this matter a bit more seriously than normal. I was around a lot of lawyers last summer when I clerked for a defense litigation firm, and each case was pretty much like the next. You work hard, bill hard, but take the outcome in stride. There are always a dozen new cases waiting for you.

I sense an air of panic over there, and I'm sure it's not created by my presence. It's standard procedure in insurance litigation for the defense firms to assign two lawyers to a case. They always come in pairs. Regardless of the case, the facts, the issues, the work to be done, you get two of them.

But five? Seems like overkill to me. There's something going on over there. These guys are scared.

"Your request to remove to federal court is denied, Mr. Drummond. The case stays here," Kipler says firmly, already signing his name. This is not well received across the aisle, though they try not to show it.

"Anything else?" Kipler asks.

"No, Your Honor." Drummond gathers his papers, and leaves the podium. I watch out of the corner of my eye. As he steps to the defense table, he gazes for a quick second at the two executives, and I see the unmistakable look of fear in his eyes. Goose bumps cover my forearms and legs.

Kipler switches gears. "Now, the plaintiff has two remaining motions. The first is to fast-track this case, the second to expedite the deposition of Donny Ray Black. The two are sort of related, so, Mr. Baylor, why don't we handle them together?"

I'm on my feet. "Sure, Your Honor." As if I'm going to suggest otherwise.

"Can you wrap it up in ten minutes?"

In light of the carnage I've just witnessed, I immediately indulge another strategy. "Well, Your Honor, my briefs speak for themselves. I really have nothing new to add."

Kipler gives me a warm smile, such a bright young lawyer, then he immediately attacks the defense. "Mr. Drummond, you have objected to the fast-tracking of this case. What's the problem?"

There's a flurry of activity around the defense table, and finally T. Pierce Morehouse rises slowly and adjusts his tie.

"Your Honor, if I may address this, we feel that this

case will take some time to prepare for trial. Fast-tracking it will unduly burden both sides, in our opinion." Morehouse is speaking slowly and choosing his words with caution.

"Nonsense," Kipler says, glaring.

"Sir?"

"I said nonsense. Let me ask you something, Mr. Morehouse. As a defense lawyer, have you ever agreed to the fast-tracking of a lawsuit?"

Morehouse finches and shifts his weight. "Well, uh, sure, Your Honor."

"Fine. Give me the case name and the court it was in."

T. Pierce looks desperately at B. Dewey Clay Hill the Third, who in turn looks longingly at M. Alec Plunk Junior. Mr. Drummond refuses to look up, preferring instead to keep his eyes buried in some awfully important file.

"Well, Your Honor, I'll have to get back with you on that one."

"Call me this afternoon, by three, and if I haven't heard from you by three, then I'll call you. I'm really anxious to hear about this case you agreed to fast-track."

T. Pierce slumps at the waist and exhales as if he's been kicked in the gut. I can almost hear the Trent & Brent computers roaring at midnight as they search vainly for such a case. "Yes, Your Honor," he says weakly.

"Fast-tracking is completely within my discretion, as you know. The plaintiff's motion is hereby granted. The defendant's answer is due in seven days. Discovery will commence then and end one hundred and twenty days from today."

This gets them hopping over at the defense table. Papers are being slid and shoved from one lawyer to the next. Drummond and company whisper and frown at each other. The corporate boys huddle and hunker behind the bar. This is almost fun.

T. Pierce Morehouse squats with his rear hovering just centimeters above the leather seat, arms and elbows braced for the next motion.

"The last motion is to expedite the deposition of Donny Ray Black," His Honor says, looking directly at the defense table. "Surely, you cannot be opposed to this," he says. "Which one of you gentlemen would like to respond?"

Along with this motion, I included a two-page affidavit signed by Dr. Walter Kord, in which he states in plain terms that Donny Ray will not live much longer. Drummond's response was a baffling collection of mishmash, the upshot of which seemed to be that he was simply too busy to be bothered.

T. Pierce slowly unfolds, opens his hands, spreads his arms, starts to say something, when Kipler wades in. "Don't tell me you know more about his medical condition than his own doctor."

"No sir," T. Pierce says.

"And don't tell me you guys are seriously opposed to this motion."

It's quite obvious how His Honor is about to rule, and so T. Pierce deftly moves to middle ground. "Just a matter of scheduling, Your Honor. We haven't even filed our answer yet."

"I know exactly what your answer's gonna be, okay? No surprises there. And you've certainly had time to file everything else. Now, give me a date." He suddenly looks at me. "Mr. Baylor?"

"Any day, Your Honor. Any time." I say this with a smile. Ah, the advantages of having nothing else to do.

All five of the lawyers at the defense table are scrambling for their little black books as if it just might be possible to locate a date on which they can all be available.

"My trial calendar is full, Your Honor," Drummond says without standing. The life of a very important lawyer revolves around only one thing: the trial calendar. Drummond is arrogantly telling Kipler and me that he simply will be too busy in the near future to bother with a deposition.

His four lackeys all frown, nod and rub their chins in unison because they too have trial calendars which, remarkably, are packed and unrelenting.

"Do you have a copy of Dr. Kord's affidavit?" Kipler asks.

"I do," Drummond replies.

"Have you read it?"

"I have."

"Do you question its validity?"

"Well, I, uh—"

"A simple yes or no, Mr. Drummond. Do you question the validity of it?"

"No."

"Then this young man is about to die. Do you agree that we need to record his testimony so that the jury may one day see and hear what he has to say?"

"Of course, Your Honor. It's just that, well, right now, my trial calendar is—"

"How about next Thursday?" Kipler interrupts, and there's dead silence across the aisle.

"Looks fine to me, Your Honor," I say loudly. They ignore me.

"One week from today," Kipler says, watching them with great suspicion. Drummond finds what he's looking for in a file, and studies a document.

"I have a trial starting Monday in federal court, Your

Honor. This is the pretrial order, if you'd like to see it. Estimated length is two weeks."

"Where?"

"Here. Memphis."

"Chances of settlement?"

"Slim."

Kipler studies his schedule for a moment. "What about next Saturday?"

"Sounds fine to me," I add again. Everyone ignores me.

"Saturday?"

"Yes, the twenty-ninth."

Drummond looks at T. Pierce, and it's obvious that the next excuse belongs to him. He rises slowly, holds his black appointment book as if it's gold, says, "I'm sorry, Your Honor, I'm scheduled to be out of town that weekend."

"What for?"

"A wedding."

"Your wedding?"

"No. My sister's."

Strategically, it's to their advantage to postpone the deposition until Donny Ray dies, thus preventing the jury from seeing his withered face and hearing his tortured voice. And there's little doubt that, between the five of them, these guys can orchestrate enough excuses to stall until I die of old age.

Judge Kipler knows this. "The deposition is set for Saturday, the twenty-ninth," he says. "Sorry if it inconveniences the defense, but God knows there are enough of you guys to handle it. One or two won't be missed." He closes a book, leans forward on his elbows, grins down at Great Benefit's lawyers and says, "Now, what else?"

It's almost cruel the way he sneers at them, but he's not mean-spirited. He's just ruled against them on five of six motions, but his reasonings are sound. I think he's per-

fect. And I know there will be other days in this courtroom, other pretrial motions and hearings, and I'm sure
I'll get my share of drubbings.

Drummond is on his feet, shrugging while examining
the spread of paperwork before him on the table. I'm sure
he wants to say something like, "Thanks for nothing,
Judge." Or, "Why don't you just go ahead and hand the
plaintiff a million bucks?" But, as usual, he's the consummate barrister. "No, Your Honor, that will be all for now,"
he says, as if Kipler has in fact helped him immensely.

"Mr. Baylor?" His Honor asks me.

"No sir," I say with a smile. Enough for one day. I've
slaughtered the big boys in my first legal skirmish, and I'm
not pressing my luck. Me and old Tyrone up there have
kicked some ass.

"Very well," he says, rapping his gavel quietly. "Court's
adjourned. And, Mr. Morehouse, don't forget to call me
with the name of that case you agreed to fast-track."

T. Pierce grunts in pain.

Twenty-eight

HE FIRST MONTH IN BUSINESS WITH Deck has produced dismal results. We collected twelve hundred dollars in fees—four hundred from Jimmy Monk, a shoplifter Deck hustled at City Court, two hundred from a DUI case which Deck raked in by some shady and still unexplained method and five hundred from a workers' compensation case Deck stole from Bruiser's office the day we bolted. The remaining hundred bucks was produced when I prepared the wills for a middle-aged couple who stumbled into our office. They were shopping for antiques, took a wrong turn downstairs and happened to catch me napping at my desk. We had a pleasant visit, one thing led to another, and they waited as I typed their wills. They paid me in cash, which I duly reported to Deck, the bookkeeper. My first fee was ethically produced.

We spent five hundred dollars on rent, four hundred on stationery and business cards, about five-fifty on utility hookups and deposits, eight hundred for a leased phone system and the first month's bill, three hundred for the

first installment for desks and a few other furnishings pro-
cured from the landlord downstairs, two hundred on bar
dues, three hundred for assorted and hard to pinpoint
expenses, seven-fifty for a fax machine, four hundred for
the setup and first month's rent on a cheap computer, and
fifty bucks for an ad in a local restaurant guide.

We spent a total of forty-two hundred and fifty dollars,
most of it, thankfully, being initial and nonrecurring expenses. Deck has it figured to the penny. He projects a
monthly overhead, after start-up, of around nineteen hundred dollars. He pretends to be thrilled with the way
things are going.

It's hard to ignore his enthusiasm. He lives at the office.
He's single, far away from his children and living in a city
that's not his home. I don't imagine him spending much
time partying around town. The only diversion he's mentioned is the casinos in Mississippi.

He usually arrives at work an hour or so after me, and
spends most mornings in his office, on the phone, calling
heaven knows who. I'm sure he's soliciting someone, or
checking on accident reports, or just networking with his
contacts. He asks me every morning if I have any typing
for him to do. We realized quickly that he's by far the
better typist, and he's always eager to do my letters and
documents. He breaks his neck to answer the phone, runs
out for coffee, sweeps the office, takes care of the copying
at the printer. Deck has no pride and wants me happy.

He does not study for the bar exam. We've discussed
this once, and he was quick to change the subject.

By late morning, he's usually making plans to go to
some unspecified place and take care of some mysterious
business. I'm certain there's a hive of legal activity, maybe
bankruptcy or municipal court, where he finds folks who
need lawyers. We don't talk about it. He makes his hospital rounds at night.

It was only a matter of days before we sectioned off our little suite of offices and established our turfs. Deck thinks I should spend most of the day patrolling the innumerable halls of justice, trolling for clients. I detect his frustration because I'm not more aggressive. He's tired of my questions about ethics and tactics. It's a rough and tumble world out there, lots of hungry lawyers who know how the cutthroat game is played. Sit on your butt around here all day and you'll starve to death. The good cases don't have a prayer of getting here.

On the other hand, Deck needs me. I have a license to practice. We may split the money, but this is not an equal partnership. He views himself as expendable, and this is why he volunteers for the grunt work. Deck is perfectly willing to chase ambulances and loiter around federal parlors and hide in hospital emergency rooms because he's content with an arrangement that allows him fifty percent. He can't find a better deal anywhere.

It takes just one, he says over and over. You hear that all the time in this business. One big case, and you can retire. That's one reason lawyers do so many sleazy things, like full-color ads in the yellow pages, and billboards, and placards on city buses, and telephone solicitation. You hold your nose, ignore the stench of what you're doing, ignore the snubs and snobbery of big-firm lawyers, because it takes only one.

Deck's determined to find the big one for our little firm.

While he's out shaking down Memphis, I manage to keep busy. There are five small, incorporated municipalities tucked along the Memphis city limits. Each of these little towns has a municipal court, and each has a system of appointing young lawyers to represent indigent criminal defendants in misdemeanor cases. The judges and prosecutors are young and part-time, most went to Memphis State, most work for less than five hundred dollars a month. They have growing practices in the suburbs, and spend a few hours each week parceling out criminal justice. I've visited these folks, smiled and glad-handed them, pled my case about needing some business in their courts, and the results have been mixed. I've now been appointed to represent six indigents, charged with a variety of crimes from drug possession to petty larceny to public profanity. I'll get paid one hundred dollars max for each case, and they should be closed within two months. By the time I meet the clients, discuss their guilty pleas, negotiate with the prosecutors and drive to the suburbs for their court appearances, I'll spend at least four hours on each case. That's twenty-five bucks an hour, before overhead and taxes.

But at least it keeps me busy and brings in something. I'm meeting people, passing out cards, telling my new clients to tell their friends that I, Rudy Baylor, can solve all their legal problems. I shudder to think what problems afflict their friends. It can only be more misery. Divorce, bankruptcy, more criminal charges. The life of a lawyer.

Deck wants to advertise when we can afford it, thinks we ought to declare ourselves personal injury studs and get on cable TV, run our spots early in the morning in order to catch the working classes as they eat breakfast and before they go off to get maimed. He's also been listening to a black rap station, not because he likes the music but because the station is highly rated and, astoundingly, no lawyers have tapped into it. He's found a niche. The rap lawyers!

God help us.

I LIKE TO HANG OUT in the Circuit Clerk's office, flirting with the deputy clerks, feeling my way around. The court files are public record, and their indexes are computerized. Once I figured out the computer, I located several old cases handled by Leo F. Drummond. The most recent is eighteen months old, the oldest, eight years. None involve Great Benefit, but all involve his defense of various insurance companies. All went to trial, all resulted in favorable verdicts for his clients.

I've spent many hours during the past three weeks studying these files, taking pages of notes, making hundreds of copies. With these files, I prepared a lengthy list of interrogatories, written questions one party sends to another to be answered in writing and under oath. There are countless ways to word interrogatories, and I found myself modeling mine after his. I picked my way through the files and made a long list of the documents I plan to request from Great Benefit. In some of the cases, Drummond's opponent was quite good, in others, rather pitiful. But Drummond always seemed to have the upper hand.

I study his pleadings, briefs, motions, his written discovery and his responses to the same received from the plaintiffs. I read his depositions in bed at night. I memorize his pretrial orders. I even read his letters to the court.

AFTER A MONTH of subtle hints and gentle coaxing, I finally persuaded Deck to take a quick road trip to Atlanta. He spent two days there beating the bushes. He spent two nights in very cheap motels. The trip was firm business.

He returned today with the news I'd been expecting. Miss Birdie's fortune is slightly in excess of forty-two thousand dollars. Her second husband did indeed inherit from an estranged brother in Florida, but his share of the estate was less than a million dollars. Before he married Miss Birdie, Anthony Murdine had two other wives, and they produced for him six children. The children, the lawyers and the IRS devoured almost all of the estate. Miss

Birdie got forty thousand, and for some reason left it in the trust department of a large Georgia bank. After five years of fearless investing, the principal has grown by about two thousand dollars.

Only a portion of the court file has been sealed, and Deck was able to dig around and pester enough people to find what we wanted.

"Sorry," he says after he summarizes his findings and hands me copies of some of the court orders.

I'm disappointed, but not surprised.

THE DEPOSITION of Donny Ray Black was originally scheduled to be taken in our new offices, a scenario that caused me no small amount of anguish. Deck and I don't work in squalor, but the offices are small and virtually bare. The windows have no curtains. The toilet in the cramped rest room flushes sporadically.

I'm not ashamed of the place, in fact, it's almost quaint. A modest starter office for a rising young legal eagle. But it's destined to be sneered at by the boys from Trent & Brent. They're accustomed to the finest, and I hate the thought of enduring their snobbery as they slum here in the hinterlands. We don't have enough chairs to crowd around the narrow conference table.

On Friday, the day before the deposition, Dot tells me that Donny Ray is bedridden and cannot leave the house. He's been worrying about the depo, and it's left him weak. If Donny Ray can't leave home, then there's only one place to take it. I call Drummond and he says he cannot agree to move the deposition from my office to the home of my client. Says the rules are the rules, and I'll simply have to postpone it and renotify everyone. He's very sorry about this. He, of course, would like to postpone it until after the funeral. I hang up, then I call Judge Kipler. Minutes later, Judge Kipler calls Drummond, and after a few quick remarks the deposition is moved to the home of Dot and Buddy Black. Oddly, Kipler plans to attend the deposition. This is extremely unusual, but he has his reasons. Donny Ray is gravely ill, and this might be our only chance to depose him. Time, therefore, is crucial. It's not uncommon in depositions for huge fights to erupt between counsel. It's often necessary to run to the phone and locate the judge, who's expected to settle the matter during a conference call. If the judge cannot be found, and if the dispute cannot be worked around, then the deposition will be canceled and rescheduled. Kipler thinks Drummond et al. will attempt to disrupt the proceedings by picking a meaningless fight, then storm off in a huff.

But if Kipler is present, the deposition will proceed without a hitch. He'll rule on objections, and keep Drummond on course. Plus, he says, it's Saturday and he has nothing else to do.

Also, I think he's worried about my performance in my first deposition. He has good reason to be concerned.

Friday night I lost sleep trying to figure out exactly how we could take a deposition in the Black home. It's dark, damp and the lighting is terrible, which is critical because Donny Ray's testimony will be videotaped. The jury must be able to see how tragic he looks. The house has little air conditioning, and the temperature runs in the mid-nineties. It's hard to imagine five or six lawyers and a judge, along with a court reporter and a video camera operator and Donny Ray, all being able to sit together in semicomfort anywhere in the house.

I had nightmares of Dot choking us with vast clouds of blue smoke, and of Buddy in the backyard throwing empty gin bottles at the window. I slept less than three hours.

I arrive at the Black home an hour before the deposition. It seems much smaller, and hotter. Donny Ray is sitting in bed, his spirits improved, claims to be up to the challenge. We've talked about this for hours, and a week ago I gave him a detailed list of my questions and what I expect from Drummond. He says he's ready, and I detect a bit of nervous excitement. Dot is brewing coffee and washing walls. A group of lawyers and a judge are about to visit, and Donny Ray says she's been cleaning all night. Buddy passes through the den as I move a sofa. He's been cleaned and scrubbed. His shirt is white and the tail is tucked in. I cannot imagine the shrill bitching Dot laid on him to obtain this effect.

My clients are attempting to be presentable. I'm proud of them.

Deck arrives with a load of equipment. He's borrowed an obsolete video camera from a friend. It's at least three times larger than most current models. He assures me it will operate properly. He meets the Blacks for the first time. They watch him suspiciously, especially Buddy, who's been relegated to dusting a coffee table. Deck surveys the den, living room and kitchen, and confides quietly to me that there's simply not enough room. He hauls a tripod into the den, kicks over a magazine rack, draws a nasty look from Buddy.

The house is quite cluttered with small tables and footstools and other early sixties furniture covered with cheap knickknack souvenirs. It grows hotter by the minute.

Judge Kipler arrives, meets everyone, starts sweating, and after a minute or so says, "Let's take a look outside." He follows me through the kitchen door, onto the small brick patio. Along the back fence, in the corner opposite Buddy's Fairlane, is an oak tree that was probably planted when the house was built. It provides nice shade. Deck and I follow Kipler through the freshly mowed but unraked grass. He notices the Fairlane with the cats on the windshield as we walk in front of it.

"What's wrong with this?" he asks, under the tree.

Across the back fence is a hedgerow so thick it prevents the view of the adjoining lot. In the middle of this unruly growth are four tall pine trees. They're blocking the morning sun from the east, making this spot under the oak somewhat tolerable, at least for the moment. There's plenty of light.

"Looks fine to me," I say, though in my hugely limited experience I have never heard of an outdoor deposition. I say a quick prayer of thanks for the presence of Tyrone Kipler.

"Do we have an extension cord?" he asks.

"Yes. I brought one," Deck says, already shuffling through the grass. "It's a hundred-footer."

The entire lot is less than eighty feet wide and maybe a hundred feet deep. The front yard is larger than the back, so the rear patio is not far away. Neither is the Fairlane. In fact, it's sitting right there, not far away at all. Claws, the watchcat, is perched majestically on top, watching us warily.

"Let's get some chairs," Kipler says, very much in control. He rolls up his sleeves. Dot, the judge and myself haul the four chairs from the kitchen while Deck struggles with the extension cord and the equipment. Buddy has disappeared. Dot allows us to use her patio furniture, then she locates three stained and mildewed lawn chairs in the utility room.

Within minutes of carrying and lifting, Kipler and I are both soaked with sweat. And we've drawn attention. Some of the neighbors have emerged from under their rocks and are examining us with great curiosity. A black male in jeans hauling chairs to a spot under the Blacks' oak tree? A strange little creature with an oversized head fighting electrical cords which he's managed to wrap around his ankles? What's going on here?

Two female court reporters arrive a few minutes before nine, and, unfortunately, Buddy answers the door. They almost leave before Dot rescues them and leads them through the house to the backyard. Thankfully, they've worn slacks instead of skirts. They chat with Deck about the equipment and the electrical supply.

Drummond and his crew arrive precisely at nine, not a minute early. He brings only two lawyers with him, B. Dewey Clay Hill the Third and Brandon Fuller Grone, and they're dressed like twins: navy blazers, white cotton shirts, starched khakis, loafers. Only their ties refuse to match. Drummond is tieless.

They find us in the backyard, and seem stunned at the surroundings. By now, Kipler and Deck and myself are hot and wet, and don't care what they think. "Only three?" I ask, counting the defense team, but they're not amused.

"You'll sit here," His Honor says, pointing to three kitchen chairs. "Watch those wires." Deck has strung wires and cords all around the tree, and Grone in particular seems apprehensive about electrocution.

Dot and I assist Donny Ray from his bed, through the house, into the yard. He's very weak and trying valiantly to walk on his own. As we approach the oak tree, I watch closely as Leo Drummond sees Donny Ray for the first time. His smug face is noncommittal, and I want to snap something like, "Get a good look, Drummond. See what your client's done." But it's not Drummond's fault. The decision to deny the claim was made by a still undetermined person at Great Benefit long before Drummond knew about it. He just happens to be the nearest person to hate.

We seat Donny Ray in a cushioned patio rocker. Dot

fluffs and pats and takes her time making sure he's as comfortable as possible. His breathing is heavy and his face is wet. He looks worse than usual.

I politely introduce him to the participants: Judge Kipler, both court reporters, Deck, Drummond and the other two from Trent & Brent. He's too weak to shake their hands, so he just nods, tries his best to smile.

We move the camera directly into his face, the lens about four feet away. Deck tries to focus it. One of the court reporters is a licensed videographer, and she's trying to get Deck out of the way. The video will show no one but Donny Ray. There will be other voices off-camera, but his will be the only face for the jury to see.

Kipler places me to Donny Ray's right, Drummond on the left. His Honor himself sits next to me. We all take our places and squeeze our chairs toward the witness. Dot stands several feet behind the camera, watching every move her son makes.

The neighbors are overcome with curiosity and lean on the chain-link fence not twenty feet away. A loud radio down the street blares Conway Twitty, but it's not a distraction, yet. It's Saturday morning, and the hum of distant lawn mowers and hedge trimmers echoes through the neighborhood.

Donny Ray takes a sip of water, and tries to ignore the four lawyers and one judge straining toward him. The purpose of his deposition is obvious: the jury needs to hear from him because he'll be dead when the trial starts. He's supposed to arouse sympathy. Not too many years ago, his deposition would have been taken in the normal manner. A court reporter would record the questions and answers, type up a neat deposition and at trial we would read it to the jury. But technology has arrived. Now, many depositions, especially those involving dying witnesses, are recorded on video and played for the jury. This one will also be taken by a stenographic machine in the standard procedure, pursuant to Kipler's suggestion. This will give all parties and the judge a quick reference without having to watch an entire video.

The cost of this deposition will vary, depending on its length. Court reporters charge by the page, so Deck told me to be efficient with my questions. It's our deposition, we have to pay for it, and he estimates the cost at close to four hundred dollars. Litigation is expensive.

Kipler asks Donny Ray if he's ready to proceed, then instructs the court reporter to swear him. He promises to tell the truth. Since he's my witness, and this is for evidentiary purposes as opposed to the normal unbridled fishing expedition, my direct examination of him must conform to the rules of evidence. I'm jittery, but comforted mightily by Kipler's presence.

I ask Donny Ray his name, address, birthdate, some things about his parents and family. Basic stuff, easy for him and me. He answers slowly and into the camera, just as I've instructed him. He knows every question I'll ask, and most that Drummond might come up with. His back is to the trunk of the oak, a nice setting. He occasionally dabs his forehead with a handkerchief, and ignores the curious stares of our little group.

Although I didn't tell him to act as sick and weak as possible, he certainly appears to be doing it. Or maybe Donny Ray has only a few days left to live.

Across from me, just inches away, Drummond, Grone and Hill balance legal pads on their knees and try to write every word spoken by Donny Ray. I wonder how much they bill for Saturday depositions. Not long into the depo, the navy blazers come off and the ties are loosened.

During a long pause, the back door slams suddenly and Buddy stumbles onto the patio. He's changed shirts, now wears a familiar red pullover with dark stains, and he carries a sinister-looking paper bag. I try to concentrate on my witness, but out of the corner of my eye I can't help but watch as Buddy walks across the yard, eyeing us suspiciously. I know exactly where he's going.

The driver's door to the Fairlane is open, and he backs into the front seat, cats jumping from every window. Dot's face tightens, and she gives me a nervous look. I shake my head quickly, as if to say, "Just leave him alone. He's harmless." She'd like to kill him.

Donny Ray and I talk about his education, work experience, the fact that he's never left home, never registered to vote, never been in trouble with the law. This is not nearly as difficult as I had envisioned last night when I was swinging in the hammock. I'm sounding like a real lawyer.

I ask Donny Ray a series of well-rehearsed questions about his illness and the treatment he didn't receive. I'm careful here, because he can't repeat anything his doctor told him and he can't speculate or give medical opinions. It would be hearsay. Other witnesses will cover this at trial, I hope. Drummond's eyes light up. He absorbs each answer, analyzes it quickly, then waits for the next one. He is completely unruffled.

There's a limit to how long Donny Ray can last, both mentally and physically, and there's a limit to how much of this the jury wants to see. I finish in twenty minutes without drawing the first objection from the other side. Deck winks at me, as if I'm the greatest.

Leo Drummond introduces himself, on the record, to Donny Ray, then explains who he represents and how much he regrets being here. He's not talking to Donny Ray, but rather to the jury. His voice is sweet and condescending, a man of real compassion.

Just a few questions. He gently pokes around the issue of whether Donny Ray has ever left this house, even for a week or a month, to live elsewhere. Since he's above the age of eighteen, they'd love to establish that he left home and thus shouldn't be covered under the policy purchased by his parents.

Donny Ray answers repeatedly with a polite and sickly, "No sir."

Drummond briefly covers the area of other coverage. Did Donny Ray ever purchase his own medical policy? Ever work for a company where health insurance was provided? A few more questions along this line are all met with a soft "No sir."

Though the setting is a bit odd, Drummond has been here many times before. He's probably taken thousands of depositions, and he knows to be careful. The jury will resent any rough treatment of this young man. In fact, it's a wonderful opportunity for Drummond to curry a little favor with the jury, to show some real compassion for poor little Donny Ray. Plus, he knows that there's not much hard information to be gathered from this witness. Why drill him?

Drummond finishes in less than ten minutes. I have no redirect examination. The deposition is over. Kipler says so. Dot is quick to wipe her son's face with a wet cloth. He looks at me for approval, and I give him a thumbs-up. The defense lawyers quietly gather their jackets and briefcases and excuse themselves. They can't wait to leave. Nor can I.

Judge Kipler begins hauling chairs back to the house, eyeing Buddy as he walks in front of the Fairlane. Claws is perched on the middle of the hood, ready to attack. I hope there's no bloodshed. Dot and I assist Donny Ray to the house. Just before we step into the door, I look to my left. Deck is working the crowd on the fence, passing out my cards, just a good ole boy.

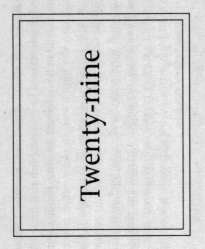

Twenty-nine

THE WOMAN IS ACTUALLY IN MY APART-
ment, standing in the den holding one of my magazines when I open the door. She jumps through
her skin and drops the magazine when she sees me. Her
mouth flies open. "Who are you!?" she almost screams. Who
the hell are you?"

She doesn't appear to be a criminal. "I live here. Who
the hell are you?"

"Oh my gosh," she says, panting with great exaggera-
tion and clutching her heart.

"What're you doing here?" I ask again, really angry.

"I'm Delbert's wife."

"Who the hell is Delbert? And how'd you get in here?"
"Who are you?"

"I'm Rudy. I live here. This is a private residence."

With that, she rolls her eyes quickly around the room,
as if to say, "Yeah, some place."

"Birdie gave me the key, said I could look around."

"She did not!"

"Did too!" She pulls a key out of her tight shorts and
waves it at me. I close my eyes and think of strangling

Miss Birdie. "Name's Vera, from Florida. Just visiting Birdie for a few days."

Now I remember. Delbert is Miss Birdie's youngest son, the one she hasn't seen in three years, never calls, never writes. I can't remember if Vera here is the one Miss Birdie refers to as a tramp, but it would certainly fit. She's around fifty, with the bronze leathered skin of a serious Florida sun worshiper. Orange lips that glow in the center of a narrow copper face. Withered arms. Tight shorts over badly wrinkled but gloriously tanned, spindly legs. Hideous yellow sandals.

"You have no right to be here," I say, trying to relax.

"Get a grip." She walks past me, and I get a nose full of a cheap perfume that's scented with coconut oil. "Birdie wants to see you," she says as she leaves my apartment. I listen as she flops down the stairs in her sandals.

Miss Birdie is sitting on the sofa, arms crossed, staring at another idiotic sitcom, ignoring the rest of the world. Vera is rummaging through the refrigerator. At the kitchen table is another brown creature, a large man with permed hair, badly dyed, and gray, Elvis lamb chop sideburns. Gold-rimmed glasses. Gold bracelets on both wrists. A regular pimp.

"You must be the lawyer," he says as I close the door behind me. Before him on the table are some papers he's been examining.

"I'm Rudy Baylor," I say, standing at the other end of the table.

"I'm Delbert Birdsong. Birdie's youngest." He's in his late fifties and trying desperately to look forty.

"Nice to meet you."

"Yeah, a real pleasure." He waves at a chair. "Have a seat."

"Why?" I ask. These people have been here for hours. The kitchen and adjacent den are heavy with conflict. I can see the back of Miss Birdie's head. I can't tell if she's listening to us, or to the television. The volume is low.

"Just trying to be nice," Delbert says, as if he owns the place.

Vera can't find anything in the fridge, so she decides to join us. "He yelled at me," she whimpers to Delbert. "Told me to get out of his apartment. Really rude like."

"That so?" Delbert asks.

"Hell yes it's so. I live there, and I'm telling you two to stay out. It's a private residence."

He jerks his shoulders backward. This is a man who's had his share of barroom fights. "It's owned by my mother," he says.

"And she happens to be my landlord. I pay rent each month."

"How much?"

"That's really none of your business, sir. Your name is not on the deed to this house."

"I'd say it's worth four, maybe five hundred dollars a month."

"Good. Any other opinions?"

"Yeah, you're a real smartass."

"Fine. Anything else? Your wife said Miss Birdie wanted to see me." I say this loud enough for Miss Birdie to hear, but she doesn't move an inch.

Vera takes a seat and scoots it close to Delbert. They eye each other knowingly. He picks at the corner of a piece of paper. He adjusts his glasses, looks up at me and says, "You been messin' with Momma's will?"

"That's between me and Miss Birdie." I look on the table, and barely see the top of a document. I recognize it as her will, the most current, I think, the one prepared by her last lawyer. This is terribly disturbing because Miss Birdie has always maintained that neither son, Delbert nor Randolph, knows about her money. But the will plainly seeks to dispose of something around twenty million dollars. Delbert knows it now. He's been reading the will for the past few hours. Paragraph number three, as I recall, gives him two million.

Even more disturbing is the issue of how Delbert got his hands on the document. Miss Birdie would never voluntarily give it to him.

"A real smartass," he says. "You wonder why people hate lawyers. I come home to check on Momma, and, damned, she's got a stinking lawyer living with her. Wouldn't that worry you?"

Probably. "I live in the apartment," I say. "A private residence with a locked door. You go in again, I'll call the police."

It hits me that I keep a copy of Miss Birdie's will in a file under my bed. Surely they didn't find it there. I suddenly feel ill with the thought that I, not Miss Birdie, breached such a private matter.

No wonder she's ignoring me.

I have no idea what she put in her previous wills, so there's no way to know whether Delbert and Vera are thrilled to know they might be millionaires, or whether they're angry because they're not getting more. And there's no way in the world I can tell them the truth. I really don't want to, to be honest.

Delbert snorts at my threat to call the cops. "I'll ask you again," he says, a bad imitation of Brando in *The Godfather.* "Have you prepared a new will for my mother?"

"She's your mother. Why don't you ask her?"

"She won't say a word," Vera chimes in.

"Good. Then neither will I. It's strictly confidential."

Delbert does not fully comprehend this, and he's not bright enough to attack from different angles. For all he knows, he might be violating the law.

"I hope you're not meddling, boy," he says as fiercely as possible.

I'm ready to leave. "Miss Birdie!" I call out. She does not move for a second, then slowly raises the remote control and increases the volume.

Fine with me. I point at Delbert and Vera. "If you get near my apartment again, I'll call the police. You understand?"

Delbert forces a laugh first, and Vera quickly giggles too. I slam the door.

I can't tell if the files under my bed have been tampered with. Miss Birdie's will is here, just the way I left it, I think. It's been several weeks since I last looked at it. Everything appears in order.

I lock the door, and wedge a chair under the doorknob.

I'M IN THE HABIT of getting to the office early, around seven-thirty, not because I'm overworked and not because my days are filled with court appearances and office appointments, but because I enjoy a quiet cup of coffee and the solitude. I spend at least an hour each day organizing and working on the Black case. Deck and I try to avoid each other around the office, but at times it's difficult. The phone is slowly beginning to ring more.

I like the stillness of this place before the day starts.

On Monday, Deck arrives late, almost ten. We chat for a few minutes. He wants to have an early lunch, says it's important.

We leave at eleven and walk two blocks to a vegetarian food co-op with a small diner in the rear. We order meatless pizza and orange tea. Deck is very nervous, his face twitching more than usual, his head jerking at the slightest sound.

"Gotta tell you something," he says, barely above a

whisper. We're in a booth. There are no customers at the other six tables.

"We're safe, Deck," I say, trying to assure him. "What is it?"

"I left town Saturday, just after the deposition. Flew to Dallas, then to Las Vegas, checked into the Pacific Hotel."

Oh, great. He's been on a binge, gambling and drinking again. He's broke.

"Got up yesterday morning, talked to Bruiser on the phone, and he told me to leave. Said the feds had followed me from Memphis, and that I should leave. Said someone had been watching me all the way, and that it was time to get back to Memphis. Said to tell you the feds are watching every move because you're the only lawyer who worked for both Bruiser and Prince."

I take a gulp of tea to wet my parched mouth. "You know where . . . Bruiser is?" I say this louder than I planned to, but no one's listening.

"No. I don't," he says, eyes oscillating around the room. "Well, is he in Vegas?"

"I doubt it. I think he sent me to Vegas because he wanted the feds to think that's where he is. Seems a likely spot for Bruiser, so he wouldn't go there."

My eyes won't focus and my brain won't slow down. I think of a dozen questions at once, but I can't ask them all. There are many things I'd like to know, but many things I shouldn't. We watch each other for a moment.

I honestly thought Bruiser and Prince were in Singapore or Australia, never to be heard from again.

"Why did he contact you?" I ask, very carefully.

He bites his lip as if he's about to cry. The tips of the four beaver teeth are visible. He scratches his head as minutes pass. Time, though, is frozen. "Well," he says, even lower, "seems as if they left some money behind. Now they want it."

"They?"

"Sounds like they're still together, doesn't it?"

"It does. And they want you to do what?"

"Well, we never got around to the details. But it sounds like they wanted *us* to help *them* get the money."

"Us?"

"Yeah."

"Me and you?"

"Yep."

"How much money?"

"Never got around to that, but you gotta figure it's a pile or they wouldn't be worried about it."

"And where is it?"

"He didn't give specifics, just said it was in cash, locked up somewhere."

"And he wants us to get it?"

"Right. What I figure is this: the money's hidden somewhere in town, probably close to us right now. The feds haven't found it by now, so they probably won't find it. Bruiser and Prince trust me and you, plus we're semi-legit now, you know, a real firm, not just a couple of street thugs who'd steal the money soon as we saw it. They figure the two of us can load the money in a truck, drive it to them and everybody's happy."

It's impossible to tell how much of this is Deck's speculation and how much was actually presented to him by Bruiser. I don't want to know.

But I'm curious. "And what do we get for our troubles?"

"We never got that far. But it would be plenty. We could take our cut up front."

Deck's already figured it out.

"No way, Deck. Forget it."

"Yeah, I know," he says sadly, surrendering after the first shot.

"It's too risky."

"Yeah."

"Sounds great now, but we could spend time in jail."

"Sure, sure, just had to tell you, you know," he says, waving me off as if he wouldn't dare consider it. A plate of blue corn chips and hummus is placed before us. We both watch the waiter until he's gone.

I have thought about the fact that I'm surely the only person who worked for both fugitives, but I honestly never dreamed the feds would be watching me. My appetite has vanished. My mouth remains dry. Every slight sound causes me to jump.

We both withdraw into our thoughts, and stare at various items on the table. We don't speak again until the pizza arrives, and we eat in complete silence. I'd like to know the details: How did Bruiser contact Deck? Who paid for his trip to Vegas? Is this the first time they've talked since the fugitives disappeared? Will it be the last? Why is Bruiser still concerned about me?

Two thoughts emerge from the fog. One, if Bruiser had enough help tracking Deck's movements to Vegas to know that he was followed the entire way, then he would certainly be able to hire people to fetch the money from Memphis. Why worry about us? Because he doesn't care if we get caught, that's why. Second, the feds haven't bothered to interview me because they didn't want to alert me. It's been much easier to watch me because I haven't been worried about them.

And another thought. There's no doubt my little buddy across the table wanted to open the door to a serious discussion about the money. Deck knows more than he's told me, and he started this conference with a plan. I'm not foolish enough to believe he's giving up this easily.

□ □ □ □

THE DAILY MAIL is an event I'm learning to dread. Deck picks it up after lunch, as usual, and brings it to the office. There's a thick, legal-sized envelope from the good folks at Tinley Britt, and I hold my breath as I rip it open. It's Drummond's written discovery: a set of interrogatories, a series of requests for every document known to the plaintiff or his lawyer and a set of requests for admissions. The latter is a neat device to force an opposing party to admit or deny certain facts set forth in writing within thirty days. If the facts are not denied, then they are forever deemed admitted. The package also contains a notice to take the deposition of Dot and Buddy Black, in two weeks, in my office. Normally, I'm told, lawyers chat for a bit on the phone and agree on the date, time and place for a deposition. This is called professional courtesy, takes about five minutes, and makes things run much smoother. Evidently, Drummond either forgot his manners or has adopted a hardball strategy. Either way, I'm determined to alter the date and place. Not that I have a conflict, it's just for the sake of principle.

Remarkably, the package contains no motions! I'll wait for tomorrow.

Written discovery must be answered within thirty days, and can be filed simultaneously. My own is almost complete, and the receipt of Drummond's spurs me into action. I'm determined to show Mr. Bigshot that I can play the paper war. He'll either be impressed, or he'll once again realize he's competing with a lawyer who has nothing else to do.

IT'S ALMOST DARK when I pull quietly into the driveway. There are two strange cars next to Miss Birdie's Cadillac, two shiny Pontiacs with Avis stickers on the rear bumpers. I hear voices as I tiptoe around the house, hoping to make it to my apartment without being seen.

I stayed at the office until late, mainly because I wanted to avoid Delbert and Vera. I should be so lucky. They're on the patio with Miss Birdie, drinking tea. And there's more company.

"There he is," Delbert says loudly as soon as I'm visible. I break stride, look toward the patio. "Come on over, Rudy." It's more of a command than an invitation.

He rises slowly as I walk over, and another man also gets to his feet. Delbert points to the new guy. "Rudy, this here is my brother Randolph."

Randolph and I shake hands. "My wife June," he says, waving at another aging leathered tart in the Vera vein, this one with bleached hair. I nod at her. She gives me a look that would boil cheese.

"Miss Birdie," I say politely, nodding to my landlord, waving at another aging leathered tart in the Vera vein, this one with bleached hair. I nod at her. She gives me a look that would boil cheese.

"Hello, Rudy," she says sweetly. She's sitting on the wicker sofa with Delbert.

"Join us," Randolph says, waving at an empty chair.

"No thanks," I say. "I need to get to my apartment, see if anybody's been pilfering." I glance at Vera as I say this. She's sitting behind the sofa, away from the rest, probably as far away from June as she can get.

June is between forty and forty-five. Her husband, as I recall, is almost sixty. Now I remember that she's the one Miss Birdie referred to as a tramp. Randolph's third wife. Always asking about the money.

"We haven't been in your apartment," Delbert says testily.

In contrast with his gaudy brother, Randolph is aging with dignity. He's not fat, permed, dyed or laden with gold. He's wearing a golf shirt, bermuda shorts, white socks, white sneakers. Like everybody else, he's tanned. He could easily pass for a retired corporate executive, complete with a plastic little trophy wife. "How long are you gonna be living here, Rudy?" he asks.

"Didn't know I was leaving."

"Didn't say you were. Just curious. Mother says there's no lease, so I'm just asking."

"Why are you asking?" Things are changing rapidly. As of last night, Miss Birdie wasn't discussing the lease.

"Because from now on, I'm helping Mother handle her affairs. The rent is very low."

"It certainly is," June adds.

"You haven't complained, have you, Miss Birdie?" I ask her.

"Well no," she says, waffling, as if maybe she's thought about complaining but just hasn't found the time.

I could bring up mulching and painting and weed-pulling, but I'm determined not to argue with these idiots.

"So there," I say. "If the landlord's happy, then what are you worried about?"

"We don't want Momma taken advantage of," Delbert says.

"Now, Delbert," Randolph says.

"Who's taking advantage of her?" I ask.

"Well, no one, but—"

"What he's trying to say," Randolph interrupts, "is that things are gonna be different now. We're here to help Mother, and we're just concerned about her business. That's all."

I watch Miss Birdie while Randolph is talking, and her face is glowing. Her sons are here, worrying about her, asking questions, making demands, protecting their momma. Though I'm sure she despises her two current daughters-in-law, Miss Birdie is a very content woman.

"Fine," I say. "Just leave me alone. And stay out of my apartment." I turn and walk quickly away, leaving behind many unspoken words and many questions they'd planned to ask. I lock my apartment, eat a sandwich, and in the darkness, through a window, hear them chatter in the distance.

I spend a few minutes trying to reconstruct this gathering. At some point yesterday, Delbert and Vera arrived from Florida, for what purpose I'll probably never know. Somehow they found Miss Birdie's last will, saw that she had twenty million or so to give away and became deeply concerned about her welfare. They learned she had a lawyer living on the premises, and this concerned them too. Delbert called Randolph, who also lives in Florida, and Randolph hurried home, trophy wife in tow. They spent today grilling their mother about everything imaginable, and have now reached the point of being her protectors.

I really don't care. I can't help but chuckle to myself at the entire gathering. Wonder how long it'll take for them to learn the truth.

For now, Miss Birdie is happy. And I'll be happy for her.

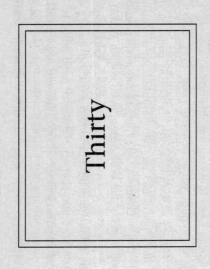

Thirty

I ARRIVE EARLY FOR MY NINE O'CLOCK AP-
pointment with Dr. Walter Kord. A lot of good it
does. I wait for an hour, reading Donny Ray's medical records, which I've already memorized. The waiting
room fills with cancer patients. I try not to look at them.

A nurse comes for me at ten. I follow her to a windowless exam room deep in a maze. Of all the medical specialties, why would anyone choose oncology? I guess someone has to do it.

Why would anyone choose the law?

I sit in a chair with my file and wait another fifteen
minutes. Voices in the hall, then the door opens. A young
man of about thirty-five rushes in. "Mr. Baylor?" he says,
sticking out a hand. We shake as I stand.

"Yes."

"Walter Kord. I'm in a hurry. Can we do this in five
minutes?"

"I guess."

"Let's hurry if we can. I have a lot of patients," he says,

actually managing a smile. I'm very aware of how doctors hate lawyers. For some reason, I don't blame them.

"Thanks for the affidavit. It worked. We've already taken Donny Ray's deposition."

"Great." He's about four inches taller, and stares down at me as if I'm a fool.

I grit my teeth and say, "We need your testimony."

His reaction is typical of doctors. They hate courtrooms. And to avoid them, they sometimes agree to give evidentiary depositions to be used in lieu of their live testimony. They don't have to agree. And when they don't, lawyers occasionally are forced to use a deadly device—the subpoena. Lawyers have the power to have subpoenas issued to almost anyone, including doctors. Thus, to this limited extent, lawyers have power over doctors. This makes doctors despise lawyers even more.

"I'm very busy," he says.

"I know. It's not for me, it's for Donny Ray."

He frowns and breathes heavily as if this is physically very uncomfortable. "I charge five hundred dollars an hour for a deposition."

This doesn't shock me because I expected it. In law school, I heard stories of doctors charging even more. I'm here to beg. "I can't afford that, Dr. Kord. I opened my office six weeks ago, and I'm about to starve to death. This is the only decent case I have."

It's amazing what the truth can do. This guy probably earns a million bucks a year, and he is instantly disarmed by my candor. I see pity in his eyes. He hesitates for a second, maybe he thinks of Donny Ray and the frustration of being unable to help, maybe he feels sorry for me. Who knows?

"I'll send you a bill, okay? Pay whenever you can."

"Thanks, Doc."

"Get with my secretary and pick a date. Can we do it here?"

"Certainly."

"Good. Gotta run."

DECK HAS A CLIENT in his office when I return. She's a middle-aged woman, heavyset, nicely dressed. He waves at me as I walk by his door. He introduces me to Mrs. Madge Dresser, who wants a divorce. She's been crying, and as I lean on the desk next to Deck he slides me a note on a legal pad: "She has money."

We spend an hour with Madge, and it's a sordid tale. Booze, beatings, other women, gambling, bad kids, and she's done nothing wrong. She filed for divorce two years ago and her husband shot out the front window of her lawyer's office. He plays with guns and is dangerous. I glance at Deck when she tells this story. He won't look at me.

She pays six hundred dollars in cash and promises more. We'll file for divorce tomorrow. She's in good hands with the law firm of Rudy Baylor, Deck assures her.

Moments after she leaves, the phone rings. A male voice asks for me. I identify myself.

"Yes, Rudy, this is Roger Rice, attorney. I don't think we've met."

I met almost every lawyer in Memphis when I was looking for work, but I don't remember Roger Rice. "No, I don't think so. I'm new."

"Yeah. I had to call directory assistance to get your number. Listen, I'm in the middle of a meeting with two brothers, Randolph and Delbert Birdsong, and their mother, Birdie. I understand you know these people."

I can just see her sitting there between her sons, grinning stupidly and saying, "How nice."

"Sure, I know Miss Birdie well," I say as if this call has been expected all day.

"Actually, they're next door in my office. I've sneaked off to the conference room so we can talk. I'm working on her will, and, well, there's a pot full of money involved. They said you've tried to do her will."

"That's true. I prepared a rough draft several months ago, but, frankly, she hasn't been inclined to sign it."

"Why not?" He's friendly enough, just doing his job, and it's not his fault they're there. And so I give him the quick version of Miss Birdie's desire to leave her fortune to the Reverend Kenneth Chandler.

"Does she have the money?" he asks.

I simply cannot tell him the truth. It would be terribly unethical for me to divulge any information about Miss Birdie without her prior consent. And the information Rice is after was obtained by me through dubious, though not illegal, means. My hands are tied.

"What has she told you?" I ask.

"Not much. Something about a fortune in Atlanta, money left by her second husband, but when I try to pin her down she gets real flaky."

Certainly sounds familiar. "Why does she want a new will?" I ask.

"She wants to leave everything to her family—kids and grandkids. I just want to know if she has the money."

"I'm not sure of the money. There's a probate court file in Atlanta that's been sealed, and that's as far as I've been."

He's still not satisfied, and I have even less to say. I promise to fax over the lawyer's name and phone number in Atlanta.

THERE ARE EVEN MORE rental cars in the driveway when I arrive home after nine. I'm forced to park in the street, and this really ticks me off. I sneak through the darkness, and go unnoticed by the party on the patio.

It must be the grandkids. From the window of my small den, I sit in the dark, eat a chicken pot pie and listen to the voices. I can distinguish Delbert's and Randolph's. Miss Birdie's occasional cackling rips through the humid air. The other voices are younger.

It must've been handled like a frantic 911 call. Come quick! She's loaded! We thought the old biddy had a few bucks, but not a fortune. One call led to another as the family was tracked down. Come quick! Your name's in the will, and it's got a million dollars next to it. And she's thinking of redrafting it. Circle the wagons. It's time to love Granny.

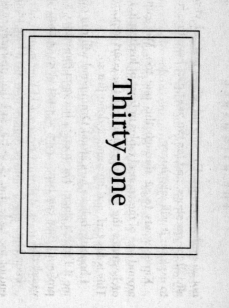

Thirty-one

PURSUANT TO JUDGE KIPLER'S ADVICE, and with his blessing, we gather in his courtroom for Dot's deposition. After Drummond had scheduled it for my office without consulting me, I refused to agree on either the date or place. Kipler stepped in, called Drummond, and the matter was settled within a matter of seconds.

When we deposed Donny Ray, everyone got an eyeful of Buddy sitting in the Fairlane. I've explained to Kipler, and also to Drummond, that I don't think we should depose Buddy. He ain't right, as Dot put it. Poor guy is harmless, and he knows nothing about the insurance mess. Throughout the entire file, there is nothing to indicate Buddy has been remotely involved. I've never heard him utter a complete sentence. I can't imagine him surviving the strain of an extended deposition. Buddy might erupt and maul a few lawyers.

Dot leaves him at home. I spent two hours with her yesterday preparing for Drummond's questions. She'll be around to testify at trial, so this will be a discovery depo, not an evidentiary one. Drummond will go first, ask virtually all the questions, and for the most part have free rein to explore. It will take hours.

Kipler wants to sit through this one too. We gather around one of the counsel tables in front of his bench. He orchestrates the video operator and the court reporter. This is his turf, and he wants it done just so.

I honestly believe he's afraid Drummond will run over me if I'm left alone. The friction between these two is so profound they can barely look at each other. I think it's wonderful.

Poor Dot's hands are shaking as she sits alone at the end of the table. I'm close by, and that probably makes her even more nervous. She's wearing her best cotton blouse, and her best jeans. I explained to her that she did not have to dress up because the video will not be shown to the jury. At trial, however, it will be important for her to wear a dress. God knows what we'll do with Buddy.

Kipler sits on my side of the table, but as far away as possible, next to the video camera. Across is Drummond and only three assistants—B. Dewey Clay Hill the Third, M. Alec Plunk Junior, and Brandon Fuller Grone.

Deck's in the building, down the hallway somewhere, stalking unsuspecting clients. He said he might drop by later.

So there are five lawyers and a judge staring at Dot Black as she raises her right hand and swears to tell the truth. My hands would be trembling too. Drummond flashes a toothy grin, introduces himself to Dot, for the record, and spends the first five minutes in a warm explanation of the purpose of a deposition. We're looking for truth. He won't try to mislead or confuse her. She's free to counsel with her fine lawyer, and on and on. He's in no hurry. The clock is ticking.

The first hour is spent on family history. Drummond,

typically, is impeccably prepared. He moves slowly from one subject to the next—education, employment, homes, hobbies—and asks questions I could never dream of. Most of this is mindless drivel, but it's what good lawyers do in discovery depositions. Ask, dig, peek away, dig some more and who knows what you'll find. And if he found something incredibly juicy, say, a teenage pregnancy, it would be of absolutely no benefit. He couldn't use it at trial. Totally irrelevant. But the rules allow such nonsense, and his client is paying him a truckload of money to plunder in the darkness.

Kipler announces a recess, and Dot makes a mad dash for the hallway. The cigarette is between her lips before she gets through the doors. We huddle near a water fountain.

"You're doing fine," I tell her, and she really is handling it well.

"Sumbitch gonna ask me about my sex life?" she growls.

"Probably." An image of Dot and her husband in bed doing it flashes before me, and I almost have to excuse myself.

She's puffing rapidly as if this one might be the last.

"Can't you stop him?"

"If he gets out of line, I will. But he has the right to ask almost anything."

"Nosy bastard."

The second hour is as slow as the first. Drummond gets into the Blacks' finances, and we learn about the purchase of their home and the purchases of their cars, including the Fairlane, and the purchases of the major appliances. Kipler has had enough at this point, and tells Drummond to move on. We learn a lot about Buddy, his war injuries and his jobs and his pension. And his hobbies, and how he spends his days.

Kipler acidly tells Drummond to try and find something relevant.

Dot informs us she has to go to the rest room. I told her to do this whenever she was tired. She chain-smokes three cigarettes in the hall as I chat with her and dodge the fumes.

Halfway through the third hour, we finally get around to the claim. I have prepared a complete copy of every document relating to the file, including Donny Ray's medicals, and these are in a neat stack on the table. Kipler has reviewed these. We are in the rare and enviable position of having no bad documents. There is nothing we'd like to hide. Drummond can see it all.

According to Kipler, and also to Deck, it's not unusual in these cases for the insurance companies to hide things from their own lawyers. In fact, it's quite common, especially when the company has really dirty laundry and would like to bury it.

During a trial procedure class last year, we studied, in disbelief, case after case where corporate wrongdoers got nailed because they tried to hide documents from their own lawyers.

As we move to the paperwork, I'm terribly excited. So is Kipler. Drummond has already asked for these documents when he filed his written discovery, but I have another week before they're due. I want to watch his face when he sees the Stupid Letter. So does Kipler.

We're assuming he's already seen most, if not all, of what's on the table in front of Dot. He got his documents from his client, I took mine from the Blacks. But many are the same, we think. In fact, I've filed a written request for production of documents identical to his request. When he answers my request, he'll send me copies of documents I've had for three months. The paper trail.

Later, if things go as planned, I'll be introduced to a fresh batch of documents at the home office in Cleveland.

We start with the application and the policy. Dot hands it to Drummond, who reviews it quickly, then hands it to Hill; then it gets passed to Plunk, then, finally, to Grone. This takes time as these damned clowns flip through each page. They've had the damned policy and application for months. But time is money. Then the stenographer makes it an exhibit to Dot's deposition.

The next document is the first letter of denial, and it gets passed along the table. The same procedure is repeated for the other letters of denial. I'm trying desperately to stay awake.

The Stupid Letter is next. I've instructed Dot to simply hand this to Drummond without commenting on its contents. I don't want to tip him off in case he's never seen it. It's difficult for her because the letter is so inflammatory. Drummond takes it, reads it:

Dear Mrs. Black:

On seven prior occasions, this company has denied your claim in writing. We now deny it for the eighth and final time. You must be stupid, stupid, stupid!

Having spent the last thirty years in courtrooms, Drummond is a superb actor. I know instantly that he's never seen this letter. His client didn't include it in the file. It hits him hard. His mouth falls slightly open. Three large wrinkles across his forehead instantly fold together. His eyes squint fiercely. He reads it a second time.

Then he does something that the later wishes he could have avoided. He raises his eyes above the letter and looks at me. I, of course, am staring at him, a rather sneering type of glare that says, "Caught you, big boy."

Then he worsens his agony by looking at Kipler. His Honor is watching every facial move, every blink and twitch, and he catches the obvious. Drummond is stunned by what he's holding.

He recovers nicely, but the damage is done. He passes the letter to Hill, who's half asleep and unaware that his boss is handing him a bomb. We watch Hill for a few seconds, then it hits.

"Let's go off the record," Kipler says. The stenographer stops and the video camera operator clicks off the machine. "Mr. Drummond, it's obvious to me that you've never seen this letter before. And I have a hunch it won't be the first or last document your client tries to conceal. I've sued insurance companies enough to know that documents have a way of getting lost." Kipler leans forward and begins pointing at Drummond. "If I catch you or your client hiding documents from the plaintiff, I'll sanction both of you. I'll impose severe penalties which will include costs and attorney fees at an hourly rate equal to what you bill your client. Do you understand me?"

The sanction route is the only way I'll ever earn two hundred and fifty bucks an hour.

Drummond and crew are still reeling. I can only imagine how the letter will be received by a jury, and I'm sure they're thinking the same.

"Are you accusing me of hiding documents, Your Honor?"

"Not yet." Kipler is still pointing. "Right now, I'm just warning."

"I think you should recuse yourself from this case, Your Honor."

"Is that a motion?"

"Yes sir."

"Denied. Anything else?"

Drummond shuffles papers and kills a few seconds. The tension subsides. Poor Dot is petrified, probably thinks she did something to set off these sparks. I'm a bit stiff myself.

"Back on the record," Kipler says, never taking his eyes off Drummond.

A few questions are asked and answered. A few more documents are passed along the assembly line. We break for lunch at twelve-thirty, and an hour later we're back for the afternoon. Dot is exhausted.

Kipler instructs Drummond, rather severely, to speed things up. He tries, but it's difficult. He's done this for so long, and made so much money in the process, that he could literally ask questions forever.

My client adopts a strategy which I adore. She explains to the group, off the record, that she has a bladder problem, nothing serious, you know, but, hell, she's almost sixty. And anyway, as the day progresses, she needs to visit the ladies' room more often. Drummond, typically, has a dozen questions about her bladder, but Kipler finally cuts him off. So every fifteen minutes, Dot excuses herself and leaves the courtroom. She takes her time.

I'm sure there's nothing wrong with her bladder, and I'm sure she's hiding in a stall smoking like a chimney. The strategy allows her to pace herself, and it eventually wears down Drummond.

At three-thirty, six and a half hours after we started, Kipler declares the depo to be over.

FOR THE FIRST TIME in over two weeks, all the rental cars are gone. Miss Birdie's Cadillac sits alone. I park behind it, in my old space, and walk around the house. No one.

They've finally left. I haven't talked to Miss Birdie since the day Delbert arrived, and we have things to discuss. I'm not angry, I just want to have a chat.

I get to the steps leading to my apartment when I hear a voice. It's not Miss Birdie.

"Rudy, got a minute?" It's Randolph, rising from a rocker on the patio.

I place my briefcase and jacket on the steps and walk over.

"Have a seat," he says. "We need to talk." He seems to be in a wonderful mood.

"Where's Miss Birdie?" I ask. The lights are off in the house.

"She's, uh, well she's gone for a while. Wants to spend some time with us in Florida. She flew out this morning."

"When's she coming back?" I ask. It's really none of my business, but I can't help but ask.

"Don't know. She might not. Look, me and Delbert will be looking after her business from now on. Guess we sorta dropped the ball lately, but she wants us to take care of things.

"And we want you to stay right here. In fact, we gotta deal for you. You stay here, look after the house, tend to the place, and there's no rent."

"What do you mean by tending to the place?"

"General upkeep, nothing heavy. Momma says you've been a good yard boy this summer, just keep doing what you've been doing. We're having the mail forwarded, so that won't be a problem. Anything major comes up, call me. It's a sweet deal, Rudy."

It is indeed. "I'll take it," I say.

"Good. Momma really likes you, you know, says you're a fine young man who can be trusted. Even though you are a lawyer. Ha, ha."

"What about her car?"

"I'm driving it to Florida tomorrow." He hands me a large envelope. "Here are the keys to the house, phone numbers for the insurance agent, alarm company, stuff like that. Plus my address and phone number."

"Where is she staying?"

"With us, near Tampa. We have a nice little house with a guest room. She'll be well taken care of. A couple of my kids are nearby, so she'll have lots of company."

I can see them now, falling all over themselves to be of service to Granny. They'll be happy to smother her for a while, they're just hoping she doesn't live too long. They can't wait for her to die so they'll all be rich. It's very hard to suppress a grin.

"That's good," I say. "She's been a lonely old woman."

"She really likes you, Rudy. You've been good to her."

His voice is soft and sincere, and I'm touched with sadness.

We shake hands and say good-bye.

I SWAY IN THE HAMMOCK, swat mosquitoes, stare at the moon. I seriously doubt if I'll ever see Miss Birdie again, and I feel the odd loneliness of losing a friend. These people will keep her under their thumb until she's dead, making damned sure she doesn't get a chance to monkey around with her will. I feel a twinge of guilt for knowing the truth about her wealth, but it's a secret I cannot share.

At the same time, I can't help but smile at her fate. She's out of this lonely old house and now surrounded by her family. Miss Birdie is suddenly the center of attention, a position she craves. I think of her at the Cypress Gardens Senior Citizens Building, the way she worked the crowd, led the songs, made the speeches, fussed over Bosco and the other geezers. She has a heart of gold, but she also hungers for attention.

I hope the sunshine's good for her. I pray she's happy. I wonder who'll take her place at Cypress Gardens.

Thirty-two

I SUSPECT THE REASON BOOKER CHOSE this fancy restaurant is that he has good news. The table is covered with silver. The napkins are linen. He must have a client who's paying for this.

He arrives fifteen minutes late, very unlike him, but he's a busy man these days, and the first words out of his mouth are "I passed it." We sip our water while he goes through an animated history of his appeal to the Board of Law Examiners. His exam was regraded, his score was raised three points and he's now a full-fledged lawyer. I've never seen him smile so much. Only two others from our group had successful appeals. Sara Plankmore was not one of them. Booker's heard a rumor that her score was miserable, and that her job with the U.S. Attorney's office might be in jeopardy.

Against his wishes, I order a bottle of champagne, and I instruct the waiter to hand me the bill. You just can't hide money.

The food arrives, incredibly tiny slivers of salmon but beautifully presented, and we admire it for a while before eating. Shankle's got Booker running in thirty directions, fifteen hours a day, but Charlene is a woman of great patience. She realizes he must make sacrifices in these early years to reap rewards later. For the moment, I'm thankful I have no wife and kids.

We talk about Kipler, who's talked a bit to Shankle and word has leaked. Lawyers have great trouble keeping secrets. Shankle mentioned to Booker that Kipler mentioned to him that this buddy, me, has a case that could be worth millions. Evidently, Kipler has become convinced that I've got Great Benefit nailed to a rock, and it's simply a question of how much the jury will give us. Kipler is determined to get me to the jury in one piece.

This is splendid gossip.

Booker wants to know what else I'm doing. It sounds as though Kipler might have also mentioned something to the effect that I apparently have little else to do, or something like this.

Over cheesecake, Booker says he has some files that I might want to look at. He explains. The second-largest furniture store in Memphis is called Ruffin's, a black-owned company with stores all over town. Everybody knows Ruffin's, mainly because they saturate late night TV with ads screaming out all sorts of bargains for no money down. They do about eight million a year, Booker says, and Marvin Shankle is their lawyer. They extend their own credit, and they have lots of bad debts. It's the nature of their business. The Shankle firm has become burdened with hundreds of collection files for Ruffin's customers.

Would I like a few of these files?

Collection law is not the reason bright young students flock to law school. The defendants are past-due folks who bought cheap furniture to begin with. The client doesn't want the furniture back, just the money. In most cases, no answer is filed, no appearance is made by the defendant, so the lawyer has to attach personal assets, or wages. This can be dangerous. Three years ago a Memphis lawyer was shot but not killed by an angry young man whose paycheck had just been garnished.

To make it work, a lawyer needs a bunch of files because each suit is worth but a few hundred dollars. The law allows the recovery of attorney fees and costs.

It's grimy work, but, and this is the reason Booker is offering, fees can be squeezed from these files. Modest fees, but volume can produce enough to pay overhead and buy groceries.

"I can send over fifty," he says, "along with the necessary forms. And I'll help you get the first batch filed. There's a system."

"What's the average fee?"

"It's hard to say, because on some files you won't collect a dime. They've either skipped town or they'll go bankrupt. But on the average, I'd say a hundred dollars a file."

A hundred times fifty is five thousand dollars.

"The average file takes four months," he explains, "and if you want, I can send over twenty or so a month. File them all at one time, same court, same judge, returnable the same day in the future, and you make only one court appearance. Take the defaults, go from there. It's ninety percent paperwork."

"I'll do it," I say. "Anything else you guys want to unload?"

"Maybe. I'm always looking."

The coffee arrives, and we backslide into what lawyers do best—talking about other lawyers. In our case, we gossip about our classmates and how they're faring in the real world.

Booker has been revived.

□ □ □

DECK CAN SNEAK through the tiniest crack in an open door without making a sound. He does this to me all the time. I'll be at my desk, deep in thought or buried in one of the rare files I own, and, Presto!, here's Deck! I wish he would knock, but I hate to fuss at him.

Here he is, suddenly standing in front of my desk, holding an armload of mail. He notices the stack of shiny new collection files on the corner. "What's this?" he asks. "Work."

He picks up a file. "Ruffin's?"

"Yes sir. We're now counsel for the second-largest furniture store in Memphis."

"It's a collection file," he says in disgust, as if he's dirtied his hands. This from a man who dreams of more paddle wheel disasters.

"It's honest work, Deck."

"It's beating your head against a wall."

"Go chase an ambulance."

He drops my mail on the desk and vanishes as silently as he appeared. I take a deep breath and tear open a heavy envelope from Trent & Brent. It's a stack of legalsized papers, at least two inches thick.

Drummond has answered my interrogatories, denied my requests for admissions and produced some of the documents I requested. It'll take hours to plow through this, and even more time to figure out what he hasn't produced.

Of particular importance are his answers to my interrogatories. I have to depose a corporate spokesman, and he designates a gentleman by the name of Jack Underhall at the corporate headquarters in Cleveland. I also asked for the official titles and addresses of several Great Benefit employees, names I found repeatedly in Dot's paperwork.

Using a form Judge Kipler gave me, I prepare a notice to depose six people. I pick a date a week away, knowing full well that Drummond will have a conflict. This is what he did to me with Dot's depo, and this is how the game is played. He'll run to Kipler, who'll have little sympathy.

I'm about to spend a couple of days in Cleveland at the corporate headquarters of Great Benefit. This is not something I want to do, but I have no choice. It will be an expensive trip—travel, lodgings, food, court reporters. Deck and I have not discussed it yet. Frankly, I've been waiting for him to reel in a quickie car wreck.

The Black case has now moved into the third expandable file. I keep it in a cardboard box on the floor next to my desk. I look at it many times each day and ask myself if I know what I'm doing. Who am I to dream of a huge courtroom victory? Of handing the great Leo F. Drummond a humbling defeat?

I've never said a word to a jury.

DONNY RAY was too weak to talk on the phone an hour ago, so I drive to their house in Granger. It's late September, and I don't remember the exact date, but Donny Ray was first diagnosed over a year ago. Dot's eyes are red when she comes to the door. "I think he's about gone," she says through sniffles. I didn't think it was possible for him to look worse, but his face is even paler and more fragile. He's asleep in the unlighted room. The sun is low to the west, and the shadows fall in perfect rectangles across the white sheets on his narrow bed. The TV is off. The room is silent.

"He hasn't eaten a bite today," she whispers as we stare down at him.

"How much pain?"

"Not too bad. I've given him two shots."

"I'll sit for a while," I whisper as I ease into a folding chair. She leaves the room. I hear her sniffing in the hallway.

He could be dead for all I know. I concentrate on his chest, wait for it to move up and down slightly, but I can't detect anything. The room gets darker. I turn on a small lamp on a table near the door, and he moves slightly. His eyes open, then close.

So this is how the uninsured die. In a society filled with wealthy doctors and gleaming hospitals and state-of-the-art medical gadgetry and the bulk of the world's Nobel winners, it seems outrageous to allow Donny Ray Black to wither away and die without proper medical care.

He could've been saved. By law, he was solidly under the umbrella, leaky as it was, of Great Benefit when his body became afflicted with this terrible disease. At the moment he was diagnosed, he was covered by a policy which his parents paid good money for. By law, Great Benefit had a contractual obligation to provide medical treatment.

One day very soon I hope to meet the person responsible for this death. He or she might be a lowly claims handler who was simply following orders. He or she might be a vice president who gave the orders. I wish I could take a picture of Donny Ray right now, then hand it to this pathetic person when we finally meet.

He coughs, moves again, and I think he's trying to tell me that he's still alive. I turn off the light and sit in darkness.

I'm alone and outgunned, scared and inexperienced, but I'm *right*. If the Blacks do not prevail in this lawsuit, then there is nothing fair with the system.

A streetlight comes on somewhere in the distance, and a stray ray flickers through the window and across Donny

Ray's chest. It's moving now, up and down slightly. I think he's trying to wake.

There will not be many more moments sitting in this room. I stare at his bony frame barely visible under the sheets, and I vow revenge.

Thirty-three

I T IS AN ANGRY JUDGE WHO TAKES THE bench with his black robe settling around him. It's a Motion Day, a time set aside for brief, nonstop arguments on multitudes of motions in dozens of cases. The courtroom is filled with lawyers.

We go first because Judge Kipler is perturbed. I filed a notice to take the deposition of six employees of Great Benefit, beginning next Monday in Cleveland. Drummond objected, claiming he, of course, is unavailable because of his sacred trial calendar. But not only is he tied up, all six of the prospective deponents are too busy to be bothered. All six!

Kipler arranged a phone conference with Drummond and me, and things went badly, at least for the defense. Drummond has legitimate courtroom obligations, and he faxed over the pretrial order from the other case to prove this. What angered the judge was Drummond's assertion that it would be two months before he could spare three days in Cleveland. Furthermore, the six employees up there are very busy people, and it might be months before they could all be caught at one place.

Kipler ordered this hearing so he could formally chew Drummond's ass, and get it on the record. Since I've talked to His Honor every day for the past four, I know precisely what's about to happen. It will be ugly. I won't have to say much.

"On the record," Kipler snaps at the court reporter, and the clones across the aisle lurch forward and hover over their legal pads. Four, today. "In case number 214668, *Black versus Great Benefit*, the plaintiff has noticed the deposition of the corporate designee, along with five other employees of the defendant, to be taken next Monday, October 5, at the corporate offices in Cleveland, Ohio. Defense counsel, not surprisingly, has objected on the grounds that there's a scheduling conflict. Correct, Mr. Drummond?"

Drummond stands slowly, "Yes sir. I have previously submitted to the court a copy of a pretrial order for a case in federal court starting Monday. I am lead counsel for the defense in that case."

Drummond and Kipler have had at least two raging arguments on this issue, but it's important to do it now for the record.

"And when might you be able to work this into your schedule?" Kipler asks with heavy sarcasm. I'm sitting alone at my table. Deck is not here. There are at least forty lawyers seated behind me in the benches, all watching the great Leo F. Drummond in the process of getting trashed. They must be wondering who I am, this unknown rookie who's so good he's got the judge fighting for him.

Drummond shifts his weight from one foot to the next, then says, "Well, Your Honor, I'm really booked. It might be——"

"I believe you said two months. Did I hear this correctly?" Kipler asks this as if he's in shock, that surely no single lawyer is that busy.

"Yes sir. Two months."

"And these are trials?"

"Trials, depositions, motions, appellate arguments. I'll be happy to show you my calendar."

"At the moment, I can't think of anything worse, Mr. Drummond," Kipler says.

"Here's what we're gonna do, Mr. Drummond, and please listen carefully because I'm going to put this in writing, in the form of an order. I remind you, sir, that this case is on the fast-track, and in my court this means no delays. These six depositions will commence first thing Monday morning in Cleveland." Drummond sinks into his seat and starts scribbling. "And if you can't make it, I'm sorry. But at last count, you have four other lawyers tending to this case—Morehouse, Plunk, Hill and Grone, all of whom, I might add, have much more experience than Mr. Baylor who, I believe, got his license this past summer. Now, I realize you guys can't send just one lawyer to Cleveland, realize it must be done with no less than two, but I'm sure you can arrange to have enough lawyers present to adequately represent your client."

These words singe the air. The lawyers behind me are incredibly still and quiet. Many, I sense, have been waiting for this for years.

"Furthermore, the six employees listed in the notice will be available Monday morning, and they shall remain available until Mr. Baylor releases them. This corporation has qualified to do business in Tennessee. I have jurisdiction over it in this matter, and I'm ordering these six individuals to cooperate fully."

Drummond and company sink lower and write faster.

"Furthermore, the plaintiff has requested files and documents." Kipler pauses for a second, glares down at the defense table. "Listen to me, Mr. Drummond, no hanky-panky with the documents. I insist on full disclosure, full cooperation. I will be close to my phone Monday and Tuesday, and if Mr. Baylor calls and says he's not getting the documents to which he's entitled, then I'll get on the phone and make sure he does. Do you understand me?"

"Yes sir," Drummond says.

"Can you make your client understand this?"

"I think so."

Kipler relaxes a bit, takes a breath. The courtroom is still perfectly quiet. "On second thought, Mr. Drummond, I'd like to see your trial calendar. That is, if you don't mind."

Drummond offered it just minutes ago, so there's no way he can decline now. It's a thick, black, leather-bound chronicle of the life and times of a very busy man. It's also very personal, and I suspect Drummond didn't really mean to offer it.

He carries it proudly to the bench, gives it to His Honor and waits. Kipler flips rapidly through the months without reading the specifics. He's looking for empty days. Drummond hangs around the podium in the center of the courtroom.

"I notice here you have nothing scheduled for the week of February 8."

Drummond walks to the bench and looks at his book while Kipler holds it over the edge. He nods affirmatively without saying anything. Kipler hands him the book, and Drummond returns to his seat.

"The trial of this case is hereby set for Monday, February 8," His Honor declares. I swallow hard, take a deep breath, try to look confident. Four months sounds like plenty of time, a nice distance away, but for one who's never tried even a simple fender-bender it's terribly frightening. I've memorized the file a dozen times. I've memorized the rules of procedure and the rules of evidence. I've read countless books on how to handle discovery and how to pick juries and how to cross-examine witnesses and how to win trials; but I don't know beans about how things will unfold in this courtroom on February 8.

Kipler dismisses us, and I quickly gather my mess and leave. As I exit, I notice quite a few stares from the gallery of lawyers waiting their turn.

Who is this guy?

THOUGH HE'S NEVER actually confessed it, I now know that Deck's closest acquaintances are a couple of two-bit private dicks he met while working for Bruiser. One, Butch, is an ex-cop who shares Deck's affinity for casinos. They travel to Tunica once or twice a week for poker and blackjack.

Butch somehow located Bobby Ott, the debit agent who sold the policy to the Blacks. He found him in the Shelby County Penal Farm serving ten months for bad checks. Further investigation revealed Ott is freshly divorced and bankrupt.

Deck expressed dismay at having missed this fish. Ott has world-class legal problems. So many fees to be earned.

A JUNIOR ADMINISTRATOR of some variety at the penal farm collects me after a thorough search of my briefcase and my body by a bulky guard with thick hands. I'm led to a room near the front of the main building. It's square with cameras mounted high in each corner. A partition down the center keeps the convicts away from their guests. We'll talk through a screen, which is fine with me. I hope this visit is extremely brief. After five minutes, Ott is brought in from the other side. He's around forty, wire-rimmed glasses, Marine haircut, slight build, and wearing navy prison overalls. He studies me carefully as he takes his seat across the partition. The guard leaves and we are alone.

I slide a business card through an opening at the bottom of the screen. "My name's Rudy Baylor. I'm an attorney." Why does this sound so ominous?

He takes it well, tries to smile. This guy once made his living knocking on doors and selling cheap insurance to poor folks, so, in spite of his obvious bad luck, he's at heart a friendly sort, the type who could talk his way into homes.

"Nice to meet you," he says out of habit. "What brings you here?"

"This," I say, pulling a copy of the lawsuit from my briefcase. I slide it through the opening. "It's a lawsuit I've filed on behalf of some of your former customers."

"Which ones?" he asks, taking the lawsuit, looking at the cover sheet, which is a summons.

"Dot and Buddy Black, and their son Donny Ray."

"Great Benefit huh?" he says. Deck has explained to me that many of these street agents represent more than one company. "Mind if I read this?"

"Sure. You're named as a defendant. Go ahead."

His voice and movements are very deliberate. No wasted energy here. He reads very slowly, flipping pages with great reluctance. Poor guy. He's been through a divorce, lost everything else in a bankruptcy, now sits in jail on felony convictions, and I've just trotted my cocky ass in here and sued him for another ten million.

But he seems unfazed. He finishes and places it on the counter in front of him. "You know I'm protected by the bankruptcy court," he says.

"Yes, I know." Not really. According to court records, he filed for bankruptcy in March, actually two months before I did, and has now been discharged. An old BK filing will not always prevent future lawsuits, but the point is moot. This guy's as broke as a refugee. He's immune. "We were forced to include you as a defendant because you sold the policy."

"Oh, I know. You're just doing your job."

"That's it. When do you get out?"

"Eighteen days. Why?"

"We might want to take your deposition."

"In here?"

"Maybe."

"What's the rush? Lemme get out, and I'll give you a deposition."

"I'll think about it."

This little visit is a brief vacation for him, and he's in no hurry to see me go. We chat about prison life for a few minutes, and I start looking for the door.

I'VE NEVER BEEN UPSTAIRS in Miss Birdie's house, and it's just as dusty and mildewed as the downstairs. I open the door to each room, flip on the light switch, look around hurriedly, then turn off the light and close the door. The floor in the hallway creaks as I walk on it. There's a narrow stairway to a third level, but I'm skittish about going up there.

The house is much larger than I thought. And much lonelier. It's hard to imagine her living here alone. I feel a sense of profound guilt for not spending more time with her, for not sitting with her through her sitcoms and TV revival services, for not eating more of her turkey sandwiches and drinking more of her instant coffee.

The downstairs appears just as free of burglars as the upstairs, and I lock the patio doors behind me. It's odd now that she's gone. I do not remember being comforted by her presence, but it was always nice to know she was here, in the big house, just in case I needed anything. Now I feel isolated.

In the kitchen, I stare at the telephone. It's an old rotary model, and I almost dial Kelly's number. If she answers, I'll think of something to say. If he answers, I'll hang up. The call can be traced to this house, but I don't live here.

I thought about her more today than I did yesterday. More this week than last.

I need to see her.

Thirty-four

I'M RIDING TO THE BUS TERMINAL WITH Deck in his minivan. It's early Sunday morning. The weather is clear and beautiful, the first hint of autumn in the air. Mercifully, the stifling humidity is behind us for a few months. Memphis is a lovely place in October.

A round-trip plane ticket to Cleveland costs just under seven hundred dollars. We figured a room in an inexpensive yet safe motel will be forty dollars a night, food will be minimal since I can get by with little. We're doing the cheapest court reporter I talked to in Cleveland gets a hundred dollars a day for showing up, two dollars a page for taking down and transcribing the testimony. It's not unusual for these depositions to run for a hundred pages or more. We'd like to video them, but it's out of the question.

So, it seems, is the idea of air travel. The law firm of Rudy Baylor simply cannot afford to fly me to Cleveland. There's no way I'd risk the Toyota on the open road. If it stopped, then I'd be stranded and the depositions postponed. Deck sort of offered his minivan, but I wouldn't trust it for a thousand miles either.

Greyhound is quite reliable, though awfully slow. The buses eventually get there. It's not my first choice, but what the hell. I'm in no great hurry. I can see some of the countryside. We're saving some valuable money. I've thought of lots of reasons.

Deck drives and says little. I think he's somewhat embarrassed because we can't afford better. And he knows he should be going too. I'm about to confront hostile witnesses and lots of fresh documents which will need instant review. It would be nice to have another mind close by.

We say good-bye in the parking lot by the station. He promises to take care of the office and hustle up some business. I have no doubt that he'll try. He drives off, in the direction of St. Peter's.

I've never been on a Greyhound before. The terminal is small but clean, bustling with Sunday morning travelers, most of whom are old and black. I find the proper clerk and receive my reserved ticket. It costs my firm $139.

The bus leaves on time at eight, and heads west into Arkansas, then north to St. Louis. Luckily, I manage to avoid the nuisance of someone sitting next to me.

The bus is almost full, only three or four empty seats. We're scheduled to be in St. Louis in six hours, Indianapolis by eleven tonight. That's fifteen hours. Cleveland by seven P.M., The depositions start at nine in the morning.

I'm sure my opponents at Trent & Brent are still sleeping, and will arise to a lovely breakfast, then the Sunday paper on the patio with their wives, perhaps church for a couple of them, then a nice lunch and a round of golf. Around five or so, their wives will drive them to the airport, where they'll be kissed good-bye properly and sent off together in the first-class section. An hour later, they'll land in Cleveland, no doubt be met by a gofer from Great Benefit who'll chauffeur them to the finest hotel in the city. After a delicious dinner, with drinks and wine, they'll gather in a plush executive conference room and plot against me until late. About the time I check into a Motel 6 or whatever, they'll be retiring to bed, refreshed, prepared, ready for war.

THE GREAT BENEFIT BUILDING is in an affluent Cleveland suburb, one created by white flight. I explain to my cabdriver that I want an inexpensive motel in the vicinity, and he knows exactly where to go. He stops in front of the Plaza Inn. Next door is a McDonald's, across the street, a Blockbuster Video. It's nothing but sprawl—strip shops, fast food, flashing billboards, shopping centers, cheap motels. A mall can't be far away. It appears safe.

There are plenty of vacant rooms, and I pay thirty-two dollars, cash, for one night. I ask for a receipt because Deck instructed me to.

At two minutes after midnight, I get into bed, stare at the ceiling and realize, among other things, that, other than the motel clerk, not a single person in this world knows where I am. There's no one to call and check in with.

Of course, I can't go to sleep.

EVER SINCE I BEGAN to hate Great Benefit, I've had a mental image of their corporate headquarters. I could see a tall, modern building with lots of shiny glass, a fountain by the front entrance, flagpoles, the corporate name and logo emblazoned in bronze. Wealth and corporate prosperity everywhere.

Not exactly. The building is easy enough to find because the address is in bold black letters on a concrete entrance: 5550 Baker Gap Road. But the name Great Benefit is nowhere to be seen. In fact, the building is unidentifiable from the street. No fountains or flagpoles, just a huge five-story hodgepodge of square block buildings wedged together and seemingly built into one another. It's all very modern and unbelievably ugly. The exterior is white cement and black-tinted windows.

Thankfully, the front entrance is marked, and I step into a small foyer with a few plastic potted plants along one wall and a cute receptionist against another. She wears a chic headset with a tiny felt-tipped wire curved around her jaw and sticking just inches from her lips. On the wall behind her are the names of three nondescript companies: PinnConn Group, Green Lakes Marine and Great Benefit Life Insurance. Which owns which? Each has a self-conscious logo etched in bronze.

"My name is Rudy Baylor, and I'm supposed to see a Mr. Paul Moyer," I say politely.

"One moment please." She punches a button, waits, then says, "Mr. Moyer, a Mr. Baylor here to see you." She never stops smiling.

His office must be close, because I wait less than a minute before he's all over me with handshakes and how-are-you's? I follow him around a corner, down a hallway to an elevator. He's almost as young as I am, talks incessantly about nothing. We exit on four, and I'm already hopelessly lost in this architectural horror. The floors are carpeted on the fourth floor, the lights are dimmer, the walls have paintings. Moyer rattles away as we walk along a hallway, then pulls open a heavy door, and shows me to my place.

Welcome to the Fortune 500. It's a boardroom, long and wide with a shiny oblong table in the center and at least fifty chairs around it. Leather chairs. A glistening chandelier hangs just a few feet from the center of the table. In a corner to my left is a bar. To my right is a coffee tray with biscuits and bagels. Around the food is a cluster of conspirators, at least eight of them, every one in a dark suit, white shirt, striped tie, black shoes. Eight against one. The nervous tremors in my major organs become serious quakes. Where is Tyrone Kipler when I need him? Right now, even Deck's presence would be comforting.

Four of them are my buddies from Trent & Brent. One is a familiar face from the hearings in Memphis, the other three are strangers, and they all instantly clam up when they realize I've arrived. For a second, they stop sipping and chewing and talking, and just gawk at me. I've interrupted a very serious conversation.

T. Pierce Morehouse recovers first. "Rudy, come on in," he says, but only because he has to. I nod to B. Dewey Clay Hill the Third and to M. Alec Plunk Junior and to Brandon Fuller Grone, then shake hands with the four new acquaintances as Morehouse spits out their names, names that I immediately forget. Jack Underhall is the familiar face from the skirmishes in Kipler's courtroom. He's one of the in-house lawyers for Great Benefit, and the designated corporate spokesman.

My opponents look bright-eyed and fresh, lots of sleep last night after a quick flight up and a relaxing dinner. They're all creased and starched, just as if their clothes came out of their closets this morning and not a travel bag. My eyes are red and tired, my shirt wrinkled. But I have more important things on my mind.

The court reporter arrives, and T. Pierce herds us to the end of the table. He points here and there, saving the end seat for the witnesses, pondering for a second about just exactly how to seat everyone. He finally figures it out. I dutifully take my chair and try to pull it closer to the table. It's a strain, because the damned thing weighs a ton. Across from me, at least ten feet away, the four boys from Trent & Brent open their briefcases with as much noise as they can create—latches clicking, zippers zipping, files snatched out, papers ruffling. Within seconds, the table is littered with piles of paper.

The four corporate suits are loitering behind the court reporter, uncertain about their next move and waiting for T. Pierce. His papers and pads finally arranged, he says, "Now, Rudy, we thought we'd start with the deposition of our corporate designee, Jack Underhall."

I anticipated this, and I've already decided against it. "No, I don't think so," I say, somewhat nervously. I'm trying desperately to act cool in spite of being on strange turf and surrounded by enemies. There are several reasons I don't want to start with the corporate designee, not the least of which is that it's what they want. These are my depositions, I keep telling myself.

"Beg your pardon?" T. Pierce says.

"You heard me. I want to start with Jackie Lemancyzk, the claims handler. But first I want the file."

The heart of any bad-faith case is the claim file, the collection of letters and documents kept by the claims handler in the home office. In a good bad-faith case, the claim file is an amazing historical account of one screwup after another. I'm entitled to it, and should've received it ten days ago. Drummond pled his innocence, said his client was dragging its feet. Kipler stated unequivocally in a court order that the file must be waiting for me first thing this morning.

"We think it would be best to start with Mr. Underhall," T. Pierce says without authority.

"I don't care what you think," I say, sounding remarkably perturbed and indignant. I can get by with this because the judge is my buddy. "Shall we call the judge?" I ask, taunting, a real swaggering ass.

Though Kipler is not here, his presence still dominates. His order states, in very plain terms, that the six witnesses I've requested are to be available at nine this morning, and that I have sole discretion as to the order in which they're deposed. They must remain on call until I release them. The order also leaves the door open for additional depos once I start asking questions and digging deeper. I couldn't wait to threaten them with a phone call to His Honor.

"Uh, we, well, we, uh, have a problem with Jackie Lemancyzk," T. Pierce says, glancing nervously at the four suits who've eased backward closer to the door. They're collectively studying their feet, shuffling and twitching. T. Pierce is directly across the table from me, and he's struggling.

"What kind of problem?" I ask.

"She doesn't work here anymore."

I catch my mouth falling open. I am genuinely stunned, and for a second can't think of anything to say. I stare at him and try to collect my thoughts. "When did she leave?" I ask.

"Late last week."

"How late? We were in court last Thursday. Did you know it then?"

"No. She left Saturday."

"Was she terminated?"

"She resigned."

"Where is she now?"

"She's no longer an employee, okay? We can't produce her as a witness."

I study my notes for a second, scanning for more names. "Okay, how about Tony Krick, junior claims examiner?"

More twitching and shuffling and struggling.

"He's gone too," T. Pierce says. "He's been downsized."

I take a second blow to the nose. I'm dizzy with thoughts of what to do next.

Great Benefit has actually fired people to keep them from talking to me.

"What a coincidence," I say, floored. Plunk, Hill and Grone refuse to look up from their legal pads. I can't imagine what they're writing.

"Our client is going through a periodical downsizing," T. Pierce says, managing to keep a serious face.

"What about Richard Pellrod, senior claims examiner? Lemme guess, he's been downsized too."

"No. He's here."

"And Russell Krokit?"

"Mr. Krokit left us for another company."

"So he wasn't downsized."

"No."

"He resigned, like Jackie Lemancyzk."

"That's correct."

Russell Krokit was the Senior Claims Supervisor when he wrote the Stupid Letter. As nervous and scared as I've been about this trip, I was actually looking forward to his deposition.

"And Everett Lufkin, Vice President of Claims? Downsized?"

"No. He's here."

There's an incredibly long period of silence as everyone busies himself with nothing-work while the dust settles. My lawsuit has caused a bloodletting. I write carefully on my legal pad, listing the things I should do next.

"Where's the file?" I ask.

T. Pierce reaches behind himself and picks up a stack

of papers. He slides these across the table. They're neatly copied and bound with thick rubber bands.

"Is it in chronological order?" I ask, Kipler's order requires this.

"I think so," T. Pierce says, looking at the four Great Benefit suits as if he could choke them.

The file is almost five inches thick. Without removing the rubber bands, I say, "Give me an hour. Then we'll continue."

"Sure," T. Pierce says. "There's a small conference room right there." He rises and points to the wall behind me.

I follow him and Jack the Suit into an adjacent room, where they quickly leave me. I sit at the table and immediately begin plowing through the documents.

AN HOUR LATER, I reenter the boardroom. They're drinking coffee and suffering through small talk. "We need to call the judge," I say, and T. Pierce snaps to attention. "In here," I say, pointing to my little room.

With him on one phone and me on another, I dial Kipler's office number. He answers on the second ring. We identify ourselves and say good morning. "Got some problems here, Your Honor," I say, anxious to start the conversation with the right tone.

"What kinda problems?" he demands. T. Pierce is listening and staring blankly at the floor.

"Well, of the six witnesses specified in my notice, and in your order, three have suddenly disappeared. They've either resigned, been downsized or suffered some other equal fate, but they aren't here. Happened very late last week."

"Who?"

I'm sure he has the file in front of him, looking at the names.

"Jackie Lemancyzk, Tony Krick and Russell Krokit no longer work here. Pellrod, Lufkin, and Underhall, the designee, miraculously survived the carnage."

"How about the file?"

"I have the claim file, and I've scanned it."

"And?"

"There's at least one missing document," I say, watching T. Pierce carefully. He frowns hard at me, as if he can't believe this.

"What is it?" Kipler asks.

"The Stupid Letter. It's not in the file. I haven't had time to check everything else."

The attorneys for Great Benefit saw the Stupid Letter for the first time last week. The copy Dot handed to Drummond during her depo had the word copy stamped three times across the top. I did this on purpose so if the letter turned up later we'd know where it came from. The original is locked safely away in my files. It would've been too risky for Drummond et al. to forward their marked copy of the letter to Great Benefit to belatedly add it to the claim file.

"Is this true, Pierce?" Kipler demands.

Pierce is genuinely at a loss. "I'm sorry, Your Honor, I don't know. I've gone through the file, but, well, I guess so, you know. I haven't checked everything,"

"Are you guys in the same room?" Kipler asks.

"Yes sir," we answer in unison.

"Good. Pierce, leave the room. Rudy, stay on the phone."

T. Pierce starts to say something, but thinks better of it. Confused, he hangs up his phone and leaves the room.

"Okay, Judge, it's just me," I say.

"What's their mood?" he asks.

"Pretty tense."

"I'm not surprised. This is what I'm gonna do. By kill-ing off witnesses and hiding documents, they've given me the authority to order all depositions to be taken down here. It's discretionary, and they've earned themselves the punishment. I think you should depose Underhall and no one else. Ask him everything under the sun, but try and pin him down on the terminations of the three missing witnesses. Throw everything at him. When you're finished with him, come home. I'll order a hearing for later this week and get to the bottom of this. Get the underwriting file too."

I'm taking notes as fast as I can.

"Lemme talk to Pierce now," he says, "and lay him out."

JACK UNDERHALL is a compact little man with a clipped mustache and clipped speech. He sheds light on the company itself. Great Benefit is owned by PinnConn, a privately held corporation whose owners are hard to pin down. I question him at length about the affiliations and connections of the three companies that call this place home, and it becomes hopelessly confused. We talk for an hour about the corporate structure, starting with the CEO on down. We talk about products, sales, markets, divi-sions, personnel, all interesting to a point but mostly use-less. He produces two letters of resignation from the miss-ing witnesses, and assures me their departures had absolutely nothing to do with this case.

I grill him for three hours, then quit. I had resigned myself to the reality of spending at least three days in Cleveland, enclosed in a room with the boys from Trent & Brent, wrangling with one hostile witness after another, and plowing through reams of documents at night.

But I leave this place just before two, never to return,

loaded with fresh documents for Deck to scour, secure in the knowledge that now these assholes will be forced to come to my turf and give their depositions in my court-room, with my judge nearby.

The bus ride back to Memphis seems much faster.

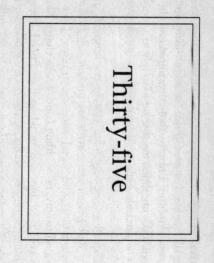

Thirty-five

DECK HAS A BUSINESS CARD WHICH DE-scribes him as a *Paralawyer*, an animal new to me. He roams the hallways outside City Court and hustles small-time criminals who are waiting for their first appearances before the various judges. He picks out a guy who looks scared and is holding a piece of paper, and he makes his move. Deck calls this the Buzzard Two-Step, a quick little solicitation perfected by many of the street lawyers who hang around City Court. He once invited me to go with him so I could learn the ropes. I declined.

DERRICK DOGAN was originally targeted as a victim of the Buzzard Two-Step, but the hustle fell apart when he asked Deck, "What the hell's a paralawyer?" Deck, ever quick with a canned response, failed to satisfy this inquiry, and left in a hurry. But Dogan kept the card with Deck's name on it. Later the same day, Dogan was broadsided by a teenager who was speeding. About twenty-four hours after he told Deck to get lost outside City Court, he dialed the number on the card from his semiprivate room at St.

Peter's. Deck took the call at the office, where I was sifting through an impenetrable web of insurance documents. Minutes later, we were racing down the street toward the hospital. Dogan wanted to talk to a real lawyer, not a paralawyer.

THIS IS a semi-legitimate visit to the hospital, my first. We find Dogan alone with his broken leg, broken ribs, broken wrist and facial cuts and bruises. He's young, around twenty, no wedding band. I take charge like a real lawyer, feed him the usual well-practiced lines about avoiding insurance companies and saying nothing to anybody. It's just us against them, and my firm handles more car wrecks than anybody else in town. Deck smiles. He's taught me well.

Dogan signs a contract and a medical release which will allow us to obtain his records. He's in significant pain, so we don't stay long. His name's on the contract. We say good-bye and promise to see him tomorrow.

By noon, Deck has a copy of the accident report and has already talked to the teenager's father. They're insured by State Farm. The father, against his better judgment, offers Deck the opinion that he thinks the policy has a limit of twenty-five thousand dollars. He and the kid are really sorry about this. No problem, says Deck, quite thankful that the accident occurred.

One third of twenty-five thousand is eight thousand and change. We eat lunch at a place called Dux, a wonderful restaurant in The Peabody. I have wine. Deck has dessert. It's the biggest moment in the history of our firm. We count and spend our money for three hours.

ON THE THURSDAY after the Monday I spent in Cleveland, we're in Kipler's courtroom at five-thirty in the afternoon. His Honor picked this time so the great Leo F.

Drummond could rush over after a long day in court and receive another tongue lashing. His presence completes the defense team—all five are present and looking sufficiently smug though everybody knows they're in for the worst. Jack Underhall, one of the in-house lawyers for Great Benefit, is here, but the rest of the corporate suits have elected to stay in Cleveland. I don't blame them.

"I warned you about the documents, Mr. Drummond." His Honor is scolding from the bench. He called us to order less than five minutes ago, and Drummond's already bleeding. "I thought I was rather specific, even put it all in writing, in an order, you know. Now, what happened?"

This is probably not Drummond's fault. His client is playing games with him, and I strongly suspect he's already done some lashing of his own at the guys in Cleveland. Leo Drummond is a study in ego, and he doesn't take humiliation well. I almost feel sorry for him. He's in the middle of a zillion-dollar lawsuit in federal court, probably sleeping three hours a night, a hundred things on his mind, and now he's dragged across the street to defend the suspicious actions of his wayward client.

I *almost* feel sorry for him.

"There's no excuse, Your Honor," he says, and his sincerity is convincing.

"When did you first learn that these three witnesses no longer worked for your client?"

"Sunday afternoon."

"Did you attempt to notify counsel for the plaintiff?"

"I did. We couldn't locate him. We even called the airlines in an attempt to track him. No luck."

Shoulda called Greyhound.

Kipler makes a big production out of shaking his head and acting disgusted. "Be seated, Mr. Drummond," he says. I have yet to open my mouth.

"Here's the plan, gentlemen," His Honor says. "One week from next Monday, we will gather here for depositions. The following people will appear on behalf of the defendant: Richard Pellrod, senior claims examiner; Everett Lufkin, Vice President of Claims; Kermit Aldy, Vice President of Underwriting; Bradford Barnes, Vice President of Administration and M. Wilfred Keeley, CEO." Kipler told me to make a wish list of the ones I wanted. I can almost feel the air being sucked from the room into the lungs of the boys across the aisle.

"No excuses, no delays, no continuances. They will of course travel here at their own expense. They will make themselves available for depositions at the pleasure of the plaintiff, and be released only when Mr. Baylor says so. All expenses of the depositions, including stenographer's fees and copying, will be borne by Great Benefit. Let's plan on three days for these depositions.

"Furthermore, copies of all documents shall be delivered to the plaintiff no later than Wednesday of next week, five days before the depositions. The documents are to be neatly copied and in chronological order. Failure to do so will result in severe sanctions.

"And, speaking of sanctions, I hereby order the defendant, Great Benefit, to pay to Mr. Baylor, as sanctions, the cost of his wasted trip to Cleveland. Mr. Baylor, how much is a round-trip plane ticket to Cleveland?"

"Seven hundred dollars," I say, answering truthfully.

"Is that first class or coach?"

"Coach."

"Mr. Drummond, you guys sent four lawyers to Cleveland. Did you fly first class or coach?"

Drummond glances at T. Pierce, who cringes like a kid caught stealing, then says, "First class."

"That's what I thought. How much is a first-class ticket?"

"Thirteen hundred."

"How much did you spend on food and lodging, Mr. Baylor?"

Actually, less than forty dollars. But it would be terribly embarrassing to admit this in open court. I wish I'd stayed in a penthouse suite. "Around sixty bucks," I say, fudging a little but not being greedy. I'm sure their rooms were a hundred and fifty dollars a night.

Kipler is writing this down with great drama, the calculator clicking in his brain. "What'd you spend traveling? A couple hours each way?"

"I guess," I say.

"At two hundred bucks an hour, that's eight hundred dollars. Any other expenses?"

"Two hundred fifty to the court reporter."

He writes this down, adds it all up, checks his figures and says, "I order the defendant to pay Mr. Baylor the sum of two thousand four hundred and ten dollars, as sanctions, to be paid within five days. If not received by Mr. Baylor within five days, the sum will automatically double each day until the check is received. Do you understand this, Mr. Drummond?"

I can't help smiling.

Drummond rises slowly, slightly bent at the waist, hands spreading out. "I object to this," he says. He's burning, but he's under control.

"Your objection is noted. Your client has five days."

"There's no proof that Mr. Baylor flew first class."

It's the nature of a defense lawyer to contest everything. Nitpicking is a native feature. It's also profitable. But the money is peanuts to his client, and Drummond should realize he'll get nowhere with this.

"Evidently the trip to Cleveland and back is worth thirteen hundred dollars, Mr. Drummond. That's what I'm ordering your client to pay."

"Mr. Baylor does not get paid by the hour," he replies.

"Are you saying his time is not valuable?"

"No."

What he wants to say is that I'm just a rookie street lawyer and my time is not nearly as valuable as his or his buddies.

"Then you'll pay him two hundred per hour. Consider yourself lucky. I was thinking of charging you for every hour he spent in Cleveland."

So close!

Drummond waves his arms in frustration and retakes his seat. Kipler is glaring down. After a few months on the bench, he's already famous for his dislike of the big firms. He's been quick with sanctions in other cases, and there's lots of buzz about it in legal circles. It doesn't take much.

"Anything else?" he growls in their direction.

"No sir," I say loudly, just to let everyone know I'm still here.

There's a general, collective shaking of heads among the conspirators across the aisle, and Kipler raps his gavel. I gather my papers quickly and leave the courtroom.

FOR DINNER, I eat a bacon sandwich with Dot. The sun falls slowly behind the trees in their backyard, behind the Fairlane where Buddy sits and refuses to come eat. She says he's spending more and more time out there because of Donny Ray. It's a matter of days now before he dies, and Buddy's way of dealing with it is to hide in the car out there and drink. He sits with his son for a few minutes each morning, usually leaves the room in tears, then tries to avoid everybody for the rest of the day.

Plus, he usually doesn't come in if there's company in the house. Fine with me. And fine with Dot. We chat about the lawsuit, about the actions of Great Benefit and the incredible fairness of Judge Tyrone Kipler, but she's lost interest. The fiery woman I first met six months ago at Cypress Gardens. The fiery woman I first met six months ago at Cypress Gardens seems to have given up the fight. Then, she honestly thought a lawyer, any lawyer, even me, could scare Great Benefit into doing right. There was still time for a miracle. Now all hope is gone.

Dot will always blame herself for Donny Ray's death. She's told me more than once that she should've gone straight to a lawyer when Great Benefit first denied the claim. She chose instead to write the letters herself. I now have a strong suspicion Great Benefit would've stepped in quickly, after being threatened with litigation, and provided treatment. I think this for two reasons: First, they're dead wrong and they know it. And, second, they offered seventy-five thousand dollars to settle shortly after I, a rather green rookie, sued them. They're scared. Their lawyers are scared. The boys in Cleveland are scared.

Dot serves me a cup of instant decaf, then leaves to check on her husband. I take my coffee to the back of the house, to Donny Ray's room, where he's sleeping under the sheets, curled on his right side. A small lamp in the corner gives the only light. I sit close to it with my back to the open window, catching a cool breeze. The neighborhood is quiet, the room is still.

His will is a simple two-paragraph document leaving everything to his mother. I prepared it a week ago. He neither owes nor owns anything, and the will is unnecessary. But it made him feel better. He's also planned his funeral. Dot's made the arrangements. He wants me to be a pallbearer.

I pick up the same book I've been reading intermittently for two months now, a condensed book with four novels in it. It's thirty years old, one of the few books in the house. I leave it in the same place and read a few pages on each visit.

He grunts and jerks a bit. I wonder what she'll do when she eases in one morning and he doesn't wake up.

She leaves us alone when I'm sitting with Donny Ray. I can hear her washing dishes. Buddy, I think, is in the house now. I read for an hour, glancing at Donny Ray occasionally. If he wakes, then we'll chat, or perhaps I'll turn on the TV. Whatever he wants.

I hear a strange voice in the den, then a knock on the door. It opens slowly and it takes a few seconds for me to recognize the young man standing there. It's Dr. Kord, making a house call. We shake hands and speak softly at the foot of the bed, then walk three steps to the window.

"Just passing by," he says, still whispering, as if he drives through this neighborhood all the time.

"Sit down," I say, pointing to the only other chair. We sit with our backs to the window, knees touching, eyes on the dying kid in the bed six feet away.

"How long you been here?" he asks.

"Couple of hours. I ate dinner with Dot."

"Has he been awake?"

"No."

We sit in semidarkness with a gentle wind against our necks. Clocks rule our lives, but right now there is no sense of time.

"I've been thinking," Kord says, almost under his breath. "About this trial. Any idea when it might happen?"

"February 8."

"Is that definite?"

"Looks that way."

"Don't you think it would be more effective if I testified live, as opposed to talking to the jury through a video or a written deposition?"

"Of course it would be."

Kord has been practicing for a few years. He knows

about trials and depos. He leans forward, elbows on knees. "Then let's forget the depo. I'll do it live and in color, and I won't send a bill."

"That's very generous."

"Don't mention it. It's the least I could do."

We think about this for a long time. There's a random light noise from the kitchen, but the house is silent. Kord is the type who's not bothered by long lapses in conversation.

"You know what I do?" he finally asks.

"What?"

"I diagnose people, then I prepare them for death."

"Why'd you go into oncology?"

"You want the truth?"

"Sure. Why not?"

"There's a demand for oncologists. Easy to figure out, right? It's less crowded than most other specialties."

"I guess someone has to do it."

"It's not that bad, really. I love my work." He pauses for a moment and looks at his patient. "This is a tough one, though. Watching a patient go untreated. If the marrow transplants weren't so expensive, maybe we could've done something. I was willing to donate my time and effort, but it's still a two-hundred-thousand-dollar procedure. No hospital or clinic in the country can afford to eat that kind of money."

"Makes you hate the insurance company, doesn't it?"

"Yeah. It really does." A long pause, then, "Let's stick it to them."

"I'm trying."

"Are you married?" he asks, sitting up up straight and glancing at his watch.

"No. You?"

"No. Divorced. Let's go get a beer."

"Okay. Where?"

"You know Murphy's Oyster Bar?"

"Sure."

"Let's meet there."

We tiptoe past Donny Ray, say good-bye to Dot, who's rocking and smoking on the front porch, and leave them for now.

I HAPPEN TO BE ASLEEP when the phone rings at three-twenty in the morning. Either Donny Ray's dead, or a plane's gone down and Deck's in hot pursuit. Who else would call at such an hour?

"Rudy?" a very familiar voice gushes from the other end.

"Miss Birdie!" I say, sitting and reaching for a light.

"Sorry to call at such an awful time."

"That's okay. How are you?"

"Well, they're being mean to me."

I close my eyes, breathe deeply and fall back onto the bed. Why am I not surprised by this? "Who's being mean?" I ask, but only because I'm supposed to. It's hard to care at this point.

"June's the meanest," she says, as if they're ranked. "She doesn't want me in the house."

"You're living with Randolph and June?"

"Yes, and it's awful. Just awful. I'm afraid to eat the food."

"Why?"

"Because it might have poison in it."

"Come on, Miss Birdie."

"I'm serious. They're all waiting for me to die, that's all. I signed a new will that gives them what they want, signed it up in Memphis, you know, then as soon as we got down here to Tampa they were real sweet for a few days. Grandkids stopped by all the time. Brought me flowers and chocolates. Then Delbert took me to the doctor for a physical. Doctor checked everything, and told them I was in great health. I think they were expecting something else. They seemed so disappointed at what the doctor said, and they changed overnight. June went back to being the mean little tramp she really is. Randolph took up golf again and is never home. Delbert stays at the dog track. Vera hates June and June hates Vera. The grandkids, most of them don't have jobs, you know, just up and vanished."

"Why are you calling me at this hour, Miss Birdie?"

"Because, well, I have to sneak around and use the phone. Yesterday, June told me I couldn't use it anymore, and I went to Randolph and he said I could use it twice a day. I miss my house, Rudy. Is it okay?"

"It's fine, Miss Birdie."

"I can't stay here much longer. They've got me stuck back in a little bedroom with a tiny little bathroom. I'm used to lots of room, you know, Rudy."

"Yes, Miss Birdie." She's waiting for me to volunteer to come get her, but it's not the thing to do now. She's been gone for less than a month. This is good for her.

"And Randolph is after me to sign a power of attorney that would allow him to do things on my behalf. What do you think?"

"I never advise my clients to sign those things, Miss Birdie. It's not a good idea." I've never had a client faced with this problem, but in her case it's bad business.

Poor Randolph. He's busting his butt to get his hands on her twenty-million-dollar fortune. What will he do if he finds out the truth? Miss Birdie thinks things are bad now. Just wait.

"Well, I just don't know." Her words fade.

"Don't sign it, Miss Birdie."

"And another thing. Yesterday, Delbert, oops . . . somebody's coming. Gotta go." The phone slams on the other end. I can see June with a leather strap beating Miss Birdie for an unauthorized phone call.

The phone call does not register as a significant event. It's almost comical. If Miss Birdie wants to come home, then I'll get her home.

I manage to fall asleep.

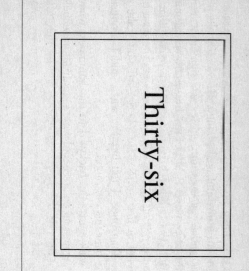

Thirty-six

I DIAL THE NUMBER AT THE PENAL FARM, and ask for the same lady I spoke with the first time I visited Ott. Regulations require all visits to be cleared with her. I want to visit him again before we take his deposition.

I can hear her pecking away at a keyboard. "Bobby Ott is no longer here," she says.

"What?"

"He was released three days ago."

"That's too bad. He's gone."

"Where'd he go?" I ask in disbelief.

"You must be kidding," she says, and hangs up.

Ott is loose. He lied to me. We got lucky the first time we found him, and now he's in hiding again.

"He told me he had eighteen days left. And that was a week ago."

THE PHONE CALL I've been dreading finally comes on a Sunday morning. I'm sitting on Miss Birdie's patio like I own the place, reading the Sunday paper, sipping coffee and enjoying a beautiful day. It's Dot, and she tells me she found him about an hour ago. He went to sleep last night, and never woke up.

Her voice wavers a little, but her emotions are under control. We talk for a moment, and I realize that my throat is getting dry and my eyes are wet. There's a trace of relief in her words. "He's better off now," she says more than once. I tell her I'm sorry, and I promise to come over this afternoon.

I walk across the backyard to the hammock, where I lean against an oak tree and wipe tears from my cheeks. I sit on the edge of the hammock, my feet on the ground, my head hung low, and say the last of my many prayers for Donny Ray.

I CALL JUDGE KIPLER at home with the news of the death. The funeral will be tomorrow afternoon at two, which presents a problem. The home office depositions are scheduled to begin at nine in the morning, and run for most of the week. I'm sure the suits from Cleveland are already in town, probably sitting in Drummond's office right now doing rehearsals before video cameras. That's how thorough he is.

Kipler asks me to be in court at nine anyway, and he'll handle things from there. I tell him I'm ready. I certainly should be. I've typed every possible question for each of the witnesses, and His Honor himself has made suggestions. Deck has reviewed them too.

Kipler hints that he might postpone the depositions because he has two important hearings tomorrow. Whatever. I really don't care right now.

BY THE TIME I get to the Blacks', the whole neighborhood has come to mourn. The street and driveway are bumper to bumper with parked cars. Old men loiter in the front yard and sit on the porch. I smile and nod and work my way inside through the crowd, where I find Dot in the kitchen, standing by the refrigerator. The house is packed with people. The kitchen table and countertops are covered with pies and casseroles and Tupperware filled with fried chicken.

Dot and I hug each other gently. I express my sympathy by simply saying that I'm sorry, and she thanks me for coming. Her eyes are red but I sense that she's tired of crying. She waves at all the food and tells me to help myself. I leave her with a group of ladies from the neighborhood.

I'm suddenly hungry. I fill a large paper plate with chicken and baked beans and coleslaw, and go to the tiny patio, where I eat in solitude. Buddy, bless his heart, is not in his car. She's probably locked him in the bedroom, where he can't embarrass her. I eat slowly, and listen to the quiet chatter emanating from the open windows of the kitchen and den. When my plate is empty, I fill it for the second time and again hide on the patio.

I'm soon joined by a young man who looks oddly familiar. "I'm Ron Black," he says, sitting in the chair next to mine. "The twin."

He's lean and fit, not very tall. "Nice to meet you," I say.

"So you're the lawyer." He's holding a canned soft drink.

"That's me. Rudy Baylor. I'm sorry about your brother."

"Thanks."

I'm very aware of how little Dot and Donny Ray talked about Ron. He left home shortly after high school, went far away and has kept his distance. I can understand this to a certain degree.

He's not in a talkative mood. His sentences are short

and forced, but we eventually get around to the bone marrow transplant. He confirms what I already believe to be true, that he was ready and willing to donate his marrow to save his brother, and that he'd been told by Dr. Kord that he was a perfect match. I explain to him that it'll be necessary for him to explain this to a jury in a few short months, and he says he'd love to. He has a few questions about the lawsuit, but never indicates any curiosity about how much money he might get from it.

I'm sure he's sad, but he handles his grief well. I open the door to their childhood and hope to hear a few warm stories all twins must share about pranks and jokes they played on others. Nothing. He grew up here, in this house and this neighborhood, and it's obvious he has no use for his past.

The funeral is tomorrow at two, and I'll bet Ron Black is on a plane back to Houston by five.

The crowd thins then swells, but the food remains. I eat two pieces of chocolate cake while Ron sips a warm soda. After two hours of sitting, I'm exhausted. I excuse myself and leave.

ON MONDAY, there's a regular throng of stern-faced and darkly dressed men sitting around Leo F. Drummond on the far side of the courtroom.

I'm ready. Scared and shaking and weary, but the questions are written and waiting. If I completely choke, I'll still be able to read the questions and make them answer.

It is amusing to see these corporate honchos cowering in fear. I can only imagine the harsh words they had for Drummond and me and Kipler and lawyers in general and this case in particular when they were informed that they had to appear en masse here today, and not only appear and give testimony, but sit and wait for hours and days until I finish with them.

Kipler takes the bench and calls our case first. We're taking the depositions next door, in a courtroom that's vacant this week, close by so His Honor can stick his head in at random and keep Drummond in line. He calls us forth because he has something to say.

I take my seat on the right. Four boys from Trent & Brent take theirs to the left.

"We don't need a record for this," Kipler tells the court reporter. This is not a scheduled hearing. "Mr. Drummond, are you aware that Donny Ray Black died yesterday morning?"

"No sir," Drummond answers gravely. "I'm very sorry."

"The funeral is this afternoon, and that poses a problem. Mr. Baylor here is a pallbearer. In fact, he should be with the family right now."

Drummond is standing, looking at me, then at Kipler.

"We're going to postpone these depositions. Have your people here next Monday, same time, same place," Kipler is glaring at Drummond, waiting for the wrong response. The five important men from Great Benefit will be forced to rearrange and rejuggle their busy lives and travel to Memphis next week.

"Why not start tomorrow?" Drummond asks, stunned.

It's a perfectly legitimate question.

"I run this court, Mr. Drummond. I control discovery, and I certainly plan to control the trial."

"But, Your Honor, if you please, and I'm not being argumentative, your presence is not necessary to the depositions. These five gentlemen have gone to great hardship to be here today. It might not be possible next week."

"This is exactly what Kipler wanted to hear. "Oh, they'll be here, Mr. Drummond. They'll be right here at nine o'clock next Monday morning."

"Well, I think it's unfair, with all due respect."

"Unfair? These depositions could've been taken in

Cleveland two weeks ago, Mr. Drummond. But your client started playing games."

A judge has unbridled discretion in matters like these, and there's no way to appeal. Kipler is punishing Drummond and Great Benefit, and, in my humble opinion, I think he's a bit overboard. There will be a trial here in a few short months, and the judge is establishing himself. He's telling the hotshot lawyer that he, His Honor, will rule at trial.

Fine with me.

BEHIND A SMALL COUNTRY CHURCH, a few miles north of Memphis, Donny Ray Black is laid to rest. Because I'm one of eight pallbearers, I'm instructed to stand behind the chairs where the family is seated. It's chilly with overcast skies, a day for a burial.

The last funeral I attended was my father's, and I try desperately not to think of it.

The crowd inches together under the burgundy canopy as the young minister reads from the Bible. We stare at the gray casket with flowers around it. I can hear Dot crying softly. I can see Buddy sitting next to Ron. I stare away, trying to mentally leave this place and dream of something pleasant.

DECK IS A NERVOUS WRECK when I return to the office. His pal Butch, the private detective, is sitting on a table, his massive biceps bulging under a tight turtleneck. He's a scruffy type with red cheeks, pointed-toe boots, the look of a man who enjoys brawls. Deck introduces us, refers to Butch as a client, then hands me a legal pad with the message, "Keep talking about nothing, okay," scrawled in black felt on the top sheet.

"How was the funeral?" Deck asks, as he takes my arm and leads me to the table where Butch is waiting.

"Just a funeral," I say, staring blankly at these two men.

"How's the family?" Deck asks.

"Doing all right, I guess." Butch quickly unscrews the cap from the phone receiver, and points inside.

"I guess the kid's better off now, don't you think?" Deck says as I look down. Butch points closer, to a small, round, black device stuck to the inside cover. I can only stare at it.

"Don't you think the kid's better off?" Deck repeats himself loudly, and nudges me in the ribs.

"Sure, yeah, right. He certainly is better off. Really sad, though."

We watch as Butch expertly puts the phone back together, then shrugs at me as if I know precisely what to do next.

"Let's walk down and get some coffee," Deck says.

"Good idea," I say, with a huge knot growing in my stomach.

On the sidewalk, I stop and look at them. "What the hell?"

"Let's walk this way," Deck says, pointing down the street. There's an artsy coffee bar a block and a half away, and we walk to it without another word. We hide in a corner as if we're being stalked by gunmen.

The story quickly unfolds. Deck and I have been worried about the feds since Bruiser and Prince disappeared. We expected them to at least stop by and ask some questions. We've talked about the feds many times, but, unknown to me, he's also been spilling his guts to Butch here. I wouldn't trust Butch with much.

Butch stopped by the office an hour ago, and Deck asked him to take a peek at our phones. Butch confesses that he's no expert on bugging devices, but he's been around. They're easy to spot. Identical devices in all three phones. They were about to search for more bugs, but decided to wait for me.

"More bugs?" I ask.

"Yeah, like little mikes hidden around the office to pick up everything the phones don't catch," Butch says. "It's fairly easy. We just have to cover every inch of the place with a magnifying glass."

Deck's hands are literally shaking. I wonder if he's spoken to Bruiser on our phones.

"What if we find more?" I ask. We haven't taken the first sip of our coffee.

"Legally, you can remove them," Butch explains. "Or, you can just be careful what you say. Sorta talk around them."

"What if we take them out?"

"Then the feds know you've found them. They'll get even more suspicious, probably increase other forms of surveillance. Best thing to do, in my opinion, is act as if nothing has happened."

"That's easy for you to say."

Deck wipes his brow and refuses to look at me. I'm very nervous about him. "Do you know Bruiser Stone?" I ask Butch.

"Of course. I've done some work for him."

I'm certainly not surprised. "Good," I say, then look at Deck. "Have you talked to Bruiser on our phones?"

"No," he says. "I haven't talked to Bruiser since the day he disappeared."

In telling me this lie, he's told me to shut up in front of Butch.

"I'd like to know if there are other bugs, you know," I say to Butch. "It'd be nice to know how much they're hearing out there."

"We'll have to comb the office."

"Let's go."

"Fine with me. Start with the tables, desk and chairs. Look in garbage cans, books, clocks, staplers, everything. These bugs can be smaller than raisins."

"Can they tell we're looking?" Deck asks, scared to death.

"No. You two guys carry on the usual office chatter. I won't say a word, and they won't know I'm there. If you find something, use hand signals."

We take the coffee back to our offices, a place that's suddenly spooky and forbidding. Deck and I begin a banal conversation about Derrick Dogan's case while we gently overturn tables and chairs. Anyone with a brain listening would know that we're out of step and trying to cover something.

We crawl around on all fours. We dig through wastebaskets and pick through files. We examine heating vents and inspect baseboards. For the first time, I'm thankful we have so little furniture and furnishings.

We dig for four hours, and find nothing. Only our phones have been defiled. Deck and I buy Butch a spaghetti dinner at a bistro down the street.

AT MIDNIGHT, I'm lying in bed, the possibility of sleep long since forgotten. I'm reading the morning paper, and occasionally staring at my phone. Surely, I keep telling myself, surely they wouldn't go to the trouble of bugging it. I've seen shadows and heard noises all afternoon and all evening. I've jumped at nonexistent sounds. My skin has crawled with goose bumps. I can't eat. I'm being followed, I know, the question is, How close are they?

And how close do they intend to get?

With the exception of the classifieds, I read every word in the paper. Sara Plankmore Wilcox gave birth to a seven-pound girl yesterday. Good for her. I don't hate her anymore. Since Donny Ray died, I've found myself being easier on everybody. Except, of course, Drummond and his loathsome client.

PFX Freight is undefeated in WinterBall.

I wonder if he makes her go to all the games.

I check the record of vital statistics every day. I pay particular attention to the divorce filings, though I'm not optimistic. I also look at the arrests to see if Cliff Riker has been picked up for beating his wife again.

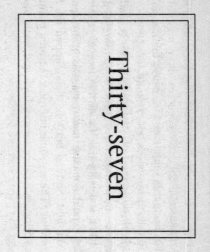

Thirty-seven

THE DOCUMENTS COVER FOUR RENTED folding tables wedged side by side in the front room of our offices. They're separated in neat stacks, in chronological order, all marked, numbered, indexed and even computerized.

And memorized. I've studied these pieces of paper so often that I now know everything on every sheet. The documents given to me by Dot total 221 pages. The policy, for instance, will be considered as only one document at trial, but it has 30 pages. The documents produced so far by Great Benefit total 748 pages, some of them duplicates of the Blacks'.

Deck too has spent countless hours with the paperwork. He's written a detailed analysis of the claim file. Most of the computer work fell on him. He'll assist me during the depositions. It's his job to keep the documents straight and quickly find the ones we need.

He's not exactly thrilled with this type of work, but he's anxious to keep me happy. He's convinced we've caught Great Benefit holding the smoking gun, but he's also convinced the case is not worth the effort I'm putting into it. Deck, I'm afraid, has grave concerns about my trial abilities. He knows that any twelve we pick for the jury will view fifty thousand bucks as a fortune.

I sip a beer in the office late Sunday night, and walk through the tables again and again. Something is missing here. Deck is certain that Jackie Lemancyzk, the claims handler, would not have had the authority to deny the claim outright. She did her job, then shipped the file to underwriting. There's some interplay between claims and underwriting, interoffice memos back and forth, and this is where the paper trail breaks down.

There was a scheme to deny Donny Ray's claim, and probably thousands of others like it. We have to unravel it.

AFTER MUCH DELIBERATION and discussion with the members of my firm, I have decided to depose M. Wilfred Keeley, CEO, first. I figure I'll start with the biggest ego and work my way down. He's fifty-six years old, a real hale-and-hearty type with a warm smile, even for me. He actually thanks me for allowing him to go first. He desperately needs to get back to the home office.

I poke around the fringes for the first hour. I'm on my side of the table in a pair of jeans, a flannel shirt, loafers and white socks. Thought it'd be a nice contrast to the severe shades of black so pervasive on the other side. Deck said I was being disrespectful.

Two hours into the depo, Keeley hands me a financial statement, and we talk about money for a while. Deck scours the financials and slides me one question after another. Drummond and three of his boys pass a few notes but seem completely bored. Kipler is next door presiding over a Motion Day.

Keeley knows of several other lawsuits against Great Benefit now pending across the country. We talk about these for a while; names, courts, other lawyers, similar facts. He's not been forced to give a deposition in any of them. I can't wait to talk to the other lawyers who've sued Great Benefit. We can compare documents and trial strategies.

The glamorous part of running an insurance company is definitely not the mundane business of selling policies and handling claims. It's taking the premiums and investing. Keeley knows much more about the investment side, says he got his start there and worked his way up. He knows little about claims.

Since I'm not paying for these depositions, I'm in no hurry. I ask a thousand useless questions, just digging and shooting in the dark. Drummond looks bored and at times frustrated, but he wrote the book on how to conduct all-day depos, and his meter is ticking too. He'd like to object occasionally, but he knows I'll simply run next door and tattle to Judge Kipler, who'll rule in my favor and admonish him.

The afternoon brings another thousand questions, and when we adjourn at five-thirty I'm physically exhausted. Keeley's smile disappeared just after lunch, but he was determined to answer for as long as I could ask. He again thanks me for allowing him to finish first, and thanks me for releasing him from further questions. He's headed back to Cleveland.

THINGS PICK UP A BIT on Tuesday, partly because I'm getting tired of wasting time, partly because the witnesses either know little or can't remember much. I start with Everett Lufkin, Vice President of Claims, a man who'll not utter a single syllable unless it's in response to a direct question. I make him look at some documents, and halfway through the morning he finally admits it's company policy to do what is known as "post-claim underwriting," an odious but not illegal practice. When a claim is filed by an insured, the initial handler orders all medical records for the preceding five years. In our case, Great Benefit obtained records from the Black family physician who had treated Donny Ray for a nasty flu five years earlier. Dot did not list the flu on the application. The flu had nothing to do with the leukemia, but Great Benefit based one of its early denials on the fact that the flu was a preexisting condition.

I'm tempted to hammer a nail through his heart at this point, and it would be easy. It's also unwise. Lufkin will testify at trial, and it's best to save the brutal cross-examination until then. Some lawyers like to try their cases in deposition, but with my vast experience I know to save the good stuff for the jury. Actually, I read it in a book somewhere. Plus, it's the strategy used by Jonathan Lake.

Kermit Aldy, Vice President of Underwriting, is as glum and noncommittal as Lufkin. Underwriting is the process of accepting and reviewing the application from the agent, and ultimately making the decision of whether or not to issue the policy. It's a lot of paper shuffling with small rewards, and Aldy seems the perfect guy to oversee it. I finish him off in under two hours, and without inflicting any wounds.

Bradford Barnes is the Vice President of Administration, and it takes almost an hour to pin down exactly what he does. It's early Wednesday. I'm sick of these people. I'm nauseated at the sight of the same boys from Trent & Brent sitting six feet away across the table wearing the same damned dark suits and the exact scowling smirks they've had for months now. I even despise the court reporter. Barnes knows nothing about anything, I jab, I duck, not a glove is laid on him. He will not testify at trial because he's clueless.

Wednesday afternoon I call the last witness, Richard

Pellrod, the senior claims examiner who wrote at least two letters of denial to the Blacks. He's been sitting in the hallway since Monday morning, so he hates my guts. He barks at me a few times during the early questions, and this reinvigorates me. I show him his letters of denial, and things get testy. It's his position, and the position still maintained by Great Benefit, that bone marrow transplants are simply too experimental to be taken seriously as a method of treatment. But he denied once on the grounds that Donny Ray had failed to disclose a preexisting condition. He blames this on someone else, just an oversight. He's a lying bastard, and I decide to make him suffer. I slide a stack of documents in front of me, and we go through them one by one. I make him explain them, and take responsibility for each. He was, after all, in charge of supervising Jackie Lemancyzk, who, of course, is no longer with us. He says he thinks she moved back to her hometown somewhere in southern Indiana. Periodically, I ask pointed questions about her departure, and this really irritates Pellrod. More documents. More blame shifted to others. I'm relentless. I can ask anything anytime I want, and he never knows what's coming. After four hours of a nonstop barrage, he asks for a break.

WE FINISH PELLROD at seven-thirty Wednesday night, and the corporate depos are over. Three days, seventeen hours, probably a thousand pages of testimony. The depos, like the documents, will have to be read a dozen times.

As his boys stuff their briefcases, Leo F. Drummond pulls me to one side. "Nice job, Rudy," he says in a low voice, as if he's really impressed with my performance but would rather keep his evaluation quiet.

"Thanks."

He breathes deeply. We're both exhausted, and tired of looking at each other.

"So who do we have left?" he asks.

"I'm through," I say, and I really cannot think of anyone else I want to depose.

"What about Dr. Kord?"

"He'll testify at trial."

This is a surprise. He studies me carefully, no doubt wondering how I can afford to have the doc do it live for the jury.

"What's he gonna say?"

"Ron Black was a perfect match for his twin. Bone marrow is routine treatment. The boy could've been saved. Your client killed him."

He takes this well, and it's obvious it's not a surprise.

"We'll probably depose him," he says.

"Five hundred an hour."

"Yeah, I know. Look, Rudy, could we have a drink? There's something I'd like to discuss with you."

"What?" I can't think of anything worse at this moment than having a drink with Drummond.

"Business. Settlement possibilities. Could you run by my office, say, fifteen minutes from now? We're just around the corner, you know."

The word "settlement" has a nice ring to it. Plus, I've always wanted to see their offices. "It'll have to be quick," I say, as if there are beautiful and important women waiting for me.

"Sure. Let's go now."

I tell Deck to wait at the corner, and Drummond and I walk three blocks to the tallest building in Memphis. We chat about the weather as we ride to the fortieth floor. The suite is all brass and marble, filled with people as if it were the middle of the day. It's a tastefully appointed factory. I look for my old pal Loyd Beck, the thug from Broadnax and Speer, and hope I don't see him.

Drummond's office is smartly decorated but not exceptionally large. This building has the highest rent in town, and the space is used efficiently. "What would you like to drink?" he asks, tossing his briefcase and jacket on his desk.

I don't care for hard liquor, and I'm so tired I'm afraid one drink might knock me out. "Just a Coke," I say, and this disappoints him for a second. He mixes himself a drink at a small wet bar in the corner, scotch and water.

There's a knock on the door, and, much to my surprise, Mr. M. Wilfred Keeley steps in. We haven't seen each other since I grilled him for eight hours on Monday. He acts like he's delighted to see me again. We shake hands, say hello like old buddies. He goes to the bar and mixes himself a drink.

They sip their whiskey as we sit around a small, round table in a corner. For Keeley to return here so soon means only one thing. They want to settle this case. I'm all ears.

I cleared six hundred dollars last month from my struggling practice. Drummond makes at least a million a year. Keeley runs a company with a billion in sales, and probably gets paid more than his lawyer. And they want to talk business with me.

"Judge Kipler concerns me a great deal," Drummond says abruptly.

"I've never seen anything like it," Keeley is quick to add.

Drummond is famous for his immaculate preparation, and I'm sure this little duet has been well rehearsed.

"To be honest, Rudy, I'm afraid of what he might do at trial," Drummond says.

"We're being railroaded," Keeley says, shaking his head in disbelief.

Kipler is a legitimate cause for their concern, but they're sweating blood because they've been caught red-handed. They've killed a young man, and their murderous deed is about to be exposed. I decide to be nice, let them say what they want.

They sip in unison, then Drummond says, "We'd like to settle this thing, Rudy. We feel good about our defense, and I mean that sincerely. Given an even playing field, we're ready to tee it up tomorrow. I haven't lost in eleven years. I love a good courtroom brawl. But this judge is so biased it's frightening,"

"How much?" I ask, cutting off the drivel.

They squirm in perfect hemorrhoidal harmony. A moment of pain, then Drummond says, "We'll double it. A hundred and fifty thousand. You get fifty or so, your client gets a—"

"I can do the math," I say. It's none of his business how much my fee will be. He knows I'm broke, and fifty thousand will make me rich.

Fifty thousand dollars!

"What am I supposed to do with this offer?" I ask.

They exchange puzzled looks.

"My client is dead. His mother buried him last week, and now you expect me to tell her there's some more money on the table."

"Ethically, you're obligated to tell her—"

"Don't lecture me about ethics, Leo. I'll tell her. I'll convey the offer, and I'll bet she says no."

"We're very sorry about his death," Keeley says sadly.

"I can tell you're really broken up, Mr. Keeley. I'll pass along your condolences to the family."

"Look, Rudy, we're making a good-faith effort to settle here," Drummond says.

"Your timing is terrible."

There's a pause as we all take a drink. Drummond starts smiling first. "What does the lady want? Tell us, Rudy, what will it take to make her happy?"

"Nothing."

"Nothing?"

"There's nothing you can do. He's dead, and there's nothing you can do about it."

"So why are we going to trial?"

"To expose what you've done."

More squirming. More pained expressions. More whiskey being gulped.

"She wants to expose you, then she wants to break you," I say.

"We're too big," Keeley says smugly.

"We'll see." I stand and pick up my briefcase. "I'll find my way out," I say, and leave them sitting there.

Thirty-eight

S LOWLY, OUR OFFICES ARE ACCUMULAT-
ing the evidence of commercial activity, however
humble and nonlucrative it may be. Thin files are
stacked here and there, always in plain view so that the
occasional visiting client can see them. I have almost a
dozen court-appointed criminal cases, all serious misde-
meanors or lightweight felonies. Deck claims to have
thirty active files, though this number seems a bit high.

The phone rings even more now. It takes great discipline to talk on a phone with a bug in it, and it's something I fight every day. I keep telling myself that before
the phones were tapped a court order was signed allowing
such an invasion. A judge had to approve it, so there must
be an element of legitimacy in it.

The front room is still crowded with the rented tables,
which are covered with documents for the Black case, and
their presence gives the appearance of a truly monumen-
tal work in progress.

At least the office is looking busier. After several
months in business, our overhead is averaging a miserly

seventeen hundred dollars a month. Our gross income is averaging thirty-two hundred, so Deck and I are splitting, on paper, fifteen hundred dollars before taxes and withholding.

We're surviving. Our best client is Derrick Dogan, and if we can settle his case for twenty-five thousand, the policy limits, then we can breathe easier. We're hoping it'll hit in time for Christmas, though I'm not sure why. Neither Deck nor I have anyone we'd like to spend money on.

I'll get through the holidays by working on the Black case. February is not far away.

THE MAIL TODAY is routine, with two exceptions. There is not a single piece from Trent & Brent. This is so rare it's actually a thrill. The second surprise shocks me to the point of having to walk around the office to collect my wits.

The envelope is large and square, with my name and address handwritten. Inside is a printed invitation to attend a dazzling pre-Christmas sale of gold chains and bracelets and necklaces at a jewelry store in a local mall. It's junk mail, the type I'd normally throw away if it had a preprinted address label.

At the bottom, below the store's hours, in a rather lovely handwriting is the name: Kelly Riker. No message. Nothing. Just the name.

I WALK THE MALL for an hour after I arrive. I watch children ice-skate on an indoor rink. I watch groups of teenagers roam in large packs from one end to the other. I buy a platter of warmed-over Chinese food and eat it on the promenade above the ice-skaters.

The jewelry store is one of over a hundred shops under

this roof. I saw her punching a cash register the first time I slinked by.

I enter behind a young couple, and walk slowly to the long glass display counter where Kelly Riker is helping a customer. She glances up, sees me and smiles. I ease away a few steps, lean with my elbows on a counter, study the dazzling array of gold chains as thick as ski ropes. The store is crowded. A half-dozen clerks chatter and remove items from the cases.

"Can I help you, sir?" she says as she stands across from me, just two feet away. I look at her, and melt.

We smile at each other for as long as we dare. "Just looking," I say. No one is watching us, I hope. "How are you?"

"Fine, and you?"

"Great."

"Can I show you something? These are on sale."

She points and we're suddenly looking at chains fit for a pimp. "Nice," I say, just loud enough for her to hear. "Can we talk?"

"Not here," she says, leaning even closer. I get a whiff of her perfume. She unlocks the case, slides the door open and removes a ten-inch gold chain. She holds it for me to see, and says, "There's a cinema down the mall. Buy a ticket for the Eddie Murphy movie. Center section, back row. I'll be there in thirty minutes."

"Eddie Murphy?" I ask, holding and admiring the chain.

"Nice isn't it?"

"My favorite. Really nice. But let me look around some more." She takes it from me, says, "Come back soon," like the perfect salesperson.

My knees are weak as I float down the mall. She knew I'd come, and she had it planned—the cinema, the movie, the seat and the section. I drink coffee near an overworked Santa, try to imagine what she'll say, what's on her mind. To avoid a painful movie, I wait until the last minute to buy a ticket.

There are less than fifty people in the place. Some kids, too young for an R-rated movie, sit close to the front, snickering at each obscenity. A few other sad souls are scattered through the darkness. The back row is empty.

She arrives a few minutes late, and sits next to me. She crosses her legs, the skirt inches above her knees. I cannot help but notice.

"You come here often?" she says, and I laugh. She doesn't appear to be nervous. I certainly am.

"Are we safe?" I ask.

"Safe from whom?"

"Your husband."

"Yeah, he's out with the boys tonight."

"Drinking again?"

"Yes."

This has enormous implications.

"But not much," she says as an afterthought.

"So he hasn't—"

"No. Let's talk about something else."

"I'm sorry. I just worry about you, that's all."

"Why do you worry about me?"

"Because I think about you all the time. Do you ever think about me?"

We're staring at the screen but seeing nothing.

"All the time," she says, and my heart stops.

On-screen, a guy and a girl are suddenly ripping each other's clothes off. They're falling onto a bed, pillows and undergarments flying through the air, then they embrace hotly and the bed starts shaking. As the lovers love each other, Kelly slides her arm under mine and inches closer. We don't speak until the scene changes. Then I start breathing again.

"When did you start to work?" I ask.

"Two weeks ago. We need a little extra for Christmas." She'll probably earn more than me between now and Christmas. "He allows you to work?"

"I'd rather not talk about him."

"What do you want to talk about?"

"How's the lawyer stuff?"

"Busy. Got a big trial in February."

"So you're doing well?"

"It's a struggle, but business is growing. Lawyers starve, and then if they're lucky they make money."

"And if they're not lucky?"

"They keep starving. I'd rather not talk about lawyers."

"Fine. Cliff wants to have a baby."

"What would that accomplish?"

"I don't know."

"Don't do it, Kelly," I say with a passion that surprises me. We look at each other and squeeze hands.

Why am I sitting in a dark theater holding hands with a married woman? That's the question of the day. What if Cliff suddenly appeared and caught me here cuddling with his wife? Who would he kill first?

"He told me to stop taking the pill."

"Did you?"

"No. But I'm worried about what might happen when I don't get pregnant. It's been rather easy in the past, if you'll recall."

"It's your body."

"Yeah, and he wants it all the time. He's becoming obsessed with sex."

"Look, uh, I'd rather talk about something else, okay?"

"Okay. We're running out of topics."

"Yes, we are."

We release each other's hand and watch the movie for a few moments. Kelly slowly turns and leans on her elbow.

Our faces are just inches apart. "I just wanted to see you, Rudy," she says, almost in a whisper.

"Are you happy?" I ask, touching her cheek with the back of my hand. How can she be happy?

She shakes her head. "No, not really."

"What can I do?"

"Nothing." She bites her lip, and I think I see moist eyes.

"You have a decision to make," I say.

"Yeah?"

"Either forget about me, or file for divorce."

"I thought you were my friend."

"I thought I was too. But I'm not. It's more than friendship, and both of us know it."

We watch the movie for a moment.

"I need to go," she says. "My break is almost over. I'm sorry I bothered you."

"You didn't bother me, Kelly. I'm glad to see you. But I'm not going to sneak around like this. You either file for divorce or forget about me."

"I can't forget about you."

"Then let's file for divorce. We can do it tomorrow. I'll help you get rid of this bum, and then we can have some fun."

She leans over, pecks me on the cheek and is gone.

WITHOUT FIRST CONSULTING ME, Deck sneaks his phone from the office and takes it to Butch, then together they take it to an acquaintance who once allegedly worked for some branch of the military. According to the acquaintance, the bugging device still hidden in our phones is quite dissimilar to the bugs typically used by the FBI and other law enforcement agencies. It's manufactured in Czechoslovakia, of medium grade and quality, and feeds a transmitter located somewhere close by. He's almost certain it wasn't planted by cops or feds.

I get this report over coffee a week before Thanksgiving.

"Somebody else is listening," Deck says nervously. I'm too stunned to react.

"Who would it be?" asks Butch.

"How the hell am I supposed to know?" I snap angrily at him. This guy has no business asking these questions. As soon as he's gone, I'll take Deck to task for involving him this deep. I glare at my partner, who's looking away, jerking around, waiting for strangers to attack.

"Well, it ain't the feds," Butch says with great authority.

"Thanks."

We pay for the coffee and walk back to our offices. Butch checks the phones once again, just for the hell of it. Same little round gadgets stuck in there.

The question now is, Who's listening?

I go to my office, lock the door, kill time while waiting for Butch to leave and in the process conceive a brilliant plot. Deck eventually knocks on my door, taps just loud enough for me to hear.

We discuss my little scheme. Deck leaves and drives downtown to the courthouse. Thirty minutes later, he calls me with an update of several fictitious clients. Just checking in, he says, do I need anything from downtown?

We chat for a few minutes about this and that, then I say, "Guess who wants to settle now?"

"Who?"

"Dot Black."

"Dot Black?" he asks, incredulous and phony. Deck has few acting skills.

"Yeah, I stopped by this morning to check on her, took her a fruitcake. She said she just doesn't have the will-power to suffer through the trial, wants to settle right now."

"How much?"

"Said she'd take a hundred and sixty. She's been thinking about it, and since their top offer is one-fifty, she figures she'll win a small victory if they pay more than they want. She thinks she's a real negotiator. I tried to explain things to her, but you know how hardheaded she is."

"Don't do it, Rudy. This case is worth a fortune."

"I know. Kipler thinks we'll get a huge punitive award, but, you know, ethically I'm required to approach Drummond and try to settle. It's what the client wants."

"Don't do it. One-sixty is chicken feed." Deck is reasonably convincing with this, though I catch myself grinning. The calculator is ratting away as he figures his cut from one hundred and sixty thousand dollars. "Do you think they'll pay one-sixty?" he asks.

"Don't know. I got the impression one-fifty was max. But I never countered it." If Great Benefit will pay one-fifty to settle this case, they'll throw one-sixty at us.

"Let's talk about it when I get there," he says.

"Sure." We hang up, and thirty minutes later Deck is sitting across my desk.

AT FIVE MINUTES before nine the next morning, the phone rings. Deck grabs it in his office, then runs into mine. "It's Drummond," he says.

Our little firm splurged and purchased a forty-dollar recorder from Radio Shack. It's wired to my phone. We're hoping like hell it doesn't affect the bugging device. Butch said he thought there'd be no problem.

"Hello," I say, trying to conceal my nerves and anxiety. "Rudy, Leo Drummond here," he says warmly. "How are you?"

Ethically, I should tell him at this point that the recorder is on, and give him the chance to react. For obvious reasons, Deck and I have decided against this. Just wouldn't work. What're ethics between partners?

"Fine, Mr. Drummond. And you?"

"Doing well. Listen, we need to get together on a date for Dr. Kord's deposition. I've talked to his secretary. How does December 12 sound? At his office, of course—10 A.M."

Kord's deposition will be the last, I think, unless Drummond can think of anyone else remotely interested in the case. Odd, though, that he would bother to call me beforehand and inquire as to what might be convenient.

"That's fine with me," I say. Deck hovers above my desk, nothing but tension.

"Good. It shouldn't take long. I hope not, at five hundred dollars an hour. Obscene, isn't it?"

Aren't we buddies now? Just us lawyers against the doctors.

"Truly obscene."

"Yeah, well, anyway, say, Rudy, you know what my client really wants?"

"What?"

"Well, they *don't* want to spend a week in Memphis suffering through this trial. These guys are executives, you know, big-money people with big egos and careers to protect. They want to settle, Rudy, and this is what I've been told to pass along. This is just settlement talk, no admission of liability, you understand."

"Yep." I wink at Deck.

"Your expert says the cost of the bone marrow job would've been between a hundred and fifty and two hundred thousand, and we don't argue with these figures. Assuming, and this is just for the sake of assumption, that my client was in fact responsible for the transplant. Let's

say it was covered, just assuming, okay. Then my client
should've paid out somewhere around a hundred and seventy-five thousand."

"If you say so."

"Then we'll offer that much to settle right now. One
hundred and seventy-five thousand! No more depositions.
I'll have a check to you within seven days."

"I don't think so."

"Look, Rudy. A zillion bucks can't bring that boy back.
You need to talk some sense into your client. I think she
wants to settle. There comes a time when the lawyer has
to act like a lawyer and take charge. This poor old gal has
no idea what's gonna happen at trial."

"I'll talk to her."

"Call her right now. I'll wait here another hour before I
have to leave. Call her." Sleazy bastard's probably got the
mike wired to his phone. He'd love for me to call her so
he could eavesdrop.

"I'll get back with you, Mr. Drummond. Good day."

I hang up the phone, rewind the tape in the recorder
and play it aloud.

Deck eases backward into a chair, his mouth wide
open, his four shiny teeth glistening. "They bugged our
phones," he says in sheer disbelief when the tape stops.
We stare at the recorder, as if it alone can explain this. I'm
literally numb and paralyzed by shock for several minutes.
Nothing moves. Nothing works. The phone suddenly
rings, but neither of us reaches for it. We're terrified of it,
for the moment.

"I guess we should tell Kipler," I finally say, my words
heavy and slow.

"I don't think so," Deck says, removing his thick glasses
and wiping his eyes.

"Why not?"

"Let's think about it. We know, or at least we think we

know that Drummond and/or his client have bugged our phones. Drummond certainly knows about the bugs because we've just caught him. But there's no way to prove it for sure, no way to catch him red-handed."

"He'll deny it until he's dead."

"Right. So what's Kipler gonna do? Accuse him without solid proof? Chew his ass some more?"

"He's used to it by now."

"And it won't have any effect on the trial. The jury can't be told that Mr. Drummond and his client played dirty during discovery."

We stare at the recorder some more, both of us digesting this and trying to feel our way through the fog. In an ethics class just last year we read about a lawyer who got himself severely reprimanded because he secretly taped a phone call with another lawyer. I'm guilty, but my little sin pales in comparison with Drummond's despicable act. Trouble is, I can be nailed if I produce this tape. Drummond will never be convicted because it'll never be pinned on him. At what level is he involved? Was it his idea to tap our lines? Or is he simply using stolen information passed along by his client?

Again, we'll never know. And for some reason it makes no difference. He knows.

"We can use it to our advantage," I say.

"That's exactly what I was thinking."

"But we have to be careful, or they'll get suspicious."

"Yeah, let's save it for trial. Let's wait for the perfect moment when we need to send those clowns on a goose chase."

Both of us slowly start grinning.

I WAIT TWO DAYS, and call Drummond with the sad news that my client does not want his filthy money. She's acting a bit strange, I confide in him. One day she's afraid of going to trial, the next day she wants her day in court. Right now she wants to fight.

He's not the least bit suspicious. He retreats into his typical hardball routine, threatening me with the likelihood that the money will be taken off the table forever, that it'll be a nasty trial to the bitter end. I'm sure this sounds good to the eavesdroppers up in Cleveland. Wonder how long it takes for them to hear these conversations.

The money should be taken. Dot and Buddy would clear well over a hundred thousand, more money than they could ever spend. Their lawyer would get almost sixty thousand, a veritable mint. Money, however, means nothing to the Blacks. They've never had it, and they're not dreaming of getting rich now. Dot simply wants an official record somewhere of what Great Benefit did to her son. She wants a final judgment declaring that she was right, that Donny Ray died because Great Benefit killed him.

As for me, I'm surprised at my ability to ignore the money. It's tempting, to be sure, but I'm not consumed with it. I'm not starving. I'm young and there will be other cases.

And I'm convinced of this: if Great Benefit is scared enough to bug my phones, then they are indeed hiding dark secrets. Worried though I am, I catch myself dreaming of the trial.

BOOKER AND CHARLENE invite me to Thanksgiving dinner with the Kanes. His grandmother lives in a small house in South Memphis, and evidently she's been cooking for a week. The weather is cold and wet, so we're forced to remain inside throughout the afternoon. There are at least fifty people, ranging in age from six months to eighty, the only white face belonging to me. We eat for hours, the men crowded around the television in the den, watching one game after the other. Booker and I have our pecan pie and coffee on the hood of a car, in the garage, shivering as we catch up on the gossip. He's curious about my love life, and I assure him it's nonexistent, for the moment. Business is good, I tell him. He's working around the clock. Charlene wants another kid, but getting pregnant might be a problem. He's never at home.

The life of a busy lawyer.

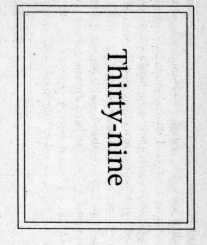

Thirty-nine

WE KNEW IT WAS IN THE MAIL, BUT I can tell by the heavy footsteps that it's here. Deck bounds through my door, waving the envelope. "It's here! It's here! We're rich!"

He rips open the envelope, delicately removes the check and places it gently on my desk. We admire it. Twenty-five thousand dollars from State Farm! It's Christmas.

Since Derrick Dogan is still on crutches, we rush to his house with the paperwork. He signs where's he's told to sign. We disburse the money. He gets exactly $16,667, and we get exactly $8,333. Deck wanted to stick him for a few expenses—copying, postage, phone charges, nitpicking stuff most lawyers try to squeeze from the clients at settlement time—but I said no.

We say good-bye to him, wish him well, try and act a bit despondent over this entire sad little episode. It's difficult.

We've decided to take three thousand each, and leave the rest in the firm, for the inevitable lean months ahead. The firm buys us a nice lunch at a fashionable restaurant in East Memphis. The firm now has a gold credit card, issued by some desperate bank obviously impressed with my status as a lawyer. I danced around the questions on the application dealing with prior bankruptcies. Deck and I shook hands on our agreement that the card will never be used unless we both consent.

I take my three thousand, and buy a car. It's certainly not new, but it's one I've been dreaming about ever since the Dogan settlement became a certainty. It's a 1984 Volvo DL, blue in color, four speed with overdrive, in great condition with only a hundred and twenty thousand miles. That's not much for a Volvo. The car's first and only owner is a banker who enjoyed servicing the car himself.

I toyed with the idea of buying something new, but I can't stand the thought of going into debt.

It's my first lawyer car. The Toyota fetches three hundred dollars, and with this money I purchase a car phone. Rudy Baylor is slowly arriving.

I MADE THE DECISION weeks ago that I would not spend Christmas in this city. The memories from last year are still too painful. I'll be alone, and it'll be easier if I simply leave. Deck has mentioned maybe getting together, but it was a blurry suggestion with no details. Told him I'd probably go to my mother's.

When my mother and Hank are not traveling in their Winnebago, they park the damned thing behind his small house in Toledo. I've never seen the house, nor the Winnebago, and I'm not spending Christmas with Hank. Mother called after Thanksgiving with a rather weak invitation to come share the holidays with them. I declined, told her I was much too busy. I'll send a card.

I don't dislike my mother. We've simply stopped talking. The rift has been gradual, as opposed to a particular nasty incident with harsh words that take years to forget.

According to Deck, the legal system shuts down from December 15 until after the new year. Judges don't schedule trials and hearings. Lawyers and their firms are busy with office parties and employee lunches. It's a wonderful time for me to leave town.

I pack the Black case in the trunk of my shiny little Volvo, along with a few clothes, and hit the road. I wander aimlessly on slow two-lane roads, in the general directions of north and west, until I hit snow in Kansas and Nebraska. I sleep in inexpensive motels, eat fast food, see whatever sights there are to see. A winter storm has swept across the northern plains. Steep snowdrifts line the roads. The prairies are as white and still as fallen cumulus. I'm invigorated by the loneliness of the road.

IT'S DECEMBER 23 when I finally arrive in Madison, Wisconsin. I find a small hotel, a cozy diner with hot food, and I walk the streets of downtown just like a regular person scurrying from one store to the next. There are some things about a normal Christmas that I don't miss.

I sit on a frozen park bench, snow under my feet, and listen to a hearty chorus belt out carols. No one in the world knows where I am right now, not the city, not the state. I love this freedom.

After dinner and a few drinks in the hotel bar, I call Max Leuberg. He has returned to his tenured position of professor of law at the university here, and I've called him about once a month for advice. He invited me to visit. I've shipped to him copies of most of the relevant documents, along with copies of the pleadings, written discovery and most of the depositions. The FedEx box weighed fourteen pounds and cost almost thirty bucks. Deck approved.

Max sounds genuinely happy that I'm in Madison. Because he's Jewish, he doesn't get too involved with Christmas, and he said on the phone the other day that it's a wonderful time to work. He gives me directions.

At nine the next morning, the temperature is eleven degrees as I walk into the law school. It's open, but deserted. Leuberg is waiting in his office with hot coffee. We talk for an hour about things he misses in Memphis, law school not being one of them. His office here is much like his office there—cluttered, disheveled, with politically provocative posters and bumper stickers stuck to the walls. He looks the same—wild bushy hair, jeans, white sneakers. He's wearing socks, but only because there's a foot of snow on the ground. He's hyper and energetic.

I follow him down the hall to a small seminar room with a long table in the center of it. He has the key. The file I shipped him is arranged on the table. We sit in chairs opposite one another, and he pours more coffee from a thermos. He knows the trial is six weeks away.

"Any offers to settle?"

"Yeah. Several. They're up to a hundred and seventy-five thousand, but my client says no."

"That's unusual, but I'm not surprised."

"Why aren't you surprised?"

"Because you got 'em nailed. They have great exposure here, Rudy. It's one of the best bad-faith cases I've ever seen, and I've looked at thousands."

"There's more," I say, then I tell him about our phone lines being tapped and the strong evidence that Drummond is listening in.

"I've actually heard of it before," he says. "Case down in Florida, but the plaintiff's lawyer didn't check his phones until after the trial. He got suspicious because the defense seemed to know what he was thinking of doing. But, wow, this is different."

"They must be scared," I say.

"They're terrified, but let's not get too carried away.

They're on friendly territory down there. Your county doesn't believe in punitive damages."

"So what are you saying?"

"Take the money and run."

"Can't do it. I don't want to. My client doesn't want to."

"Good. It's time to bring those people into the twentieth century. Where's your tape recorder?" He jumps from his seat and bounces around the room. There's a chalkboard on a wall, and the professor is ready to lecture. I remove a tape recorder from my briefcase and place it on the table. My pen and legal pad are ready.

Max takes off, and for an hour I scribble furiously and pepper him with questions. He talks about my witnesses, their witnesses, the documents, the various strategies. Max has studied the materials I sent him. He relishes the thought of nailing these people.

"Save the best for last," the professor says. "Play the tape of that poor kid testifying just before he died. I assume he looks pitiful."

"Worse."

"Great. It's a wonderful image to leave with the jury. If it tries beautifully, then you can finish in three days."

"Then what?"

"Then sit back and watch them try to explain things." He suddenly stops and reaches for something on the table. He slides it across to me.

"What is it?"

"It's Great Benefit's new policy, issued last month to one of my students. I paid for it, and we'll cancel it next month. I just wanted to get a look at the language. Guess what's now excluded, in bold print."

"Bone marrow transplants."

"All transplants, including bone marrow. Keep it, and use it at trial. I think you should ask the CEO why the policy was changed just a few months after the Blacks filed suit. Why do they now specifically exclude bone marrow? And if it wasn't excluded in the Black policy, then why didn't they pay the claim? Good stuff, Rudy. Hell, I might have to come watch this trial."

"Please do." It'd be comforting to have a friend other than Deck available for consultation.

Max has some problems with our analysis of the claim file, and we're soon lost in paperwork. I haul the four cardboard boxes from my trunk to the seminar room, and by noon the place resembles a landfill.

His energy is contagious. Over lunch, I get the first of several lectures on insurance company bookkeeping. Since the industry is exempt from federal antitrust, it has developed its own accounting methods. Virtually no competent CPA can understand a set of financials from an insurance company. They're not supposed to be understood because no insurance company wants the outside world to know what it's doing. But Max has a few pointers.

Great Benefit is worth between four hundred and five hundred million dollars, about half of it hidden in reserves and surpluses. This is what must be explained to the jury.

I don't dare suggest the unthinkable, the notion of working on Christmas Day, but Max is gung-ho. His wife is in New York visiting her family. He has nothing else to do, and he sincerely wants to work our way through the remaining two boxes of documents.

I fill three legal pads with notes, and half a dozen cassette tapes with his thoughts about everything. I'm exhausted when he finally says we're through, sometime after dark, December 25. He helps me repack the boxes and haul them to my car. Another heavy snow is falling.

Max and I say good-bye at the front door of the law school. I can't thank him enough. He wishes me well, makes me promise to call him at least once a week before the trial and once a day during it. He says again that there's a chance he might zip down for it.

I wave good-bye in the snow.

IT TAKES THREE DAYS to ramble my way to Spartanburg, South Carolina. The Volvo handles beautifully on the road, especially in the snow and ice across the Upper Midwest. I call Deck once on my car phone. The office is quiet, he says. No one's looking for me.

I've spent the past three and a half years studying long hours to get my law degree and working whenever I could at Yogi's. I've had little time off. This low-budget journey around the country might seem boring to most folks, but for me it's a luxurious vacation. It clears my head and soul, allows me to think of things other than the law. I unload some baggage. Sara Plankmore for one. Old grudges are dismissed. Life is too short to despise people who simply can't help what they've done. The grievous sins of Loyd Beck and Barry X. Lancaster are forgiven somewhere in West Virginia. I vow to stop thinking and worrying about Miss Birdie and her miserable family. They can solve their own problems without me.

I go for miles dreaming of Kelly Riker and those perfect teeth and tanned legs and sweet voice.

When I do dwell on legal matters, I focus on the looming trial. There's only one file in my office that could get anywhere near a courthouse, so there's only one trial to think about. I practice my opening remarks to the jury. I grill the crooks from Great Benefit. I damn near cry as I plead my final summation.

I get a few stares from passing motorists, but hey, nobody knows me.

I've talked to four lawyers who've sued or are currently suing Great Benefit. The first three were no help. The fourth lawyer is in Spartanburg. His name is Cooper Jackson, and there's something strange about his case. He couldn't tell me on the phone (the phone in my apartment). But he said I was welcome to stop by his office and look at his file.

He's in a bank building downtown, a firm with six lawyers in modern offices. I called yesterday from my car phone somewhere in North Carolina, and he's available today. Things are slow around Christmas, he said.

He's a burly man, with thick chest and thick limbs, dark beard and very dark eyes that glow and dance and animate every expression. He's forty-six, and he tells me he made his money in product liability. He makes sure his office door is closed before he goes any further.

He's not supposed to tell me most of what he's about to tell me. He's settled with Great Benefit, and he and his client signed a strict confidentiality agreement that provides severe sanctions if anyone discloses the terms of the settlement. He doesn't like these agreements, but they're not uncommon. He filed suit a year ago for a lady who developed a severe sinus problem and required surgery. Great Benefit denied the claim on the grounds that the lady had failed to disclose on her application the fact that she'd had an ovarian cyst removed five years before she bought the policy. The cyst was a preexisting condition, the denial letter read. The claim amounted to eleven thousand dollars. Other letters were swapped, more denials, then she hired Cooper Jackson. He made four trips to Cleveland, in his own plane, and took eight depositions.

"Dumbest and sleaziest bunch of bastards I've ever run across," he says, talking about the folks in Cleveland. Jackson loves a nasty trial, and plays the game with no holds barred. He pushed hard for a trial, and Great Benefit suddenly wanted a very quiet settlement.

"This is the confidential part," he says, relishing the idea of violating the agreement and spilling his guts to me.

I'll bet he's told a hundred people. "They paid us the eleven thousand, then threw in another two hundred thousand to make us go away." His eyes twinkle as he waits for me to respond. It is truly a remarkable settlement because Great Benefit effectively paid a bunch of money in punitive damages. No wonder they insisted on nondisclosure.

"Amazing," I say.

"Yes it is. Me, I personally didn't want to settle, but my poor client needed the money. I'm convinced we could've popped them for a big verdict." He tells a few war stories to convince me he's made a ton of money, then I follow him to a small, windowless room lined with shelves filled with identical storage boxes. He points to three of them, then leans his heavy frame against the shelves. "Here's their scheme," he says, touching a box as if great mysteries are contained therein. "The claim comes in and is assigned to a handler, just a low-level paper pusher. The people in claims are the poorest trained, least paid of all. It's that way in every insurance company. The glamour is over in investments, not claims or underwriting. The handler reviews it, and immediately begins the process of post-claim underwriting. He or she sends a letter to the insured denying the claim. I'm sure you have such a letter. The handler then orders the medical records for the past five years. The medicals are then reviewed. The insured gets another letter from claims saying, 'Claim denied, pending further review.' Here's where it gets fun. The claims handler then sends the file over to underwriting, and underwriting sends a memo back to claims which says something like 'Don't pay this claim until you hear from us.' There's more correspondence between claims and underwriting, letters and memos back and forth, paperwork builds up, disagreements ensue, clauses and subclauses in the policy become hotly in dispute as these two departments go to war. Keep in mind, these people work for the same company in the same building, but rarely know each other. Nor do they know anything about what the other department is doing. This is very intentional. Meanwhile, your client is sitting in his trailer getting these letters, some from claims, some from underwriting. Most people give up, and this, of course, is what they're counting on. About one in twenty-five will actually consult a lawyer."

I'm recollecting documents and fragments of depositions as Jackson tells me this, and, suddenly, the pieces are falling into place. "How can you prove this?" I ask.

He taps the boxes. "It's right here. Most of this stuff you don't need, but I have the manuals."

"So do I."

"You're welcome to go through this. It's all perfectly organized. I have a great paralegal, two actually."

Yes, but I, Rudy Baylor, have a *paralawyer!*

He leaves me with the boxes, and I go straight for the dark green manuals. One is for claims, the other for underwriting. At first, they appear almost identical to the ones I've obtained in discovery. The procedures are arranged by sections. There's an outline in the front, a glossary in the back, they're nothing more than handbooks for the paper pushers.

Then I notice something different. In the back of the manual for claims, I notice a Section U. My copy does not have this section. I read it carefully, and the conspiracy unravels. The manual for underwriting also has a Section U. It's the other half of the scheme, precisely as Cooper Jackson described it. The manuals, when read together, direct each department to deny the claim, pending further review, of course, then send the file to the other department with instructions not to pay until further notice.

The further notice never comes. Neither department can pay the claim until the other department says so. Both Section U's set forth plenty of directions on how to document each step, basically how to build a paper trail to show, if one day necessary, all the hard work that went into properly evaluating the claim before denying it.

Neither of my manuals has a Section U. They were conveniently removed before they were given to me. They —the crooks in Cleveland and perhaps their lawyers in Memphis—deliberately hid the Section U's from me. It is, to put it mildly, a staggering discovery.

The shock wears off quickly, and I catch myself laughing at the thought of yanking these sections out at trial and waving them before the jury.

I spend hours digging through the rest of the file, but can't keep my eyes off the manuals.

COOPER LIKES TO DRINK vodka in his office, but only after 6 P.M. He invites me to join him. He keeps the bottle in a small freezer in a closet that serves as a bar, and he sips it straight, no ice, no water. I sip mine too. About two good drops per drink, and it burns all the way down.

After he drains his first shot glass, he says, "I'm sure you have copies of the various state investigations of Great Benefit."

I feel completely ignorant, and there's no sense lying. "No, not really."

"You need to check them out. I reported the company to the Attorney General of South Carolina, a law school buddy of mine, and they're investigating now. Same in Georgia. The Commissioner of Insurance in Florida has started an official inquiry. Seems as if an excessive number of claims were denied over a short period of time." Months ago, back when I was still a student of the law,

Max Leuberg mentioned filing a complaint with the state Department of Insurance. He also said it probably wouldn't do any good because the insurance industry was notoriously cozy with those who sought to regulate it.

I can't help but feel as if I've missed something. Hey, this is my first bad-faith case.

"There's talk of a class action, you know," he says, his eyes glistening and blinking at me suspiciously. He knows I know nothing about any class action.

"Where?"

"Some lawyers in Raleigh. They have a handful of small bad-faith claims against Great Benefit, but they're waiting. The company has yet to get hit. I suspect they quietly settle the ones that worry them."

"How many policies are out there?" I've actually asked this question in discovery, and am still waiting for a reply.

"Just under a hundred thousand. If you figure a claim rate of ten percent, that's ten thousand claims a year, about the average for the industry. Let's say they deny, just for the hell of it, half of the claims. Down to five thousand. The average claim is ten thousand dollars. Five thousand times ten thousand is fifty million bucks. And let's say they spend ten million, just a figure from the air, to settle the few lawsuits that pop up. They clear forty million with their little plot, then maybe the next year they start paying the legitimate claims again. Skip a year, go back to the denial routine. Cook up another scheme. They make so damned much money they can afford to screw anybody."

I stare at him for a long time, then ask, "Can you prove this?"

"Nope. Just a hunch. It's probably impossible to prove because it's so incriminating. This company does some incredibly stupid things, but I doubt if they're dumb enough to put something this bad in writing."

I start to mention the Stupid Letter, but decide against it. He's on a roll. He'll win every battle of one-upsmanship.

"Are you active in any trial lawyer groups?" he asks.

"No. I just started practicing a few months ago."

"I'm pretty active. There's a loose network of us lawyers who enjoy suing insurance companies for bad faith. We keep in touch, you know. Lots of gossip. I'm hearing Great Benefit this and Great Benefit that. I think they've denied too many claims. Everybody's sorta waiting for the first big trial to expose them. A huge verdict will start the stampede."

"I'm not sure about the verdict, but I can guarantee there will be a trial."

He says he might call his buddies, work the network, interface, gather the gossip, see what's coming down around the country. And he might just be in Memphis in February to watch the trial. One big verdict, he says again, will burst the dam.

Why does this scare me?

I drive to Memphis in twelve hours. As I unload the Volvo behind Miss Birdie's dark house, a light snow begins to fall. Tomorrow is the new year.

I SPEND HALF of the next day backtracking through Jackson's file, then thank him and leave. He insists that I keep in touch. He has a hunch that a lot of lawyers will be watching our trial.

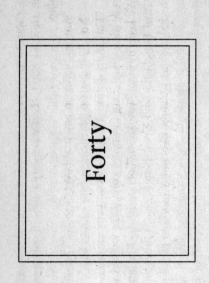

Forty

THE PRETRIAL CONFERENCE IS HELD IN the middle of January in Judge Kipler's courtroom. He arranges us around the defense table, and stations his bailiff at the door to keep wandering lawyers out. He sits at one end, without his robe, his secretary on one side, his court reporter on the other. I'm to his right, with my back to the courtroom, and across the table is the entire defense team. It's the first time I've seen Drummond since Kord's deposition on December 12, and it's a struggle to be civil. Every time I pick up my office phone I can see this well-dressed, perfectly groomed and highly respected thug listening to my conversation.

Both sides have submitted proposed pretrial orders, and we'll work out the kinks today. The final order will serve as a blueprint for the trial.

Kipler was only slightly surprised when I showed him the manuals I borrowed from Cooper Jackson. He carefully compared them to the manuals submitted to me by Drummond. According to His Honor, I am not required to notify Drummond that I know now they've withheld documents. I'm perfectly within the rules to wait until the trial, then spring this on Great Benefit in front of the jury.

It should be devastating. I'll yank down their pants before the trial and watch them run for cover.

We get to the witnesses. I've listed the names of just about everybody connected with the case.

"Jackie Lemancyzk no longer works for my client," Drummond says.

"Do you know where she is?" Kipler asks me.

"No." This is true. I've made a hundred phone calls to the Cleveland area and have not found a trace of Jackie Lemancyzk. I even convinced Butch to try and track her by phone, and he had the same luck.

"Do you?" he asks Drummond.

"No."

"So she's a maybe."

"That's correct."

Drummond and T. Pierce Morehouse think this is funny. They exchange frustrated grins. It won't be so cute if we're able to find her and get her to testify. This, however, is a long shot.

"What about Bobby Ott?" Kipler asks.

"Another maybe," I say. Both sides can list the people they reasonably expect to call at trial. Ott looks doubtful, but if he turns up I want the right to call him as a witness. Again, I've had Butch asking around for Bobby Ott.

We discuss experts. I have only two, Dr. Walter Kord and Randall Gaskin, the cancer clinic administrator. Drummond has listed one, a Dr. Milton Jiffy from Syracuse. I chose not to depose him for two reasons. First, it would be too expensive to travel up there and do it, and, more important, I know what he's going to say. He'll testify that bone marrow transplants are too experimental to be considered proper and reasonable medical treatments.

Walter Kord is incensed over this, and will help me prepare a cross-examination.

Kipler doubts if Jiffy will ever testify.

We haggle over documents for an hour. Drummond assures the judge that they've come clean and handed over everything. He would appear convincing to anyone else, but I suspect he's lying. So does Kipler.

"What about the plaintiff's request for information about the total number of policies in existence during the past two years, the total number of claims filed for the same period and the total number of claims denied?"

Drummond breathes deeply and just looks downright perplexed. "We're working on it, Your Honor, I swear we are. The information is scattered in various regional offices around the country. My client has thirty-one state offices, seventeen district offices, five regional offices, it's just hard to—"

"Does your client have computers?"

Total frustration. "Of course. But it's not a simple matter of punching a few keys somewhere and, Presto!, here's the printout."

"The trial starts in three weeks, Mr. Drummond. I want that information."

"We're trying, Your Honor. I remind my client every day."

"Get it!" Kipler insists, even pointing at the great Leo F. Drummond. Morehouse, Hill, Plunk and Grone collectively sink a few inches, but still keep up their scribbling.

We move on to less sensitive matters. We agree that two weeks should be set aside for the trial, though Kipler has confided in me he plans to push hard for a five-day trial. We finish the conference in two hours.

"Now, gentlemen, what about settlement negotiations?" Of course, I've told him their latest offer was a hundred and seventy-five thousand. He also knows Dot

Black cares nothing about settling. She doesn't want a dime. She wants blood.

"What's your best offer, Mr. Drummond?"

There are some satisfied looks among the five, as if something dramatic is about to come down. "Well, Your Honor, as of this morning, I've been authorized by my client to offer two hundred thousand dollars to settle," Drummond says with a rather weak effort at drama.

"Mr. Baylor?"

"Sorry. My client has instructed me not to settle."

"For any amount?"

"That's correct. She wants a jury in that box over there, and she wants the world to know what happened to her son."

Shock and bewilderment from the other side of the table. I've never seen so much head shaking. The judge himself manages to look puzzled.

I've barely talked to Dot since the funeral. The few brief conversations I've attempted have not gone well. She's grieving, and angry, and this is perfectly understandable. She blames Great Benefit, the system, the doctors, the lawyers, sometimes even me for Donny Ray's death. And I understand this too. She neither needs nor wants their money. She wants justice. As she said on the front porch the last time I stopped by, "I want them sumbitches outta business."

"That's outrageous," Drummond says dramatically.

"There's gonna be a trial, Leo," I say. "Get ready for it."

Kipler points to a file and his secretary gives it to him. He hands a list of some sort to both Drummond and myself. "Now, these are the names and addresses of the potential jurors. Ninety-two, I believe, though I'm sure some have moved or whatever." I grab the list and immediately start reading the names. There are a million people in this county. Do I really anticipate knowing any of these people? Nothing but strangers.

"We'll pick the jury a week before the trial, so be ready to go on February 1. You may investigate their backgrounds, but, of course, any direct contact is a serious offense."

"Where are the questionnaire cards?" Drummond asks. Each prospective juror fills out a card, giving such basic data as age, race, sex, place of employment, type of job and educational level. Often, this is all the information a lawyer has about a juror when the selection process begins.

"We're working on them. They'll be mailed tomorrow. Anything else?"

"No sir," I say.

Drummond shakes his head.

"I want that policy and claims information soon, Mr. Drummond."

"We're trying, Your Honor."

I EAT LUNCH ALONE at the food co-op near our office. Black beans and risotto, herbal tea. I feel healthier every time I come in here. I eat slowly, stirring my beans and staring at the ninety-two names on the jury list. Drummond, with his limitless resources, will use a team of investigators who'll seek out these people and explore their lives. They'll do things like secretly photograph their homes and automobiles. They'll use a team of investigators who'll seek out these people and explore their lives. They'll do things like secretly photograph their homes and automobiles, find out if they've been involved in any litigation, obtain their credit reports and employment histories, dig for dirt on possible divorces or bankruptcies or criminal charges. They'll scour public records and learn how much these people paid for their homes. The only prohibition is personal contact, either directly or through an intermediary.

By the time we're all gathered in the courtroom to select the chosen twelve, Drummond et al. will have a nice file on each of these people. The files will be evaluated not only by him and his buddies, but they'll also be thoroughly analyzed by a team of professional jury consultants. In the history of American jurisprudence, jury consultants are a relatively new animal. They're usually lawyers with some degree of skill and expertise in the study of human nature. Many are also psychiatrists or psychologists. They roam the country selling their horribly expensive skills to those lawyers who can afford them.

In law school, I heard a story about a jury consultant hired by Jonathan Lake for a fee of eighty thousand dollars. The jury brought back a verdict of several million, so the fee was peanuts.

Drummond's jury consultants will actually be in the courtroom as we select the jury. They'll be inconspicuous as they watch these unsuspecting people. They'll study faces and body language and dress and manners and God knows what else.

I, on the other hand, have Deck, who's a study in human nature in his own right. We'll get a list to Butch and to Booker, and to anybody else who might recognize a name or two. We'll make some phone calls, maybe check a few addresses, but our job is much harder. For the most part, we'll be stuck with the task of trying to select people based on their appearance in court.

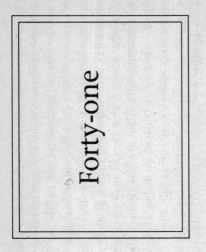

Forty-one

I GO TO THE MALL AT LEAST THREE TIMES A week now, usually in time for dinner. In fact, I have my own table on the promenade, next to the railing overlooking the ice rink, where I eat chicken chow mein from Wong's and watch the small children skate below. The table also gives me a safe view of the pedestrian traffic, so I won't get caught. She's walked by only once, alone and going nowhere in particular, it seemed. I wanted so desperately to ease beside her, take her hand and lead her off into a chic little boutique where we could hide between the racks and talk about something.

This is the largest mall for many miles, and at times it's quite crowded. I watch the people bustle about and wonder if any of them might be on my jury. How do I find ninety-two people out of a million?

Impossible. I do the best with what's available. Deck and I quickly made flash cards out of the juror questionnaires, and I keep a collection with me at all times.

I sit here tonight, on the promenade, glancing at the people walking the mall, then flashing another card from my stack: R. C. Badley is the name in bold letters. Age forty-seven, white male, plumber, high school education, lives in a southeast Memphis suburb. I flip the card to make sure my memory is perfect. It is. I've done this so much I'm already sick of these people. Their names are tacked to a wall in my office, and I stand there for at least an hour a day studying what I've already memorized. Next card: Lionel Barton, age twenty-four, black male, part-time college student and sales clerk at an auto parts store, lives in an apartment in South Memphis.

My model juror is young and black with at least a high school education. It's ancient wisdom that blacks make better plaintiff's jurors. They feel for the underdog and distrust white corporate America. Who can blame them?

I have mixed feelings about men versus women. Conventional wisdom says that women are stingier with money because they feel the pinch of the family finances. They're less likely to return a large award because none of the money will go to their personal checkbooks. But Max Leuberg tends to favor women in this case because they're mothers. They'll feel the pain of a lost child. They'll identify with Dot, and if I do my job well and get them properly inflamed, they'll try to put Great Benefit out of business. I think he's right.

So, if I had my way, I'd have twelve black women, preferably all with children.

Deck, of course, has another theory. He's afraid of blacks because Memphis is so racially polarized. White plaintiff, white defendant, everybody's white here but the judge. Why should the blacks care?

This is a perfect example of the fallacy of stereotyping jurors by race, class, age, education. The fact is, no one can predict what *anybody* might do in jury deliberations. I've read every book in the law library about jury selection, and I'm as uncertain now as I was before I read them.

There is only one type of juror to avoid in this case: the white male corporate executive. These guys are deadly in punitive damage cases. They tend to take charge of the deliberations. They're educated, forceful, organized and don't care much for trial lawyers. Thankfully, they're also usually too busy for jury duty. I've isolated only five on my list, and I'm sure each will have a dozen reasons to be excused. Kipler, under different circumstances, might give them a hard time. But Kipler, I strongly suspect, doesn't want these guys either. I'd wager my formidable net worth that His Honor wants black faces in the jury box.

I'M SURE that if I stay in this business I'll one day think of a dirtier trick, but one's hard to imagine now. I've been thinking about it for weeks, and finally mentioned it to Deck several days ago. He went berserk.

If Drummond and his gang want to listen to my phone, then we've decided to give them an earful. We wait until late in the afternoon. I'm at the office. Deck's around the corner at a pay phone. He calls me. We've rehearsed this several times, even have a script.

"Rudy, Deck here. I finally found Dean Goodlow."

Goodlow is a white male, age thirty-nine, college education, owns a carpet cleaning franchise. He's a zero on our scale, definitely a juror we don't want. Drummond would love to have him.

"Where?" I ask.

"Caught him at the office. He's been out of town for a week. Helluva nice guy. We were dead wrong about him. He's not at all fond of insurance companies, says he argues with his all the time, thinks they need to be severely regulated. I gave him the facts in our case, and, boy, did he get mad. He'll make a great juror." Deck's delivery is a bit unnatural, but to the uninformed he sounds believable. He's probably reading this.

"What a surprise," I say firmly and crisply into the phone. I want Drummond to grab every syllable.

The thought of lawyers talking to potential jurors before the selection process is incredible, almost unbelievable. Deck and I worried that our ruse might be so absurd that Drummond would know we were faking. But who would've thought one lawyer would eavesdrop on his opponent by means of an illegal wiretap? Also, we decided Drummond would fall for our ploy because I'm just an ignorant rookie and Deck is, well, Deck is nothing but a humble paralawyer. We just don't know any better.

"Was he uneasy about talking?" I ask.

"A little. I told him what I've told the rest of them. I'm just an investigator, not a lawyer. And if they don't tell anybody about our conversation, then nobody'll get in trouble."

"Good. And you think Goodlow is with us?"

"No doubt. We gotta get him."

I ruffle some paper near the phone. "Who's left on your list?" I ask loudly.

"Lemme see." I can hear Deck ruffling papers on his end. We're quite a team. "I've talked to Dermont King, Jan DeCell, Lawrence Perotti, Hilda Hinds and RaTilda Browning."

With the exception of RaTilda Browning, these are white people we don't want on our jury. If we can pollute their names enough, Drummond will try everything to exclude them.

"What about Dermont King?" I ask

"Solid. Once had to throw an insurance adjuster out of his house. I'd give him a nine."

"What about Perotti?"

"Great guy. Couldn't believe an insurance company could actually kill a person. He's with us."

"Jan DeCell?"

More paper ruffling. "Let's see. A very nice lady who wouldn't talk much. I think she was afraid it wasn't right or something like that. We talked about insurance companies and such, told her Great Benefit's worth four hundred million. I think she'll be with us. Give her a five."

It's difficult to keep a straight face. I press the phone deeper into my flesh.

"RaTilda Browning?"

"Radical black gal, no use for white people. She asked me to leave her office, works at a black bank. She won't give us a dime."

A long pause as Deck rattles papers. "What about you?" he asks.

"I caught Esther Samuelson at home about an hour ago. Very pleasant lady, in her early sixties. We talked a lot about Dot and how awful it would be to lose a child. She's with us."

Esther Samuelson's late husband was an officer with the Chamber of Commerce for many years. Marvin Shankle told me this. I cannot imagine the type of case I'd want to try with her on the jury. She'll do anything Drummond wants.

"Then I found Nathan Butts in his office. He was a little surprised to learn that I was one of the lawyers involved in the case, but he chilled out. Hates insurance companies."

If Drummond's heart is still beating at this point, there's only a faint pulse. The thought of me, the lawyer, and not my investigator out beating the bushes and discussing the facts of the case with potential jurors is enough to blow an artery. By now, however, he's realized that there is absolutely nothing he can do about it. Any response on his part will reveal the fact that he can listen to my phone calls. This would get him disbarred immediately. Probably indicted as well.

His only recourse is to stay quiet, and try to avoid these people whose names we're tossing around.

"I've got a few more," I say. "Let's chase 'em 'until ten or so, then meet here."

"Okay," Deck says, tired, his acting much better now. We hang up, and fifteen minutes later the phone rings.

A vaguely familiar voice says, "Rudy Baylor, please."

"This is Rudy Baylor."

"This is Billy Porter. You stopped by the shop today."

Billy Porter is a white male, wears a tie to work and manages a Western Auto. He's a weak one on our scale to ten. We don't want him.

"Yes, Mr. Porter, thanks for calling."

It's actually Butch. He agreed to help us with a brief cameo. He's with Deck, both probably huddled over the pay phone trying to stay warm. Butch, ever the consummate professional, went to the Western Auto and talked to Porter about a set of tires. He's trying his best to imitate his voice. They'll never see each other again.

"What do you want?" Billy/Butch demands. We told him to appear gruff, then come around quickly.

"Yes, well, it's about the trial, you know, the one you got a summons for. I'm one of the lawyers."

"Is this legal?"

"Of course it's legal, just don't tell anybody. Look, I represent this little old lady whose son was killed by a company called Great Benefit Life Insurance."

"Killed?"

"Yep. Kid needed an operation, but the company wrongfully denied the treatment. He died about three months ago of leukemia. That's why we've sued. We really need your help, Mr. Porter."

"That sounds awful."

"Worse case I've ever seen, and I've handled lots of them. And they're guilty as hell, Mr. Porter, pardon my language. They already offered two hundred thousand bucks to settle, but we're asking for a lot more. We're asking for punitive damages, and we need your help."

"Will I get picked? I really can't miss work."

"We'll pick twelve out of about seventy, that's all I can tell you. Please try to help us."

"All right. I'll do what I can. But I don't want to serve, you understand."

"Yes sir. Thanks."

DECK COMES TO THE OFFICE, where we eat a sandwich. He leaves twice more during the evening and calls me back. We kick around more names, folks we allegedly talk to, all of whom are now most anxious to punish Great Benefit for its misdeeds. We give the impression that both of us are out there on the streets, knocking on doors, pitching our appeals, violating enough ethical cannons to get me disbarred for life. And all this horribly sleazy stuff is taking place the night before the jurors gather to be examined!

Of the sixty-odd people who'll make the next round of cuts and be available for questioning, we've managed to cast heavy doubts on a third of them. And we carefully selected the ones we are most fearful of.

I'll bet Leo Drummond does not sleep a wink tonight.

Forty-two

FIRST IMPRESSIONS ARE CRUCIAL. THE JUrors arrive between eight-thirty and nine. They walk through the double wooden doors nervously, then shuffle down the aisle, staring, almost gawking at the surroundings. For many, it's their first visit to a courtroom. Dot and I sit together and alone at the end of our table, facing the rows of padded pews being filled with jurors. Our backs are to the bench. A single legal pad is on our table, nothing else. Deck is in a chair near the jury box, away from us. Dot and I whisper and try to smile. My stomach is cramped with frenzied butterflies.

In sharp contrast, across the aisle the defense table is surrounded by five unsmiling men in black suits, all of whom are poring over piles of paper which completely cover the desk.

My theme of David versus Goliath is decisive, and it begins now. The first thing the jurors see is that I'm outmanned, outgunned and obviously underfunded. My poor little client is frail and weak. We're no match for those rich folks over there.

Now that we've completed discovery, I've come to realize how unnecessary it is to have five lawyers defending this case. Five very good lawyers. Now, I'm amazed that Drummond does not realize how menacing this looks to the jurors. His client must be guilty of something. Why else would they use five lawyers against only one of me?

They refused to speak to me this morning. We kept our distance, but the sneers and scowls of contempt told me they're appalled by my direct contact with the jurors. They're shocked and disgusted, and they don't know what to do about it. With the exception of stealing money from a client, contacting potential jurors is probably the gravest sin a lawyer can commit. It ranks right up there with illegal wiretaps on your opponent's phone. They look stupid trying to appear indignant.

The clerk of the court herds the panel together on one side, then seats them in random order on the other side, in front of us. From the list of ninety-two, sixty-one people are here. Some could not be found. Two were dead. A handful claimed to be sick. Three invoked their age as an excuse. Kipler excused a few others for various personal reasons. As the clerk calls out each name I make notes. I feel like I've known these people for months. Number six is Billy Porter, the Western Auto manager who allegedly called me last night. It'll be interesting to see what Drummond does to him.

Jack Underhall and Kermit Aldy are representing Great Benefit. They sit behind Drummond and his team. That's seven suits, seven serious and forbidding faces glowering at the jury pool. Lighten up, guys! I keep a pleasant look on my face.

Kipler enters the courtroom and everybody rises. Court is opened. He welcomes the panel, and delivers a brief and effective speech on jury service and good citizenship. A few hands go up when he asks if there are valid excuses.

He instructs them to approach the bench one at a time, where they plead their cases in muted voices. Four of the five corporate execs on my blacklist whisper with the judge. Not surprisingly, he excuses them.

This takes time, but it allows us to study the panel. Based on the way they're seated, we'll probably not get past the first three rows. That's thirty-six. We need only twelve, plus two alternates.

On the benches directly behind the defense table, I notice two well-dressed strangers. Jury consultants, I presume. They watch every move from these people. Wonder what our little ploy did to their in-depth psychological profiles? Ha, ha, ha. Bet they've never had to factor in a couple of nuts out there the night before chatting with the jury pool.

His Honor dismisses seven more, so we're down to fifty. He then gives a sketchy summary of our case, and introduces the parties and the lawyers. Buddy is not in the courtroom. Buddy is in the Fairlane.

Kipler then starts the serious questioning. He urges the jurors to raise their hands if they need to respond in any way. Do any of you know any of the parties, any of the lawyers, any of the witnesses? Any of you have policies issued by Great Benefit? Any of you involved in litigation? Any of you ever sued an insurance company?

There are a few responses. They raise their hands, then stand and talk to His Honor. They're nervous, but after a few do it the ice is broken. There's a humorous comment, and everybody relaxes a bit. At times, and for very brief intervals, I tell myself that I belong here. I can do this. I'm a lawyer. Of course, I have yet to open my mouth.

Kipler gave me a list of his questions, and he'll ask everything I want to know. Nothing wrong with this. He gave me the same list to Drummond.

I make notes, watch the people, listen carefully to

what's said. Deck is doing the same thing. This is cruel, but I'm almost glad the jurors don't know he's with me.

It drags on as Kipler plows through the questions. After almost two hours, he's finished. The vicious knot returns to my stomach. It's time for Rudy Baylor to say his first words in a real trial. It'll be a brief appearance.

I stand, walk to the bar, give them a warm smile and say the words that I've practiced a thousand times. "Good morning. My name is Rudy Baylor, and I represent the Blacks." So far so good. After two hours of being hammered from the bench, they're ready for something different. I look at them warmly, sincerely. "Now, Judge Kipler has asked a lot of questions, and these are very important. He's covered everything I wanted to ask, so I won't waste time. In fact, I have only one question. Can any of you think of any reason why you shouldn't serve on this jury and hear this case?"

No response is expected, and none is received. They've been looking at me for over two hours, and I merely want to say hello, give them another nice smile and be very brief. There are few things in life worse than a long-winded lawyer. Plus, I have a hunch Drummond will hit them pretty hard.

"Thank you," I say with a smile, then I slowly turn to the bench and say loudly, "The panel looks fine to me, Your Honor." I return to my seat, patting Dot on the shoulder as I sit.

Drummond is already on his feet. He tries to look calm and affable, but the man is burning. He introduces himself and begins by talking about his client, and the fact that Great Benefit is a big company with a healthy balance sheet. It's not to be punished for this, you understand? Will this influence any of you? He's actually arguing the case, which is improper. But he's close enough to the line not to get called down. I'm not sure if I should object. I've vowed that I'll do so only when I'm certain I'm right. This line of questioning is very effective. His smooth voice begs to be trusted. His graying hair conveys wisdom and experience.

He covers a few more areas without a single response. He's planting seeds. Then it hits the fan.

"Now, what I'm about to ask you is the most important question of the day," he says gravely. "Please listen to me carefully. This is crucial." A long, dramatic pause. A deep breath. "Have any of you been contacted about this case?"

The courtroom is perfectly still as his words linger, then slowly settle. It's more of an accusation than a question. I glance at their table. Hill and Plunk are glaring at me. Morehouse and Grone are watching the jurors.

Drummond is frozen for a few seconds, ready to pounce on the first person who's brave enough to raise a hand and say, "Yes! The plaintiff's lawyer stopped by my house last night!" Drummond knows it's coming, he just knows it. He'll extract the truth, expose me and my corrupt paralawyer partner, move to have me admonished, sanctioned and ultimately disbarred. The case will be postponed for years. It's coming!

But his shoulders slowly sink. The air quietly rushes from his lungs. Buncha lying schmucks!

"This is very important," he says. "We need to know." His tone is one of distrust.

Nothing. No movement anywhere. But they're watching him intensely, and he's making them very uneasy. Keep going, big boy.

"Let me ask it another way," he says, very coolly. "Did any of you have a conversation yesterday with either Mr. Baylor here or Mr. Deck Shifflet over there?"

I lunge to my feet. "Objection, Your Honor! This is absurd!"

Kipler is ready to come over the bench. "Sustained! What are you doing, Mr. Drummond?" Kipler yells this directly into his microphone, and the walls shake.

Drummond is facing the bench. "Your Honor, we have reason to believe this panel has been tampered with."

"Yeah, and he's accusing me," I say angrily.

"I don't understand what you're doing, Mr. Drummond," Kipler says.

"Perhaps we should discuss it in chambers," Drummond says, glaring at me.

"Let's go," I shoot back, as if I'm just itching for a fight.

"A brief recess," Kipler says to his bailiff.

DRUMMOND AND I sit across the desk from His Honor. The other four Trent & Brents stand behind us. Kipler is extremely perturbed. "You better have your reasons," he says to Drummond.

"This panel has been tampered with," Drummond says.

"How do you know this?"

"I can't say. But I know it for a fact."

"Don't play games with me, Leo. I want proof."

"I can't say, Your Honor, without divulging confidential information."

"Nonsense! Talk to me."

"It's true, Your Honor."

"Are you accusing me?" I ask.

"Yes."

"You're out of your mind."

"You are acting rather bizarre, Leo," His Honor says.

"I think I can prove it," he says smugly.

"How?"

"Let me finish questioning the panel. The truth will come out."

"They haven't budged yet."

"But I've barely started."

Kipler thinks about this for a moment. When this trial's over, I'll tell him the truth.

"I would like to address certain jurors individually," Drummond says. This is usually not done, but it's within the judge's discretion.

"What about it, Rudy?"

"No objection." Personally, I can't wait for Drummond to start grilling those we allegedly polluted. "I have nothing to hide." A couple of the turds behind me cough at this.

"Very well. It's your grave you're digging, Leo. Just don't get out of line."

"WHAT'D Y'ALL DO in there?" Dot asks when I return to the table.

"Just lawyer stuff," I whisper. Drummond is at the bar. The jurors are highly suspicious of him.

"Now, as I was saying. It's very important that you tell us if anyone has contacted you and talked about this case. Please raise your hand if this has happened." He sounds like a first-grade teacher.

No hands anywhere.

"It's a very serious matter when a juror is contacted either directly or indirectly by any of the parties involved in a trial. In fact, there could be severe repercussions for both the person initiating the contact, and also for the juror if the juror fails to report it." This has a deathly ring to it.

No hands. No movement. Nothing but a bunch of people who are quickly getting angry.

He shifts weight from one foot to the next, rubs his chin and zeroes in on Billy Porter.

"Mr. Porter," he says in a deep voice, and Billy feels zapped. He bolts upright, nods. His cheeks turn red.

"Mr. Porter, I'm going to ask you a direct question. I'd appreciate an honest response."

"You ask an honest question and I'll give you an honest answer," Porter says angrily. "This is a guy with a short fuse. Frankly, I'd leave him alone.

Drummond is stopped for a second, then plunges onward. "Yes, now, Mr. Porter, did you or did you not have a phone conversation last night with Mr. Rudy Baylor?"

I stand, spread my arms, look blankly at Drummond as if I'm completely innocent and he's lost his mind, but say nothing.

"Hell no," Porter says, the cheeks getting redder.

Drummond leans on the railing, both hands clutching the thick mahogany bar. He stares down at Billy Porter, who's on the front row, less than five feet away.

"Are you sure, Mr. Porter?" he demands.

"I damned sure am!"

"I think you did," Drummond says, out of control now and over the edge. Before I can object and before Kipler can call him down, Mr. Billy Porter charges from his seat and pounces on the great Leo F. Drummond.

"Don't call me a liar, you sonofabitch!" Porter screams as he grabs Drummond by the throat. Drummond falls over the railing, his tassled loafers flipping through the air. Women scream. Jurors jump from their seats. Porter is on top of Drummond, who's grappling and wrestling and kicking and trying to land a punch or two.

T. Pierce Morehouse and M. Alec Plunk Junior dash from their seats and arrive at the melee first. The others follow. The bailiff is quick on the scene. Two of the male jurors try to break it up.

I stay in my seat, thoroughly enjoying the thrashing. Kipler makes it to the bar about the time Porter is pulled off and Drummond gets to his feet and the combatants are safely separated. A tassled loafer is found under the second bench, and returned to Leo, who's brushing himself off while keeping a wary eye on Porter. Porter is restrained and settling down quickly.

The jury consultants are shocked. Their computer models are blown. Their fancy theories are out the window. They are utterly useless at this point.

AFTER A SHORT RECESS, Drummond makes a formal motion to dismiss the entire panel. Kipler declines.

Mr. Billy Porter is excused from jury duty, and leaves in a huff. I think he wanted some more of Drummond. I hope he waits outside to finish him off.

THE EARLY AFTERNOON is spent in chambers going through the tedious process of picking jurors. Drummond and his gang firmly avoid any of the people Deck and I mentioned on the phone last night. They're convinced we somehow got to these folks, and somehow persuaded them to remain quiet. They're so bitter they will not look at me.

The result is a jury of my dreams. Six black females, all mothers. Two black males, one a college graduate, one a disabled former truck driver. Three white males, two of whom are union workers. The other lives about four blocks from the Blacks. One white female, the wife of a prominent realtor. I couldn't avoid her, and I'm not worried. It takes only nine of the twelve to agree on a verdict.

Kipler seats them at 4 P.M., and they take their oaths. He explains that the trial will start in a week. They are not to talk about the case with anyone. He then does something that at first terrifies me, but on second thought is a wonderful idea. He asks both attorneys, me and Drummond, if we'd like to make a few comments to the jury, off the record and informal. Just tell a little about your case. Nothing fancy.

I, of course, was not expecting this, primarily because it's unheard of. Nonetheless, I shake off my fear, and stand before the jury box. I tell them a little about Donny Ray, about the policy and why we think Great Benefit is wrong. In five minutes I'm finished.

Drummond walks to the box, and a blind person could see the distrust he's created with the jury. He apologizes for the incident, but stupidly blames most of it on Porter. What an ego. He talks about his version of the facts, says he's sorry about Donny Ray's death, but to suggest his client is responsible is ludicrous.

I watch his team and the boys from Great Benefit, and it's a scared bunch. They have a rotten set of facts. They have a plaintiff's jury. The judge is an enemy. And their star not only lost all credibility with the jury but got his ass whipped as well.

Kipler adjourns us, and the jury goes home.

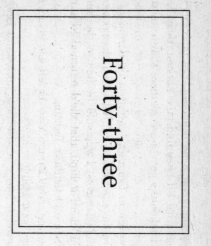

Forty-three

SIX DAYS AFTER WE PICK THE JURY AND four days before the trial begins, Deck takes a call at the office from a lawyer in Cleveland who wants to speak with me. I'm immediately suspicious because I don't know a single lawyer in Cleveland, and I chat with the guy just long enough to get his name. Takes about ten seconds, then I gently cut him off in mid-sentence and go through a little routine as if we've somehow been disconnected. It's been happening all the time lately, I tell Deck loud enough to be recorded in the receiver. We take the three office phones off the hook, and I run to the street where the Volvo is parked. Butch has checked my car phone and it appears remarkably free of bugging devices. Using directory assistance, I call the lawyer in Cleveland.

It turns out to be an immensely important phone call. His name is Peter Corsa. His speciality is labor law and employment discrimination of all types, and he represents a young lady by the name of Jackie Lemancyzk. She found her way to his office after she was suddenly fired from Great Benefit for no apparent reason, and together they plan to seek redress for a multitude of grievances. Contrary to what I'd been told, Ms. Lemancyzk has not left Cleveland. She's in a new apartment with an unlisted phone.

I explain to Corsa that we've made dozens of phone calls to the Cleveland area, but haven't found a trace of Jackie Lemancyzk. I was told by one of the corporate boys, Richard Pellrod, that she'd returned to her home somewhere in southern Indiana.

Not true, says Corsa. She never left Cleveland, though she has been hiding.

It evolves into a wonderfully juicy story, and Corsa spares no details.

His client was sexually involved with several of her bosses at Great Benefit. He assures me she's very attractive. Her promotions and pay were given or denied based on her willingness to hop into bed. At one point she was a senior claims examiner, the only female to reach that position, but got herself demoted when she broke off an affair with the VP of Claims, Everett Lufkin, who appears to be nothing more than a weasel but has a fondness for kinky sex.

I concur that he appears to be nothing more than a weasel. I had him in deposition for four hours, and I'll assault him next week on the witness stand.

Their lawsuit will be for sexual harassment and other actionable practices, but she also knows a lot about Great Benefit's dirty laundry in the claims department. She was sleeping with the VP of Claims! Lots of lawsuits are coming, he predicts.

I finally pop the big question. "Will she come testify?"

He doesn't know. Maybe. But she's scared. These are nasty people with lots of money. She's in therapy now, really fragile.

He agrees to allow me to talk to her by phone, and we

make arrangements for a late night call from my apartment. I explain that it's not a good idea to call me at the office.

IT'S IMPOSSIBLE to think about anything but the trial. When Deck's not at the office, I pace around talking to myself, telling the jury how truly awful Great Benefit is, cross-examining their people, delicately questioning Dot and Ron and Dr. Kord, pleading with the jury in a rather spellbinding closing argument. It is still difficult to ask the jury for ten million in punitive and keep a straight face.

Perhaps if I were fifty years old and had tried hundreds of cases and knew what the hell I was doing, then maybe I would have the right to ask a jury for ten million. But for a rookie nine months out of school it seems ridiculous.

But I ask them anyway. I ask them at the office, in my car and especially in my apartment, often at two in the morning when I can't sleep. I talk to these people, these twelve faces I can now put with names, these wonderfully fair folks who listen to me and nod and can't wait to get back there and dispense justice.

I'm about to strike gold, to destroy Great Benefit in open court, and I struggle every hour to control these thoughts. Damn, it's hard. The facts, the jury, the judge, the frightened lawyers on the other side. It's adding up to a lot of money.

Something has got to go wrong.

I TALK TO JACKIE LEMANCYZK for an hour. At times she sounds strong and forceful, at times she can barely hold it together. She didn't want to sleep with these men, she keeps saying, but it was the only way to advance. She's divorced with a couple of kids.

She agrees to come to Memphis. I offer to fly her down and cover her expenses, and I'm able to convey this with the calm assurance that my firm has plenty of money. She makes me promise that if she testifies, it has to be a complete surprise to Great Benefit.

She's scared to death of them. I think a surprise would be lovely.

WE LIVE AT THE OFFICE over the weekend, napping only a few hours at our respective apartments, then returning like lost sheep to the office to prepare some more.

My rare moments of relaxation can be attributed to Tyrone Kipler. I've silently thanked him a thousand times for selecting the jury a week before the trial, and for allowing me to address them with a few off-the-cuff remarks. The jury was once a great part of the unknown, an element I feared immensely. Now I know their names and faces, and I've chatted with them without the benefit of written notes. They like me. And they dislike my opponent.

However deep my inexperience runs, I truly believe Judge Kipler will save me from myself.

Deck and I say good night around midnight, Sunday. A light snow is falling as I leave the office. A light snow in Memphis usually means no school for a week and the closing of all government offices. The city has never purchased a snowplow. Part of me wants a blizzard so tomorrow will be delayed. Part of me wants to get it over with.

By the time I drive to my apartment, the snow has stopped. I drink two warm beers and pray for sleep.

"ANY PRELIMINARY MATTERS?" Kipler says to a tense group in his office. I'm sitting next to Drummond, both of us looking across the desk at His Honor. My eyes are red from a fitful night, my head aches and my brain thinks of twenty things at once.

I am surprised at how tired Drummond looks. For a

guy who spends his life in courtrooms, he looks exceptionally haggard. Good. I hope he worked all weekend too.

"I can't think of anything," I say. No surprise, I rarely add much to these little meetings.

Drummond shakes his head no.

"Is it possible to stipulate to the cost of a bone marrow transplant?" Kipler asks. "If so, then we can eliminate Gaskin as a witness. Looks like the cost is about a hundred and seventy-five thousand."

"Fine with me," I say.

Defense lawyers earn more if they stipulate to less, but Drummond has nothing to gain here. "Sounds reasonable," he says indifferently.

"Is that a yes?" Kipler demands harshly.

"Yes."

"Thank you. And what about the other costs. Looks like about twenty-five thousand. Can we agree that the amount of the claim for the actual damages sought by the plaintiff is an even two hundred thousand? Can we do this?" He's really glaring at Drummond.

"Fine with me," I say, and I'm sure it really irritates Drummond.

"Yes," Drummond says.

Kipler writes something on his legal pad. "Thank you. Now, anything else before we get started? How about settlement possibilities?"

"Your Honor," I say firmly. This has been well planned. "On behalf of my client, I'd like to offer to settle this matter for one point two million."

Defense lawyers are trained to express shock and disbelief with any settlement proposal made by a plaintiff's lawyer, and my offer is met with the expected shaking of heads and clearing of throats and even a slight chuckle from somewhere behind me, where the minions are clustered.

"You wish," Drummond says acidly. I truly believe Leo is sliding off the edge. When this case started he was quite the gentleman, a very polished pro both in the courtroom and out. Now he acts like a pouting sophomore.

"No counterproposal, Mr. Drummond?" Kipler asks.

"Our offer stands at two hundred thousand."

"Very well. Let's get this thing started. Each side will get fifteen minutes for opening statements, but of course you don't have to use it all."

My opening statement has been timed a dozen times at six and a half minutes. The jury is brought in, welcomed by His Honor, given a few instructions, then turned over to me.

If I do this sort of thing very often, then maybe one day I'll develop some talent for drama. That'll have to wait. Right now I just want to get through it. I hold a legal pad, glance at it once or twice, and tell the jury about my case. I stand beside the podium, hopefully looking quite lawyerly in my new gray suit. The facts are so strongly in my favor that I don't want to belabor them. There was a policy, the premiums were paid on time every week, it covered Donny Ray, he got sick, and then he got screwed. He died for obvious reasons. You, the jurors, will get to meet Donny Ray, but only by means of a videotape. He's dead. The purpose of this case is not only to collect from Great Benefit what it should have paid to begin with, but also to punish it for its wrongdoing. It's a very rich company, made its money by collecting premiums and not paying the claims. When all the witnesses have finished, then I'll be back to ask you, the jurors, for a large sum of money to punish Great Benefit.

It's crucial to plant this seed early. I want them to know that we're after big bucks, and that Great Benefit deserves to be punished.

The opening statement goes smoothly. I don't stutter or

shake or draw objections from Drummond. I predict Leo will keep his butt in his chair for most of the trial. He doesn't want to be embarrassed by Kipler, not in front of this jury.

I take my seat next to Dot. We're all alone at our long table.

Drummond strides confidently to the jury box and holds a copy of the policy. He gets off to a dramatic start: "This is the policy purchased by Mr. and Mrs. Black," he says, holding it up for everyone to see. "And nowhere in this policy does it say that Great Benefit has to pay for transplants." A long pause as this sinks in. The jurors don't like him, but this has their attention. "This policy costs eighteen dollars a week, does not cover bone marrow transplants, yet the plaintiffs expected my client to pay two hundred thousand dollars for, you guessed it, a bone marrow transplant. My client refused to do so, not out of any malice toward Donny Ray Black. It wasn't a matter of life or death to my client, it was a matter of what's covered in this policy." He waves the policy dramatically, and quite effectively. "Not only do they want the two hundred thousand dollars they're not entitled to, they also have sued my client for *ten million dollars* in extra damages. They call them punitive damages. I call them ridiculous. I call it greed."

This is finding its mark, but it's risky. The policy specifically excludes transplants for every organ transplantable, but doesn't mention bone marrow. Its drafters screwed up and left it out. The new policy given to me by Max Leuberg includes language that excludes bone marrow.

The defense strategy becomes clear. Instead of softpedaling by admitting a mistake was made by unknown incompetents deep within a huge company, Drummond is conceding nothing. He'll claim bone marrow transplants are very unreliable, bad medicine, certainly not an accepted and routine method of treating acute leukemia.

He sounds like a doctor talking about the odds against finding a suitable donor, millions to one in some cases, and the odds against a successful transplant. Over and over he repeats himself by saying, "It's simply not in the policy."

He decides to push me. The second time he mentions the word "greed," I leap to my feet and object. The opening statement is not the place for argument. That's saved for last. He's allowed to tell the jury only what he thinks the evidence will prove.

Kipler, the beloved, quickly says, "Sustained."

First blood is mine.

"I'm sorry, Your Honor," Drummond says sincerely. He talks about his witnesses, who they are and what they'll say. He loses steam and should quit after ten minutes. Kipler calls time on him at fifteen, and Drummond thanks the jury.

"Call your first witness, Mr. Baylor," Kipler says. I don't have time to be scared.

Dot Black walks nervously to the witness stand, takes her oath and her seat and looks at the jurors. She's wearing a plain cotton dress, a very old one, but she looks neat.

We have a script, Dot and I. I gave it to her a week ago, and we've gone over it ten times. I ask the questions, she answers them. She's scared to death, rightfully so, and her answers sound awfully wooden and practiced. I told her it's okay to be nervous. The jurors are nothing if not humans. Names, husband, family, employment, policy, life with Donny Ray before the illness, during the illness, since his death. She wipes her eyes a few times, but keeps her composure. I told her Dot tears should be avoided. Everyone can imagine her grief.

She describes the frustration of being a mother and not

being able to provide health care for a dying son. She wrote and called Great Benefit many times. She wrote and called congressmen and senators and mayors, all in a vain effort to find help. She pestered local hospitals to provide free care. She organized friends and neighbors to try and raise the money, but failed miserably. She identifies the policy and the application. She answers my questions about the purchase of it, the weekly visits by Bobby Ott to collect the payments.

Then we get to the good stuff. I hand her the first seven letters of denial, and Dot reads them to the jury. They sound worse than I hoped. Denial outright, for no reason. Denial from claims, subject to review by underwriting. Denial by underwriting, subject to review by claims. Denial from claims based on preexisting condition. Denial from underwriting based on the fact that Donny Ray was not a member of the household since he was an adult. Denial from claims based on the assertion that bone marrow transplants are not covered by the policy. Denial from claims based on the assertion that bone marrow transplants are too experimental and thus not an acceptable method of treatment.

The jurors hang on every word. The stench is descending.

And then, the Stupid Letter. As Dot reads it to the jury, I watch their faces intently. Several are visibly stunned. Several blink in disbelief. Several glare at the defense table, where, oddly enough, all members of the defense team are staring down in deep meditation.

When she finishes, the courtroom is silent.

"Please read it again," I say.

"Objection," Drummond says, quickly on his feet.

"Overruled," Kipler snaps.

Dot reads it again, this time with more deliberation and feeling. This is exactly where I want to leave Dot, so I tender the witness. Drummond takes the podium. It would be a mistake for him to get rough with her, and I'll be surprised if he does.

He starts with some vague questions about former policies she carried, and why she happened to purchase this particular policy. What did she have in mind when she bought it? Dot just wanted coverage for her family, that's all. And that's what the agent promised. Did the agent promise her the policy would cover transplants?

"I wasn't thinking of transplants," she says. "I never had need of one." This causes some smiles in the jury box, but no one laughs.

Drummond tries to press her on whether she intended to purchase a policy that would cover bone marrow transplants. She'd never heard of them, she keeps telling him.

"So you didn't specifically request a policy that would cover them?" he asks.

"I wasn't thinking of these things when I bought the policy. I just wanted full coverage."

Drummond scores a weak point on this, but I think and hope it will soon be forgotten by the jury.

"Why'd you sue Great Benefit for ten million dollars?" he asks. This question can produce disastrous results early in a trial because it makes the plaintiff appear greedy. The damages sought in lawsuits are often just figures pulled out of the air by the lawyer with no input from the clients. I certainly didn't ask Dot how much she wanted to sue for.

But I knew the question was coming because I've studied the transcripts from Drummond's old trials. Dot is ready.

"Ten million?" she asks.

"That's right, Mrs. Black. You've sued my client for ten million dollars."

"Is that all?" she asks.

"I beg your pardon."

"I thought it was more than that."

"Is that so?"

"Yeah. Your client's got a billion dollars, and your client killed my son. Hell, I wanted to sue for a lot more."

Drummond's knees buckle slightly and he shifts his weight. He keeps smiling though, a remarkable talent. Instead of retreating behind a harmless question or even taking his seat, he makes one last mistake with Dot Black. It's another of his stock questions. "What're you going to do with the money if the jury gives you ten million dollars?"

Imagine trying to answer this on the spur of the moment in open court. Dot, however, is very ready. "Give it to the American Leukemia Society. Every penny. I don't want a dime of your stinkin' money."

"Thank you," Drummond says, and quickly gets to his table.

Two of the jurors are actually snickering as Dot leaves the witness stand and takes her seat next to me. Drummond looks pale.

"How'd I do?" she whispers.

"You kicked ass, Dot," I whisper back.

"I gotta have a smoke."

"We'll break in a minute."

I call Ron Black to the stand. He too has a script, and his testimony lasts for less than thirty minutes. All we need from Ron is the fact that the tests were run on him, he was a perfect match for his twin brother and that at all times he was ready to be the donor. Drummond has no cross-examine. It's almost eleven, and Kipler orders a ten-minute recess.

Dot runs to the rest room to hide in a stall and smoke. I warned her against smoking in front of the jurors. Deck and I huddle at our table and compare notes. He sits behind me, and he's been watching the jurors. The denial letters got their attention. The Stupid Letter infuriated them.

Keep them mad, he says. Keep 'em riled. Punitive damages come down only when a jury is angry.

Dr. Walter Kord presents a striking figure as he takes the stand. He wears a plaid sport coat, dark slacks, red tie, very much the successful young doctor. He's a Memphis boy, local prep school, then off to college at Vanderbilt and med school at Duke. Impeccable credentials. I go through his résumé and have no trouble qualifying him as an expert in oncology. I hand him Donny Ray's medical records, and he gives the jury a nice summary of his treatment. Kord uses layman's terms whenever possible, and he's quick to explain the medical vernacular. He's a doctor, trained to hate courtrooms, but he's very at ease with himself and the jury.

"Can you explain the disease to the jury, Dr. Kord?" I ask.

"Of course. Acute myelocytic leukemia, or AML, is a disease that strikes two age groups, the first being young adults ranging in age from twenty to thirty, and the second being older people, usually above the age of seventy. Whites get AML more than nonwhites, and for some unknown reason, people of Jewish ancestry get the disease more than others. Men get it more than women. For the most part, the cause of the disease is unknown.

"The body manufactures its blood in the bone marrow, and this is where AML strikes. The white blood cells, which are the ones in charge of fighting infection, become malignant in acute leukemia and the white cell count often rises to one hundred times normal. When this happens, the red blood cells are suppressed, leaving the patient pale, weak and anemic. As the white cells grow uncontrollably, they also choke off the normal production of platelets, the third type of cell found in bone marrow. This leads to easy bruising, bleeding and headaches. When Donny Ray first came to my office, he complained of dizziness, shortness of breath, fatigue, fever and flu-like symptoms."

When Kord and I were practicing last week, I asked him to refer to him as Donny Ray, not as Mr. Black or patient this or that.

"And what did you do?" I ask. This is easy, I tell myself. "I ran a routine diagnostic procedure known as a bone marrow aspiration."

"Can you explain this to the jury?"

"Sure. With Donny Ray, the test was done in his hip bone. I placed him on his stomach, deadened a small area of skin, made a tiny opening, then inserted a large needle. The needle actually has two parts, the outer part is a hollow tube, and inside it is a solid tube. After the needle was inserted into the bone marrow, the solid tube was removed and an empty suction tube was attached to the opening of the needle. This acts sort of like a syringe, and I extracted a small amount of liquid bone marrow. After the bone marrow was aspirated, or removed, we ran the usual tests by measuring the white and red blood cells. There was no doubt he had acute leukemia."

"What does this test cost?" I ask.

"Around a thousand dollars."

"And how did Donny Ray pay for it?"

"When he first came to the office, he filled out the normal forms and said he was covered under a medical policy issued by Great Benefit Life Insurance Company. My staff checked with Great Benefit, and verified that such a policy did in fact exist. I proceeded with the treatment."

I hand him copies of the documents relevant to this, and he identifies them.

"Did you get paid by Great Benefit?"

"No. We were notified by the company that the claim was being denied for several reasons. Six months later the bill was written off. Mrs. Black has been paying fifty dollars a month."

"How did you treat Donny Ray?"

"By what we call induction therapy. He entered the hospital and I placed a catheter into a large vein under his collarbone. The first induction of chemotherapy was with a drug called ara-C, which goes into the body for twenty-four hours a day, seven straight days. A second drug called idarubicin was also given during the first three days. It's called 'red death' because of its red color and its extreme effect of wiping out the cells in the bone marrow. He was given Allopurinol, an anti-gout agent, because gout is common when large numbers of blood cells are killed. He received intensive intravenous fluids to flush the by-products out of his kidneys. He was given antibiotics and anti-fungus treatments because he was susceptible to infection. He was given a drug called amphotericin B, which is a treatment for funguses. This is a very toxic drug, and it ran his temperature to 104. It also caused uncontrolled shaking, and that's why amphotericin B is known as 'shake and bake.' In spite of this, he handled it well, with a very positive attitude for a very sick young man.

"The theory behind intensive induction therapy is to kill every cell in the bone marrow and hopefully create an environment where normal cells can grow back faster than leukemic cells."

"Does this happen?"

"For a short period of time. But we treat every patient with the knowledge that the leukemia will reappear, unless of course the patient undergoes bone marrow transplantation."

"Can you explain to the jury, Dr. Kord, how you perform a bone marrow transplant?"

"Certainly. It's not a terribly complicated procedure. After the patient goes through the chemotherapy I just described, and if he or she is lucky enough to find a donor whose match is close enough genetically, then we extract the marrow from the donor and infuse through an intravenous tube to the recipient. The idea is to transfer from one patient to another an entire population of bone marrow cells."

"Was Ron Black a suitable donor for Donny Ray?"

"Absolutely. He's an identical twin, and they're the easiest. We ran tests on both men, and the transplant would've been easy. It would've worked."

Drummond jumps to his feet. "Objection. Speculation. The doctor can't testify as to whether or not the transplant would've worked."

"Overruled. Save it for cross-examination."

I ask a few more questions about the procedure, and while Kord answers I pay attention to the jurors. They're listening and following closely, but it's time to wrap this up.

"Do you recall approximately when you were ready to perform the transplant?"

He looks at his notes, but he knows the answers. "August of '91. About eighteen months ago."

"Would such a transplant increase the likelihood of surviving acute leukemia?"

"Certainly."

"By how much?"

"Eighty to ninety percent."

"And the chances of surviving without a transplant?"

"Zero."

"I tender the witness."

It's after twelve, and time for lunch. Kipler adjourns us

until one-thirty. Deck volunteers to fetch deli sandwiches, and Kord and I prep for the next round. He's savoring the idea of sparring with Drummond.

I'LL NEVER KNOW how many medical consultants Drummond employed to prepare for trial. He's not obligated to disclose this. He has only one expert listed as a potential witness. Dr. Kord has repeatedly assured me that bone marrow transplantation is now so widely accepted as the preferred means of treatment that no one but a quack would claim otherwise. He's given me dozens of articles and papers, even books, to support our position that this is simply the best way to treat acute leukemia.

Evidently, Drummond discovered pretty much the same thing. He's not a doctor, and he's asserting a weak position, so he doesn't quarrel too much with Kord. The skirmish is brief. His main point is that very few acute leukemia patients receive bone marrow transplants compared with those who don't. Less than five percent, Kord says, but only because it's hard to find a donor. Nationwide, about seven thousand transplants occur each year.

Those lucky enough to find a donor have a much greater chance of living. Donny Ray was a lucky one. He had a donor.

Kord looks almost disappointed when Drummond surrenders after a few quick questions. I have no redirect, and Kord is excused.

The next moment is very tense because I'm about to announce which corporate executive I want to testify. Drummond asked me this morning, and I said I hadn't made up my mind. He complained to Kipler, who said I didn't have to reveal it until I was ready. They're sequestered in a witness room down the hall, just waiting, and fuming.

"Mr. Everett Lufkin," I announce. As the bailiff disappears to fetch him, there's a burst of activity at the defense table, most of it, as far as I can tell, worth nothing. Just papers being pushed around, notes being passed, files being located.

Lufkin enters the courtroom, looks around wildly as if he's just been roused from hibernation, straightens his tie and follows the bailiff down the aisle. He glances nervously at his support group to his left, and makes his way to the witness stand.

Drummond is known to train his witnesses by subjecting them to brutal cross-examinations, sometimes using four or five of his lawyers to pepper the witness with questions, all of it recorded on video. He'll then spend hours with the witness watching the tape and working on technique, prepping for this moment.

I know these corporate people will be immaculately prepared.

Lufkin looks at me, looks at the jury and tries to appear calm, but he knows he can't answer all the questions that are coming. He's about fifty-five, gray hair that starts not far above his eyebrows, nice features, quiet voice. He could be trusted with the local Boy Scout troop. Jackie Lemancyzk told me he wanted to tie her up.

They have no idea she'll testify tomorrow.

We talk about the claims department and its role in the scheme of things at Great Benefit. He's been there eight years, VP of Claims for the past six, has the department firmly in control, a real hands-on type of manager. He wants to sound important for the jury, and within minutes we've established that it's his job to oversee every aspect of claims. He doesn't oversee every single claim, but he has the responsibility of running the division. I'm able to lull him into a boring discussion about nothing but corporate bureaucracy, when suddenly I ask him, "Who is Jackie Lemancyzk?"

His shoulders actually jerk a bit. "A former claims handler."

"Did she work in your department?"

"Yes."

"When did she stop working for Great Benefit?"

He shrugs, just can't remember the date.

"How about October 3 of last year?"

"Sounds close."

"And wasn't that two days before she was scheduled to give a deposition in this case?"

"I really don't remember."

I refresh his memory by showing him two documents; the first is her letter of resignation, dated October 3, the second is my notice to take her deposition on October 5. Now he remembers. He reluctantly admits that she left Great Benefit two days before she was scheduled to give testimony in this trial.

"And she was the person responsible for handling this claim for your company?"

"That's correct."

"And you fired her?"

"Of course not."

"How'd you get rid of her?"

"She resigned. It's right here in her letter."

"Why'd she resign?"

He pulls the letter close like a real smartass, and reads for the jury: "I hereby resign for personal reasons."

"So it was her idea to leave her job?"

"That's what it says."

"How long did she work under you?"

"I have lots of people under me. I can't remember all these details."

"So you don't know?"

"I'm not sure. Several years."

"Did you know her well?"

"Not really. She was just a claims handler, one of many."

Tomorrow, she'll testify that their dirty little affair lasted for three years.

"And you're married, Mr. Lufkin?"

"Yes, happily."

"With children?"

"Yes. Two adult children."

I let him hang here for a minute as I walk to my table and retrieve a stack of documents. It's the Blacks' claim file, and I hand it to Lufkin. He takes his time, looks through it, then says it appears to be complete. I make sure he promises that this is the entire claim file, nothing is missing.

For the benefit of the jury, I take him through a series of dry questions with equally dry answers, all designed to provide a basic explanation of how a claim is supposed to be handled. Of course, in our hypothetical, Great Benefit does everything properly.

Then we get to the dirt. I make him read, into the microphone and into the record, each of the first seven denial letters. I ask him to explain each letter: Who wrote it? Why was it written? Did it follow the guidelines set forth in the claims manual? What section of the claims manual? Did he personally see the letter?

I make him read to the jury each of Dot's letters. They cry out for help. Her son is dying. Is anybody up there listening? And I grill him on each letter: Who received this one? What was done with it? What does the manual require? Did he personally see it?

The jury seems anxious to get to the Stupid Letter, but of course Lufkin has been prepped. He reads it to the jury, then explains, in a rather dry monotone and without the slightest flair for compassion, that the letter was written by a man who later left the company. The man was wrong, the company was wrong, and now, at this moment, in open court, the company apologizes for the letter.

I allow him to prattle on. Give him enough rope, he'll hang himself.

"Don't you think it's a bit late for an apology?" I finally ask, cutting him off.

"Maybe."

"The boy's dead, isn't he?"

"Yes."

"And for the record, Mr. Lufkin, there's been no written apology for the letter, correct?"

"Not to my knowledge."

"No apology whatsoever until now, correct?"

"That's correct."

"To your limited knowledge, has Great Benefit ever apologized for anything?"

"Objection," Drummond says.

"Sustained. Move along, Mr. Baylor."

Lufkin has been on the stand for almost two hours. Maybe the jury's tired of him. I certainly am. It's time to be cruel.

I've purposefully made a big deal out of the claims manual, referring to it as if it's the inviolable pronouncement of corporate policy. I hand Lufkin my copy of the manual that I received in discovery. I ask him a series of questions, all of which he answers perfectly and establishes that, yes, this is the holy word on claims procedures. It's been tested, tried and true. Periodically reviewed, modified, updated, amended with the changing times, all in an effort to provide the best service for their customers.

After reaching the point of near tedium about the damned manual, I ask: "Now, Mr. Lufkin, is this the entire claims manual?"

He flips through it quickly as if he knows every section, every word. "Yes."

"Are you certain?"

"Yes."

"And you were required to give me this copy during discovery?"

"That's correct."

"I requested a copy from your attorneys, and this is what they gave me?"

"Yes."

"Did you personally select this particular copy of the manual to be sent to me?"

"I did."

I take a deep breath and walk a few steps to my table. Under it is a small cardboard box filled with files and papers. I fumble through it for a second, then abruptly stand up straight, empty-handed, and say to the witness, "Could you take the manual and flip over to Section U, please?" As this last word comes out, I look directly at Jack Underhall, the in-house counsel seated behind Drummond. His eyes close. His head falls forward, then he leans on his elbows, staring at the floor. Beside him, Kermit Aldy appears to be gasping for breath.

Drummond is clueless.

"I beg your pardon?" Lufkin says, his voice an octave higher. With everybody watching me, I remove Cooper Jackson's copy of the claims manual and place it on my table. Everybody in the courtroom stares at it. I glance at Kipler, and he's thoroughly enjoying this.

"Section U, Mr. Lufkin. Flip over there and find it. I'd like to talk about it."

He actually takes the manual and flips through it again. At this crucial moment, I'm sure he'd sell his children if a miracle somehow could happen and a nice, neat Section U materialized.

Doesn't happen.

"I don't have a Section U," he says, sadly and almost incoherent.

"I beg your pardon," I say loudly. "I didn't hear you."

"Uh, well, this one doesn't have a Section U." He's absolutely stunned, not by the fact that the section is missing, but by the fact that he's been caught. He keeps looking wildly at Drummond and Underhall as if they should do something, like call Time Out!

Leo F. Drummond has no idea what his client has done to him. They doctored the manual, and didn't tell their lawyer. He's whispering to Morehouse. What the hell's going on?

I make a big production of approaching the witness with the other manual. It looks just like the one he's holding. A title page in the front gives the same date for the revised edition: January 1, 1991. They're identical, except that one has a final section called U, and one doesn't.

"Do you recognize this, Mr. Lufkin?" I ask, handing him Jackson's copy and retrieving mine.

"Yes."

"Well, what is it?"

"A copy of the claims manual."

"And does this copy contain a Section U?"

He turns pages, then nods his head.

"What was that, Mr. Lufkin? The court reporter can't record the movements of your head."

"It has a Section U."

"Thank you. Now, did you personally remove the Section U from my copy, or did you instruct someone else to do it?"

He gently places the manual on the railing around the witness stand, and very deliberately folds his arms across his chest. He stares at the floor between us, and waits. I think he's drifting away. Seconds pass, as everyone waits for a response.

"Answer the question," Kipler barks from above.

"I don't know who did it."

"But it was done, wasn't it?" I ask.

"Evidently."

"So you admit that Great Benefit withheld documents."

"I admit nothing. I'm sure it was an oversight."

"An oversight? Please be serious, Mr. Lufkin. Isn't it true that someone at Great Benefit intentionally removed the Section U from my copy of the manual?"

"I don't know. I, uh, well, it just happened, I guess. You know."

I walk back to my table in search of nothing in particular. I want him to hang here for a few seconds so the jury can hate him sufficiently. He stares blankly at the floor, whipped, defeated, wishing he was anywhere but here.

I confidently walk to the defense table and hand Drummond a copy of Section U. I give him a toothy, nasty smile, and give Morehouse one as well. Then I hand a copy to Kipler. I take my time so the jury can watch and wait with great anticipation.

"Well, Mr. Lufkin, let's talk about the mysterious Section U. Let's explain it to the jury. Would you look at it, please?"

He takes the manual, turns the pages.

"It went into effect January 1, 1991, correct?"

"Yes."

"Did you draft it?"

"No." Of course not.

"Okay, then who did?"

Another suspicious pause as he gropes for a suitable lie.

"I'm not sure," he says.

"You're not sure? But I thought you just testified that this fell squarely under your responsibility at Great Benefit?"

He's staring at the floor again, hoping I'll go away.

"Fine," I say. "Let's skip paragraphs one and two, and read paragraph three."

Paragraph three directs the claims handler to immediately deny *every claim* within three days of receiving it. No exceptions. Every claim. Paragraph four allows for the subsequent review of some claims, and prescribes the paperwork necessary to indicate that a claim might be inexpensive, very valid and therefore payable. Paragraph five tells the handler to send all claims with a potential value in excess of five thousand dollars to underwriting, with a letter of denial to the insured, subject to review by underwriting, of course.

And so it goes. I make Lufkin read from his manual, then I grill him with questions he can't answer. I use the word "scheme" repeatedly, especially after Drummond objects and Kipler overrules him. Paragraph eleven sets forth a veritable glossary of secret code signals the handlers are supposed to use in the file to indicate a strong reaction from the insured. It's obvious the scheme is designed to play the odds. If an insured threatens with lawyers and lawsuits, the file is immediately reviewed by a supervisor. If the insured is a pushover, then the denial sticks.

Paragraph eighteen b. requires the handler to cut a check for the amount of the claim, send the check and the file to underwriting with instructions not to mail the check until further word from claims. Word, of course, never comes. "So what happens to the check?" I ask Lufkin. He doesn't know.

The other half of the scheme is in Section U of the underwriting manual, and so I get to do this again tomorrow with another VP.

It's really not necessary. If we could stop right now, the jury would give whatever I ask, and they haven't even seen Donny Ray yet.

We break for a quick recess at four-thirty. I've had Lufkin on the stand for two and a half hours, and it's time to finish him off. As I step into the hall on my way to the rest room, I see Drummond pointing angrily to a room he wants Lufkin and Underhall to enter. I'd love to hear this mauling.

Twenty minutes later, Lufkin is back on the stand. I'm through with the manuals for now. The jury can read the fine print when it deliberates.

"Just a few more quick questions," I say, smiling and refreshed. "In 1991, how many health insurance policies did Great Benefit have issued and in effect?"

Again, the weasel looks helplessly at his lawyer. This information was due me three weeks ago.

"I'm not sure," he says.

"And how many claims were filed in 1991?"

"I'm not sure."

"You're the Vice President of Claims, and you don't know?"

"It's a big company."

"How many claims were denied in 1991?"

"I don't know."

At this point, perfectly on cue, Judge Kipler says, "The witness may be excused for today. We're going to recess for a few minutes so the jury can go home."

He says good-bye to the jury, thanks them again, and gives them their instructions. I get a few smiles as they file past our table. We wait for them to leave, and when the last juror disappears through the double doors, Kipler says, "Back on the record. Mr. Drummond, both you and your client are in contempt of court. I insisted that this information be forwarded to the plaintiff several weeks ago. It hasn't been done. It's very relevant and pertinent, and you have refused to provide it. Are you and your client prepared to be incarcerated until this information is received?"

Leo is on his feet, very tired, aging quickly. "Your Honor, I've tried to get this information. I've honestly done my best." Poor Leo. He's still trying to comprehend Section U. And, at this moment, he is perfectly believable. His client has just proven to the world that it will hide documents from him.

"Is Mr. Keeley nearby?" His Honor asks.

"In the witness room," Drummond says.

"Go get him." Within seconds, the bailiff leads the CEO into the courtroom.

Dot has had enough. She needs to pee and must have a smoke.

Kipler points to the witness stand. He swears Keeley himself, then asks him if there's any good reason why his company has refused to provide the information I've asked for.

He stutters, stammers, tries to blame it on the regional offices and the district offices.

"Do you understand the concept of contempt of court?" Kipler asks.

"Maybe, well, not really."

"It's very simple. Your company is in contempt of court, Mr. Keeley. I can either fine your company, or place you, as the CEO, in jail. Which shall it be?"

I'm sure some of his pals have pulled time at the federal country clubs, but Keeley knows that jail here means one downtown with lots of street types. "I really don't want to go to jail, Your Honor."

"Didn't think so. I hereby fine Great Benefit the sum of ten thousand dollars, due and payable to the plaintiff by 5 P.M. tomorrow. Call the home office and get a check FedExed, okay?"

Keeley can do nothing but nod.

"Furthermore, if this information is not faxed in here by nine in the morning, then you'll be taken to the Memphis City Jail, where you'll remain until you comply. Plus, while you're there, your company will be fined five thousand dollars a day."

Kipler turns and points downward at Drummond. "I have repeatedly warned you about these documents, Mr. Drummond. This behavior is grossly unacceptable."

He raps his gavel angrily, and leaves the bench.

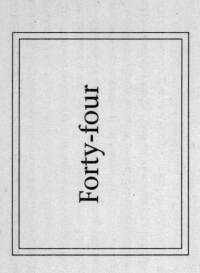

Forty-four

UNDER NORMAL CIRCUMSTANCES, I might feel silly wearing a blue and gray cap with a tiger on it, along with my suit, and leaning on a wall in Concourse A of the Memphis airport. But this day has been anything but normal. It's late, and I'm dead tired, but the adrenaline is hopping. A better first day of trial would be impossible.

The flight from Chicago arrives on time, and I'm soon spotted by my cap. A woman behind a large pair of dark sunglasses approaches, looks me up and down, finally says, "Mr. Baylor?"

"That's me." I shake hands with Jackie Lemancyzk, and with her male companion, a man who introduces himself only as Carl. He has a carry-on bag, and they're ready to go. These people are nervous.

We talk on the way to the hotel, a Holiday Inn downtown, six blocks from the courthouse. She sits in the front with me. Carl lurks in the backseat, saying nothing but guarding her like a rottweiler. I replay most of the first day's excitement. No, they do not know she's coming. Her hands shake. She's brittle and frail, and scared of her shadow. Other than revenge, I can't figure out her motive for being here.

The hotel reservation is in my name, at her request. The three of us sit around a small table in her room on the fifteenth floor, and go over my direct examination. The questions are typed and in order.

If there's beauty here, it's well concealed. The hair is chopped off and badly dyed to some dark red shade. Her lawyer said she was in therapy, and I'm not about to ask questions. Her eyes are bloodshot and sad, not at all enhanced with makeup. She's thirty-one, two small children, one divorce, and from outward appearances and demeanor it's hard to believe she spent her career at Great Benefit in one bed and out of another.

Carl is very protective. He pats her arm, occasionally gives his opinion about a particular answer. She wants to testify as soon as possible in the morning, then get back to the airport and get out of town.

I leave them at midnight.

AT NINE Tuesday morning, Judge Kipler calls us to order but instructs the bailiff to keep the jury in its room for a few moments. He asks Drummond if the claims information has been received. At the rate of five thousand bucks a day, I almost hope it hasn't.

"Came in about an hour ago, Your Honor," he says, obviously relieved. He hands me a neat stack of documents an inch thick, and even smiles a little when he hands Kipler his set.

"Mr. Baylor, you'll need some time," His Honor says.

"Give me thirty minutes," I say.

"Fine. We'll seat the jury at nine-thirty."

Deck and I dash to a small attorney's conference room down the hall, and wade through the information. Not unexpectedly, it's in Greek and almost impossible to decode. They'll be sorry.

At nine-thirty, the jury is brought into the courtroom and greeted warmly by Judge Kipler. They report in good condition, no sicknesses, no contact last night from anybody regarding the case.

"Your witness, Mr. Baylor," Kipler says, and day two is under way.

"We'd like to continue with Everett Lufkin," I say.

Lufkin is retrieved from the witness room, and takes the stand. After the Section U fiasco yesterday, nobody will believe a word he says. I'm sure Drummond chewed on him until midnight. He looks rather haggard. I hand him the official copy of the claims information, and ask him if he can identify it.

"It's a printout of a computer summary of various claims information."

"Prepared by the computers at Great Benefit?"

"That's correct."

"When?"

"Late yesterday afternoon and last night."

"Under your supervision as Vice President of Claims?"

"You could say that."

"Good. Now, Mr. Lufkin, please tell the jury how many medical policies were in existence in 1991."

He hesitates, then starts to play with the printout. We wait while he searches through the pages. The only sound for a long, awkward gap is the shuffling of paper in Lufkin's lap.

The "dumping" of documents is a favorite tactic of insurance companies and their lawyers. They love to wait until the last minute, preferably the day before the trial, and unload four storage boxes full of paperwork on the plaintiff's lawyer's doorstep. I avoided this because of Tyrone Kipler.

This is just a taste of it. I guess they thought they could trot in here this morning, hand me seventy pages of printout, most of it apparently meaningless, and be done with it.

"It's really hard to tell," he says, barely audible. "If I had some time."

"You've had two months," Kipler says loudly, his microphone working splendidly. The tone and volume of his words are startling. "Now answer the question." They're already squirming at the defense table.

"I want to know three things, Mr. Lufkin," I say. "The number of policies in existence, the number of claims on these policies and the number of these claims which were denied. All for the year 1991. Please."

More pages are flipped. "If I recall correctly, we had something in the neighborhood of ninety-seven thousand policies."

"You can't look at your numbers there and tell us for certain?"

It's obvious he can't. He pretends to be so engrossed in the data he can't answer my question.

"And you're the Vice President of Claims?" I ask, taunting.

"That's right!" he responds.

"Let me ask you this, Mr. Lufkin. To the best of your knowledge, is the information I want contained in that printout?"

"Yes."

"So, it's just a matter of finding it."

"If you'll shut up a second, I'll find it." He smarls this at me like a wounded animal, and in doing so comes across very badly.

"I'm not required to shut up, Mr. Lufkin."

Drummond rises, pleads with his hands. "Your Honor,

in all fairness, the witness is trying to find the information."

"Mr. Drummond, the witness has had two months to gather this information. He's the Vice President of Claims, surely he can read the numbers. Overruled."

"Forget the printout for a second, Mr. Lufkin," I say. "In an average year, what would be the ratio of policies to claims? Just give us a percentage."

"On the average, we get claims filed on between eight and ten percent of our policies."

"And what percentage of the claims would ultimately be denied?"

"Around ten percent of all claims are denied," he says. Though he suddenly has answers, he's not the least bit pleased to share them.

"What's the dollar amount of the average claim, whether it's paid or denied?"

There's a long pause as he thinks about this. I think he's given up. He just wants to get through, get himself off the witness stand and out of Memphis.

"On the average, somewhere around five thousand dollars a claim."

"Some claims are worth just a few hundred dollars, correct?"

"Yes."

"And some claims are worth tens of thousands, correct?"

"Yes."

"So it's hard to say what's average, right?"

"Yes."

"Now, these averages and percentages you've just given me, are they fairly typical throughout the industry, or are they unique to Great Benefit?"

"I can't speak for the industry."

"So you don't know?"

"I didn't say that."

"So you do know? Just answer the question."

His shoulders sag a bit. The man just wants out of this room. "I'd say they're pretty average."

"Thank you." I pause for effect here, study my notes for a second, change gears, wink at Deck, who eases from the courtroom. "Just a couple more, Mr. Lufkin. Did you suggest to Jackie Lemancyzk that she should quit?"

"I did not."

"How would you rate her performance?"

"Average."

"Do you know why she was demoted from the position of senior claims examiner?"

"As I recall, it had something to do with her skills in handling people."

"Did she receive any type of termination pay when she resigned?"

"No. She quit."

"No compensation of any kind?"

"No."

"Thank you. Your Honor, I'm through with this witness."

Drummond has two choices. He can either use Lufkin now, on direct exam with no leading questions, or he can save him for later. It will be impossible to prop up this guy, and I have no doubt Drummond will get him out of here as soon as possible.

"Your Honor, we're going to keep Mr. Lufkin for later," Drummond says. No surprise. The jury will never see him again.

"Very well. Call your next witness, Mr. Baylor."

I say this at full volume. "The plaintiff calls Jackie Lemancyzk."

I turn quickly to see the reaction of Underhall and Aldy. They're in the process of whispering to each other, and they freeze when they hear her name. Their eyes bulge, mouths open in complete and total surprise.

Poor Lufkin is about halfway to the double doors when he hears the news. He stops cold, whirls wild-eyed at the defense table, then walks even faster from the courtroom.

As his boys scramble around him, Drummond is on his feet. "Your Honor, may we approach the bench?"

Kipler waves us up where he is to huddle away from the microphone. My opponent is pretending to be incensed. I'm sure he's surprised, but he has no right to cry foul. He's almost hyperventilating. "Your Honor, this is a complete surprise," he hisses. It's important for the jury not to hear his words or see his shock.

"Why?" I ask smugly. "She's listed as a potential witness in the pretrial order."

"We have a right to be forewarned. When did you find her?"

"Didn't know she was lost."

"It's a fair question, Mr. Baylor," His Honor says, frowning at me for the first time in history. I give them both an innocent look as if to say, "Hey, I'm just a rookie. Gimme a break."

"She's in the pretrial order," I insist, and, frankly, all three of us know she's going to testify. Perhaps I should've informed the court yesterday that she was in town, but, hey, this is my first trial.

She follows Deck into the courtroom. Underhall and Aldy refuse to look at her. The five stiffs from Trent & Brent watch every step. She cleans up nicely. A loose-fitting blue dress hangs on her thin body and falls just above her knees. Her face looks much different from last night, much prettier. She takes her oath, sits in the witness chair, shoots one hateful look at the boys from Great Benefit and is ready to testify.

I wonder if she's slept with Underhall or Aldy. Last

night she mentioned Lufkin and one other, but I know I didn't get a full history.

We cover the basics quickly, then move in for the kill.

"How long did you work for Great Benefit?"

"Six years."

"And when did your employment end?"

"October 3."

"How did it end?"

"I was fired."

"You didn't resign?"

"No. I was fired."

"Who fired you?"

"It was a conspiracy. Everett Lufkin, Kermit Aldy, Jack Underhall and several others." She nods at the guilty parties, and all necks twist toward the boys from Great Benefit.

I approach the witness and hand her a copy of her letter of resignation. "Do you recognize this," I ask.

"This is a letter I typed and signed," she says.

The letter states that you're quitting for personal reasons."

"The letter is a lie. I was fired because of my involvement in the claim of Donny Ray Black, and because I was scheduled to give a deposition on October 5. I was fired so the company could claim I no longer worked there."

"Who made you write this letter?"

"The same ones. It was a conspiracy."

"Can you explain it to us?"

She looks at the jurors for the first time, and they are all looking at her. She swallows hard, and starts talking. "On the Saturday before my deposition was scheduled, I was asked to come to the office. There I met with Jack Underhall, the man sitting over there in the gray suit. He's one of the in-house lawyers. He told me I was leaving immediately, and that I had two choices. I could call it a firing, and leave with nothing. Or, I could write that letter, call it a resignation and the company would give me ten thousand dollars in cash to keep quiet. And I had to make the decision right there, in his presence."

She was able to talk about this last night without emotion, but things are different in open court. She bites her lip, struggles for a minute, then is able to move on. "I'm a single mother with two children, and there are lots of bills. I had no choice. I was suddenly out of work. I wrote the letter, took the cash and signed an agreement to never discuss any of my claims files with anybody."

"Including the Black file?"

"Specifically the Black file."

"Then if you took the money and signed the agreement, why are you here?"

"After I got over the shock, I talked to a lawyer. A very good lawyer. He assured me the agreement I signed was illegal."

"Do you have a copy of the agreement?"

"No. Mr. Underhall wouldn't let me keep one. But you can ask him. I'm sure he has the original." I slowly turn and stare at Jack Underhall, as does every other person in the courtroom. His shoelaces have suddenly become the center of his life, and he's fiddling with them, seemingly oblivious to her testimony.

I look at Leo Drummond, and for the first time see the look of complete defeat. His client, of course, didn't tell him about the cash bribery or the agreement signed under duress.

"Why did you see a lawyer?"

"Because I needed advice. I was wrongfully terminated. But before that, I was discriminated against because I was a woman, and I was sexually harassed by various executives at Great Benefit."

"Anybody we know?"

"Objection, Your Honor," Drummond says. "This might be fun to talk about, but it's not relevant to the case."

"Let's see where it goes. I'll overrule for now. Please answer the question, Ms. Lemancyzk."

She takes a deep breath, says, "I had sex with Everett Lufkin for three years. As long as I was willing to do whatever he wanted, my pay was increased and I was promoted. When I got tired of it and stopped, I was demoted from senior claims examiner to claims handler. My pay was cut by twenty percent. Then, Russell Krokit, who was at that time the senior claims supervisor but was fired when I was, decided he'd like to have an affair. He forced himself on me, told me if I didn't play along then I'd be out of work. But if I'd be his girl for a while, he'd make sure I got another promotion. It was either put out, or get out."

"Both of these men are married?"

"Yes, with families. They were known to prey on the young girls in claims. I could give you a lot of names. And these weren't the only two hotshots who traded promotions for sex."

Again, all eyes turn to Underhall and Aldy.

I pause here to check something on my desk. It's just a little courtroom ploy I've sort of learned to allow juicy testimony to hang in the air before moving on.

I look at Jackie, and she dabs her eyes with a tissue. They're both red right now. The jury is with her, ready to kill for her.

"Let's talk about the Black file," I say. "It was assigned to you."

"That's correct. The initial claim form from Mrs. Black was assigned to me. Pursuant to company policy at that time, I sent her a letter of denial."

"Why?"

"Why? Because all claims were initially denied, at least in 1991."

"All claims?"

"Yes. It was our policy to deny every claim initially, then review the smaller ones that appeared to be legitimate. We eventually paid some of those, but the big claims were never paid unless a lawyer got involved."

"When did this become policy?"

"January 1, 1991. It was an experiment, sort of a scheme." I'm nodding at her. Get on with it. "The company decided to deny every claim over one thousand dollars for a twelve-month period. It didn't matter how legitimate the claim was, it was simply denied. Many of the smaller claims were also ultimately denied if we could find any arguable reason. A very few of the larger claims were paid, and, again, only after the insured hired a lawyer and started threatening."

"How long was this policy in effect?"

"Twelve months. It was a one-year experiment. It had never been done before in the industry, and it was generally viewed by management as a wonderful idea. Deny for a year, add up the money saved, deduct the amount spent on quickie court settlements, and there's a pot of gold left."

"How much gold?"

"The scheme netted an extra forty million or so."

"How do you know this?"

"You stay in bed long enough with these miserable men and you hear all sorts of trash. They'll tell everything. They'll talk about their wives, their jobs. I'm not proud of this, okay? I didn't get one moment of pleasure from it. I was a victim." Her eyes are red again, and her voice shakes a little.

Another long pause as I review my notes. "How was the Black claim treated?"

"Initially, it was denied like all the rest. But it was a big claim, and coded differently. When the words 'acute leukemia' were noticed, everything I did was monitored by Russell Krokit. At some point early on, they realized that the policy did not exclude bone marrow transplants. It became a very serious file for two reasons. First, it was suddenly worth a ton of money, money the company obviously didn't want to pay. And secondly, the insured was terminally ill."

"So the claims department knew Donny Ray Black was going to die?"

"Of course. His medical records were clear. I remember one report from his doctor saying the chemo went well but the leukemia would be back, probably within a year, and that it eventually would be fatal unless his patient received the bone marrow transplant."

"Did you show this to anyone?"

"I showed it to Russell Krokit. He showed it to his boss, Everett Lufkin. Somewhere up there the decision was made to continue the denial."

"But you knew the claim should be paid?"

"Everybody knew it, but the company was playing the odds."

"Could you explain this?"

"The odds that the insured wouldn't consult a lawyer."

"Did you know what the odds were at the time?"

"It was commonly believed that no more than one out of twenty-five would talk to a lawyer. That's the only reason they started this experiment. They knew they could get by with it. They sell these policies to people who are not that educated, and they count on their ignorance to accept the denials."

"What would happen when you received a letter from an attorney?"

"It became a very different situation. If the claim was

under five thousand dollars and legitimate, we paid it immediately with a letter of apology. Just a corporate mix-up, you know, that type of letter. Or maybe our computers were to blame. I've sent a hundred such letters. If the claim was over five thousand dollars, then the file left my hands and went to a supervisor. I think they were almost always paid. If the lawyer had filed suit or was on the verge of filing, the company would negotiate a confidential settlement."

"How often did this happen?"

"I really don't know."

I step back from the podium, say, "Thanks," then turn to Drummond, and with a pleasant smile say, "Your witness."

I sit by Dot, who's in tears and sobbing quietly. She's always blamed herself for not finding a lawyer sooner, and to hear this testimony is especially painful. Regardless of the outcome, she will never forgive herself.

Fortunately, several of the jurors see her crying.

Poor Leo walks slowly to a spot as far away from the jury as he can stand and still be allowed to ask questions. I cannot imagine what he might ask, but I'm sure he's been ambushed before.

He introduces himself, very cordially, tells Jackie that of course they've never met. This is an effort to inform the jury that he hasn't had the benefit of knowing what in the world she might say. She gives him a blistering look. She not only hates Great Benefit but any lawyer sorry enough to represent it.

"Now, is it true, Ms. Lemancyzk, that you have been committed recently to an institution for various problems?" He asks this question very delicately. In a trial you're not supposed to ask a question unless you know the answer, but I have a hunch Leo has no idea what's coming. His source has been a few desperate whispers during the past fifteen minutes.

"No! That's not true." She's bristling.

"I beg your pardon. But you have been receiving treatment?"

"I was not committed. I voluntarily checked into a facility and stayed for two weeks. I was permitted to leave whenever I wanted. The treatment was supposedly covered under my group policy at Great Benefit. I was supposed to be covered for twelve months after my departure. They, of course, are denying the claim."

Drummond chews on a nail, stares down at his legal pad as if he didn't hear this. Next question, Leo.

"Is that why you're here? Because you're angry with Great Benefit?"

"I hate Great Benefit, and most of the worms who work there. Does that answer your question?"

"Is your testimony here today prompted by your hatred?"

"No. I'm here because I know the truth about how they deliberately screwed thousands of people. This story needs to be told."

Better give it up, Leo.

"Why did you go to the treatment facility?"

"I'm struggling with alcoholism and depression. Right now, I'm okay. Next week, who knows? For six years I was treated like a piece of meat by your clients. I was passed around the office like a box of candy, everybody taking what they wanted. They preyed on me because I was broke, single with two kids and I had a nice ass. They robbed me of my self-esteem. I'm fighting back, Mr. Drummond. I'm trying to save myself, and if I have to seek treatment, then I won't hesitate. I just wish your client would pay the damned bills."

"No further questions, Your Honor." Drummond

scoots quickly back to his table. I walk Jackie through the railing and almost to the door. I thank her more than once, and promise to call her attorney. Deck leaves to drive her to the airport.

It's almost eleven-thirty. I want the jury to ponder her testimony over lunch, so I ask Judge Kipler to break early. My official reason is that I need time to study computer printouts before I can call any more witnesses.

The ten thousand dollars in sanctions arrived while we were in the courtroom, and Drummond has submitted it in escrow, along with a twenty-page motion and brief. He plans to appeal the sanctions, so the money will sit, untouchable, in a court account pending the outcome. I have other things to worry about.

Forty-five

I GET A FEW SMILES FROM THE JURORS AS they file to their seats after lunch. They're not supposed to discuss the case until it's officially handed to them, but everyone knows they whisper about it every time they leave the courtroom. A few years ago, two jurors got in a fistfight while debating the veracity of a certain witness. Problem was, it was the second witness in a trial scheduled for two weeks. The judge declared a mistrial and started over.

They've had two hours to simmer and boil over Jackie's testimony. It's time for me to show them how to rectify some of these wrongs. It's time to talk about money.

"Your Honor, the plaintiff calls Mr. Wilfred Keeley to the stand." Keeley is found nearby, and bounces into the courtroom, just itching to testify. He seems vigorous and friendly, in sharp contrast to Lufkin and in spite of the indelible lies already exposed against his company. He obviously wants to assure the jury that he's in charge, and that he's a soul to be trusted.

I ask a few general questions, establish the fact that he's

the CEO, the number-one boss at Great Benefit. He heartily confesses to this. Then I hand him a copy of the company's latest financial statement. He acts as if he reads it every morning.

"Now, Mr. Keeley, can you tell the jury how much your company is worth?"

"What do you mean by worth?" he shoots back.

"I mean net worth."

"That's not a clear concept."

"Yes it is. Look at your financial statements there, take the assets on one hand, subtract the liabilities on the other, and tell the jury what's left. That's net worth."

"It's not that simple."

I shake my head in disbelief. "Would you agree that your company has a net worth of approximately four hundred and fifty million dollars?"

Aside from the obvious advantages, one additional benefit in catching a corporate thug lying is that its subsequent witnesses need to be refreshingly honest. Keeley needs to be refreshingly honest, and I'm sure Drummond has beaten him over the head with this. I'm sure it's been difficult.

"That's a fair assessment. I'll agree with that."

"Thank you. Now, how much cash does your company have?"

This question was not expected. Drummond stands and objects, Kipler overrules.

"Well, that's difficult to say," he says, and lapses into the Great Benefit angst we've come to expect.

"Come on, Mr. Keeley, you're the CEO. You've been with the company for eighteen years. You came out of finance. How much cash you got lying around up there?"

He's flipping pages like crazy, and I wait patiently. He finally gives me a figure, and this is where I thank Max Leuberg. I take my copy, and ask him to explain a particular Reserve Account. When I sued them for ten million dollars, they set aside that amount as a reserve to pay the claim. Same with every lawsuit. It's still their money, still being invested and earning well, but now it's classified as a *liability*. Insurance companies love it when they get sued for umpteen zillion bucks, because they can reserve the money and claim they're basically broke.

And it's all perfectly legal. It's an unregulated industry with its own set of murky accounting practices.

Keeley starts using long financial words that no one understands. He'd rather confuse the jury than admit the truth.

I quiz him about another Reserve, then we move to the Surplus accounts. Restricted Surplus. Unrestricted Surplus. I grill him pretty good, and I sound rather intelligent. Using Leuberg's notes, I tally up the figures and ask Keeley if the company has about four hundred and eighty-five million in cash.

"I wish," he says with a laugh. There's not so much as a grin from anyone else.

"Then how much cash do you have, Mr. Keeley?"

"Oh, I don't know. I'd say probably around a hundred million."

That's enough for now. During my closing argument, I can put my figures on a chalkboard and explain where the money is.

I hand him a copy of the printout on the claims data, and he looks surprised. I made the decision at lunch to ambush him while I had him on the stand, and stay away from an encore by Lufkin. He looks at Drummond for help, but there's nothing he can do. Mr. Keeley here is the CEO, and he certainly should be able to aid us in our search for the truth. I'm assuming they're thinking I'll bring back Lufkin to explain this data. As much as I love Lufkin, I'm through with him. I won't give him the chance to refute the statements of Jackie Lemancyzk.

"Do you recognize that printout, Mr. Keeley? It's the one your company gave me this morning."

"Certainly."

"Good. Can you tell the jury how many medical policies your company had in effect in 1991?"

"Well, I don't know. Let me see." He turns pages, holds one up, then puts it down, takes another, then another.

"Does the figure of ninety-eight thousand sound correct, give or take a few?"

"Maybe. Sure, yeah, I think that's right."

"And how many claims on these policies were filed in 1991?"

Same routine. Keeley flounders through the printout, mumbling figures to himself. It's almost embarrassing. Minutes pass, and I finally say, "Does the figure of 11,400 sound correct, give or take a few?"

"Sounds close, I guess, but I'd need to verify it, you know."

"How would you verify it?"

"Well, I'd need to study this some more."

"So the information is right there?"

"I think so."

"Can you tell the jury how many of these claims were denied by your company?"

"Well, again, I'd have to study all this," he says, lifting the printout with both hands.

"So this information is also contained in what you're now holding?"

"Maybe. Yes, I think so."

"Good. Look on pages eleven, eighteen, thirty-three and forty-one." He's quick to obey, anything to keep from testifying. Pages rattle and shuffle.

"Does the figure of 9,100 sound correct, give or take a few?"

He's just plain shocked at this outrageous suggestion. "Of course not. That's absurd."

"But you don't know?"

"I know it's not that high."

"Thank you." I approach the witness, take the printout and hand him the Great Benefit policy given to me by Max Leuberg. "Do you recognize this?"

"Sure," he says gladly, anything to get away from that wretched printout.

"What is it?"

"It's a medical policy issued by my company."

"Issued when?"

He examines it for a second. "September of 1992. Five months ago."

"Please look at page eleven, Section F, paragraph four, sub-paragraph c, clause number thirteen. Do you see that?"

The print is so small he has to pull the policy almost to his nose. I chuckle at this and glance at the jurors. The humor is not missed.

"Got it," he says finally.

"Good. Now read it, please."

He reads, squinting and frowning as if it's truly tedious. When he's finished, he forces a smile. "Okay."

"What's the purpose of that clause?"

"It excludes certain surgical procedures from the coverage."

"Specifically?"

"Specifically all transplants."

"Is bone marrow listed as an exclusion?"

"Yes. Bone marrow is listed."

I approach the witness and hand him a copy of the Black policy. I ask him to read a certain section. The minuscule print strains his eyes again, but he valiantly plows through it.

"What does this policy exclude in the way of transplants?"

"All major organs; kidney, liver, heart, lungs, eyes, they're all listed here."

"What about bone marrow?"

"It's not listed."

"So it's not specifically excluded?"

"That's correct."

"When was this lawsuit filed, Mr. Keeley? Do you remember?"

He glances at Drummond, who of course cannot be of any assistance at this moment. "During the middle of last summer, as I recall. Could it be June?"

"Yes sir," I say. "It was June. Do you know when the language of the policy was changed to include the exclusion of bone marrow transplants?"

"No. I do not. I'm not involved in the writing of the policies."

"Who writes your policies? Who creates all this fine print?"

"It's done in the legal department."

"I see. Would it be safe to say that the policy was changed sometime after this lawsuit was filed?"

He analyzes me for a moment, then says, "No. It might have been changed before the suit was filed."

"Was it changed after the claim was filed, in August of 1991?"

"I don't know."

His answer sounds suspicious. Either he's not paying attention to his company, or he's lying. It really makes no difference to me. I have what I want. I can argue to the jury that this new language is clear evidence that there was no intent to exclude bone marrow from the Blacks' policy. They excluded everything else, and they exclude everything now, so they got nailed by their own language.

I have only one quick matter left for Keeley. "Do you have a copy of the agreement Jackie Lemancyzk signed on the day she was fired?"

"No."

"Have you ever seen this agreement?"

"No."

"Did you authorize the payment of ten thousand dollars in cash to Jackie Lemancyzk?"

"No. She's lying about that."

"Lying?"

"That's what I said."

"What about Everett Lufkin? Did he lie to the jury about the claims manual?"

Keeley starts to say something, then catches himself. No answer will benefit him at this point. The jurors know full well that Lufkin lied to them, so he can't tell the jurors they really didn't hear what they really heard. And he certainly can't admit that one of his vice presidents lied to the jury.

I didn't plan this question, it just happened. "I asked you a question, Mr. Keeley. Did Everett Lufkin lie to this jury about the claims manual?"

"I don't think I have to answer that question?"

"Answer the question," Kipler says sternly.

There's a painful pause as Keeley glares at me. The courtroom is silent. Every single juror is watching him and waiting. The truth is obvious to all, and so I decide to be the nice guy.

"Can't answer it, can you, because you can't admit a vice president of your company lied to this jury?"

"Objection."

"Sustained."

"No further questions."

"No direct at this time, Your Honor," Drummond says. Evidently, he wants the dust to settle before he brings these guys back during the defense. Right now, Drummond wants time and distance between Jackie Lemanczyk and our jury.

KERMIT ALDY, the Vice President for Underwriting, is my next to last witness. At this point, I really don't need his testimony, but I need to fill some time. It's two-thirty on the second day of the trial, and I'll easily finish this afternoon. I want the jury to go home thinking about two people, Jackie Lemanczyk and Donny Ray Black.

Aldy is scared and short with his words, afraid to say much more than is absolutely necessary. I don't know if he slept with Jackie, but right now everybody from Great Benefit is a suspect. I sense the jury feels this way too.

We zip through enough background to suffice. Underwriting is so horribly boring I'm determined to provide only the barest of details for the jury. Aldy is also boring and thus up to the task. I don't want to lose the jury, so I go fast.

Then, it's time for the fun stuff. I hand him the underwriting manual that was given to me during discovery. It's in a green binder, and looks very much like the claims manual. Neither Aldy nor Drummond nor anyone else knows if I also have in my possession another copy of the underwriting manual, this one fully equipped with a Section U.

He looks at it as if he's never seen it before, but identifies it when I ask him to. Everybody knows the next question.

"Is this a complete manual?"

He flips through it slowly, takes his time. He obviously has had the benefit of Lufkin's experience yesterday. If he says it's complete, and if I whip out the copy I borrowed from Cooper Jackson, then he's dead. If he admits something's missing, then he'll pay a price. I'm betting that Drummond has opted for the latter.

"Well, let's see. It looks complete, but, no, wait a minute. There's a section missing in the back."

"Might that be Section U?" I ask, incredulous.

"I think so, yes."

I pretend to be amazed. "Why in the world would any-one want to remove Section U from this manual?"

"I don't know."

"Do you know who removed it?"

"No."

"Of course not. Who selected this particular copy to be delivered to me?"

"I really don't remember."

"But it's obvious Section U was removed before it was given to me?"

"It's not here, if that's what you're after."

"I'm after the truth, Mr. Aldy. Please help me. Was Section U removed before this manual was given to me?"

"Apparently so."

"Does that mean yes?"

"Yes. The section was removed."

"Would you agree that the underwriting manual is very important to the operations of your department?"

"Of course."

"So you're obviously very familiar with it?"

"Yes."

"So it would be easy for you to summarize the basics of Section U for the jury, wouldn't it?"

"Oh, I don't know. It's been a while since I looked at it."

He still doesn't know if I have a copy of Section U from the underwriting manual. "Why don't you try? Just give the jury a brief rundown on what's in Section U."

He thinks for a moment, then explains that the section

deals with a system of checks and balances between claims and underwriting. Both departments are supposed to monitor certain claims. It requires a good deal of paperwork to ensure a claim is handled properly. He rambles, picks up a little confidence, and since I have yet to produce a copy of Section U, I think he starts to believe I don't have one.

"So the purpose of Section U is to guarantee that each claim is handled in a proper manner."

"Yes."

I reach under the table, pull out the manual and walk to the witness stand. "Then let's explain it to the jury," I say, handing him the complete manual. He sinks a bit. Drummond tries to maintain a confident bearing, but it's impossible.

The Section U in underwriting is just as dirty as the Section U in claims, and after an hour of embarrassing Aldy it's time to stop. The scheme has been laid bare for the jury to fume over.

Drummond has no questions. Kipler recesses us for fifteen minutes so Deck and I can set up the monitors.

Our final witness is Donny Ray Black. The bailiff dims the courtroom lights, and the jurors ease forward, anxious to see his face on the twenty-inch screen in front of them. We've edited his deposition down to thirty-one minutes, and every scratchy and weak word is absorbed by the jurors.

Instead of watching it for the hundredth time, I sit close to Dot and study the faces in the jury box. I see lots of sympathy. Dot wipes her cheeks with the backs of her hands. Toward the end, I have a lump in my throat.

The courtroom is very quiet for a full minute as the screens go blank and the bailiff goes for the lights. In the dimness, the soft but unmistakable sound of a crying mother emanates from our table.

We have inflicted all the damage I can think of. I have the case won. The challenge now is not to lose it.

The lights come on, and I announce solemnly, "Your Honor, the plaintiff rests."

LONG AFTER the jury leaves, Dot and I sit in an empty courtroom and talk about the remarkable testimony we've heard over the past two days. It's been clearly proven that she is right, they were wrong, but there's little satisfaction in this. She will go to her grave tormented because she didn't fight harder when it counted.

She tells me she doesn't care what happens next. She's had her day in court. She'd like to go home now, and never come back. I explain this is not possible. We're only halfway through. Just a few more days.

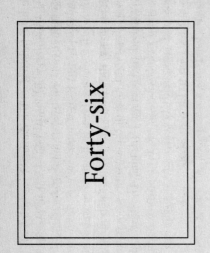

Forty-six

I AM FASCINATED BY WHAT DRUMMOND will try with his defense. He risks further damage if he trots out others from the home office and tries to explain away their claim denial schemes. He knows that I'll simply pull out the Section U's and ask all sorts of nasty questions. For all I know, there might be more blatant lies and cover-ups buried somewhere. The only way to expose them will be in a wide-open cross-examination.

He has eighteen people listed as possible witnesses. I can't imagine who he'll call first. When I presented our case, I had the luxury of knowing what would happen next, the next witness, the next document. It's very different now. I have to react, and quickly.

I make a late call to Max Leuberg in Wisconsin, and replay with great gusto the events of the first two days. He offers some advice and a few opinions about what might happen next. He gets terribly excited and says he might catch a flight.

I walk the floors until three in the morning, talking to myself and trying to imagine what Drummond will try.

□ □ □ □

I AM PLEASANTLY SURPRISED to see Cooper Jackson sitting in the courtroom when I arrive at eight-thirty. He introduces me to two more lawyers, both from Raleigh, North Carolina. They've flown in to watch my trial. How's it going, they ask? I give them a cautious summary of what's happened. One of the lawyers was here on Monday, watched the Section U drama. The three of them have about twenty cases so far, been advertising in newspapers and such, and the cases are popping up everywhere. They plan to file very soon.

Cooper hands me a newspaper and asks if I've seen it. It's *The Wall Street Journal*, dated yesterday, and there's a front-page story about Great Benefit. I tell them I haven't read a newspaper in a week, don't even know what day it is. They know the feeling.

I read the story quickly. It centers around the growing number of complaints about Great Benefit and its tendency to deny claims. Many states are now investigating. Lots of lawsuits are being filed. The last paragraph says that a certain little trial down in Memphis is being watched because it could produce the first substantial verdict against the company.

I show the story to Kipler in his office, and he's unconcerned. He'll simply ask the jurors if they've seen it. They were warned against reading newspapers. We both seriously doubt if the *Journal* is widely read by our panel.

THE DEFENSE first calls André Weeks, a Deputy Commissioner of Insurance for the state of Tennessee. He's a high-level bureaucrat in the Department of Insurance, a witness Drummond's used before. His job is to place the government squarely on the side of the defense.

He's a very attractive man of about forty with a nice suit, easy smile, honest face. Plus, at this moment he possesses a crucial asset: he doesn't work for Great Benefit. Drummond asks him a lot of mundane questions about the regulatory duties of his office, tries to make it sound as though these boys are riding roughshod over the insurance industry, really cracking the whip. Since Great Benefit is still a company in good standing in this state, then it's obvious they're really behaving themselves. Otherwise, André here and his pack of watchdogs would be in hot pursuit.

Drummond needs time. He needs a small mountain of testimony dumped on our jurors so maybe they'll forget some of the horrible things they've already heard. He goes slow. He moves slow, talks slow, very much like an aging professor. And he's very good. Given another set of facts, he would be deadly.

He hands Weeks the Black policy, and they spend half an hour explaining to the jury how each policy, *every policy*, has to be approved by the Department of Insurance. Heavy emphasis is placed on the word "approved."

Since I'm not on my feet, I can spend more time looking around. I study the jurors, a few of whom maintain eye contact. They're with me. I notice strangers in the courtroom, young men in suits I've never seen before. Cooper Jackson and his buddies are on the back row, near the door. There are less than fifteen spectators. Why would anyone want to watch a civil trial?

After an hour and a half of truly excruciating testimony about the intricacies of statewide insurance regulation, the jurors drift away. Drummond doesn't care. He desperately wants to stretch the trial into next week. He finally tenders the witness just before eleven, effectively killing the morning. We recess for fifteen minutes, and it's my turn to take a few shots in the dark.

Weeks says that there are now over six hundred insurance companies operating in the state, that his office has a staff of forty-one and that of this number only eighteen actually review policies. He reluctantly estimates that each of the six hundred companies has at least ten different types of policies in effect, so there's a minimum of six thousand policies on file with the department. And he admits that the policies are constantly being modified and amended.

We do some more math, and I'm able to convey my message that it's impossible for any bureaucratic unit to monitor the ocean of fine print created by the insurance industry. I hand him the Black policy. He claims to have read it, but admits he did so only in preparation for this trial. I ask him a question about the Weekly Accident Benefit—Non-Hospital Confinement. The policy suddenly seems heavier, and he turns pages quickly, hoping to find the section and fire off an answer. Doesn't happen. He flips and shuffles, squints and frowns, finally says he's got it. His answer is sort of correct, so I let it pass. Then I ask him about the proper method of changing beneficiaries under the policy, and I almost feel sorry for him. He studies the policy for a very long time as everybody waits. The jurors are amused. Kipler is smirking. Drummond is burning but can do nothing about it.

He gives us an answer, the correctness of which is not important. The point is made. I place the two green manuals on my table as if Weeks and I are about to trudge through them again. Everybody watches. Holding the claims manual, I ask him if he periodically reviews the internal claims handling processes of any of the companies he so zealously regulates. He wants to say yes, but evidently he's heard about Section U. So he says no, and I, of course, am just plain shocked. I pop him with a few sarcastic questions, then let him off the hook. Damage is done and duly recorded.

I ask him if he's aware that the Commissioner of Insurance in Florida is investigating Great Benefit. He does not know this. How about South Carolina? No, again, this is news to him. What about North Carolina? Seems he might've heard something about that one, but hasn't seen anything. Kentucky? Georgia? Nope, and for the record, he's really not concerned with what the other states are doing. I thank him for this.

DRUMMOND'S NEXT WITNESS is another nonemployee of Great Benefit, but just barely. His name is Payton Reisky, and his daunting title is Executive Director and President of the National Insurance Alliance. He has the look and manner of a very important person. We quickly learn his outfit is a political organization based in Washington, funded by insurance companies to be their voice on Capitol Hill. Just a bunch of lobbyists, no doubt with a gold-plated budget. They do lots of wonderful things, we're told, all in an effort to promote fair insurance practices.

This little introduction goes on for a very long time. It starts at one-thirty in the afternoon, and by two we're convinced the NIA is on the verge of saving humanity. What fabulous people!

Reisky has spent thirty years in the business, and his résumé and pedigree are soon shared with us. Drummond wants him to be qualified as an expert in the field of insurance claims practice and procedure. I have no objection. I've studied his testimony from one other trial, and I think I can handle him. It would take an exceptionally gifted expert to make Section U sound good.

With virtually no prompting, he leads us through a complete checklist of how such a claim should be handled. Drummond gravely nods his head, as if they're really kicking some ass now. Guess what? Great Benefit stuck to the book on this one. Maybe a couple of minor mistakes, but hey, it's a big company with lots of claims. No major departure from what's reasonable.

The gist of Reisky's opinions is that Great Benefit had every right to deny this claim because of its magnitude. He explains very seriously to the jury how a policy that costs eighteen dollars a week cannot reasonably be expected to cover a transplant that costs two hundred thousand dollars. The purpose of a debit policy is to provide only the basics, not all the bells and whistles.

Drummond broaches the subject of the manuals and their missing sections. Unfortunate, Reisky believes, but not that important. Manuals come and go, in a state of perpetual modification, usually ignored by seasoned claims handlers because they know what they're doing. But, since it's become such an issue, let's talk about it. He eagerly takes the claims manual and explains various sections to the jury. It's all laid out here in black and white. Everything works wonderfully!

They move from the manuals to the numbers. Drummond asks if he's had the chance to review the information regarding policies, claims and denials. Reisky nods seriously, then takes the printout from Drummond.

Great Benefit certainly had a high rate of denials in 1991, but there could be reasons for this. It's not unheard of in the industry. And you can't always trust the numbers. In fact, if you look at the past ten years, Great Benefit's average denial rate is slightly under twelve percent, which is certainly within the industry average. Numbers follow more numbers, and we're quickly confused, which is precisely what Drummond wants.

Reisky steps down from the witness stand, and begins pointing here and there on a multicolored chart. He talks to the jury like a skilled lecturer, and I wonder how often he does this. The numbers are well within the average. Kipler mercifully gives us a break at three-thirty. I huddle in the hallway with Cooper Jackson and his friends. They're all veteran trial lawyers and quick with advice. We agree that Drummond is stalling and hoping for the weekend.

I do not utter a single word during the afternoon session. Reisky testifies until late, finally finishing with a flurry of opinions about how fairly everything was handled. Judging from the faces of the jurors, they're happy the man's finished. I'm thankful for a few extra hours to prepare for his cross-examination.

DECK AND I enjoy a long meal with Cooper Jackson and three other lawyers at an old Italian restaurant called Grisanti's. Big John Grisanti, the colorful proprietor, puts us in a private dining room called the Press Box. He brings us a wonderful wine we didn't order, and tells us precisely what we should eat.

The wine is soothing, and for the first time in many days I almost relax. Maybe I'll sleep well tonight.

The check totals over four hundred dollars, and is quickly grabbed by Cooper Jackson. Thank goodness. The law firm of Rudy Baylor may be on the verge of serious money, but right now it's still broke.

Forty-seven

SECONDS AFTER PAYTON REISKY TAKES the witness stand bright and early Thursday morning, I hand him a copy of the Stupid Letter and ask him to read it. Then I ask, "Now, Mr. Reisky, in your expert opinion, is this a fair and reasonable response from Great Benefit?"

He's been forewarned. "Of course not. This is horrible."

"It's shocking, isn't it?"

"It is. And I understand the author of this letter is no longer with the company."

"Who told you this?" I ask, very suspicious.

"Well, I'm not sure. Someone at the company."

"Did this unknown person also tell you the reason why Mr. Krokit is no longer with the company?"

"I'm not sure. Maybe it had something to do with the letter."

"Maybe? Are you sure of yourself, or simply speculating?"

"I'm really not sure."

"Thank you. Did this unknown person tell you that Mr. Krokit left the company two days before he was to give a deposition in this case?"

"I don't believe so."

"You don't know why he left, do you?"

"No."

"Good. I thought you were trying to imply to the jury that he left the company because he wrote this letter. You weren't trying to do that, were you?"

"No."

"Thank you."

It was decided over the wine last night that it would be a mistake to beat Reisky over the head with the manuals. There are several reasons for this line of thinking. First, the evidence is already before the jury. Second, it was first presented in a very dramatic and effective manner, i.e., we caught Lufkin lying through his teeth. Third, Reisky is quick with words and will be hard to pin down. Fourth, he's had time to prepare for the assault and will do a better job of holding his own. Fifth, he'll seize the opportunity to further confuse the jury. And, most important, it will take time. It would be easy to spend all day haggling with Reisky over the manuals and the statistical data. I'd kill a day and get nowhere in the process.

"Who pays your salary, Mr. Reisky?"

"My employer. The National Insurance Alliance."

"Who funds the NIA?"

"The insurance industry."

"Does Great Benefit contribute to the NIA?"

"Yes."

"And how much does it contribute?"

He looks at Drummond, who's already on his feet.

"Objection, Your Honor, this is irrelevant."

"Overruled. I think it's quite relevant."

"How much, Mr. Reisky?" I repeat, helpfully.

He obviously doesn't want to say, and looks squeamish.

"Ten thousand dollars a year."

"So they pay you more than they paid Donny Ray Black."

"Objection!"

"Sustained."

"Sorry, Your Honor. I'll withdraw that comment."

"Move to have it stricken from the record, Your Honor," Drummond says angrily.

"So ordered."

We take a breath as tempers subside. "Sorry, Mr. Reisky," I say humbly with a truly repentant face.

"Does all of your money come from insurance companies?"

"We have no other funding."

"How many insurance companies contribute to the NIA?"

"Two hundred and twenty."

"And what was the total amount contributed last year?"

"Six million dollars."

"And you use this money to lobby with?"

"We do some lobbying, yes."

"Are you getting paid extra to testify in this trial?"

"No."

"Why are you here?"

"Because I was contacted by Great Benefit. I was asked to come testify."

Very slowly, I turn and point to Dot Black. "And, Mr. Reisky, can you look at Mrs. Black, look her squarely in the eyes, and tell her that her son's claim was handled fairly and properly by Great Benefit?"

It takes him a second or two to focus on Dot's face, but he has no choice. He nods, then finally says crisply, "Yes. It certainly was."

I, of course, had planned this. I wanted it to be a dramatic way to quickly end Reisky's testimony, but I certainly didn't expect it to be humorous. Mrs. Beverdee Hardaway, a stocky black woman of fifty-one, who's juror number three and sitting in the middle of the front row, actually laughs at Reisky's absurd response. It's an abrupt burst of laughter, obviously spontaneous because she cuts it off as rapidly as possible. Both hands fly up to her mouth. She grits her teeth and clenches her jaws and looks around wildly to see how much damage she's done. Her body, though, keeps gyrating slightly.

Unfortunately for Mrs. Hardaway, and quite blessedly for us, the moment is contagious. Mr. Ranson Pelk who sits directly behind her gets tickled at something. So does Mrs. Ella Faye Salter who sits next to Mrs. Hardaway. Within seconds of the initial eruption, there is widespread laughing throughout the jury box. Some jurors glance at Mrs. Hardaway as if she's still the source of the mischief. Others look directly at Reisky and shake their heads in amused bewilderment.

Reisky assumes the worst, as if he's the reason they're laughing. His head falls and he studies the floor. Drummond chooses simply to ignore it, though it must be awfully painful. Not a face can be seen from his group of bright young eagles. They've all got their noses stuck in files and books. Aldy and Underhall examine their socks.

Kipler wants to laugh himself. He tolerates the comedy for a bit, and as it begins to subside he raps his gavel, as if to officially record the fact that the jury actually laughed at the testimony of Payton Reisky.

It happens quickly. The ridiculous answer, the burst of laughter, the cover-up, the chuckling and giggling and head-shaking skepticism, all last but a few seconds. I detect, though, a certain forced relief on the part of some of the jurors. They want to laugh, to express disbelief, and in doing so they can, if only for a second, tell Reisky and

Great Benefit exactly what they think about what they're hearing.

Brief though it is, it's an absolutely golden moment. I smile at them. They smile at me. They believe everything from my witnesses, nothing from Drummond's.

"Nothing else, Your Honor," I say with disgust, as if I'm tired of this lying scoundrel.

Drummond is obviously surprised. He thought I'd spend the rest of the day hammering Reisky with the manuals and the statistics. He shuffles paper, whispers to T. Price, then stands and says, "Our next witness is Richard Pellrod."

Pellrod was the senior claims examiner over Jackie Lemancyzk. He was a terrible witness during deposition, a real chip on his shoulder, but his appearance now is no surprise. They must do something to cast mud on Jackie. Pellrod was her immediate boss.

He's forty-six, of medium build with a beer gut, little hair, bad features, liver spots and nerdish eyeglasses. There's nothing physically attractive about the poor guy, and he obviously doesn't care. If he says Jackie Lemancyzk was nothing but a whore who tried to snare his body as well, I'll bet the jury starts laughing again.

Pellrod has the irascible personality you'd expect from a person who's worked in claims for twenty years. Just slightly friendlier than the average bill collector, he simply cannot convey any warmth or trust to the jury. He's a low-level corporate rat who's probably been working in the same cubicle for as long as he can remember.

And he's the best they have! They can't bring back Lufkin or Aldy or Keeley because they've already lost all credibility with the jury. Drummond has a half-dozen home office people left on his witness list, but I doubt if he calls all of them. What can they say? The manuals don't exist? Their company doesn't lie and hide documents?

Drummond and Pellrod Q&A through a well-rehearsed script for half an hour, more breathless inner workings of the claims department, more heroic efforts by Great Benefit to treat its insureds fairly, more yawns from the jury.

Judge Kipler decides to insert himself into the boredom. He interrupts this little tag-team, says, "Counselor, could we move along?"

Drummond appears shocked and wounded. "But, Your Honor, I have the right to conduct a thorough examination of this witness."

"Sure you do. But most of what he's said so far is already before the jury. It's repetitive."

Drummond just can't believe this. He's incredulous, and he pretends, quite unsuccessfully, to act as if the judge is picking on him.

"I don't recall your telling plaintiff's counsel to hurry up."

He shouldn't have said this. He's trying to prolong this flare-up, and he's picking a fight with the wrong judge. "That's because Mr. Baylor kept the jury awake, Mr. Drummond. Now move along."

Mrs. Hardaway's outburst and the snickering it created has obviously loosened up the jurors. They're more animated now, ready to laugh again at the expense of the defense.

Drummond glares at Kipler as if he'll discuss this later and straighten things out. Back to Pellrod, who sits like a toad, eyes half-open, head tilted to one side. Mistakes were made, Pellrod admits with a weak effort at remorse, but nothing major. And, believe it or not, most of the mistakes can be attributed to Jackie Lemancyzk, a troubled young woman.

Back to the Black claim for a while as Pellrod discusses

some of the less-damning documents. He never gets around to the denial letters, but instead spends a lot of time with paperwork that is irrelevant and unimportant.

"Mr. Drummond," Kipler interrupts sternly, "I've asked you to move along. These documents are in evidence for the jury to examine. This testimony has already been covered with other witnesses. Now, move it."

Drummond's feelings are hurt by this. He's being harangued and picked on by an unfair judge. He takes time to collect himself. His acting is not up to par.

They decide to fashion a new strategy with the claims manual. Pellrod says it's just a book, nothing more or less. Personally, he hasn't looked at the damned thing in years. They keep changing it so much that most of the veteran claims handlers just ignore it. Drummond shows him Section U, and, son of a gun, he's never seen it before. Means nothing to him. Means nothing to the many handlers under his supervision. Personally, he doesn't know a single claims handler who bothers with the manual.

So how are claims really handled? Pellrod tells us. Under Drummond's prompting, he takes a hypothetical claim, walks it through the normal channels. Step by step, form by form, memo by memo. Pellrod's voice remains in the same octave, and he bores the hell out of the jury. Lester Days, juror number eight, on the back row, nods off to sleep. There are yawns and heavy eyelids as they try vainly to stay awake.

It does not go unnoticed.

If Pellrod is crushed by his failure to dazzle the jury, he doesn't show it. His voice doesn't change, his manner remains the same. He finishes with some alarming revelations about Jackie Lemancyzk. She was known to have a drinking problem, and often came to work smelling of liquor. She missed more work than the other claims handlers. She grew increasingly irresponsible, and her termination was inevitable. What about her sexual escapades?

Pellrod and Great Benefit have to be careful here because this topic will be discussed again on another day in another courtroom. Whatever is said here will be recorded and preserved for future use. So, instead of making her a whore who readily slept with anybody, Drummond wisely takes the higher ground.

"I really don't know anything about that," Pellrod says, and scores a minor point with the jury.

They kill some more clock, and make it almost until noon before Pellrod is handed to me. Kipler wants to break for lunch, but I assure him I won't take long. He reluctantly agrees.

I start by handing Pellrod a copy of a denial letter he signed and sent to Dot Black. It was the fourth denial, and was based on the grounds that Donny Ray's leukemia was a preexisting condition. I make him read it to the jury, and admit it's his. I allow him to try and explain why he sent it, but, of course, there's no way to explain. The letter was a private matter between Pellrod and Dot Black, never intended to be seen by anybody else, certainly not in this courtroom.

He talks about a form that was mistakenly filled in by Jackie, and about a misunderstanding with Mr. Krokit, and, well, hell, the whole thing was just a mistake. And he's very sorry about it.

"It's a little too late to be sorry, isn't it?" I ask.

"I guess."

"When you sent that letter, you didn't know that there would be four more letters of denial, did you?"

"No."

"So, this letter was intended to be the final letter of denial to Mrs. Black, correct?"

The letter contains the words "final denial."

"I guess so."

"What caused the death of Donny Ray Black?"

He shrugs. "Leukemia."

"And what medical condition prompted the filing of his claim?"

"Leukemia."

"In your letter there, what preexisting condition do you mention?"

"The flu."

"And when did he have the flu?"

"I'm not sure."

"I can get the file if you want to go through it with me."

"No, that's okay." Anything to keep me out of the file.

"I think he was fifteen or sixteen," he says.

"So he had the flu when he was fifteen or sixteen, before the policy was issued, and this was not mentioned on the application."

"That's correct."

"Now, Mr. Pellrod, in your vast experience in claims, have you ever seen a case in which a bout with the flu was somehow related to the onset of acute leukemia five years later?"

There's only one answer, but he just can't give it. "I don't think so."

"Does that mean no?"

"Yes it means no."

"So the flu had nothing to do with the leukemia, did it?"

"No."

"So you lied in your letter, didn't you?"

Of course he lied in his letter, and he'll lie now if he says he didn't lie then. The jury will see it. He's trapped, but Drummond's had time to work with him.

"The letter was a mistake," Pellrod says.

"A lie or a mistake?"

"A mistake."

"A mistake that helped kill Donny Ray Black?"

"Objection!" Drummond roars from his seat.

Kipler thinks about this for a second. I expected an objection, and I expect it to be sustained. His Honor, however, feels otherwise. "Overruled. Answer the question."

"I'd like to enter a continuing objection to this line of questioning," Drummond says angrily.

"Noted. Please answer the question, Mr. Pellrod."

"It was a mistake, that's all I can say."

"Not a lie?"

"No."

"How about your testimony before this jury? Is it filled with lies or mistakes?"

"Neither."

I turn and point to Dot Black, then look at the witness. "Mr. Pellrod, as the senior claims examiner, can you look Mrs. Black squarely in the eyes and tell her that her son's claim was handled fairly by your office? Can you do this?"

He squints and twitches and frowns, and glances at Drummond for instructions. He clears his throat, tries to act offended, says, "I don't believe I can be forced to do that."

"Thank you. No further questions."

I finish in less than five minutes, and the defense is scrambling. They figured we'd spend the day with Reisky, then consume tomorrow with Pellrod. But I'm not wasting time with these clowns. I want to get to the jury.

Kipler declares a two-hour lunch break. I pull Leo to one side, and hand him a list of six additional witnesses.

"What the hell is this?" he says.

"Six doctors, all local, all oncologists, all ready to come testify live if you put your quack on." Walter Kord is incensed over Drummond's strategy to portray bone marrow transplants as experimental. He's twisted the arms of his partners and friends, and they're ready to come testify.

"He's not a quack."

"You know he's a quack. He's a nut from New York or some foreign place. I've got six local boys here. Put him on. This could be fun."

"These witnesses are not in the pretrial order. This is an unfair surprise."

"They're rebuttal witnesses. Go cry to the judge, okay." I leave him standing by the bench, staring at my list.

AFTER LUNCH, but before Kipler calls us to order, I chat near my table with Dr. Walter Kord and two of his partners. Seated alone in the front row behind the defense table is Dr. Milton Jiffy, Drummond's quack. As the lawyers prepare for the afternoon session, I call Drummond over and introduce him to Kord's partners. It's an awkward moment. Drummond is visibly unnerved by their presence here. The three of them take their places on the front row behind me. The five boys from Trent & Brent can't help but stare.

The jury is brought in, and Drummond calls Jack Underhall to the stand. He's sworn in, takes his seat, grins idiotically at the jury. They've been staring at him for three days now, and I don't understand how or why Drummond thinks this guy will be believed.

His purpose becomes plainly obvious. It's all about Jackie Lemancyzk. She lied about the ten thousand dollars in cash. She lied about signing the agreement because there is no agreement. She lied about the claim denial scheme. She lied about having sex with her bosses. She even lied about the company denying her medical claims. Underhall's tone starts as mildly sympathetic but becomes harsh and vindictive. It's impossible to say these horrible things with a smile, but he seems particularly eager to trash her.

It's a bold and risky maneuver. The fact that this corporate thug would accuse anybody of lying is glaringly ironic. They have decided that this trial is far more important than any subsequent action by Jackie. Drummond is apparently willing to risk total alienation of the jury on the prayer of causing enough doubt to muddy the waters. He's probably thinking he has little to lose by this rather nasty attack on a young woman who's not present and cannot defend herself.

Jackie's job performance was lousy, Underhall tells us. She was drinking and having trouble getting along with her co-workers. Something had to be done. They offered a chance to resign so it wouldn't screw up her record. Had nothing to do with the fact that she was about to give a deposition, nothing whatsoever to do with the Black claim.

His testimony is remarkably brief. They hope to get him on and off the stand without significant damage. There's not much I can do but hope the jury despises him as much as I do. He's a lawyer, not someone I want to spar with.

"Mr. Underhall, does your company keep personnel files on its employees?" I ask, very politely.

"We do."

"Did you keep one on Jackie Lemancyzk?"

"We did."

"Do you have it with you?"

"No sir."

"Where is it?"

"At the office, I presume."

"In Cleveland?"

"Yes. At the office."

"So we can't look at it?"

"I don't have it, okay. And I wasn't told to bring it."

"Does it include performance evaluations and stuff like that?"

"It does."

"If an employee received a reprimand or a demotion or a transfer, would these be in the personnel file?"

"Yes."

"Does Jackie's have any of these?"

"I believe so."

"Does her file have a copy of her letter of resignation?"

"Yes."

"But we'll have to take your word about what's in the file, correct?"

"I wasn't told to bring it here, Mr. Baylor."

I check my notes and clear my throat. "Mr. Underhall, do you have a copy of the agreement Jackie signed when you gave her the cash and she promised never to talk?"

"You must not hear very well."

"I beg your pardon."

"I just testified that there was no such agreement."

"You mean it doesn't exist?"

He shakes his head emphatically. "Never did. She's lying."

I act surprised, then slowly walk to my table, where papers are scattered everywhere. I find the one I want, scan it thoughtfully as everybody watches, then return to the podium with it. Underhall's back stiffens and he looks wildly at Drummond, who at the moment is staring at the paper I'm holding. They're thinking about the Section U's! Baylor's done it again! He's found the buried documents and caught us lying.

"But Jackie Lemancyzk was quite specific when she told the jury what she was forced to sign. Do you remember her her testimony?" I dangle the paper off the front of the podium.

"Yes, I heard her testimony," he says, his voice a bit higher, his words tighter.

"She said you handed her ten thousand dollars in cash and made her sign an agreement. Do you remember that?" I glance at the paper as if I'm reading from it. Jackie told me the dollar amount was actually listed in the first paragraph of the document.

"I heard her," he says, looking at Drummond. Underhall knows I don't have a copy of the agreement because he buried the original somewhere. But he can't be certain. Strange things happen. How in the world did I find the Section U's?

He can't admit there's an agreement. And he can't deny it either. If he denies, and if I suddenly produce a copy, then the damage cannot be estimated until the jury returns with its verdict. He fidgets, twists, wipes sweat from his forehead.

"And you don't have a copy of the agreement to show to the jury?" I ask, waving the paper in my hand.

"I do not. There is none."

"Are you certain?" I ask, rubbing my finger around the edges of the paper, fondling it.

"I'm certain."

I stare at him for a few seconds, thoroughly enjoying the sight of him suffering. The jurors haven't thought about sleeping. They're waiting for the ax to fall, for me to whip out the agreement and watch him croak.

But I can't. I wad the meaningless piece of paper and dramatically toss it on the table. "No further questions," I say. Underhall exhales mightily. A heart attack has been avoided. He leaps from the witness stand and leaves the courtroom.

Drummond asks for a five-minute recess. Kipler decides the jury needs more, and dismisses us for fifteen.

□

□ □ □

THE DEFENSE STRATEGY of dragging out testimony and hopefully confusing the jury is plainly not working. The jurors laughed at Reisky and slept through Pellrod. Underhall was a near fatal disaster because Drummond was terrified I had a copy of a document his client assured him did not exist.

Drummond's had enough. He'll take his chances with a strong closing argument, something he can control. He announces after recess that the defense rests.

The trial is almost over. Kipler schedules closing arguments for nine o'clock Friday morning. He promises the jurors they'll have the case by eleven.

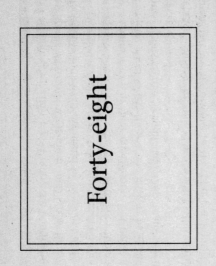

Forty-eight

LONG AFTER THE JURY'S GONE, AND LONG after Drummond and his crew hurriedly left for their offices and what will undoubtedly be another dicey session of what-went-wrong, we sit around the plaintiff's table in the courtroom and talk about tomorrow. Cooper Jackson and the two lawyers from Raleigh, Hurley and Grunfeld, are careful not to dispense too much unsolicited advice, but I don't mind listening to their opinions. Everyone knows it's my first trial. They seem amazed at the job I've done. I'm tired, still quite nervous and very realistic about what's happened. I was handed a beautiful set of facts, a rotten but rich defendant, an incredibly sympathetic trial judge and one lucky break after another at trial. I also have a handsome jury, but it's yet to perform.

Litigation will only get worse for me, they say. They're convinced the verdict will be in seven figures. Jackson had been trying cases for twelve years before he got his first one-million-dollar verdict.

They tell war stories designed to boost my confidence.

It's a pleasant way to spend the afternoon. Deck and I will work all night, but right now I enjoy the comfort of kindred spirits who truly want me to nail Great Benefit.

Jackson is somewhat dismayed by news out of Florida. A lawyer down there jumped the gun and filed four lawsuits against Great Benefit this morning. They thought the guy was about to join their class action, but evidently he got greedy. As of today, these three lawyers have nineteen claims against Great Benefit, and their plans are to file early next week.

They're pulling for me. They want to buy us a nice dinner, but we have work to do. The last thing I need tonight is a heavy dinner with wine and drinks.

AND SO WE DINE at the office on deli sandwiches and soft drinks. I make Deck sit in a chair in my office, and I rehearse my closing argument to the jury. I've memorized so many versions of it that they're all running together. I use a small chalkboard and write the crucial figures neatly on it. I appeal for fairness, yet ask for outrageous sums of money. Deck interrupts a lot, and we argue like schoolchildren.

Neither of us has ever made a closing argument to a jury, but he's seen more than I so of course he's the expert. There are moments when I feel invincible, downright arrogant because I've made it this far in such wonderful shape. Deck can spot these airs and is quick to chop at the knees. He reminds me repeatedly that the case can still be won or lost tomorrow morning.

Most of the time, however, I'm simply scared. The fear is controllable, but it never leaves. It motivates me and inspires me to keep forging ahead, but I'll be very happy once it's gone.

We turn off the office lights around ten and go home. I drink one beer as a sleeping aid, and it works. Sometime after eleven, I drift away, visions of success dancing in my head.

LESS THAN AN HOUR LATER, the phone rings. It's an unfamiliar voice, a female, young and very anxious. "You don't know me, but I'm a friend of Kelly's," she says, almost in a whisper.

"What's wrong?" I ask, waking quickly.

"Kelly's in trouble. She needs your help."

"What's happened?"

"He beat her again. Came home drunk, the usual."

"When?" I'm standing in the dark beside my bed, trying to find the lamp switch.

"Last night. She needs your help, Mr. Baylor."

"Where is she?"

"She's here with me. After the police left with Cliff, she went to an emergency clinic to see a doctor. Luckily, nothing's broken. I picked her up, and she's hiding here at my place."

"How bad is she hurt?"

"It's pretty ugly, but no broken bones. Cuts and bruises."

I get her name and address, hang up the phone and dress hurriedly. It's a large apartment complex in the suburbs, not too far from Kelly's, and I drive around several one-way loops before I find the right building.

Robin, the friend, cracks the door with the chain in place, and I have to identify myself sufficiently before I'm admitted. She thanks me for coming. Robin is just a kid too, probably divorced and working for slightly more than minimum wage. I step into the den, a small room with rented furniture. Kelly is sitting on the sofa, an ice pack to her head.

I guess it's the woman I know. Her left eye is completely swollen shut, the puffy skin already turning shades of blue. There's a bandage above the eye with a spot of blood on it. Both cheeks are swollen. Her bottom lip has been busted and protrudes grotesquely. She wears a long tee shirt, nothing else, and there are large bruises on both thighs and above the knees.

I bend over and kiss her on the forehead, then sit on a footstool across from her. There's already a tear in the right eye. "Thanks for coming," she mumbles, her words hindered by the wounded cheeks and the damaged lips. I pat her very gently on the knee. She rubs the back of my hand.

I could kill him.

Robin sits beside her, says, "She doesn't need to talk, okay. Doctor said as little movement as possible. He used his fists this time, couldn't find the baseball bat."

"What happened?" I ask Robin, but keep looking at Kelly.

"It was a credit card fight. The Christmas bills were due. He's been drinking a lot. You know the rest." She's quick with the narrative, and I suspect Robin's been around. She has no wedding ring. "They fight. He wins as usual, neighbors call the cops. He goes to jail, she goes to see the doctor. Would you like a Coke or something?"

"No, thanks."

"I brought her here last night, and this morning I took her to an abuse crisis center downtown. She met with a counselor who told her what to do, gave her a bunch of brochures. They're over there if you need them. Bottom line is she needs to file for divorce and run like hell."

"Did they photograph you?" I ask, still rubbing her knee. She nods. Tears have made their way out of the swollen eye and run down both cheeks.

"Yeah, they took a bunch of pictures. There's a lot you can't see. Show him, Kelly. He's your lawyer. He needs to see."

With Robin's assistance, she carefully gets to her feet, turns her back to me, and lifts the tee shirt above her waist. There's nothing underneath, nothing but solid bruises on her rear and the backs of her legs. The shirt goes higher and reveals more bruises on her back. The shirt comes down, and she carefully sits on the sofa.

"He beat her with a belt," Robin explains. "Forced her across his knee and just beat the shit out of her."

"Do you have a tissue?" I ask Robin as I gently wipe tears from Kelly's cheeks.

"Sure." She hands me a large box and I dab Kelly's cheeks with great care.

"What are you gonna do, Kelly?" I ask.

"Are you kidding?" Robin says. "She has to file for divorce. If not, he'll kill her."

"Is this true? Are we going to file?"

Kelly nods, and says, "Yes. As soon as possible."

"I'll do it tomorrow."

She squeezes my hand and closes her right eye.

"Which brings up the second problem," Robin says. "She can't stay here. Cliff got out of jail this morning, and he started calling her friends. I skipped work today, something I can't do again, and he called me around noon. I told him I knew nothing. He called back an hour later and threatened me. Kelly, bless her heart, doesn't have a lot of friends, and it won't be long before he finds her. Plus, I have a roommate, and it just won't work."

"I can't stay here," Kelly says softly and awkwardly.

"So where do you go?" I ask.

Robin has been thinking about this. "Well, the counselor we talked to this morning told us about a shelter for abused women, sort of a secret place that's not officially registered with the county and state. It's some type of home here in the city, sort of a word-of-mouth place. The women are safe because their beloved men can't find them. Problem is, it costs a hundred bucks a day, and she can stay only for a week. I don't earn a hundred dollars a day."

"Is that where you want to go?" I ask Kelly. She nods painfully.

"Fine. I'll take you tomorrow."

Robin breathes a heavy sigh of relief. She disappears into the kitchen, where she finds a card with the shelter's address.

"Let me see your teeth," I say to Kelly.

She opens her mouth as wide as possible, just wide enough for me to see her front teeth. "Nothing's broken?" I ask.

She shakes her head. I touch the bandage above her closed eye. "How many stitches?"

"Six."

I lean even closer and squeeze her hands. "This is never going to happen again, understand?"

She nods and whispers, "Promise?"

"I promise."

Robin returns to her place next to Kelly and hands me the card. She has some more advice. "Look, Mr. Baylor, you don't know Cliff, but I do. He's crazy and he's mean and he's wild when he's drunk. Please be careful."

"Don't worry."

"He might be outside right now watching this place."

"I'm not worried." I stand and kiss Kelly on the forehead again. "I'll file the divorce in the morning, then I'll come get you, okay. I'm in the middle of a big trial, but I'll get it done."

Robin walks me to the door, and we thank each other. It closes behind me, and I listen to the sounds of chains and locks and dead bolts.

It's almost 1 A.M. The air is clear and very cold. No one's lurking in the shadows.

Sleep would be a joke at this point, so I drive to the office. I park at the curb directly under my window, and race to the front door of the building. This is not a safe part of town after dark.

I lock the doors behind me, and go to my office. For all the terrible things it might be, a divorce is a fairly simple action to initiate, at least legally. I begin typing, a chore I struggle with, but the effort is made easier by the purpose at hand. In this case, I truly believe I'm helping to save a life.

DECK ARRIVES at seven and wakes me. Sometime after four I fell asleep in my chair. He tells me I look haggard and tired, and what happened to the good night's rest?

I tell the story, and he reacts badly. "You spent the night working on a stinking divorce? Your closing argument is less than two hours away!"

"Relax, Deck, I'll be fine."

"What's with the smirk?"

"We're gonna kick ass, Deck. Great Benefit's going down."

"No, that's not it. You're finally gonna get the girl, that's why you're smiling."

"Nonsense. Where's my coffee?"

Deck twitches and jerks. He's a nervous wreck. "I'll get it," he says, and leaves the office.

The divorce is on my desk, ready to be filed. I'll get a process server to pin it on my buddy Cliff while he's at work, otherwise he might be hard to find. The divorce also asks for immediate injunctive relief to keep him away from her.

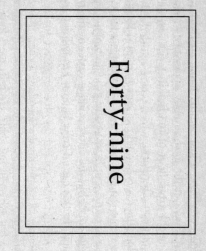

Forty-nine

ONE GREAT ADVANTAGE IN BEING A rookie is that I'm expected to be scared and jittery. The jury knows I'm just a kid with no experience. So expectations are low. I've developed neither the skill nor the talent to deliver great summations.

It would be a mistake to attempt to be something I'm not. Maybe in my later years when my hair is grayer and my voice is oily and I have hundreds of courtroom brawls under my belt, maybe then I can stand before a jury and give a splendid performance. But not today. Today I'm just Rudy Baylor, a nervous kid asking his friends in the jury box to help.

I stand before them, quite tense and frightened, and try to relax. I know what I'll say because I've said it a hundred times. But it's important not to sound rehearsed. I begin by explaining that this is a very important day for my clients because it's their only chance to receive justice from Great Benefit. There's no tomorrow, no second chance in court, no other jury waiting to help them. I ask them to consider Dot and what she's been through. I talk a little about Donny Ray without being overly dramatic. I ask the jurors to imagine what it would be like to be slowly and painfully dying when you know you should be getting the treatment to which you're entitled. My words are slow and measured, very sincere, and they find their mark. I'm talking in a relaxed tone, and looking directly into the faces of twelve people who are ready to roll.

I cover the basics of the policy without much detail, and briefly discuss bone marrow transplants. I point out that the defense offered no proof contrary to Dr. Kord's testimony. This medical procedure is far from experimental, and quite probably would've saved Donny Ray's life.

My voice picks up a bit as I move to the fun stuff. I cover the hidden documents and the lies that were told by Great Benefit. This played out so dramatically in trial that it would be a mistake to belabor it. The beauty of a four-day trial is that the important testimony is still fresh. I use the testimony from Jackie Lemancyzk and the statistical data from Great Benefit, and put some figures on a chalk-board: the number of policies in 1991, the number of claims and, most important, the number of denials. I keep it quick and neat so a fifth-grader could grasp it and not forget it. The message is plain and irrefutable. The unknown powers in control of Great Benefit decided to implement a scheme to deny legitimate claims for a twelve-month period. In Jackie's words, it was an experiment to see how much cash could be generated in one year. It was a cold-blooded decision made out of nothing but greed, with absolutely no thought given to people like Donny Ray Black.

Speaking of cash, I take the financial statements and explain to the jury that I've been studying them for four months and still don't understand them. The industry has its own funny accounting practices. But, using the company's own figures, there's plenty of cash around. On the chalkboard, I add the available cash, reserves and undistributed surpluses, and tally up the figure of four hundred and seventy-five million. The admitted net worth is four hundred and fifty million.

How do you punish a company this wealthy? I ask this question, and I see gleaming eyes staring back at me. They can't wait!

I use an example that's been around for many years. It's a favorite of trial lawyers, and I've read a dozen versions of it. It works because it's so simple. I tell the jury that I'm just a struggling young lawyer, scratching to pay my bills, not too far removed from law school. What if I work hard and am very frugal, save my money, and two years from now I have ten thousand dollars in the bank? I worked very hard for this money and I want to protect it. And what if I do something wrong, say, lose my temper and pop somebody in the nose, breaking it? I, of course, will be required to pay the actual damages incurred by my victim, but I will also need to be punished so I won't do it again. I have only ten thousand dollars. How much will it take to get my attention? One percent will be a hundred dollars, and that may or may not hurt me. I wouldn't want to fork over a hundred bucks, but it wouldn't bother me too much. What about five percent? Would a fine of five hundred dollars be enough to punish me for breaking a man's nose? Would I suffer enough when I wrote the check? Maybe, maybe not. What about ten percent? I'll bet that if I was forced to pay a thousand dollars, then two things would happen. Number one, I'd truly be sorry. Number two, I'd change my ways.

How do you punish Great Benefit? The same way you'd punish me or the guy next door. You look at the bank statement, decide how much money is available, and you levy a fine that will hurt, but not break. Same for a rich corporation. They're no better than the rest of us.

I tell the jury the decision is best left to them. We've sued for ten million, but they're not bound by that number. They can bring back whatever they want, and it's not my place to suggest an amount.

I close with a smile of thanks, then I tell them that if they don't stop Great Benefit, they could be next. A few nod and a few smile. Some look at the figures on the board.

I walk to my table. Deck is in the corner grinning from ear to ear. On the back row, Cooper Jackson gives me a thumbs-up. I sit next to Dot, and anxiously wait to see if the great Leo F. Drummond can snatch victory from defeat.

He begins with a drippy apology for his performance during jury selection, says he fears he got off on the wrong foot, and now wants to be trusted. The apologies continue as he talks about his client, one of the oldest and most respected insurance companies in America. But it made mistakes with this claim. Serious mistakes. Those dreadful denial letters were horribly insensitive and downright abusive. His client was dead wrong. But his client has over six thousand employees and it's hard to monitor the movements of all these people, hard to check all the correspondence. No excuses, though, no denials. Mistakes were made.

He pursues this theme for a few minutes, and does a fine job of painting his client's actions as merely accidental, certainly not deliberate. He tiptoes around the claim file, the manuals, the hidden documents, the exposed lies. The facts are a minefield for Drummond, and he wants to go in other directions.

He frankly admits that the claim should've been paid, all two hundred thousand dollars of it. This is a grave admission, and the jurors absorb it. He's trying to soften them up, and it's effective. Now, for the damage control. He's nothing but bewildered at my suggestion that the jury should consider awarding Dot Black a percentage of Great Benefit's net worth. It's shocking! What good would that do? He's admitted his client was wrong. Those responsible for this injustice have been terminated. Great Benefit has cleaned up its act.

So what will a large verdict accomplish? Nothing, absolutely nothing.

Drummond carefully eases into an argument against unjust enrichment. He has to be careful not to offend Dot, because he will also offend the jury. He states some facts about the Blacks; where they live, for how long, the house, the neighborhood, etcetera. In doing so, he portrays them as a very average, middle-class family living simple but happy lives. He's quite generous. Norman Rockwell couldn't paint a better picture. I can almost see the shady streets and the friendly paperboy. His setup is perfect, and the jurors are listening. He's describing either the way they live or the way they want to live.

Why would you, the jurors, want to take money from Great Benefit and give it to the Blacks? It would upset this pleasant picture. It would bring chaos to their lives. It would make them vastly different from their neighbors and friends. In short, it would wreck them. And is anyone entitled to the kind of money that I, Rudy Baylor, am suggesting? Of course not. It's unjust and unfair to take money from a corporation simply because the money's available.

He walks to the chalkboard and writes the figure of $746, and tells the jury this is the monthly income for the Blacks. Next to it he writes the sum of $200,000, and multiplies it by six percent to get the figure of $12,000. He then tells the jury what he really wants, and that's to double the Blacks' monthly income. Wouldn't we all like that? It's easy. Award the Blacks the $200,000 that the transplant would've cost, and if they'll invest the money in tax-free bonds at six percent, then they'll have $1,000 a month in tax-free income. Great Benefit will even agree to do the investing for Dot and Buddy.

What a deal!

He's done this enough to make it work. The argument is very compelling, and as I study the faces I see the jurors considering it. They study the board. It seems like such a nice compromise.

It is at this point that I hope and pray they remember Dot's vow to give the money to the American Leukemia Society.

Drummond ends with an appeal for sanity and fairness. His voice deepens and his words get slower. He's nothing but sincerity. Please do what is fair, he asks, and takes his seat.

Since I'm the plaintiff, I get the last word. I've saved ten minutes of my allotted half-hour for rebuttal, and as I walk to the jury I'm smiling. I tell them that I hope one day I'll be able to do what Mr. Drummond has just done. I praise him as a skilled courtroom advocate, one of the best in the country. I'm such a nice kid.

I have just a couple of comments. First, Great Benefit now admits it was wrong and in effect offers two hundred thousand dollars as a peace offering. Why? Because right now they're chewing their fingernails as they fervently pray that they get hit with nothing more than two hundred thousand. Second, did Mr. Drummond admit these mistakes and offer the money when he addressed the jury Monday morning? No, he did not. He knew everything then that he knows now, so why didn't he tell you up front that his client was wrong? Why? Because they were hoping then that you wouldn't learn the truth. And now that you know the truth, they've become downright humble.

I close by actually provoking the jury. I say, "If the best you can do is two hundred thousand dollars, then just keep it. We don't want it. It's for an operation that will never take place. If you don't believe that Great Benefit's actions deserve to be punished, then keep the two hundred thousand and we'll all go home." I slowly look into the eyes of each juror as I step along the box. They will not let me down.

"Thank you," I say, and take my seat next to my client. As Judge Kipler gives them their final instructions, an intoxicating feeling of relief comes over me. I relax as never before. There are no more witnesses or documents or motions or briefs, no more hearings or deadlines, no more worries about this juror or that. I breathe deeply and sink into my chair. I could sleep for days.

This calm lasts for about five minutes, until the jurors leave to begin their deliberations. It's almost ten-thirty.

The waiting now begins.

DECK AND I walk to the second floor of the courthouse and file the Riker divorce, then we go straight to Kipler's office. The judge congratulates me on a fine performance, and I thank him for the hundredth time. I do, however, have something else on my mind, and I show him a copy of the divorce. I quickly tell him about Kelly Riker and the beatings and her crazy husband, and ask him if he'll agree to emergency injunctive relief to prohibit Mr. Riker from getting near Mrs. Riker. Kipler hates divorces, but I have him captive. This is fairly routine in domestic abuse cases. He trusts me, and signs the order. No word on the jury. They've been out for fifteen minutes.

Butch meets us in the hallway and takes a copy of the divorce, the order just signed by Kipler and the summons.

He has agreed to serve Cliff Riker at work. I ask him again to try and do it without embarrassing the boy.

We wait in the courtroom for an hour; Drummond and his gang huddled on one side. Me, Deck, Cooper Jackson, Hurley and Grunfeld all grouped together on the other. I'm amused to observe the suits from Great Benefit keeping their distance from their lawyers, or maybe it's the other way around. Underhall, Aldy and Lufkin sit on the back row, their faces glum. They're waiting for a firing squad.

At noon, lunch is sent into the jury room, and Kipler sends us away until one-thirty. I couldn't possibly keep food in my stomach, the way it's flipping and whirling. I call Kelly on the car phone as I race across town to Robin's apartment. Kelly is alone. She's dressed in a pair of baggy sweats and borrowed sneakers. She has neither clothing nor toiletries with her. She walks gingerly, in great pain. I help her to my car, open the door, ease her inside, lift her legs and swing them around. She grits her teeth and doesn't complain. The bruises on her face and neck are much darker in the sunlight.

As we leave the apartment complex, I catch her glancing around, as if she expects Cliff to jump from the shrubs. "We just filed this," I say, handing her a copy of the divorce. She holds it to her face and reads it as we move through traffic.

"When does he get it?" she asks.

"Right about now."

"He'll go crazy."

"He's already crazy."

"He'll come after you."

"I hope he does. But he won't, because he's a coward. Men who beat their wives are the lowest species of cowards. Don't worry. I have a gun."

□
□ □
□ □

THE HOUSE IS OLD, unmarked and does not stand out from the others on the street. The front lawn is deep and wide and heavily shaded. The neighbors would have to strain to see any movement. I stop at the end of the drive and park behind two other cars. I leave Kelly in the car and knock on a side door. A voice over an intercom asks me to identify myself. Security is a priority here. The windows are all completely shaded. The backyard is lined with a wooden fence at least eight feet high.

The door opens halfway, and a hefty young woman looks at me. I'm in no mood for confrontation. I've been in trial for five days now, and I'm ready to snap. "Looking for Betty Norvelle," I say.

"That's me. Where's Kelly?"

I nod to the car.

"Bring her in."

I could easily carry her, but the backs of her legs are so tender it's easier for her to walk. We inch along the sidewalk, and onto the porch. I feel as though I'm escorting a ninety-year-old grandmother. Betty smiles at her and shows us into a small room. It's an office of some sort. We sit next to each other at a table with Betty on the other side. I talked to her early this morning, and she wants copies of the divorce papers. She reviews these quickly. Kelly and I hold hands.

"So you're her lawyer," Betty says, noticing the hand-holding.

"Yes. And a friend too."

"When are you supposed to see the doctor again?"

"In a week," Kelly says.

"So you have no ongoing medical needs?"

"No."

"Medication?"

"Just some pain pills."

The paperwork looks fine. I write a check for two hundred dollars—a deposit, plus the first day's fee.

"We are not a licensed facility," Betty explains. "This is a shelter for battered women whose lives are in danger. It's owned by a private individual, an abused woman herself, and it's one of several in this area. Nobody knows we're here. Nobody knows what we do. We'd like to keep it that way. Do both of you agree to keep this confidential?"

"Sure." We both nod, and Betty slides a form over for us to sign.

"This is not illegal, is it?" Kelly asks. It's a fair question given the ominous surroundings.

"Not really. The worst they could do would be to shut us down. We'd simply move somewhere else. We've been here for four years, and nobody's said a word. You realize that seven days is the maximum stay?"

We understand this.

"You need to start making plans for your next stop."

I'd love for it to be my apartment, but we haven't discussed this yet.

"How many women are here?" I ask.

"Today, five. Kelly, you'll have your own room with a bath. Food's okay, three meals a day. You can eat in your room or with the rest. We don't offer medical or legal advice. We don't counsel or have sessions. All we offer is love and protection. You're very safe here. No one will find you. And we have a guard with a gun around here someplace."

"Can he come visit?" Kelly asks, nodding at me.

"We allow one visitor at a time, and each visit has to be approved. Call ahead for clearance, and make sure you're not followed. Sorry, though, we can't allow you to spend the night."

"That's fine," I say.

"Any more questions? If not, I need to show Kelly around. You're welcome to visit tonight."

I can take a hint. I say good-bye to Kelly, and promise to see her later tonight. She asks me to bring a pizza. It is, after all, Friday night.

As I drive away, I feel as though I've introduced her to the underground.

A REPORTER from a newspaper in Cleveland catches me in the hallway outside the courtroom, and wants to talk about Great Benefit. Did I know that the Ohio Attorney General is rumored to be investigating the company? I say nothing. He follows me into the courtroom. Deck is alone at the counsel table. The defense lawyers are telling jokes across the room. No sign of Kipler. Everyone's waiting.

Butch served papers on Cliff Riker as he was leaving for a quick lunch. Riker offered some lip. Butch didn't back down, declared himself ready to rumble and Riker left in a hurry. My name is on the summons, so from this point on I'll be watching my back.

Others drift in as the time approaches two o'clock. Booker shows up and sits with us. Cooper Jackson, Hurley and Grunfeld return from a long lunch. They've had several drinks. The reporter sits on the back row. No one will talk to him.

There are lots of theories about jury deliberations. A quick verdict is supposed to favor the plaintiff in a case like this. The passing of time means the jury's deadlocked. I listen to these unfounded speculations and I cannot sit still. I walk outside for a drink of water, then to the rest room, then to the snack bar. Walking is better than sitting in the courtroom. My stomach churns violently and my heart pounds like a piston.

Booker knows me better than anyone, and he joins

these walks. He's nervous too. We poke along the marble hallways going nowhere, just killing time. And waiting. In times of great turmoil, it's important to be with friends. I thank him for coming. He said he wouldn't miss it for the world.

By three-thirty, I'm convinced I've lost. It should've been a slam-dunk decision, a simple matter of picking a percentage and calculating the result. Maybe I've been too confident. I recall one awful story after another about pathetically low verdicts in this county. I'm about to become a statistic, another example of why a lawyer in Memphis should take any decent offer to settle. Time passes with excruciating delay.

From somewhere far away, I hear my name being called. It's Deck, outside the courtroom doors, waving desperately for me. "Oh my God," I say.

"Just be cool," Booker says, then both of us practically race to the courtroom. I take a deep breath, say a quick prayer and step inside. Drummond and the other four are in their seats. Dot sits alone at our table. Everyone else is in place. The jury is filing into the box as I walk through the gate in the railing and sit next to my client. The faces of the jurors reveal nothing. When they're seated, His Honor asks, "Has the jury reached a verdict?"

Ben Charnes, the young black college graduate, and foreman of the jury, says, "We have, Your Honor."

"Is it written on paper according to my instructions?"

"Yes sir."

"Please stand and read it."

Charnes rises slowly. He's holding a sheet of paper that's visibly shaking. It is not shaking as violently as my hands. My breathing is quite labored. I'm so dizzy I feel faint. Dot, however, is remarkably calm. She's already won her battle with Great Benefit. They admitted in open court that they were wrong. Nothing else matters to her.

I'm determined to keep a straight face and display no emotion, regardless of the verdict. I do this the way I've been trained. I scribble on a legal pad. A quick glance to my left reveals the same strategy being employed by all five defense lawyers.

Charnes clears his throat, and reads, "We, the jury, find for the plaintiff and award actual damages in the amount of two hundred thousand dollars." There is a pause. All eyes are on the sheet of paper. So far, no surprises. He clears his throat again, says, "And, we, the jury, find for the plaintiff, and award punitive damages in the amount of fifty million dollars."

There's a gasp from behind me, and general stiffening around the defense table, but all else is quiet for a few seconds. The bomb lands, explodes and after a delay everyone does a quick search for mortal wounds. Finding none, it's possible to breathe again.

I actually write these sums on my legal pad, though the chicken scratch is illegible. I refuse to smile, though I'm forced to bite a hole in my bottom lip to achieve this effect. There are lots of things I want to do. I'd love to bound onto the table and gyrate like an idiot football player in the end zone. I'd love to dash to the jury box and start kissing feet. I'd love to strut around the defense table with some obnoxious in-your-face taunting. I'd love to leap onto the bench and hug Tyrone Kipler.

But I maintain my composure, and simply whisper, "Congratulations," to my client. She says nothing. I look at the bench and His Honor is inspecting the written verdict which the clerk has handed him. I look at the jury, and most of them are looking at me. It's impossible at this point not to smile. I nod and silently say thanks.

I make a cross on my legal pad and under it write the name—Donny Ray Black. I close my eyes and recall my favorite image of him; I see him sitting in the folding chair at the softball game, eating popcorn and smiling just because he was there. My throat thickens and my eyes water. He didn't have to die.

"The verdict appears to be in order," Kipler says. Very much in order, I'd say. He addresses the jury, thanks them for their civic service, tells them their meager checks will be mailed out next week, asks them not to talk about the case with anyone and says they are free to leave. Under the direction of the bailiff, they file from the courtroom for the last time. I'll never see them again. Right now, I'd like to give them each a cool million.

Kipler too is struggling to keep a straight face. "We'll argue post-trial motions in a week or so. My secretary will send you a notice. Anything further?"

I just shake my head. What more could I ask for?

Without standing, Leo says softly, "Nothing, Your Honor." His team is suddenly busy stuffing papers in briefcases and files in boxes. They can't wait to get out of here. It is, by far, the largest verdict in the history of Tennessee, and they'll be forever tagged as the guys who got clobbered with it. If I wasn't so tired and so stunned, I might walk over and offer to shake their hands. This would be the classy thing to do, but I just don't feel like it. It's much easier to sit here close to Dot and stare at Donny Ray's name on my legal pad.

I'm not exactly rich. The appeal will take a year, maybe two. And the verdict is so enormous that it will face a vicious attack. So, I have my work cut out for me.

Right now, though, I'm sick of work. I want to get on a plane and find a beach.

Kipler raps his gavel, and this trial is officially over. I look at Dot and see the tears. I ask her how she feels. Deck is quickly upon us with congratulations. He's pale but grinning, his four perfect front teeth shining. My attention is on Dot. She's a hard woman who cries with great reluctance, but she's slowly losing it. I pat her arm, and hand her a tissue.

Booker squeezes the back of my neck, and says he'll call me next week. Cooper Jackson, Hurley and Grunfeld stop by the table, beaming and full of praise. They need to catch a plane. We'll talk Monday. The reporter approaches, but I wave him off. I half-ignore these people because I'm worried about my client. She's collapsing now, the sobbing is getting louder.

I also ignore Drummond and his boys as they load themselves like pack mules and make a speedy exit. Not a word is spoken between us. I'd love to be a fly on the wall at Trent & Brent right now.

The court reporter and bailiff and clerk tidy up their mess and leave. The courtroom is empty except for me, Dot and Deck. I need to go speak to Kipler, to thank him for holding my hand and making it possible. I'll do it later. Right now I'm holding Dot's hand as she's unloading a torrent. Deck sits beside us, saying nothing. I say nothing. My eyes are moist, my heart is aching. She cares nothing for the money. She just wants her boy back.

Someone, probably the bailiff, hits a switch in the narrow hallway near the jury room, and the lights go off. The courtroom is semidark. None of us moves. The crying subsides. She wipes her cheeks with the tissue and sometimes with her fingers.

"I'm sorry," she says hoarsely. She wants to go now, so we decide to leave. I pat her arm as Deck gathers our junk and packs it in three briefcases.

We exit the unlit courtroom, and step into the marble hallway. It's almost five, Friday afternoon, and there's not much activity. There are no cameras, no reporters, no mob waiting for me to capture a few words and images from the lawyer of the moment.

In fact, no one notices us.

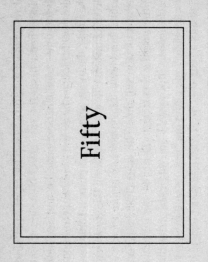

Fifty

THE LAST PLACE I WANT TO GO IS THE OFfice. I'm too tired and too stunned to celebrate in a bar, and my only pal for the moment is Deck, a nondrinker. Two stiff drinks would put me in a coma anyway, so I'm not tempted. There should be a wild celebration party somewhere, but these things are hard to plan when dealing with juries.

Maybe tomorrow. I'm sure the trauma will be gone by tomorrow, and I'll have a delayed reaction to the verdict. Reality will set in by then. I'll celebrate tomorrow.

I say good-bye to Deck in front of the courthouse, tell him I'm dead, promise to get together later. We're both still in shock, and we need time to think, alone. I drive to Miss Birdie's and go through my daily routine of checking every room in her house. It's just another day. No big deal. I sit on her patio, stare at my little apartment, and for the first time start spending money. How long will it be before I buy or build my first fine home? What new car shall I buy? I try to dismiss these thoughts, but it is impossible. What do you do with sixteen and a half million bucks? I cannot begin to comprehend. I know a dozen things can go wrong; the case could be reversed and sent back for a new trial; the case could be reversed and rendered, leaving me nothing; the punitive award could be cut dramatically by an appellate court, or it could be eliminated all together. I know these awful things can happen, but for the moment the money is mine.

I dream as the sun sets. The air is clear but very cold. Maybe tomorrow I can begin to realize the magnitude of what I've done. For now, I am warmed by the thought that a great deal of venom has been purged from my soul. For almost a year I've lived with a burning hatred of the mystical entity that is Great Benefit Life. I've carried a bitter poison for the people who work there, the people who set in motion a chain of events which took the life of an innocent victim. I hope Donny Ray's resting in peace. Surely an angel will tell him what happened today.

They've been exposed and proven wrong. I don't hate them anymore.

KELLY CUTS her thin slice of pizza with a fork and takes tiny bites. Her lips are still swollen and her cheeks and jaws are very sore. We're sitting on her single bed, our backs against the wall, our legs stretched out, the pizza box shared between us. We're watching a John Wayne western on an eighteen-inch Sony perched atop the dresser, not far across the small room.

She's wearing the same gray sweats, no socks or shoes, and I can see a small scar on her right ankle where he broke it last summer. She's washed her hair and put it in a ponytail. She's painted her fingernails, a light red. She is trying to be happy and make conversation, but she's in such physical pain it's very difficult to have fun. There's not much talk. I've never suffered through a thorough beating, and it's difficult to imagine the aftershocks. The aches and soreness are fairly easy to comprehend. The mental horror is not. I wonder at what point he decided to stop it, to call it off and admire his handiwork.

I try not to think about it. We certainly haven't discussed it, and I have no plans to bring it up. No word from Cliff since he was served with papers.

She's met one other lady here at this shelter, as it's referred to, a middle-aged mother of three teenagers who was so scared and traumatized she had trouble finishing a simple sentence. She's next door. The place is deathly quiet. Kelly left her room only once, to sit on the back porch and breathe fresh air. She's tried reading but it's difficult. Her left eye is still virtually closed, and her right one is at times blurred. The doctor said there was no permanent damage.

She's cried a few times, and I keep promising her this will be the last beating. It'll never happen again if I have to kill the bastard myself. And I mean this. If he got near her, I truly believe I could blow his brains out.

Arrest me. Indict me. Put me on trial. Give me twelve people in the jury box. I'm on a roll.

I don't mention the verdict to her. Sitting here with her in this dark little room, watching John Wayne ride his horse, seems like days and miles from Kipler's courtroom.

And this is exactly where I want to be.

We finish the pizza and snuggle closer together. We're holding hands like two kids. I have to be careful, though, because she's literally bruised from her head to her knees.

The movie goes off and the ten o'clock news is on. I'm suddenly anxious to see if the Black case is mentioned. After the obligatory rapes and murders, and after the first commercial break, the anchorman announces, rather grandly, "History was made today in a Memphis courtroom. A jury in a civil case awarded a record fifty million dollars in punitive damages against the Great Benefit Life

Insurance Company of Cleveland, Ohio. Rodney Frate has the story." I can't help but smile. We immediately see Rodney Frate standing and shivering live outside the Shelby County Courthouse, which of course has been abandoned for several hours now. "Arnie, I spoke with Pauline MacGregor, the Circuit Clerk, about an hour ago, and she confirmed that around four this afternoon a jury in Division Eight, that's Judge Tyrone Kipler, returned with a verdict of two hundred thousand dollars in actual damages, and fifty million in punitive. I also spoke with Judge Kipler, who declined to be interviewed on camera, and he said the case involved a bad-faith claim against Great Benefit. That's all he would say, except that he believes the verdict is by far the largest ever awarded in Tennessee. I spoke with several trial lawyers in the city, and no one has ever heard of a verdict this large. Leo F. Drummond, attorney for the defendant, had no comment. Rudy Baylor, attorney for the plaintiff, was unavailable for comment. Back to you, Arnie."

Arnie moves quickly to a truck wreck on Interstate 55.

"You won?" she asks. She's not amazed, just unsure.

"I won."

"Fifty million dollars?"

"Yep. But the money's not in the bank yet."

"Rudy!"

"I won."

I shrug like it's all in a day's work. "I got lucky," I say. "But you just finished school."

What can I say? "It's not that difficult. We had a great jury, and the facts fell into place."

"Yeah, right, like it happens every day."

"I wish."

She takes the remote and mutes the television. She wants to pursue this. "Your modesty is not working. It's fake."

"You're right. Right now I'm the greatest lawyer in the world."

"That's better," she says, trying to smile. I'm almost accustomed to her bruised and battered face. I don't stare at the wounds the way I did in the car this afternoon. I can't wait for a week to pass so she'll be gorgeous again. I swear I could kill him.

"How much of it do you get?" she asks.

"Get right to the point, don't you?"

"I'm just curious," she says in a voice that's almost childish. In spirit we're lovers now, and it's cute to giggle and coo.

"One third, but it's a very long way off."

She twists toward me, and is suddenly racked with pain to the point of groaning. I help her lie on her stomach. She's fighting back tears and her body is tense. She can't sleep on her back because of the bruises.

I rub her hair and whisper in her ear until the intercom interrupts. It's Betty Norvelle downstairs. My time is up. Kelly squeezes my hand tightly as I kiss her bruised cheek and promise to return tomorrow. She begs me not to go.

THE ADVANTAGES in winning such a verdict in my first trial are obvious. The only disadvantage I've been able to perceive during these past hours is that there's no place to go but down. Every client from now on will expect the same magic. I'll worry about that later.

I'm alone in the office late Saturday morning, waiting for a reporter and his photographer, when the phone rings. "This is Cliff Riker," a husky voice says, and I immediately punch the record button.

"What do you want?"

"Where's my wife?"

"You're lucky she's not at the morgue."

"I'm gonna stomp your ass, big shot."

"Keep talking, old boy. The recorder's on."

He hangs up quickly, and I stare at the phone. It's a different one, a cheap model the firm purchased at a Kmart. During the trial, we substituted it occasionally when we didn't want Drummond listening.

I call Butch at home, and tell him about my brief chat with Mr. Riker. Butch wants a piece of the kid because of their confrontation yesterday when he served the divorce papers. Cliff called him all sorts of vile names, even insulted his mother. The presence of two of Cliff's co-workers nearby in the parking lot prevented Butch from drawing blood. Butch told me last night that if there were any threats, he'd like to get involved. He has a sidekick called Rocky, a part-time bouncer, and together they make an imposing pair, Butch assured me. I make him promise he can only scare the kid, not hurt him. Butch tells me he plans to find Cliff alone somewhere, mention the phone call, tell him that they are my bodyguards, and one more threat will be dealt with harshly. I'd love to see this. I am determined not to live in fear.

This is Butch's idea of a good time.

The reporter from the *Memphis Press* arrives at eleven. We talk while a photographer shoots a role of film. He wants to know all about the case and the trial, and I fill his ear. It's public information now. I say nice things about Drummond, wonderful things about Kipler, glorious things about the jury.

It'll be a big story in the Sunday paper, he promises.

I PIDDLE around the office, reading the mail and looking at the few phone messages that came in during this past week. It's impossible to work, and I'm reminded of how few clients and cases I have. Half the time is spent replaying the trial, the other half is spent dreaming of my future with Kelly. How could I be more fortunate?

I call Max Leuberg and give him the details. A blizzard closed O'Hare and he couldn't get to Memphis in time for the trial. We talk for an hour.

OUR DATE Saturday night is very similar to the one we had on Friday, except the food and the movie are different. She loves Chinese food and I bring a sackful. We watch a comedy with few laughs while sitting in our same positions on the bed.

It's anything but boring, however. She's easing out of her private nightmare. The physical wounds are healing. The laughs are a bit easier, her movements a little quicker. There's more touching, but not much. Not nearly enough.

She is desperate to get out of the sweatsuit. They wash it for her once a day, but she's sick of it. She longs to be pretty again, and she wants her clothes. We talk of sneaking into her apartment and rescuing her things.

We still don't talk about the future.

Fifty-one

MONDAY MORNING. NOW THAT I'M A man of wealth and leisure, I sleep until nine, dress casually in khakis, loafers, no tie, and arrive at the office at ten. My partner is busy packing away the Black documents and removing the folding tables which have cramped our front office for months. We're both grinning and smiling at everything. Pressure's off. We're rested and it's time to gloat. He runs down the street for coffee, and we sit at my desk and relive our finest hour.

Deck's clipped the story from yesterday's *Memphis Press*, just in case I need an extra copy. I say thanks, I might need it, though there are a dozen copies in my apartment. I made the front page of Metro, with a long, well-written story about my triumph, as well as a rather large photo of me at my desk. I couldn't take my eyes off myself all day yesterday. The paper went into three hundred thousand homes. Money can't buy this exposure.

There are a few faxes. A couple from classmates with words of congratulations, and jokingly asking for loans. A sweet one from Madeline Skinner at the law school. And two from Max Leuberg. The first is a copy of a short article in a Chicago newspaper about the verdict. The second is a copy of a story dated yesterday from a paper in Cleveland. It describes the Black trial at length, then relates the growing troubles at Great Benefit. At least seven states are now investigating the company, including Ohio. Policyholder suits are being filed around the country, and many more are expected. The Memphis verdict is expected to prompt a flood of litigation.

Ha, ha, ha. We delight in the misery we've instigated. We laugh at the image of M. Wilfred Keeley looking at the financial statements again and trying to find more cash. Surely it's in there somewhere!

The florist arrives with a beautiful arrangement, a congratulatory gift from Booker Kane and the folks at Marvin Shankle's firm.

I had expected the phone to be ringing like mad with clients looking for solid legal representation. It's not happening yet. Deck said there were a couple of calls before ten, one of which was a wrong number. I'm not worried.

Kipler calls at eleven, and I switch to the clean phone just in case Drummond is still listening. He has an interesting story, one in which I might be involved. Before the trial started last Monday, while we were all gathered in his office, I told Drummond that we would settle for one point two million. Drummond scoffed at this, and we went to trial. Evidently, he failed to convey this offer to his client, who now claims it would have seriously considered paying just what I wanted. Whether or not the company would have settled at that point is unknown, but in retrospect, one point two million is much more digestible than fifty point two. At any rate, the company is now claiming it would have settled, and it's claiming its lawyer, the great Leo F. Drummond, committed a grievous error when he failed or refused to pass along my offer.

Underhall, the in-house lawyer, has been on the phone all morning with Drummond and Kipler. The company is furious, and humiliated, and wounded and obviously looking for a scapegoat. Drummond at first denied it ever happened, but Kipler nipped that in the bud. This is where I come in. They might need an affidavit from me setting out the facts as I remember them. Gladly, I say. I'll prepare one right now.

Great Benefit has already fired Drummond and Trent & Brent, and things could get much worse. Underhall has mentioned the filing of a malpractice claim against the firm. The implications are enormous. Like all firms, Trent & Brent carries malpractice insurance, but it has a limit. A fifty-million-dollar policy is unheard of. A fifty-million-dollar mistake by Leo F. Drummond would place a severe strain on the firm's finances.

I can't help but smile at this. After I hang up, I relay the conversation to Deck. The idea of Trent & Brent being sued by an insurance company is hilarious.

The next call is from Cooper Jackson. He and his pals filed suit this morning in federal court in Charlotte. They represent over twenty policyholders who got screwed by Great Benefit in 1991, the year of the scheme. When it's convenient for me, he would like to visit my office and go through my file. Anytime, I say, anytime.

Deck and I do lunch at Moe's, an old restaurant downtown near the courthouses where the lawyers and judges like to eat. I get a few looks, one handshake, a slap on the back from a classmate in law school. I should eat here more often.

THE MISSION IS ON for tonight, Monday, because the ground is dry and the temperature is around forty. The last three games were canceled because of bad weather. What kind of nuts play softball in the winter? Kelly doesn't answer. It's obvious what kind of nut we're dealing with. She's certain they'll play tonight because it's so important to them. They've suffered through two weeks with no ball and no beer parties afterward and no heroics to brag about. Cliff wouldn't dare miss the game.

It starts at seven, and just to be safe we drive by the softball field. PFX Freight is indeed on the field. I speed away. I've never done anything like this before, and I'm quite nervous. In fact, we're both scared. We don't say much. The closer we get to the apartment, the faster I drive. I have a .38 under my seat, and I plan to keep it close by.

Assuming he hasn't changed the locks, Kelly thinks we can be in and out in less than ten minutes. She wants to grab most of her clothes and a few other items. Ten minutes is the max, I tell her, because there might be neighbors watching. And these neighbors might be inclined to call Cliff, and, well, who knows.

Her wounds were inflicted five nights ago, and most of the soreness is gone. She can walk without pain. She says she's strong enough to grab clothing and move about quickly. It'll take both of us.

The apartment complex is fifteen minutes from the softball field. It consists of a half-dozen three-story buildings scattered around a pool and two tennis courts. Sixty-eight units, the sign says. Thankfully, her former apartment is on the ground floor. I can't park anywhere near her door, so I decide that we'll first enter the apartment, quietly gather the things we want, then I'll pull onto the grass, throw everything into the backseat, and we'll fly away.

I park the car, and take a deep breath.

"Are you scared?" she asks.

"Yes." I reach under the seat and get the gun. "Relax, he's at the ball field. He wouldn't miss it for the world."

"If you say so. Let's do it."

We sneak through the darkness to her unit without seeing another person. Her key fits, the door is open, we're inside. A light in the kitchen and one in the hallway are on and provide sufficient lighting. Clothing is strewn across two chairs in the den. Empty beer cans and corn chip bags litter the end tables and the floor under them. Cliff the bachelor has been quite a slob. She stops for a second, looks around in disgust, says, "I'm sorry."

"Hurry, Kelly," I say. I place the gun on a narrow snack bar separating the den from the kitchen. We go to the bedroom, where I turn on a small lamp. The bed hasn't been made in days. More beer cans and a pizza box. A *Playboy*. She points to the drawers in a small cheap dresser. "That's my stuff," she says. We're whispering.

I remove the pillowcases and begin stuffing them with lingerie, socks and pajamas. Kelly is pulling clothes from the closet. I take a load of dresses and blouses to the den and drape them across a chair, then go back to the bedroom. "You can't take everything," I say, looking at the packed closet. She says nothing, hands me another load, and I take it to the den. We work quickly, silently.

I feel like a thief. Every movement makes too much noise. My heart is pounding as I race back and forth to the den with each load.

"That's enough," I finally say. She carries a stuffed pillowcase and I carry several dresses on hangers, and I follow her to the den. "Let's get out of here," I say, nervous as hell.

There's a slight noise at the door. Someone's trying to get in. We freeze and look at each other. She takes a step toward the door, when it suddenly bursts open, striking her and knocking her into the wall. Cliff Riker crashes into the room. "Kelly! I'm home!" he yells as he sees her falling over a chair. I am standing directly in front of him, less than ten feet away, and he's moving quickly, a blur, all I can see is his yellow PFX Freight jersey, his red eyes and his weapon of choice. I freeze in absolute terror as he coils the aluminum softball bat and whirls it around mightily at my head. "You sonofabitch!" he screams as he unloads a massive swing. Frozen though I am, I'm able to duck just milliseconds before the bat blows by above me. I hear it whistle by. I feel its force. His home run stroke connects with a hapless little wooden column on the edge of the snack bar, shattering it into a million pieces and knocking over a pile of dirty dishes. Kelly screams. The swing was designed to crush my skull, and when it missed, his body kept whirling so that his back is to me. I charge like a madman, and knock him over the chair filled with hangers and clothes. Kelly screams again somewhere behind us. "Get the gun!" I yell.

He's quick and strong and on his feet before I can regain my balance. "I'll kill you!" he yells, swinging again, missing again as I barely dodge another hit. The second stroke gets nothing but air. "You sonofabitch!" he growls as he jerks the bat around.

He will not get a third chance, I decide quickly. Before he can cock the bat, I lunge at his face with a right hook. It lands on his jaw and stuns him just long enough for me to kick him in the crotch. My foot lands perfectly. I can hear and feel his testicles pop as he explodes in an agonized cry. He lowers the bat, I grab it and twist it away.

I swing hard and catch him directly across his left ear, and the noise is almost sickening. Bones crunch and break. He falls to all fours, his head dangling for a second, then he turns and looks at me. My second swing starts at the ceiling and falls with all the force I can muster. I drive the bat down with all the hatred and fear imaginable, and it lands solidly across the top of his head.

I start to swing again, when Kelly grabs me. "Stop it, Rudy!"

I stop, glare at her, then look at Cliff. He's flat on his stomach, shaking and moaning. We watch in horror as he grows still. An occasional twitch, then he tries to say something. A nauseating guttural sound comes out. He tries to move his head, which is bleeding like crazy.

"I'm going to kill the bastard, Kelly," I say, breathing heavily, still scared, still in a rage.

"No."

"Yes. He would've killed us."

"Give me the bat," she says.

"What?"

"Give me the bat, and leave."

I'm amazed at how calm she is at this moment. She knows precisely what has to be done.

"What . . . ?" I try to ask, looking at her, looking at him.

She takes the bat from my hands. "I've been here before. Leave. Go hide. You were not here tonight. I'll call you later."

I can do nothing but stand still and look at the struggling, dying man on the floor.

"Please go, Rudy," she says, gently pushing me toward the door. "Okay, okay. I'll call you later."

"Okay, okay." I step into the kitchen, pick up the .38 and walk back to the den. We look at each other, then our eyes fall to the floor. I step outside. I close the door quietly behind me, and look around for nosy neighbors. I see no one. I hesitate for a moment and hear nothing from inside the apartment.

I feel nauseated. I sneak away in the darkness, my skin suddenly covered with perspiration.

IT TAKES TEN MINUTES for the first police car to arrive. A second quickly follows. Then an ambulance. I sit low in the Volvo in a crowded parking lot, watching it all. The paramedics scramble into the apartment. Another police car. Red and blue lights illuminate the night and attract a large crowd. Minutes pass, and there's no sign of Cliff. A paramedic appears in the doorway and takes his time retrieving something from the ambulance. He's in no hurry.

Kelly's in there alone and scared and answering a hundred questions about how it happened, and here I sit, suddenly Mr. Chickenshit, ducking low behind my steering wheel and hoping no one sees me. Why did I leave her in there? Should I go save her? My head spins wildly and my vision is blurred, and the frantic flashing of the red and blue lights blinds me.

He can't be dead. Maimed maybe. But not dead.
I think I'll go back in there.

The shock wears off and the fear hits hard. I want them to bring Cliff out on a stretcher and race away with him, take him to the hospital, patch him up. I suddenly want him to live. I can deal with him as a living person, though a crazy one. Come on, Cliff. Come on, big boy. Get up and walk out of there.

Surely I haven't killed a man.

The crowd gets larger, and a cop moves everybody back.

I lose track of time. A coroner's van arrives, and this sends a wave of excited gossip through the gawkers. Cliff won't be riding in the ambulance. Cliff will be taken to the morgue.

I crack the door, and vomit as quietly as possible on the

side of the car next to mine. No one hears me. Then I wipe my mouth, and ease into the crowd. "He's finally killed her," I hear someone say. Cops stream in and out of the apartment. I'm fifty feet away, lost in a sea of faces. The police string yellow tape around the entire end of the building. The flash of a camera inside streaks across the windows every few seconds.

We wait. I need to see her, but there's nothing I can do. Another rumor races through the crowd, and this one is correct. He's dead. And they think she killed him. I listen carefully to what's being said because if anyone saw a stranger leave the apartment not long after the shouts and screams, then I want to know it. I move around slowly, listening ever so closely. I hear nothing. I back away for a few seconds, and vomit again behind some shrubs.

There's a flurry of movement around the door, and a paramedic backs out pulling a stretcher. The body is in a silver bag. They roll it carefully down the sidewalk to the coroner's van, then take it away. Minutes later, Kelly emerges with a cop on each side. She looks tiny, and scared. Thankfully, she's not handcuffed. She managed to change clothes, and now wears jeans and a parka.

They place her in the backseat of a patrol car, and leave. I walk quickly to my car, and head for the police station.

I INFORM THE SERGEANT at the front counter that I am a lawyer, that my client has just been arrested, and that I insist on being with her while she's being questioned. I say this forcefully enough, and he places a call to who knows where. Another sergeant comes after me, and I'm taken to the second floor, where Kelly sits alone in an interrogation room. A homicide detective named Smotherton is looking at her through a one-way window. I hand him one of my cards. He refuses to shake hands.

"You guys travel fast, don't you?" he says with absolute contempt.

"She called me right after she called 911. What'd you find?"

We're both looking at her. She's at the end of a long table, wiping her eyes with tissue.

Smotherton grunts while he decides how much he should tell me. "Found her husband dead on the den floor, skull fracture, looks like with a baseball bat. She didn't say much, told us they were getting a divorce, she sneaked home to get her clothes, he found her, they fought. He was pretty drunk, somehow she got the bat and now he's at the morgue. You doing her divorce?"

"Yeah. I'll get you a copy of it. Last week the judge ordered him to stay away from her. He's beaten her for years."

"We saw the bruises. I just wanna ask her a few questions, okay?"

"Sure." We enter the room together. Kelly is surprised to see me, but manages to play it cool. We exchange a polite lawyer-client hug. Smotherton is joined by another plainclothes detective, Officer Hamlet, who has a tape recorder. I have no objections. After he turns it on, I take the initiative. "For the record, I'm Rudy Baylor, attorney for Kelly Riker. Today is Monday, February 15, 1993. We're at Central Police Headquarters, downtown Memphis. I'm present because I received a call from my client at approximately seven forty-five tonight. She had just called 911, and said she thought her husband was dead."

I nod at Smotherton as if he may proceed now, and he looks at me as if he'd like to choke me. Cops hate defense lawyers, and right now I couldn't care less.

Smotherton starts with a bunch of questions about Kelly and Cliff—basic info like birth dates, marriage, employment, children and on and on. She answers patiently, with a detached look in her eyes. The swelling is gone in her face, but her left eye is still black and blue. The bandage is still on her eyebrow. She's scared half to death.

She describes the abuse in sufficient detail to make all three of us cringe. Smotherton sends Hamlet to pull the records of Cliff's three arrests for the beatings. She talks about assaults in which no records were kept, no paperwork was created. She talks about the softball bat and the time he broke her ankle with it. He also punched her a few times when he didn't want to break bones.

She talks about the last beating, then the decision to leave and go hide, then to file divorce. She is infinitely believable because it's all true. It's the upcoming lies that have me worried.

"Why'd you go home tonight?" Smotherton asks.

"To get my clothes. I was certain he wouldn't be there."

"Where have you been staying for the past few days?"

"In a shelter for abused women."

"What's the name of it?"

"I'd rather not say."

"Is it here in Memphis?"

"It is."

"How'd you get to your apartment tonight?"

My heart skips a beat at this question, but she's already thought about it. "I drove my car," she says.

"And what kind of car is it?"

"Volkswagen Rabbit."

"Where is it now?"

"In the parking lot outside my apartment."

"Can we take a look at it?"

"Not until I do," I say, suddenly remembering that I'm a lawyer here, not a co-conspirator.

Smotherton shakes his head. If looks could kill.

"How'd you get in the apartment?"

"I used my key."

"What'd you do when you got inside?"

"Went to the bedroom and started packing clothes. I filled three or four pillowcases with my things, and hauled a bunch of stuff to the den."

"How long were you there before Mr. Riker came home?"

"Ten minutes, maybe."

"What happened then?"

I interrupt at this point. "She's not gonna answer that until I've had a chance to talk to her and investigate this matter. This interrogation is now over." I reach across and push the red Stop button on the recorder. Smotherton simmers for a minute as he reviews his notes. Hamlet returns with the printout, and they study it together. Kelly and I ignore each other. Our feet, though, touch under the table.

Smotherton writes something on a sheet of paper and hands it to me. "This will be treated as a homicide, but it'll go to Domestic Abuse in the prosecutor's office. Lady's name there is Morgan Wilson. She'll handle things from here."

"But you're booking her?"

"I have no choice. I can't just let her go."

"On what charges?"

"Manslaughter."

"You can release her to my custody."

"No I can't", he answers angrily. "What kinda lawyer are you?"

"Then release her on recognizance."

"Won't work," he says, with a frustrated smile at Hamlet. "We got a dead body here. Bond has to be set by a judge. You talk him into ROR, then she walks. I'm just a humble detective."

"I'm going to jail?" Kelly says.

"We have no choice, ma'am," Smotherton says, suddenly much nicer. "If your lawyer here is worth his salt, he'll get you out sometime tomorrow. That is, if you can post bond. But I can't just release you because I want to." I reach across and take her hand. "It's okay, Kelly. I'll get you out tomorrow, as soon as possible." She nods quickly, grits her teeth, tries to be strong.

"Can you put her in a private cell?" I ask Smotherton.

"Look, asshole, I don't run the jail, okay? You gotta better way to do things, then go talk to the jailers. They love to hear from lawyers."

Don't provoke me, buddy. I've already cracked one skull tonight. We glare hatefully at each other. "Thanks," I say.

"Don't mention it." He and Hamlet kick their chairs back and stomp toward the door. "You got five minutes," he says over his shoulder. They slam the door.

"Don't make any moves, okay," I say under my breath. "They're watching through that window. And this place is probably bugged, so be careful what you say."

She doesn't say anything.

I continue in my role as the lawyer. "I'm sorry this happened," I say stiffly.

"What does manslaughter mean?"

"Means a lot of things, but basically it's murder without the element of intent."

"How much time could I get?"

"You have to be convicted first, and that's not going to happen."

"Promise?"

"I promise. Are you scared?"

She carefully wipes her eyes, and thinks for a long time. "He has a large family, and they're all just like him. All heavy-drinking, violent men. I'm scared to death of them."

I can't think of anything to say to this. I'm scared of them too.

"They can't make me go to the funeral, can they?"

"No."

"Good."

They come for her a few minutes later, and this time they use handcuffs. I watch them lead her down the hall. They stop at an elevator, and Kelly strains around one of the cops to see me. I wave slowly, then she's gone.

Fifty-two

WHEN YOU COMMIT A MURDER YOU make twenty-five mistakes. If you can think of ten of them, then you're a genius. At least that's what I heard in a movie once. It wasn't actually a murder but more of an act of self-defense. The mistakes, though, are beginning to add up.

I pace around my desk at the office, which is covered with neat rows of yellow legal paper. I've diagrammed the apartment, the body, the clothes, the gun, the bat, the beer cans, everything that I can remember. I've sketched the position of my car, her car and his truck in the parking lot. I've written pages recalling every step and every event of the evening. My best guess is that I was in the apartment for less than fifteen minutes but on paper it looks like a thin novel. How many screams or yells that were capable of being heard from the outside? No more than four, I think. How many neighbors saw a strange man leave just after the screams? Who knows.

That, I think, was mistake number one. I shouldn't have left so soon. I should have waited for ten minutes or so to see if the neighbors heard anything. Then I should have called the cops and told the truth. Kelly and I had every right to be in the apartment.

Or maybe I should have called the cops and told the truth. Kelly and I had every right to be in the apartment. It's obvious he was lying in ambush somewhere nearby at a time when he should have been elsewhere. I was well within my rights to fight back, to disarm him and to hit him with his own weapon. Given his violent nature and history, no jury in the world would convict me. Plus, the only other witness would be squarely on my side.

So why didn't I stay? She was pushing me out of the door for one thing, and it just seemed like the best course of action. Who can think rationally when, in the span of fifteen seconds, you go from being brutally attacked to being a killer?

Mistake number two was the lie about her car. I drove through the parking lot after I left the police station, and found her Volkswagen Rabbit and his four-wheel-drive pickup. This lie will work if no one tells the cops that her car hasn't been moved in days.

But what if Cliff and a friend somehow disabled her car while she was at the shelter, and this friend comes forth in a few hours and talks to the cops? My imagination runs wild.

The worst mistake that's hit me in the past four hours is the lie about the phone call Kelly allegedly made to me after she dialed 911. This was my excuse for being at the police station so quick. It's an incredibly stupid lie because there is no record of the call. If the cops check the phone records, I'm in serious trouble.

Other mistakes pop up as the night wears on. Fortunately, most are the result of a scared mind, most go away after careful analysis and sufficient scribbling on the legal pad.

I allow Deck to sleep until five before I wake him. An

hour later he's at the office with coffee. I give him my version of the story, and his initial response is beautiful. "No jury in the world will convict her," he says, without a doubt.

"The trial is one thing," I say. "Getting her out of jail is another."

We formulate a plan. I need records—arrest reports, court files, medical records and a copy of their first divorce filing. Deck can't wait to gather the dirt. At seven, Deck goes out for more coffee and a newspaper.

The story is on page three of Metro, a brief three paragraphs with no photo of the deceased. It happened too late last night to be much of a story. WIFE ARRESTED IN HUSBAND'S DEATH is the headline, but Memphis has three of these a month. If I wasn't searching for it I wouldn't see it.

I call Butch and raise him from the dead. He's a latenighter, single after three divorces, and likes to close down bars. I tell him that his pal Cliff Riker has met an untimely death, and this seems to perk him up. He's at the office shortly after eight, and I explain that I want him to scour the area around the apartment and see if anybody saw or heard anything. See if the cops are on the scene doing the same thing. Butch cuts me off. He's the investigator. He knows what to do.

I call Booker at the office and explain that a divorce client of mine killed her husband last night, but she's really a sweet girl and I want her out of jail. I need his help. Marvin Shankle's brother is a criminal court judge, and I want him to either release her on recognizance or set a ridiculously low bond.

"You've gone from a fifty-million-dollar verdict to a sleazy divorce case?" Booker asks jokingly.

I manage a laugh. If he only knew.

Marvin Shankle is out of town, but Booker promises to

start making calls. I leave the office at eight-thirty and speed toward downtown. Throughout the night, I've tried to avoid the thought of Kelly in a jail cell.

I ENTER the Shelby County Justice Complex and go straight for the office of Lonnie Shankle. I'm greeted with the news that Judge Shankle, like his brother, is out of town, and won't return until late afternoon. I make a few phone calls and try to locate Kelly's paperwork. She was just one of dozens arrested last night, and I'm sure her file is still at the police station.

I meet Deck at nine-thirty in the lobby. He has the arrest records. I send him to the police station to locate her file.

The Shelby County District Attorney's office is on the third floor of the complex. It has over seventy prosecutors in five divisions. Domestic Abuse has only two, Morgan Wilson and another woman. Fortunately, Morgan Wilson is in her office, it's just a matter of getting back there. I flirt with the receptionist for thirty minutes, and to my surprise, it works.

Morgan Wilson is a stunning woman of about forty. She has a firm handshake and a smile that says, "I'm busy as hell. Get on with it." Her office is impossibly stacked with files, but very neat and organized. I get tired just looking at all this work to be done. We take our seats, then, it hits her.

"The fifty-million-dollar guy?" she says, with a much different smile now.

"That's me." I shrug. It was just another day's work.

"Congratulations." She's visibly impressed. Ah, the price of fame. I suspect she's doing what every other lawyer is doing—calculating one third of fifty million.

She earns forty thousand a year max, so she wants to talk about my good fortune. I give a brief review of the trial and what it was like when I heard the verdict. I wrap it up quickly, then tell her why I'm here.

She's a thorough listener, and takes lots of notes. I hand her copies of the current divorce file, the old one and the records of Cliff's three arrests for beating his wife. I promise to have Kelly's medical records by the end of the day. I describe the injuries left by a few of the worst beatings.

Virtually all of these files around me involve men who've beaten their wives, children or girlfriends, so it's easy to predict whose side Morgan is on. "That poor kid," she says, and she ain't talking about Cliff.

"How big is she?" she asks.

"Five-five or so. A hundred-ten pounds dripping wet."

"How'd she beat him to death?" Her tone is almost in awe, not the least bit accusatory.

"She was scared. He was drunk. Somehow she got her hands on the bat."

"Good for her," she says, and goose bumps cover my thighs. This is the prosecutor!

"I'd love to get her out of jail," I say.

"I need to get the file and review it. I'll call the bail clerk and tell him we have no objection to a low bond. Where's she living?"

"She's in a shelter, one of those underground homes with no names."

"I know them well. They're really quite useful."

"She's safe there, but the poor kid's in jail right now, and she's still black and blue from the last beating."

Morgan waves at the files surrounding us. "That's my life."

We agree to meet at nine tomorrow morning.

DECK, BUTCH AND I meet at the office for a sandwich and to plot our next moves. Butch knocked on every door of every apartment near the Rikers', and found only one person who might've heard something crash. She lives directly above, and I doubt if she could see me exit the apartment. I suspect what she heard was the column disintegrate when the Babe swung and missed with strike one. The cops have not talked to her. Butch was at the complex for three hours and saw no signs of police activity. The apartment is locked and sealed, and seems to be drawing a crowd. At one point, two large young men who appeared to be related to Cliff were joined by a truckload of boys from work, and the group stood beyond the police tape, staring at the apartment door, cursing and vowing revenge. It was a rough-looking bunch, Butch assures me.

He's also lined up a bail bondsman, a friend of his who'll do us a favor and write the bond for only five percent as opposed to the customary ten. This will save me some money.

Deck's spent most of the morning at the police station getting arrest records and tracking Kelly's paperwork. He and Smotherton are getting along well, primarily because Deck is professing an extreme dislike for lawyers. He's just an investigator now, far from being a paralawyer. Interestingly, Smotherton reported that by mid-morning, they were receiving death threats against Kelly.

I decide to go to the jail to check on her. Deck will find an available judge to set her bond. Butch will be ready with his bondsman. As we're leaving the office, the phone rings. Deck grabs it and gives it to me.

It's Peter Corsa, Jackie Lemancyzk's lawyer in Cleveland. I last talked to him after her testimony, a conversation in which I thanked him profusely. He told me at that time that he was just days away from filing suit himself.

Corsa congratulates me on the verdict, says it was big news in the Sunday paper up there. My fame is spreading. He then tells me that some weird stuff is happening at

Great Benefit. The FBI, working in conjunction with the Ohio Attorney General and the state Department of Insurance, raided the corporate offices this morning and started removing records. With the exception of the computer analysts in accounting, all the employees were sent home and told not to come back for two days. According to a recent newspaper story, PinnConn, the parent company, has defaulted on some bonds and has been laying off loads of employees.

There's not much I can say. I killed a man eighteen hours ago, and it's hard to concentrate on unrelated matters. We chat. I thank him. He promises to keep me posted.

IT TAKES AN HOUR and a half to find Kelly somewhere back in the maze and bring her into the visitor's room. We sit on opposite sides of a glass square and talk through telephones. She tells me I look tired. I tell her she looks great. She's in a cell by herself, and safe, but it's noisy and she can't sleep. She really wants to get out. I tell her I'm doing all I can. I tell her about my visit with Morgan Wilson. I explain how bail works. I do not mention the death threats.

We have so much to talk about, but not here.

After we say good-bye, and as I'm leaving the visitor's room, a uniformed jailer calls my name. She asks if I'm the lawyer for Kelly Riker, then she hands me a printout. "It's our phone records. We've had four calls about that girl in the past two hours."

I can't read the damned printout. "What kind of calls?"

"Death threats. From some crazy people."

JUDGE LONNIE SHANKLE arrives at his office at three-thirty, and Deck and I are waiting. He has a hundred things to do, but Booker has called and schmoozed with the judge's secretary, so the wheels are greased. I give the judge a flurry of paperwork, a five-minute history of the case and finish with the plea for a low bail because I, the lawyer, will be required to post it. Shankle sets the bond at ten thousand dollars. We thank him and leave.

Thirty minutes later we're all at the jail. I know for a fact that Butch has a gun in a shoulder harness, and I suspect that the bondsman, a guy named Rick, is also armed. We're ready for anything.

I write Rick a check for five hundred dollars for the bond, and I sign all the paperwork. If the charges against her are not dismissed, and if she fails to appear for any court dates, then Rick has the choice of either forking over the remaining ninety-five hundred dollars, or finding her and physically hauling her back to jail. I've convinced him the charges will be dropped.

It takes forever to process her, but we eventually see her walking toward us, no handcuffs, nothing but a smile. We quickly escort her to my car. I've asked Butch and Deck to follow us for a few blocks just to be safe.

I tell Kelly about the death threats. We suspect it's his crazy family and redneck friends from work. We talk little as we hurriedly leave downtown and head for the shelter. I don't want to discuss last night, and she's not ready for it either.

AT 5 P.M. TUESDAY, lawyers for Great Benefit file for protection under the bankruptcy code in federal court in Cleveland. Peter Corsa calls the office while I'm hiding Kelly, and Deck takes the news. When I return a few minutes later, Deck looks like death.

We sit in my office with our feet on the desk for a long time without a word. Total silence. No voices. No phones. No traffic sounds below. We'd been postponing our discussion about how much of the fee Deck would get, so he's not sure how much he's lost. But we both know that we've gone from being paper millionaires to near insolvents. Our giddy dreams of yesterday seem silly now.

There's a flicker of hope. Just last week Great Benefit's balance sheet looked stout enough to convince a jury it had fifty million bucks to spare. M. Wilfred Keeley estimated the company had a hundred million in cash. Surely there's some truth in this. I remember the warnings of Max Leuberg: Never trust an insurance company's own figures because they make their own accounting rules.

But surely somewhere down the road there'll be a spare million or so for us.

I don't really believe this. Neither does Deck.

Corsa left his home number, and I finally muster the strength to call him. He apologizes for the bad news, says the legal and financial communities up there are buzzing. It's too early to know the truth, but it looks as though PinnConn took some heavy hits trading foreign currencies. It then started syphoning off the huge cash reserves of its subsidiaries, including Great Benefit. Things got worse, and the money was simply skimmed by PinnConn and sent to Europe. The bulk of PinnConn's stock is controlled by a group of American pirates operating in Singapore. It sounds like the whole world is conspiring against me.

It's quickly evolving into a huge mess, may take months to unravel it, but the local U.S. Attorney was on TV this afternoon promising indictments. A lot of good it'll do us.

Corsa will call me in the morning.

I relay all this to Deck, and we both know it's hopeless. The money's been skimmed by crooks too sophisticated to get caught. Thousands of policyholders who had legitimate claims and have already been screwed once will now get it again. Deck and I will get screwed. Same for Dot and Buddy. Donny Ray got the ultimate screwing. Drummond will get screwed when he submits his hefty bills for legal services. I mention this to Deck, but it's hard to laugh.

The employees and agents of Great Benefit will get screwed. People like Jackie Lemancyzk will take a hit.

Misery loves company, but for some reason I feel as if I've lost more than most of these other folks. The fact that others will suffer is of small comfort.

I think of Donny Ray again. I see him sitting under the tree trying gamely to be strong during his deposition. He paid the ultimate price for Great Benefit's thievery.

I've spent most of the past six months working on this case, and now that time has been wasted. The firm has averaged about a thousand bucks a month in net profits since we started, but we were driven by the dream of paydirt on the Black case. There aren't enough fees in our files to survive another two months, and I'm not about to hustle people. Deck has one decent car wreck that won't settle until the client is released from his doctor's care, probably six months from now. At best, it's a twenty-thousand-dollar settlement.

The phone rings. Deck answers it, listens, then quickly hangs up. "Some guy says he's gonna kill you," he says matter-of-factly.

"That's not the worst phone call of the day."

"I wouldn't mind getting shot right now," he says.

THE SIGHT OF KELLY lifts my spirits. We eat Chinese again in her room, with the door locked, with my gun on a chair under my coat.

There are so many emotions hanging around our necks and competing for attention that conversation is not easy. I tell her about Great Benefit, and she's disappointed only because I'm so discouraged. The money means nothing to her.

At times we laugh, at times we almost cry. She's worried about tomorrow and the next day and what the police might do or find. She's terrified of the Riker clan. These people start hunting when they're five years old. Guns are a way of life for them. She's frightened at the prospect of going back to jail, though I promise it won't happen. If the cops and the prosecutors pursue with a vengeance, I will step forward and tell the truth.

I mention last night, and she can't handle it. She starts crying and we don't speak for a long time.

I unlock the door, and step quietly through the dark hall, through the rambling house until I find Betty Norvelle watching television alone in the den. She knows the barest details of what happened last night. I explain that Kelly is too fragile at this moment to be left alone. I need to stay with her, and I'll sleep on the floor if necessary. The shelter has a strict prohibition against men sleeping over, but in this case she makes an exception.

We lie together on the narrow bed, on top of the sheets and blankets, and hold each other closely. I had no sleep last night, a brief nap this afternoon, and I feel as though I haven't slept ten hours in the past week. I can't squeeze her because I'm afraid I'll hurt her. I drift away.

Fifty-three

G REAT BENEFIT'S DEMISE MIGHT BE BIG news in Cleveland, but Memphis is hardly concerned. There's no word of it in Wednesday's paper. There is a brief story about Cliff Riker. The autopsy revealed he died of multiple blows to the head with a blunt instrument. His widow has been arrested and released. His family wants justice. His funeral is tomorrow in the small town which he and Kelly fled.

As Deck and I scour the paper, a fax arrives from Peter Corsa's office. It's a copy of a long front-page story in the Cleveland paper, and it's filled with the latest developments in the PinnConn scandal. At least two grand juries are swinging into action. Lawsuits are being filed by the truckload against the company and its subsidiaries, most specifically Great Benefit, whose bankruptcy filing merits a sizable story of its own. Lawyers are scrambling everywhere.

M. Wilfred Keeley was detained yesterday afternoon at JFK as he was waiting to board a flight to Heathrow. His wife was with him and they claimed to be sneaking away for a quick holiday. They could not, however, produce the name of a hotel anywhere in Europe at which they were expected.

It appears as though the companies have been looted in the past two months. The cash initially went to cover bad investments, then it was preserved and wired to havens around the world. At any rate, it's gone.

The first phone call of the day comes from Leo Drummond. He tells me about Great Benefit as if I know nothing. We chat briefly, and it's hard to tell who's the more depressed. Neither of us will get paid for the war we've just waged. He does not mention his dispute with his former client over my offer to settle, and at this point it's moot. His former client is in no condition to maintain a malpractice action. It has effectively avoided the Black verdict, so it can't claim it suffered because of Drummond's bad legal work. Trent & Brent has dodged a major bullet.

The second call is from Roger Rice, Miss Birdie's new lawyer. He congratulates me on the verdict. If he only knew. He says he's been thinking about me since he saw my face in the Sunday paper. Miss Birdie's trying to change her will again, and they're sick of her in Florida. Delbert and Randolph finally succeeded in obtaining her signature on a homemade document which they took to the lawyers in Atlanta and demanded the full disclosure of their dear mother's assets. The lawyers stonewalled. The brothers besieged Atlanta for two days. One of the lawyers called Roger Rice, and the truth came out. Delbert and Randolph asked this lawyer point-blank if their mother had twenty million dollars. The lawyer couldn't help but laugh, and this upset the boys. They eventually concluded that Miss Birdie was playing games, and they drove back to Florida.

Late Monday night, Miss Birdie called Roger Rice, at

home, and informed him she was headed to Memphis. She said she'd been trying to call me, but I seemed very busy. Mr. Rice told her about the trial and the fifty-million-dollar verdict, and this seemed to excite her. "How nice," she said. "Not bad for a yard boy." She seemed terribly excited by the fact that I am now rich.

Anyway, Rice wants to forewarn me that she might arrive any day now. I thank him.

MORGAN WILSON has thoroughly reviewed the Riker file, and is not inclined to prosecute. However, her boss, Al Vance, is undecided. I follow her into his office.

Vance was elected district attorney many years ago, and gets himself reelected with ease. He's about fifty, and at one time had serious aspirations of a higher political life. The opportunity never arose, and he's been content to stay in this office. He possesses a quality that is quite rare among prosecutors—he doesn't like cameras.

He congratulates me on the verdict. I'm gracious and don't want to talk about it, for reasons best kept to myself at this moment. I suspect that in less than twenty-four hours the news about Great Benefit will be reported in Memphis, and the awe in which I'm now held will instantly disappear.

"These people are nuts," he says, tossing the file on his desk. "They've been calling here like crazy, twice this morning. My secretary has talked to Riker's father and one of his brothers."

"What do they want?" I ask.

"Death for your client. Forgo the trial, and just strap her in the electric chair now, today. Is she out of jail?"

"Yes."

"Is she hiding?

"Yes."

"Good. They're so damned stupid they make threats

against her. They don't know it's against the law to do this. These are really sick people."

The three of us are unanimous in our opinion that the Rikers are quite ignorant and very dangerous.

"Morgan doesn't want to prosecute," Vance continues. Morgan nods her head.

"It's very simple, Mr. Vance," I say. "You can take it to the grand jury, and you might get lucky and get an indictment. But if you take it to trial, you'll lose. I'll wave that damned aluminum bat in front of the jury, and I'll bring in a dozen experts on domestic abuse. I'll make her a symbol, and you guys will look terrible trying to convict her. You won't get one vote out of twelve from the jury."

I continue. "I don't care what his family does. But if they bully you into prosecuting this case, you'll be sorry. They'll hate you even more when the jury slam-dunks it and we walk."

"He's right, Al," Morgan says. "There's no way to get a conviction."

Al was ready to throw in the towel before we walked in here, but he needed to hear it from both of us. He agrees to dismiss all charges. Morgan promises to fax me a letter to this effect by late morning.

I thank them and leave quickly. The moods are shifting rapidly. I'm alone in the elevator, and I can't help but grin at myself in the polished brass above the numbered buttons. All charges will be dismissed! Forever!

I practically run through the parking lot to my car.

THE BULLET was fired from the street, pierced the window in the front office, left a neat hole no more than half an inch wide, left another hole in the Sheetrock, and ended its journey deep in the wall. Deck happened to be in the front office when he heard the shot. The bullet missed him by no more than ten feet, but this was close enough. He did not run to the window immediately. He dove under the table, and waited for a few minutes.

Then he locked the door, and waited for someone to check on him. No one did. It happened around ten-thirty, while I was meeting with Al Vance. Apparently, no one saw the gunman. If the shot was heard by anyone else, we'll never know it. The sounds of random bullets are not uncommon in this part of town.

The first call Deck made was to Butch, who was asleep. Twenty minutes later, Butch was in the office, heavily armed and working to calm Deck.

They're examining the hole in the window when I arrive, and Deck tells me what happened. I'm sure Deck shakes and twitches when he's sound asleep, and he's really trembling now. He tells us he's fine, but his voice is squeaky. Butch says he'll wait just below the window and catch them if they come back. In his car he has two shotguns and an AK-47 assault rifle. God help the Rikers if they plan another drive-by shooting.

I can't get Booker on the phone. He's out of town taking depositions with Marvin Shankle, so I write him a brief letter in which I promise to call later.

DECK AND I decide on a private lunch, away from admiring throngs, out of the range of stray bullets. We buy deli sandwiches and eat in Miss Birdie's kitchen. Butch is parked in the drive behind my Volvo. If he doesn't get to shoot the AK-47 today, he'll be devastated.

The weekly cleaning service was in yesterday, so the house is fresh and temporarily without the smell of mildew. It's ready for Miss Birdie.

The deal we cut is painless and simple. Deck gets the files he wants, and I get two thousand dollars, to be paid within ninety days. He'll associate other lawyers if he has to. He'll also farm out any of my active files he doesn't want. The Ruffins' collection cases will be sent back to Booker. He won't like it, but he'll get over it.

Sorting through the files is easy. It's sad how few cases and clients we've generated in six months.

The firm has thirty-four hundred dollars in the bank, and a few outstanding bills.

We agree on the details as we eat, and the business aspect of the separation is easy. The personal untangling is not. Deck has no future. He cannot pass the bar exam, and there's no place for him to go. He'll spend a few weeks cleaning up my files, but he can't operate without a Bruiser or a Rudy to front for him. We both know this, but it's left unsaid.

He confides in me that he's broke. "Gambling?" I ask.

"Yeah. It's the casinos. I can't stay away from them." He's relaxed now, almost sedate. He takes a large bite from a dill pickle and crunches loudly.

When we started our firm last summer, we had just been handed an equal split in the Van Landel settlement. We had fifty-five hundred dollars each, and we both put up two thousand. I was forced to dip into my savings a few times, but I have twenty-eight hundred in the bank, money I've saved by living frugally and burying it when I could. Deck doesn't spend it either. He just blows it at the blackjack tables.

"I talked to Bruiser last night," he says, and I'm not surprised.

"Where is he?"

"Bahamas."

"Is Prince with him?"

"Yep."

This is good news, and I'm relieved to hear it. I'm sure Deck has known it for some time.

"So they made it," I say, looking out the window, trying

to imagine those two with straw hats and sunglasses. They both lived in such darkness here.

"Yeah. I don't know how. Some things you don't ask." Deck has a blank look on his face. He's deep in thought. "The money's still here, you know."

"How much?"

"Four million, cash. It's what they skimmed from the clubs."

"Four million?"

"Yep. In one spot. Locked in the basement of a warehouse. Right here in Memphis."

"And how much are they offering you?"

"Ten percent. If I can get it to Miami, Bruiser says he can do the rest."

"Don't do it, Deck."

"It's safe."

"You'll get caught and sent to jail."

"I doubt it. The feds aren't watching anymore. They don't have a clue about the money. Everybody assumes Bruiser took enough with him and he doesn't need anymore."

"Does he need it?"

"I don't know. But he sure as hell wants it."

"Don't do it, Deck."

"It's a piece of cake. The money will fit in a small U-Haul truck. Bruiser says it'll take two hours max to load it. Drive the U-Haul to Miami, and wait for instructions. It'll take two days, and it'll make me rich."

His voice has a faraway tone to it. There's no doubt in my mind that Deck will try this. He and Bruiser have been planning it. I've said enough. He's not listening.

We leave Miss Birdie's house and walk to my apartment. Deck helps me haul a few clothes to my car. I load the trunk and half the backseat. I'm not going back to the office, so we say our good-byes by the garage.

"I don't blame you for leaving," he says.

"Be careful, Deck."

We embrace for an awkward second or two, and I almost choke up.

"You made history, Rudy, do you know that?"

"We did it together."

"Yeah, and what do we have to show for it?"

"We can always brag."

We shake hands, and Deck's eyes are wet. I watch him shuffle and jerk down the drive, and get in the car with Butch. They drive away.

I write a long letter to Miss Birdie, and promise to call later. I leave it on the kitchen table because I'm sure she'll be home soon. I check the house once again, and say good-bye to my apartment.

I drive to a branch bank and close my savings account. A stack of twenty-eight one-hundred-dollar bills has a nice feel to it. I hide it under the floor mat.

IT'S NEARLY DARK when I knock on the Blacks' front door. Dot opens it, and almost smiles when she sees it's me.

The house is dark and quiet, still very much in mourning. I doubt if it will ever change. Buddy's in bed with the flu.

Over instant coffee, I gently break the news that Great Benefit has gone belly-up, that she's been shafted once more. Barring a miracle far off in the distance, we won't get a dime. I'm not surprised at her reaction.

There appear to be several complex reasons for Great Benefit's death, but right now it's important for Dot to think she pulled the trigger. Her eyes gleam and her entire face is happy as it sinks in. She put them out of business. One little, determined woman in Memphis, Tennessee, bankrupted them sumbitches.

She'll go to Donny Ray's grave tomorrow and tell him about it.

KELLY IS WAITING anxiously in the den with Betty Norvelle. She clutches a small leather bag I bought her yesterday. In it are a few toiletries and a few items of clothing donated by the shelter. It holds everything she owns.

We sign the paperwork, and thank Betty. We hold hands as we walk quickly to the car. We take a deep breath once inside, then we drive away.

The gun's under the seat, but I've stopped worrying.

"Dear, which direction?" I ask when we get on the interstate loop that circles the city. We laugh at this, because it is so absolutely wonderful. It doesn't matter where we go!

"I'd like to see mountains," she says.

"Me too. East or West?"

"Big mountains."

"Then West it is."

"I want to see snow."

"I think we can find some."

She cuddles closer and rests her head on my shoulder. I rub her legs.

We cross the river and enter Arkansas. The Memphis skyline fades behind us. It's amazing how little we've planned for this. We didn't know until this morning that she'd be able to leave the county. But the charges were dropped, and I have a letter from the district attorney himself. Her bond was canceled at three this afternoon.

We'll settle in a place where no one can find us. I'm not afraid of being followed, but I just want to be left alone. I don't want to hear about Deck and Bruiser. I don't want to hear about the fallout at Great Benefit. I don't want Miss Birdie calling me for legal advice. I don't want to worry about Cliff's death and everything related to it. Kelly and I will talk about it one of these days, but not anytime soon.

We'll pick a small college town because she wants to go to school. She's only twenty. I'm still a kid myself. We're unloading some serious baggage here, and it's time to have fun. I'd love to teach history in high school. That shouldn't be hard to do. After all, I have seven years of college.

I will not, under any circumstances, have anything whatsoever to do with the law. I will allow my license to expire. I will not register to vote so they can't nail me for jury duty. I will never voluntarily set foot in another courtroom.

We smile and giggle as the land flattens and the traffic lightens. Memphis is twenty miles behind us. I vow never to return.